SOULBOUND
DRUADAN LEGACY
BOOK TWO

AMELIA COLE

DAISY JANE PUBLISHING

Copyright © 2024 by Amelia Cole

All rights reserved.

Interior illustrator: and formatting by Amelia Cole

Book cover by Seventhstar Art

This book is licensed for your personal enjoyment only.

This is a work of fiction. Names, characters, pleases, brands, media, and incidents are either the product of the author's imagination or are used fictitiously. The author acknowledges the trademark status and trademark owners of various products referred to in this work of fiction which have been used without permission.

No part of this book may be reproduced in any form or by any electronic or mechanical means, including information storage and retrieval systems, without written permission from the author, except for the use of brief quotations in a book review.

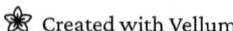 Created with Vellum

Also by Amelia Cole

VELA SERIES

URBAN FANTASY INSPIRED BY ANCIENT MYTHOLOGY

An ancient magic, A mysterious artifact, She was chosen for a reason...

Ella Dawson, a tenacious photojournalist, stumbles upon a mysterious enchanted statue. Fearing others will come to look for it and with no other options, Ella enlists the help of her secret agent and very much ex-boyfriend to journey through treacherous landscapes and ancient ruins to uncover the secrets the statue contains.

CONTENT WARNINGS

Soulbound is an adult, dystopian sci-fi set on a future Earth. It is a 'why choose' romance, where the main character will end up with more than one love interest. It may have triggers for some, including violence, threat of death, blood, sexual themes, sexual acts, pregnancy, infertility, harm to animals, death, suicidal ideation, grief, and depression.

It is intended for mature 18+ readers

Druadan Lineages

Bloodline	Temperment	SKILL	COLORS	Horse Base
GALAXY	Hot	Endurance, Fast, spirited	Duns, Buckskins, Teal manes or tails	Mustang
GEMINI	Medium	Easy to bond, well balanced	Bays, Browns	Quarter Horse
GHOST	Medium	Intelligent, trainable, fast	White, Gray, blue eyes	Quarter Horse
INFERNO	Medium	Agile, sure-footed, intelligent	Chestnut	Arabian
OBSIDIAN	Hot	Hardy, trainable, thick coat	Blacks, dark browns, bay	Morgan
RAVEN	Docile	Intelligent, trainable	Blacks	Friesian
SHADE	Docile	Trainable, brave, durable	Spotted black, white, dapple gray	Thoroughbred
SOLARA	Unknown	Unknown	Palomino, Cremello	Unknown

Venovia

Bergen Region

Blackhawk Village

Delford

North Bay

Blackhawk Druadan Station

Levilee

North Bay Eradication Center

George Eradication Center

Tox Zone Beta

Newworld

Ashburn Lake

Lake Crimela

Tox Zone Delta

Meridian Druadan Station

Tox Zone Alpha

Lotus Colony

Southern Ashburn Eradication Center

Ungy'eia

Parnia

Amber Coast

To Michael, for showing me the meaning of soulmate

Prologue

BRIGID

Two years ago

"I hope it's alright I invited a few friends," Sharice tells me as we settle into the seats by our table. "I think you'll like them."

"Uh, okay, yeah. No problem," I say, even as I wilt inside. I've been bugging my sister to take me to this restaurant since it opened and had looked forward to dinner being just the two of us. It seemed like every time we met up, which had been less and less, Sharice always had some new group of brilliant friends I needed to meet.

And they stole all her attention.

Palouse is an old building with a modern vibe. Its walls are adorned with paintings and photographs commemorating its namesake: a historic area where hundreds of wheat farms fell victim to the first of the great floods. The artwork captures the region's iconic landscape: rolling hills of golden grain fields, red-brick main streets, and tree-covered mountains. It evokes a nostalgic, almost bittersweet feeling, even for a place and time I've never experienced. The thought of vast stretches of land so far that you could walk for days without seeing the ocean is hard to comprehend.

A server hands us an unnecessary chalkboard menu, given it's on Network, but it adds a rustic charm. Sharice orders an expensive bottle of wine, and a goat cheese and smoked chicken appetizer for the table. They serve beef here, too, on a limited basis and at an exorbitant price. I promise myself once I graduate, I'll spend my first paycheck on a juicy hamburger.

"So," my sister asks me once the server leaves, "what classes are you taking this semester?"

"Circuit Foundations Two, Gaërgan art history, and Post-Rise Venovian Geography."

She tsks. "Circuit Foundations, but not a single science class?"

"Chemistry was full," I say, a little defensively. "And I don't need any more for my history major."

She wrinkles her nose, not hiding her displeasure. "History? Really? You can't do anything with that. Teaching positions are hard to come by, and unless you get a fellowship at one of the museums, you're going to wind up in an underfunded classroom at a filtration plant."

Our server brings the bottle of wine, and despite being furious, I smile politely at her. This is *not* the conversation I want to have. I didn't need another mom telling me I was making poor life choices; I needed a sister.

"There's this guy in my geography class," I say, changing the subject.

Sharice pours herself a glass before sliding me the bottle. "Oh? What's his major?"

"Engineering," I say proudly. "We meet at the library for study dates."

A hint of a rare smile touches Sharice's lips. She knows how big of a deal this is. I haven't dated anyone since Dane.

"His name is Coby, and I was hoping maybe next week you could meet him?"

She sips the wine, taking her time to savor it on her tongue. "We'll see."

Before I can tell her anything more, however, her friends arrive—Marcus, her roommate from college, and a few others I don't know. They greet her enthusiastically, kissing her on the cheeks and telling her how healthy she looks. Only after they've greeted her do they turn to me, shaking my hand and introducing themselves. I smile and appear friendly, but I can't help feeling out of place. Sharice surrounds herself with these ultra-cultured, super-intelligent people, and I never feel like I can contribute to the conversation.

"This is Paula and Shawn. They're biology grad students at DU," Sharice points to the two seated to her left. "And Danny and Nathanial are down at the end. They're working on a grassroots campaign to enforce Circuit board members to have term limits."

Paula's blonde curls frame an intense gaze, reminding me of a teacher during an exam. While Shawn, with his bloodshot eyes and pale skin, is clearly succumbing to the whole grad student experience.

At the opposite end of the table, Danny and Nathanial eagerly help themselves to the wine.

"Did you guys hear they're putting in a new filtration plant up north?" Marcus says. "Word is it'll be just outside Blackhawk."

Danny fills his glass and then passes the bottle to Paula. "Of course they are," she says. "The Drakefords would open one in every city if Circuit asked them to. The government subsidies are too good."

"I thought we didn't need one by North Bay because of the air currents?" I ask, taking a sip of wine. It's dry at first but finishes sweet enough, so I don't pucker too much.

"That's what we've always been told, isn't it?" Sharice responds. "I guess they were wrong. Or maybe they were lying to us the whole time, and we've been breathing toxic air without even knowing it."

"No way," Marcus says.

"Circuit controls Network," Paula adds. "So, it's not that unreasonable. Network is information, therefore, *they* control it. With no way to prove them right or wrong, they could literally lie to us about anything."

"Paula's right," Shawn says. "Who knows what else they're hiding?"

I shift uncomfortably in my seat, glancing around to see if anyone nearby is listening. Talk of conspiracies and rebellion always makes me nervous. Even just discussing these things can be risky these days.

"Should we really be talking about this?" I whisper to Sharice.

Sharice waves a dismissive hand. "Ah, don't worry so much, Brigid. We're just talking, that's all. Nobody's going to arrest us for having a conversation."

I bite my lip. Part of me wants to argue, but another part is curious to hear more about what Sharice and her friends think is going on. They're more educated than me and older. Maybe they are onto something.

"All right, just playing along here," Marcus says. "What do you think they're trying to hide from us with this filtration plant?" He leans forward intently. "I mean, if we really don't need it, then why are they building it?"

"That's the million-credit question, isn't it," Paula says. "My guess is they're trying to cover up some environmental disaster. Maybe there's been a leak or a spill that they don't want us to know about."

I shake my head. "But wouldn't people have noticed something like that? Wouldn't there be reports or evidence?"

"Not if Circuit had a hand in it," Sharice points out. "They could bury any reports or keep the media from covering it."

I feel a growing sense of unease as the conversation continues, my mind racing with all the implications. What if they're right? What if there really is some conspiracy or cover-up going on?

I've always been curious about the inner workings of the Network and Circuit, but I've never had the nerve to question them openly. I continue to listen to the discussion drift from new subject to new subject. Circuit board member who is retiring. New dean at DU. A shuttlecraft that set a new speed record.

When our server arrives with another bottle of wine, they all fall quiet for a moment, and I take a sip, using the alcohol to steady my nerves.

Marcus starts the conversation again to discuss the weeklong rain and the levies leaking. As the subject turns to the construction of more canals to divert water away from houses, the server soon returns, handing out our dishes. Once everyone has portioned out some food on their plate, Sharice clears her throat. "Okay. I have a confession to make."

Everyone pauses their chewing to listen. When Sharice

chooses, she effortlessly wields her charisma, capturing everyone's attention with a single sentence.

"I had dual motivations for inviting you all out tonight." The others exchange a curious look but don't interrupt. Sharice wipes her face with a napkin and briefly glances my way. Her eyes soften as if apologizing for keeping me in the dark, too. "You all remember I did that four-week internship at Blackhawk Station last year? Well, I didn't want to say anything until things were official, but I applied for a public relations position at Meridian. I interviewed yesterday, and they contacted me today to tell me I got it."

"I thought you hated Blackhawk?"

"I never said I hated it," Sharice scoffs. "I said I didn't like how they treated interns. I would be an employee there. I could have some control and authority."

"Meridian? Why on Earth would you want to work at some backwoods place like that?"

Sharice's finger traces the rim of her glass. "Because it'll be quiet."

Shawn shakes his head. "Every rich asshole I've known that flew out there for a demonstration complains about sand in their luggage when they get back."

"You guys are missing the point," Sharice says. "These days, they're doing groundbreaking genetic engineering with druadan cloning and figured what better way to apply my PR skills and my science background? Lannett is ridiculously hard to land a position at, and this will only boost my resume."

"I'd be the worst employee at a place like that," Paula says. "How could you even focus on your job with all those riders walking around? The demonstration ads make the riders look like they're spokesmen promoting fitness supplements. It makes you wonder if being 6'4" and being ripped is a prerequisite for their academy."

"I'm at low risk of being distracted," Sharice says, narrowing her eyes.

Paula laughs. "True. Still, you can't deny they're all sexy as hell."

Sharice's mouth curves into a smirk. "I'll be sure to send you photos when I get there."

Paula waves her drink. "You better."

Even the warm flush from my wine isn't enough to keep the sudden news that my sister will move hundreds of miles away from rattling me. After finishing my glass of wine, I find the words to speak. "When do you leave?"

Sharice plucks a piece of lint off the napkin before setting it down on the table. "Day after tomorrow."

We've never been super close, but since she moved to Delford, I'd secretly hoped we could grow to be that way.

Over the past six months, I'd enjoyed our weekly lunches and even the few times we'd gone to a stage play together. And now she'll be gone. Again. It's selfish to think she would have thought about telling me this before applying. Sharice never discussed her choices with anything with anyone. She opted instead to make her decisions, then spontaneously spout them to people, like switching her major from biology to communications three years in or taking a gap year after high school to roam Venovia by backpack.

Sharice looks at me out of the corner of her eye as if anticipating my next question.

"Have you told Mom?"

Sharice sighs. "She knows."

"What did she say?" I ask, suddenly feeling the heat of everyone's gazes on the side of my face. Sharice rarely talks about Mom with anyone but me, claiming she wanted her merits to be her own and not that of the prestigious biologist.

Sharice's eyes narrow, flaring with annoyance. "Nothing,

Brigid. And unlike you, I don't need her permission for where I go or what I do," Sharice snaps, causing me to jolt in my seat. "The sooner you realize you're never going to get Mom's approval, no matter what you do, the better."

My throat clamps down.

Don't cry. I command myself. I will not break in front of her or her friends.

"Excuse me," I say, voice cracking as I toss my napkin on the table and hurry to the bathroom.

Behind me, I hear Sharice say, "Let's order dessert."

One

BRIGID

I'd ridden a druadan.
 I should have blisters and burns everywhere my bare skin had touched him. I should've fallen off and cracked my skull on a rock. I should've suffocated when he'd phased—how many times, I'd lost count. But here I am. Breathing. Alive.

Moments like these, the ones that change everything, so often catch us off guard. Like my mom's warning about sneaker waves on the beach – they ambush you, dragging you under before you even realize what's happening.

That's how last night felt.

Just when I thought I'd found solid footing, another unexpected obstacle arose. The gala, my sister, the mystyl, riding

Galaxian, and the egg protecting me — all part of the unpredictable tide that had swept me away.

Sitting cross-legged in the sandy soil, I study the two-inch crack marring the druadan egg's blue shell — a glaring sign that everything has changed.

There's no coming back from this. No way to un-ring this bell.

The morning light beats down relentlessly, but despite the warmth, I shiver.

It was sheer luck I'd lived. Some primal instinct had forced me to leap clear of the truck before it crashed. And I had done more than survived, and I'd saved another life as well.

As if sensing my thoughts, the egg hums gently against my palms. The vibration is weaker now as if the little guy inside is exhausted from the night's events and has drifted off to sleep.

God, how I wish I could join him. A nap sounds *incredible* right now.

Heath, Logan, and Carter all stand before me, watching me. Finally, Carter steps closer and kneels, concern pinching his face. "Can you stand? Are you hurt?"

"I think so, just a little sore."

Relief smooths the lines on his forehead. "Good."

I reach out, running my thumb over the purple bruise on his left cheekbone. None of us escaped the attack last night unscathed. He leans forward, allowing me to cup his face, and closes his eyes, resting against my palm. That intense rider heat spreads from him and into my hand, and I wish that this moment could last forever.

But too soon, it passes, and his eyes open, revealing their hazel-green irises once more. I drop my hand back to the egg. His eyes remain steady on me as he gently clears loose strands that have fallen over my face.

Behind him, a fly circles Ember's leg, and he stamps his

hoof. It's impressive that their stallions stand without being tied, willingly choosing to be here, or because they're so thoroughly trained. Even Galaxian is lingering a little way off. He lowers his head and paws at the ground before lying down to roll in the dirt. As he shakes off the excess, he creates a cloud of dust. It's such an ordinary act, and it's hard to fathom he's anything dangerous.

Logan smashes two of the biting flies between his hands, then wipes the guts on his pants. "So, what do we do now?"

"The decision is clear," Heath says. "We have no choice but to take the egg back to Meridian." He casually rests his hands on his hips, but the slight tremor in his voice turns my blood to ice. He's the station manager. The one who's supposed to be in control. Who is assured and confident. Who makes the choices without hesitation.

"Assuming there's a station to take it back to," Logan adds.

Carter stands and holds out a hand. Carefully, I adjust the egg in my arms as he lifts my elbows and helps me up. The muscles in my legs threaten to give out, spurred on by that bone-gnawing fatigue that only comes after foregoing a night without sleeping. Sand clings to the corners of my eyes, and I wipe it away.

Heath and Logan's gazes are on me from where they stand, tall and imposing. The sun leaks around their muscular bodies, creating an almost ethereal glow around them.

Carter taps on his comm, and when it responds with a string of static, he curses under his breath.

Logan barks a laugh, waving to the surrounding dunes. "No towers, numb nuts."

Carter shoots him a glare and swivels the comm on his wrist so it shuts off.

"That answers that," Heath says. "Since we can't contact

them, let's assume Meridian is still intact. In which case, we will need to bring the egg back with us."

I open my mouth to protest, hoping to pounce on his indecision and convince him we should run with the egg or at least hide it, but Carter beats me to it. "You can't be serious? They're going to take it from us the second we're back."

Heath swipes a hand over his face. "I know. And they have every right to. That egg, the station, all of it is Circuit property."

"Please," I plead, wrapping my arms around the egg. I can feel my heart splitting at his words. We put our lives on the line for this egg, and now we're going to give it away. I have no idea where this overprotective urge to keep it safe is coming from, but I'm too exhausted to fight it.

Logan's stare scalds my face, and from the edge of my vision, I see him cross his arms. His biceps flex under his torn and dirt-stained shirt. "Seriously, Blondie. What are you going to do with it? Take it home to your apartment and keep it like a pet? You can't take care of it. Hell, *we* can't take care of it."

"I understand," I argue. "But it's a druadan hatching from an *egg*. Doesn't that mean something? Shouldn't it mean something?"

Carter rests a hand on my arm, his thumb gently stroking the sensitive skin on my wrist. "I know you don't want to hear this right now, but there's a reason they're born at the labs. They're so damn fragile. It's too dangerous for us to let it hatch anywhere but a station."

Tears prick the back of my eyes as the truth of their words strikes home.

They're right. I'm no rider. What right do I have to keep this egg? What knowledge or skills could I possibly offer to keep it alive? I don't know anything about raising a baby druadan. Hell, my friend Laura is the one who religiously watered my house plants when I forgot—which was often.

Heath lifts his chin. "I'll try to pull some strings and keep it here at the station, but you should prepare yourself if I'm unsuccessful and they do take it."

No. This is wrong.

I feel it in the very center of my being. This egg, somehow, in some impossible way, is supposed to be with me. And now it's just going to be ripped away, taken to some druadan lab where scientists will raise it in a glass box, and it will never see sunlight until it's grown.

I clutch the precious egg closer to my chest, glaring defiantly at Heath and the others. "I won't let you take it."

Carter steps forward. "Brigid, you're not thinking rationally right now. You're exhausted from everything that's happened."

"Don't patronize me!" I snap, every instinct screaming at me to protect this egg. Damn the consequences. If anyone should be on my side, it should be him. "I saved it, and it protected me."

Heath watches the standoff impassively; no doubt he's thinking the traumatic experience has broken me.

Maybe it has. The realization hits me like a sandbag to the gut. Is this how I'm avoiding dealing with Sharice? By fixating on this egg instead of confronting the truth that my sister wasn't coerced or manipulated — but had been the one orchestrating the rebel attacks all along? My heartbeat echoes in my eardrums as doubts assail me.

What *am* I doing? This isn't me. I'm a twenty-two-year-old nobody clinging to a druadan egg like some lifeline.

The whole path I've chosen feels so wrong as if I'm living a lie. My degree in history is useless for my PR job. And to make matters worse, my sister is a fugitive. A warm tear trickles down my cheek, and I lick my lips, tasting the salty flavor mixed with the dirt coating my mouth.

Carter exchanges a worried look with Heath. "We all want what's best for the egg," Carter says. "We'll figure this out together. I promise."

Heath stares into the distance while beside him, Carter begins pacing. "Say the station isn't destroyed," Carter says. "What if the rebels completely took it over, and everyone who didn't escape or die is now their prisoner? They could be hostages that Circuit at this very moment is trying to negotiate, and we'd be walking right into a death trap."

"He's right," Logan says. "We need to think this through before we rush back with our dicks in our hands. This egg is the only leverage we have, and it might be the only way to keep more people from dying."

"I witnessed at least one shuttle depart with guests from the gala," Heath says. "And another was being boarded when you took off on the truck, but we know what happened with that one, which leaves the majority of the staff still there."

Logan folds his arms. "No way they'd bring in more shuttles until the area was secure."

"Did you get a head count on rebels?" Heath asks.

"Two dozen, give or take."

"I took out at least three and winged a fourth," Carter says. "And I saw you hit two, Heath."

"I downed four, and my team chased down another three."

My stomach turns, listening to them rattle off the number of people they killed like a grocery list. It shouldn't surprise me. Vanguard was a military academy, after all, and they'd been trained alongside soldiers.

And while last night was all a blur, I'm relatively sure three rebels escaped on that boat, including my sister. How far she made it beyond that, I don't know. But as the lake was large and it was dark out, odds were good she'd made it to Nelworth, where she planned to escape with or without the egg in a car or shuttle waiting for her and the others. I shift my weight in the sand, feeling the grit rub against the burn on my ankle.

My heart stutters against my ribs as a thought jolts me. Here we are so preoccupied with the rebels taking over the station we hadn't even considered the other very real, very *dangerous* threat.

"I doubt we could hear any Circuit shuttles —" Carter says, but I cut him off.

"What about the mystyl?"

The three of them look at me. We might be at risk out here with any remaining rebels potentially finding us, but those venomous beasts were just as deadly, if not more so.

Cheeks burning from their rapt attention, I press on. "What if they survived? We know the terrorists released them to cause a distraction, but what about now? What if they're still there attacking anyone left alive, rebel or staff members alike?"

"Holy shit," Carter says and rubs his temples. "This is getting more complicated by the second."

We all turn to Heath.

"Ms. Corsair," he says, "brings up a good point. The station could be compromised in many ways; however, it is clear we cannot solve this until we obtain more information. Shall we remain out here? We will be subject to heat exposure and dehydration. Therefore, I propose we make our way back to the station, observing cautiously to assess the situation from a safe distance."

"And if it's not safe?" I ask.

Logan loops a thumb on his belt, where his laser pistol hangs in the holster. "Then I'll shoot anything that moves, Blondie."

Heath sighs. "It's agreed. Shall we?"

My tongue sweeps my back molars as I mull over Heath's words, yet my body refuses to move. Cradling the egg, I shakily nod. No one offers to take the egg, which is good because I'm not ready to give it to them, anyway. Not yet.

Heath shifts his gaze to me. "You need medical attention, and I wish for you to see Dr. Rajesh as soon as we're back within Meridian's walls."

"I'm fine," I quip, biting the inside of my cheek, trying to suppress the soreness in my back and shoulders. Then add, "Pretty sure you're hurt worse than me."

Heath hesitates, not bothering to look at the blood oozing from the cut on his thigh. I sense he wants to argue, but he sighs instead. "I'll get stitched up once we're all safely back at the station."

"What about the egg?" Carter asks.

"What about it?" Logan says.

"There's a crack in it," Carter says. "It's not like we can just put it back on the shelf in the hall, and no one will notice."

"Indeed. It will need to be addressed, and if Circuit isn't aware that the eggs were the intended target, we should inform them immediately. We are in uncharted waters here with the timeline for it to hatch."

I stare down at the crack. It hasn't changed, but judging by the high sun, several hours have passed. I wish I could see inside, like with an X-ray machine, and glimpse at the little creature that's trying to make its way out.

"Okay. Fine, we'll get it back to the station, but then what?"

"When we're in comm range, I'll call Marshal," Heath says. "He'll know what to do."

Logan starts walking up the nearest dune, sand shifting beneath his boots. "Daylight's burning."

Shadowmane moves closer to Heath. The stallion's

glowing pupil-less eyes seem to focus on me. They're unnerving, like those paintings that always seem to be watching you. A gentle humming whisks over my ears, and I know he's saying something only Heath can hear.

"He's asking about you and the egg," Heath supplies as if reading my mind. His hand flexes by his side as if debating about reaching out to me. Ever since we kissed, I'd felt this unresolved tension. I knew we needed to discuss it, but there hadn't been time.

His amber-brown eyes, filled with intensity, watch me and captivate my attention. He's so damn handsome. Dark, brooding, and controlling as hell.

I turn from him, warily eyeing Shadowmane. Though his gray hide may seem harmless, it's hotter than the scorching desert sand and would leave me with burns and blisters if I were to touch it. The intense vibrations I'd felt from the egg have stopped and I can guarantee whatever protections it'd given me are gone. All I'm wearing are the scraps of satin that had once been my formal dress from the gala, and my feet are bare. I don't have the protective carbon fiber pants or the bond like the other three to shield me.

Alright, so riding a druadan is out of the question.

Carter grabs a handful of Ember's mane and leaps onto his bare back while Heath leads Shadowmane to a rock so he can mount without straining his injured leg. He tries to hide it but winces as he hoists himself up.

The two stare down at me, then exchange a worried glance between each other.

"Go ahead. I'm okay to walk," I offer.

"Shit, Blondie," Logan calls down from the top of the dune. "It's a good five miles back. You're riding with me."

A surge of resentment courses through me. I hate that nickname, but even more, I hate that I need rescuing from him or am in this situation to begin with. Every inch of me is sore, every muscle exhausted. The thought of a long walk back to the station over sharp rocks and blazing hot sand is enough to keep me silent.

I sigh. "Fine."

Still carrying the egg, I scurry up the sandy bank away from the shallow pond and palm trees.

An old motorcycle leans against one of the thorny bushes that pass for trees on the island. As petroleum fuel is hard to find, motorcycles are relics. A novelty for the wealthy to use as living room centerpieces or adrenaline junkies to patch together a hybrid style, one that will use the more common methane. I've never ridden a motorcycle before, and a spike of adrenaline scorches my veins as he hands me a helmet. I hesitate, still gripping the egg, and he offers his hand.

"Hand it over," he says. "I'll tie it to the back." I pass it to him. With gentleness I didn't think he possessed, lash the egg to the back of the motorcycle with two thick canvas straps, securing it like a harness in a shuttle seat. I watch as his hands work, carefully testing the tension, ensuring it's secure but not too tight. Strong fingers move swiftly and deftly, and as he tucks his first two fingers under the strap to smooth it, a flicker of arousal ignites inside me. I must've reached the delirious state of exhaustion. Seriously, Brigid, they're just fingers.

Strong, skilled, gentle fingers. Flashbacks of Carter and I in the shower assault me, and I battle the intrusive thoughts that it was Logan's hands between my legs.

Or both of theirs.

I push aside the dirty thoughts as I put on the helmet and buckle the strap under my chin. Logan climbs onto the seat and waits for me. My dress makes it tricky, but I manage to swing a leg over and settle behind him without tearing the hem all the way up my thigh. I wrap my arms around his waist, the fatigue weighing heavier on me now that I'm seated.

"Do you know what you're doing?" I ask.

"Scared?" he replies.

"No." It's a bald-faced lie. I'm scared shitless.

He cranes his neck to look at me. "You galloped bareback on a druadan wearing nothing but a dress, but *this* scares you?"

"I wasn't thinking clearly. Now, I very much am."

Logan kickstarts the bike, and the engine rumbles to life. "Just don't fall off."

We begin to move and I tighten my grip, molding against his broad back. I cling to him. My life is in his hands, and a bevy of nerves flutter in my gut. There's an element of trust in riding with someone that hadn't crossed my mind. But I absolutely don't want to walk, so I have no option but to trust him. Logan guides the bike down the dune and onto the rocky terrain. There isn't a road, but a natural valley has formed where the runoff from the rain gathers, flowing downstream to the lake.

The motor vibrates beneath me, and I try to blend into the surroundings as best I can, like I'm trying to dance to a rhythm I don't understand. Leaning when he leans, anticipating when he accelerates. It seems to work because he remains focused, navigating the terrain, and only occasionally glances over his shoulder.

If I am doing something wrong, I have no doubt he'd tell me. Logan never keeps his opinion to himself.

Heath and Carter flank us on their galloping stallions, keeping pace with us on the motorcycle.

The air, hot and dry, carries the scent of sunbaked earth. My thoughts stretch ahead, envisioning what we're going to find once we reach the station. Straining to see, I peek over his shoulder. Shimmering heat waves stretch in the distance in the direction of the station. But there are no plumes of smoke, no hovering shuttles, just the desert's rocky horizon.

Small black moving specks appear, and my heart clenches with fear.

I pat Logan's side and point.

"I see them," he shouts over the drone of the motor.

The three black specks grow larger, and I recognize them as three dune buggies. They're at least a mile away but coming closer. Clouds of dust churn behind them as they climb over the dunes.

Logan stops the bike, and Carter and Heath pull their stallions to a halt.

"Fucking rebels," Logan growls, unclipping the strap on his holster.

"Hang on, trigger-fingers," Carter says. "They're too far away to tell who they are. Anyone could've taken the buggies."

Shadowmane jigs, tossing his head and eager to keep going. Heath tugs on the reins while pointing to a cluster of rock formations. "There."

The three of us make our way to where a pile of reddish sandstone boulders protects us from the line of sight.

"What now?" Logan asks.

"Figure we have about five minutes before they reach us," Carter says.

Heath's brow furrows. "I'll go out to greet them."

"Screw that," Carter says, nudging Ember around so the two stallions and the motorcycle form a triangle.

Logan turns off the bike and begins to climb off, swinging his leg in front. "I'm going with you."

"No," Heath says forcefully. "You two need to stay here with Brigid. If anything goes wrong, take her and the egg to safety."

"Don't be a fucking hero," Logan says but replaces his leg where it was on the foot peg.

From the back of the bike, I watch the exchange between the three men. The tense power struggle crackles in the air, and I wonder how much they're feeling each other out with the bond. Heath meets each of their eyes in turn, and when Carter opens his mouth to object, Heath silences him with a look.

Carter sighs in defeat and directs Ember past us to the far side of the rock wall.

"Fine," Logan grumbles, "but if I catch one whiff of rebel stank, I'm coming out there."

"Same," Carter adds, shifting in his saddle.

With a firm kick, Heath spurs Shadowmane to the right and out of the protective shade. The black and gray stallion's muscles ripple as he moves into a springing trot.

Heart in my throat, I can do nothing but watch as the sound of roaring engines grows louder, and in a wave of dust, three buggies encircle the two of them.

Two

Logan

Two dune buggies swarm around Heath and Shadowmane. White flags with the station's druadan-head logo sway in the air as four khaki-uniformed Circuit police quickly exit from the sides.

A woman's voice cuts through the drone of the buggy engines. "Whoa there. Put your hands up."

"Hello," Heath says, holding up the one free hand that isn't on the reins. "I'm Heath Lockwood, Meridian's station manager."

The woman falters. "Master Rider Lockwood? Oh, thank the tides." Her face visibly relaxes, and she waves at the other officers to stand down. "I'm Deputy Ewensen. My officers have been out here looking for you for hours. Are you alright?"

She's dressed in an official uniform with silver chevrons on her right shoulder, marking her as an officer.

Fifty yards of desert divide us, but if it turns out they're rebels with stolen uniforms, and shit goes sideways, that's not enough. They're armed and outnumber us. I'll hardly have a chance to start the bike before they either shoot me or take out a tire.

I keep my attention fixed on the biggest guy. He'll be the first I'll have to deal with.

Ewensen loops her thumbs in her belt next to a laser pistol, and the tension eases. She's used to this uniform and having a gun. Her odds of being a rebel just went down a notch.

"There were reports that you and two fellow riders rode out here," she says. "When none of the other search parties had luck, I decided to come out here myself and look."

A third buggy arrives, and while Heath's mouth moves, replying to her, the engine drowns out his response.

"Keep your eyes peeled," I whisper.

"You don't trust them?" Brigid says.

"Not for a goddamn second." My hands clamp down on the handlebars, refusing to obey Heath's orders any longer. "Hang tight." I start the bike and drive it out from behind the rock wall.

"Logan, wait," Carter says, but I cruise past him and Ember. I sense he's following me as I park to the right of Shadowmane and see him direct his red stallion to the left.

Ewensen shifts her gaze to us along with her officers. If they want to shoot me, they had better not miss because they won't get a second chance. I don't care who they are, but I'd rather take one between the eyes than be dumped in a tox zone prison.

"Master Riders McCelroy and James, I presume? Glad to see you're all alive and in one piece." She squints at Brigid, seated behind me. "And you are?"

"Brigid Corsair," Heath answers for her. "She works at the station. The attackers took her hostage, and we followed them out to rescue her."

"That's a surprising amount of effort for one person, Master Lockwood, from you and two master riders," Ewensen says, "rushing out here on your stallions unsaddled while the station is under attack."

"There were other factors at play, I assure you," Heath replies.

He's referring to the egg, but the boss man knows better than to show all his cards until he's sure he has the better hand. Bitch thinks we abandoned the station for a woman.

It's bullshit. She's trying to get under our skin. An interrogation tactic to see if we'll slip and admit we're part of the attack.

No fucking way are we going to make this easy for her. If she thinks we're connected, she can do her job and interrogate us one by one.

"Ms. Corsair," she says, lifting her chin. "You're welcome to ride with us back to the station?"

I start the engine and rev it. "I guarantee Blondie is safer with me."

She says nothing but pulls her hands a little snugger around my waist.

Deputy Ewensen nods. "Very well. Shall we go?"

Heath looks at Carter, then at me on the motorcycle, then at the egg strapped down on the back. They're worried that I'll do something stupid. In most situations, they'd be right, but not now. I know when to pick a fight and this is not the time.

Assured I'm not going to react, Carter and Heath urge their stallions forward. The officers climb back into their buggies, and one takes the lead while the two others circle around us.

The familiar warmth pressing against my breastbone tells

me he's near enough to sense the bond. Galaxian is nowhere to be seen. "*Smart boy,*" I whisper, although he's probably out of earshot.

"All right," I say. "Time to go."

Exhaustion sags my shoulders, but I shrug it off. Can't afford to be dragging ass right now. From the corner of my eye, Blondie's face is drawn tight and her dress looks like she went ten rounds with a flamethrower, but there's a fierceness burning in her eyes that I haven't seen before.

I'll give her this — learning her sister is part of a terrorist group and nearly cashing in her chips in trying to save the egg — hasn't broken her.

This side of her is doing something for me.

I am so fucked.

I avert my gaze, feeling her reposition into the seat before kick-starting the engine again. Plumes of dust hover ahead of us, kicked up by the buggies.

I grip the handlebars as the dark figures of Ember and Shadowmane disappear in the cloud of dirt. The buggies lead, and we follow. Brigid tightens her hold around my waist, and her bare feet are dangerously close to the heat of the engine. "Lift your legs," I call out over my shoulder but my words are immediately swept away in the rushing wind.

She raises them and rests her feet on the outside of my boots, allowing my legs to shield her. Protectiveness flares within me. She almost died last night. The thought of her lying broken turns my mouth to ash.

As she shifts into position, our bodies press even closer together, and I feel her breasts resting on my back through the thin fabric of her dress. My dick jerks to attention, and I suck in a sharp breath, focusing on the shifting sand and trying to distract myself from the growing hunger inside me.

I doubt she knows she's the first passenger I've ever had.

When I make runs out here, if I found anything, I'd return to the station or call for someone on my team to come out on a buggy. I try not to dwell too much on how seamlessly she fits against me, her body moving in time with mine. Fuck, it feels good having her tucked securely at my back. It's a dangerous path, getting attached — but each second I'm near her, she carves herself deeper into me.

I clench my jaw, forcing my mind away from the confusing thoughts. I've got enough shit to deal with. The sand under the tires shifts and moves, making the motorcycle fight against my control as we navigate the dunes. Between the jagged rocks and thorny bushes, the landscape is treacherous to an unskilled rider, but I've made dozens of passes out here chasing down reports of poachers or paparazzi trying to get shots of the riders. I know this island better than anyone.

We reach the shell of the wrecked truck submerged in a dune with its twisted metal frame and smoldering engine compartment.

Brigid's body tenses, and I gun the bike, leaving the wreck in our wake.

Carter and Heath's stallions pin their ears as they gallop beside us. The animal trail widens into a maintenance road. As soon as I'm closer to them, the bond between us flares brightly. Fleeting glimpses of their thoughts blur into mine — jealousy from Carter, from Blondie riding with me, and Heath's general undercurrent of worry.

I'm not as skilled as they are at sharing emotions, but I still try to will some of my 'don't give a shit attitude' into it. It works. Their reaction is subtle, but both stallions lift their heads a little higher and prick their ears.

Half an hour of hard riding later, the station's main gate looms ahead. The buggies slow, and the gate opens, and we all pass through the gap in the perimeter wall. Gray smoke rises from the storage building I'd blown up to take out the slimy fuckers, and Circuit police move among the rubble, guns in hand, directing maintenance staff and medics.

Once in the courtyard, I pull the bike to a stop and drop the stand. In the center, two police shuttles are parked. One of them had smashed a flower pot during landing.

Insenstive pricks.

Blondie's arms loosen around my waist as I swing my leg over, boots crunching in the sunbaked dirt. She dismounts beside me and peels off the helmet.

She sets it on the seat and then runs her hands through the tangles of her hair. It catches the morning sunlight like strands of spun silver. My eyes shamelessly drag over her, traveling upward to the gentle swell of her breasts, rising and falling with each breath.

Everything about her calls to me, like she's been ripped from my fantasies and made real.

But a fantasy is all she can remain. My parents. Vanguard, and now, Galaxian. Call it bad karma or shitty ass luck, I poison anything good.

Every instinct tells me to protect her, and yet how can I if I'm the threat? It's inevitable. No matter how much I may want to be with her, my own fucked up life is dogged by misery and failure. My darkness will only dull her radiance, so I'll do the right thing. I'll keep my mouth shut and hands to myself. If I need to get my dick wet, I've got plenty of other less complicated options.

Tearing my gaze from Blondie, I look at where Deputy Ewensen and the other officers are standing by the idling buggies. She cuts a glance my way before her eyes dart to the desert behind me, searching for any sign of Galaxian.

Nice try, but my boy is long gone.

Heath and Carter catch up, and Ewensen's eyes snap back to them as they dismount. "Now that we're all accounted for. There's a sensitive matter I need to discuss with you, Master Lockwood. I'll give you a few minutes to secure your mounts, seek first aid, and check on your staff before meeting me at the main house."

"Of course." Shadowmane lowers his head as Heath slides his reins over. "The barn is secured, I presume?"

"It is," Ewensen says. "We've had it scanned multiple times, and no mystyl remains."

She looks at one of her nearby officers. "Escort Ms. Corsair to the medical office and see to it that the egg is safe in the barn."

"Yes, ma'am," he says, and he and two others stride toward us.

One reaches out to take her elbow, and immediately, I shove myself between them. "Don't touch her." My lip curls into a snarl as I emphasize each word.

The officer's eyes widen, and his mouth gapes like a fish out of water. "Master Rider, I was only —"

"It's fine, Logan," she says, giving him a small smile that says she's anything but. She looks at the badge on his jacket. "Officer Bradley, is it?"

He nods, avoiding my gaze. "If it isn't obvious enough, we're all a bit jumpy. There's no need to escort me. I know where to go."

Carter approaches leading Ember. "You good?" he asks, keeping his voice low.

Her eyes brighten upon seeing him. "I'm better now that we're back."

My fists flex by my side. No way am I jealous of fuckboy.

"Same," he says. "Why don't you go get checked out at the clinic? I can take the egg to the barn and come by after."

Her mouth parts slightly as she hesitates but finally relents.

Carter and I work to loosen the straps but position the egg so it's in a makeshift sling. The entire time, worry and concern radiate through the bond, coating my tongue with an acrid taste. He holds the egg over his chest with the straps. "Stay with her," he commands, as if I don't already know what he's thinking.

I nod, shoving against the wave of anxiety with my cooling reassurance as I'd done on the ride here.

Carter gives Brigid one more sympathetic look, then leads Ember, Officer Bradley, Heath, and the other officers in the direction of the barn at the north end of the station. Ewensen remains, her gaze lingering a moment too long on her before she falls into step behind the group.

"Let's go." I kick-start the motorcycle.

"I'll walk," she says, and so I idle the bike beside her. Meridian's not as wrecked as I had anticipated, although it does look like a tornado swept through it. Debris is scattered everywhere; black streaks from laser blasts smear the walls of the guest houses and storage buildings. Amidst the wreckage, smoke and the stench of death hung in the air.

At the small medical clinic attached to the workout center, I park the bike.

"When you're in there, keep your mouth shut about the egg," I warn her.

Her blue eyes widen. "You can't think Doctor Rajesh and the nurses would —"

"Meridian was attacked," I cut her off. "We can't be ignorant and think that there weren't insiders involved. The whole place is compromised, and anyone could've been part of it."

She hesitates, and I know she wants to argue. The usual

brightness of her blue eyes fades, and something inside me cracks. Insiders. She thinks I'm referring to her because of her sister.

Fuck. I should've kept my goddamn mouth shut. "Come on then," I say, changing the subject and holding the door open for her. "You look like hell."

Three

BRIGID

I inhale the cool air conditioning of the clinic as a medic dressed in a white jumpsuit with a blue stripe down the arm and leg rushes over to me. She's wearing black-rimmed glasses and a polka dot scarf covering the lower half of her face to keep from choking on the insistent dust.

She's new brought in from Leviler or Delford to help with triage.

She eyes me up and down. "You staff or a guest?"

"Staff," I croak over my parched throat.

"Anything urgent?"

I shake my head. "I don't think so." Except I'm thirsty enough to drain a pool.

She tugs the scarf down and purses her lips when her eyes

land on my arms. "Let me see." She clasps my hands and turns them over. "Some of these scrapes are deep. I need to wash them, or they'll get infected."

I chew the inside of my cheek, hearing the memorized list of flesh-eating bacteria my mom forced me to commit to rote memory when she'd warned me against swimming in the lagoon. When I was thirteen, I defied her and accepted a dare from the kids at the neighboring filtration plant to dive into the water. I won the bet but also sliced the bottom of my foot open on a piece of coral. I kept it hidden for a while until the angry red stripes had climbed up past my ankle from the blood poisoning. I shiver at the thought. For days, my foot had felt like I dipped it in lava.

"That looks like a nasty bump on your head." She reaches into one of her pockets and pulls out a bottle of aspirin.

I take two gratefully and wash them down with the cup of water she hands me.

"Rest here. I'll be back with some medicine and the doctor." Then she leaves, and Logan and I are left alone in the exam room. He hasn't said a word since we've been here, hovering like a shadow while she examined me.

"You don't have to stay here," I tell him as he paces on the tile floor. "Really, I'm okay. If you want to go help Heath and Carter, I'll be fine."

He stops his pacing long enough to shoot me a hard look. *That's a no.*

I sigh, resting my hands on my lap. This is the first quiet moment I've had to sit with my thoughts, and now, with the painkillers beginning to dull the pain, my mind is catching up. The smell of burning rubber. The last words I'd spoken to my sister. The truck crash. The frantic ride on Galaxian. A tsunami of memories crashes over me. I press my hands to the backs of my eyes, trying to sift through everything.

"I'm sorry." The words flit from me before I can stop them, and I drop my hands.

Logan halts mid-stride. "What the hell for?"

"I shouldn't have chased after my sister," my voice cracks, but I push on. "I should have waited and found you or Carter or Heath first before going after her." I pause, drawing in a shaky breath. "I should have been more careful."

"Yeah. You should've."

I wince, even though I knew this was the exact response I'd get. If I'd wanted sympathy or forgiveness, Logan was the *wrong* person to ask. But I needed to say it for myself because I didn't know if I'd get another chance. Who knew what tomorrow would bring? There was a chance I no longer had a job and that soon Logan would no longer be a rider.

I could only imagine the guilt he felt right now being tied to a stallion that was considered dangerous. So, what would it hurt to offer him a small amount of encouragement? "He saved me, you know," I continue. "When I found the egg, rebels surrounded me. They were going to kill me and take it if Galaxian hadn't shown up when he did."

Logan doesn't reply and begins pacing again while staring at the floor. I'm not sure if he heard me when he suddenly stops. "Shit!" he curses, clutching his hand as if someone had jabbed a hot poker through it.

I push myself from the chair. "What's wrong?"

"Stay here," he snarls, turning away.

"Wait, where are you going?"

"To find my damn stallion." And then he's gone, the curtain fluttering shut behind him.

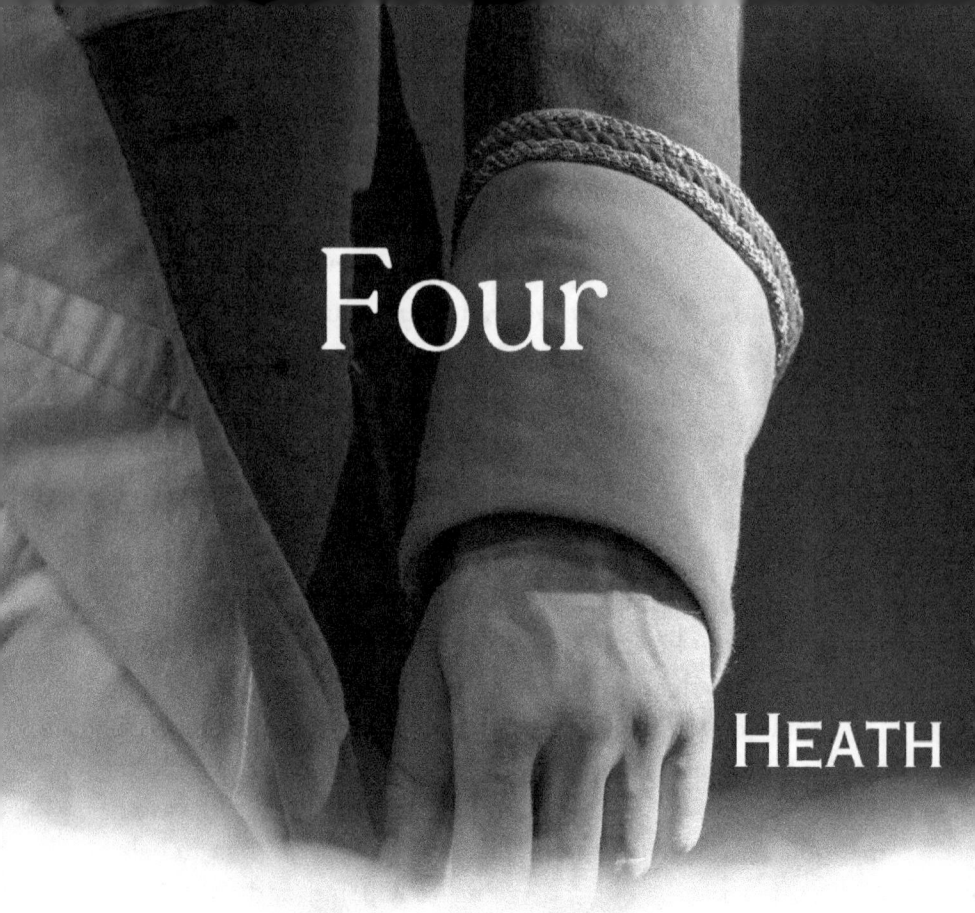

Four

Heath

I've failed.

My one job, above all others, was to protect the station, and in the moment it mattered most, I let it slip through my hands.

From the moment we returned, I was overwhelmed with questions and endless what-ifs. The careful control I've always prided myself on had unraveled, leaving me to grapple with the sting of undeniable failure. What had I done wrong? What had I missed?

Were there signs or clues that the attack was coming? Why wasn't I prepared? Should we have had a better evacuation plan? Hired more security? Had more extensive background checks on the guests?

No matter how many times I run through the questions, one remains.

Was there an insider at the station that was responsible? Someone who had betrayed us?

I trusted my staff. Considered some closer than my family. Besides Brigid, no one else had been hired recently.

We'd been so careful.

And yet, the rebels had found their way onto the station undetected and brought those monsters with them.

A disaster like this wasn't supposed to happen at a station; but it had, under my watch.

The interior of the barn is a wreck. Equipment, tack, and feed pellets are strewn everywhere. Two stall doors hang sideways from their hinges, and the aisleway is littered with shriveled, dried-up mystyl tentacles that resemble the snake-skin sheds we find in the spring outside the perimeter wall. Worried voices of druadans hum all around me, and while I am not their bonded rider, I sense their collective fear. They're all on edge, spooked and skittish.

And rightfully so.

I scan the stalls, relief flooding through me when I spot none of them empty. Ewensen had assured me we hadn't lost any druadans or riders, but I needed to see it for myself.

Carter and I put away our stallions. I spent a good ten minutes using the specially insulated metal combs, brushing Shadowmane until his white coat gleamed and the tangled bits of sagebrush were freed from his black tail.

He's the oldest stallion here, and in the bright lights of the barn, I notice the slight way in his back, the sunken space above his eyes, and the patchy hair on his face around his face nubs. I rub oil on his nose and liniment on his legs before checking his hooves for damage. I frown when I discover he's thrown his front right shoe.

However necessary we'd felt at the time, the hard gallop over the rocky terrain at night without leg protection for our druadans was a reckless decision. And while I wouldn't have changed what I'd done and encouraged Carter to do, Ember's sure-footedness and Shadowmane's experience were only half the reason we'd returned alive and with only a few nicks and scrapes.

Luck had been the other.

"Does anything hurt?" I ask him, my throat vibrating with the low sound.

"I am happy to run and can run more, but prefer a nap."

It's impossible to hear other stallions talk, but in conversing with other riders, I've learned each stallion has their own mannerisms, tone, and even accents, often mirroring their rider's style of speaking.

At some point in his forty years, Shadowmane had had a rider with a lisp, and every so often, I'd catch a trace of it, and it'd make me smile. Feeling like a part of that rider remained, even though he'd flared out years ago.

I was Shadowmane's sixth rider, and according to station records, two had made it the full ten years. He'd never spoken about them, and I'd assumed it was too painful. Unlike us, druadans *did* mourn the passing of their rider. They'd go off feed, become agitated, unpredictable, and even dangerous until the chemical reaction in their brain or alignment of the moon or whatever happened to trigger another bond.

His chest rumbles, and hot air blows from his nose. *"No more. Bad worm?"*

"No. They're all gone. We're safe."

His nostrils flare as he sniffs to ensure I am not lying to him.

I lightly stroke the soft fur on his muzzle. The skin on my hand feels like I've plunged it into almost-too-hot bathwater, and I savor the feeling, letting it radiate through me and our connection. Heat means pain, but to me, it's also a comfort. A reminder my stallion is alive and healthy. It means our bond is strong. *"I swear,"* I tell him. *"If there are more, I will take you somewhere safe."*

I dump a scoop of protein pellets into his bucket and then stay by his side as he eats them. Not even a minute later, he nudges the empty bucket. *"More?"*

A smile tugs at the corners of my mouth. *"Eat all you want,"* I murmur. *"And rest now. I'll be back later."*

As he buries his nose in the second helping, I step out of the stall. Carter is exiting Ember's across from me with a comb in his hand and his dirt-stained button-up shirt now covered in Ember's red hairs.

Roberts calls out from the center of the barn. "Carter! Heath! Over here."

At twenty-eight, Roberts is the oldest rider here, but his round baby face and the fact that his head barely reaches my chest often make him appear as the youngest. His right eye is ringed with a purplish bruise, and he has a bandage on his left forearm. He appraises us, lingering briefly on my leg.

I shield it from his vision with a hand. "Didn't move fast enough," I say when his brow furrows. He gives a small nod before switching to Carter.

"I'm all good," Carter says, "just feel like I've been dropped from a shuttle."

A tight smile appears on Roberts' face. "Sounds about right." With a look of disgust, he nudges a desiccated mystyl tentacle with his boot.

"And McCelroy?"

"Alive."

Roberts barks a laugh. "I'm not surprised. I pity the idiot who tries to take him down."

"How are the rest of the riders?" I ask.

"Nelson broke his arm trying to get Gemindusk out last night," Roberts says grimly. "Dr. Gideon treated four stallions for burns."

I let out the tense breath I'd been holding. Not good. Druadans heal fast but are still prone to infections, but because of their genetic fragility, they don't tolerate antibiotics well.

"Nice to see you made it, Lockwood," Dr. Gideon says, emerging from a stall two doors down. He yawns, then pries off the protective gloves and stuffs them into his back pocket. "Regarding McCelroy, you should make sure he's prepared if they need to sedate Galaxian. I ensured the dosage and will continue to do regular checks."

Sedate Galaxian? I let out a long sigh.

Logan is going to *love* that.

Dr. Gideon nods to me. "Now, if you don't have any concerns for Shadowmane, I'd like to check on Ember first."

"Of course," I say, shifting out of the way to let him pass.

Carter follows the druadan vet back to his stallion's stall, and the gate creaks as he lets him inside.

As Gideon goes to Ember, I instruct two novices to begin sweeping the scattered straw and mystyl parts into a biohazard bag Gideon provided.

Dr. Gideon and Carter return, and I ask how he's doing. "The wound is mending well, and as long as he can rest for a while, I think he'll be fit for training again." His eyes drift between us. "To be honest, a few days' rest would be good for all of us."

Carter flashes him a roguish grin. "Rest? Maybe when I'm dead."

Dr. Gideon shakes his head. "I know my advice is often wasted on you riders, but it's my duty as a doctor to say it, anyway."

Carrying his leather bag with supplies, he moves off to see the other stallions. He'd been away in Leviler during the gala and the attack, and I was pleasantly surprised he'd agreed to cut his trip short to return here and tend to the stallions, not to mention stay on at the station altogether. Lesser men would've been scared off, swearing that the pay wasn't worth the risk. However, he'd dedicated his life and profession to working on and around one of the world's most dangerous creatures.

Two other riders, Ve'loth and Nelson, stand in a half-circle formation, blocking the aisleway. Their clothes and faces are stained with blood and grime, and their eyes have dark circles under them from lack of sleep.

"You guys look like shit," Carter says. "I'm fine to stay here if you want to grab some shut-eye."

None of them move. Of course, they're refusing to leave. I'd do the same. A warmth of pride washes over me.

I assess the group of men, seeing the weariness etched on their faces. While Logan, Carter, and I had been out trying to save Brigid, they'd been here trying to save the stallions and themselves. "I'm encouraging you all to take the next few days off. We will postpone demonstration practice for the time being to allow you and the other staff to rest and recover from this event. You may take personal leave and the shuttle as you see fit to be with your families or partners if you wish."

No one says anything. Being separated from our stallions right now is the last thing any of us want. Stressful events are known to trigger brimming, and all of us are going to have to be extra careful until things calm down. I rub the back of my hand where the silver crescent-shaped scar is. The mark that Shadowmane branded me with two years ago. Only a mild tingle radiates up my arm, ensuring me the bond is healthy.

"I appreciate the offer," Nelson says, speaking first, "but if it's all the same, I'd like to stay here. Gemindusk is stressed as hell, and I'd hate to be far from him until he's eating again."

Nods and murmurs of agreement come from the others.

"Very well," I say, clapping him on the shoulder. "Carter and I have a meeting, but please message us if anything comes up."

I push through the heavy barn doors, stepping out into the searing heat of midday. Carter and I stride toward the guest houses when Petyr, from maintenance, intercepts me with a tablet clutched in his hands. "I've been looking for you, sir, if you have a minute? We need to talk about cleanup. The waste bin is full. Matt broke his arm and is out, so I think it's time to call in a disaster crew from Leviler."

Before I can answer, I catch a glimpse of Carter heading off behind me to the clinic. A ripple of lust tingles through our bond, unmistakable and distracting. He's off to see Brigid. I suppress a sigh, feeling the pull of desire myself.

"Sir?" Petyr repeats.

"Uh, yes, have the Circuit administrator in Leviler call me, and I'll push it through."

Satisfied, Petyr leaves. I'm stopped three more times by requests as I make my way to the main house. I'm the station manager, the one responsible for making the decisions.

Good or bad, it all falls on me.

Five

BRIGID

I barely have time to comprehend Logan's abrupt and cryptic departure when the nurse re-enters, bringing with her a metal tray holding a cotton cloth, bandages, and a brown glass bottle of disinfectant. The scent of alcohol stings my nose as she pours some on the fabric.

Dr. Rajesh is close behind her. He's unshaven and has a bandage over his left eye. He's still wearing his tux from the gala, and his bow tie is askew.

"Oh, thank the stars, you're okay, Ms. Corsair," he says. "I'd like to look you over if that's all right?" He wipes his hands on a towel and then sets it on the counter next to him.

I agree, and he starts to examine me, asking me questions about what happened. Logan's warning echoes in my ears, and

I answer in short, strained sentences, keeping details to a minimum and only those that pertain to any injuries he finds.

When he finishes, his eyes are serious as he looks at me. "You have extensive bruising on your right arm and shoulder, multiple lacerations and burns, and that cut on your head will probably scar." He notes something on his tablet. "I'll prescribe something stronger for the bruising if you want."

I shake my head. "Aspirin is fine."

"Okay." He pats my shoulder. "Good seeing you. Laney will get you cleaned up, and then I suggest you get some rest."

"Thank you," I tell him, and he pulls back the curtain and disappears. There's a light murmuring from somewhere beyond as he greets another patient.

"So, yeah, I'm Laney, by the way," the medic who'd first greeted me says cheerily. "Can I get your full name, please?"

"Brigid Corsair."

She keys in my name on her tablet. Another medic enters with hunched shoulders and graying roots under her brown hair. She gives me a passing glance before setting to restock one of the canisters on the counter with soap.

"Age?" Laney asks.

"Twenty-two."

"Any allergies to medications or food?"

"Mushrooms."

Laney gives me a questioning look.

"If I eat too many, I.. well, last time I did, me and the toilet became real good friends."

"Best avoid those, then shall we?" She laughs and swipes it on the screen.

"Current medications?"

"Anti-pregnancy implant."

Laney doesn't blink, but the other older medic pins me with a dubious look.

While perfectly legal and easily accessible, birth control is rare in Venovia, given that infertility rates are exceptionally high. Most couples are lucky to get one child, and two, like Sharice and I, are quite rare. Growing a stagnant population is the best way to rebuild humanity.

I, however, was nowhere near ready for a baby.

Especially now that my future was so uncertain. The implant was my peace of mind, but looking as though my current options were all riders, it's pretty much worthless.

Laney dabs ointment on the sores on the soles of my feet, and I wince. The stench of smoke clings to my hair, and I do my best to keep from wincing at the stinging sensation.

"The analgesic effect will kick in soon, and it should numb the pain," she says.

Her hands move with purpose, applying ointments with a touch lighter than air, soothing the fire beneath my skin. Apparently, the truck explosion had left me with more burns and abrasions than I'd realized because just when I think she's found them all, she repositions an arm or leg and finds more to smear with cream.

Satisfied she got them all, she takes my blood pressure and temperature. She marks down some notes on her tablet.

"Everything looks good." She eyes my ruined gown. "Let's say we get you changed?"

A choked laugh escapes me. "I really liked this dress."

"I'm sure it was pretty. If it's any consolation, I've heard we'll be getting hazard pay so that you can buy yourself a new one." Laney helps me down from the table before leading me to a private room.

"Can I take a bath?" The idea of cleansing away the grime and smoke with a shower is almost visceral.

"Sorry. The main water pump broke during the attack,"

Laney explains, frowning. "I heard they wanted to set the place on fire and not allow us to put it out."

A chill runs through me at the realization of how much worse it could've been. If people were trapped in the exhibition hall and buildings while lit on fire and left with no way to extinguish it., dozens could've died.

I've stayed strong the whole time since we've come back to the station. But now, for some reason, being told I couldn't rinse off the sweat and grime, despair overpowers me, clawing at me, trying to drag me down into the darkness. The task of changing out of my tattered dress seems as daunting as scaling a mountain. Laney's hands are a blessing as she carefully peels off my gown and guides me into a pair of loose medic scrubs. My body rebels, stiff and sore, every movement a stilted dance of pain and determination. I clench my teeth as I tug on the scrub pants and a too-big t-shirt.

Once changed, Laney hands me a pair of slip-on sandals like the ones they sell at the beach tourist shops, then stuffs the remnants of my dress into a drawstring laundry bag and hands it to me.

"There's dried fruit, crackers, and juice out here," she says, leading me from the private room.

I wander to the table of food in the corner and pluck one of the metal bottles of water from it. It's room temperature and has a metallic aftertaste, but I don't care.

In my whole life, water has never tasted this delicious.

Once sated, I set down the empty bottle in the recycling crate and let my gaze drift over the injured staff lying on the cots. Four in total — one with an arm in a sling, two others with gauze wrapped around various limbs, and my eyes linger on the fourth with the most extensive bandages.

Dr. Rajesh sidles up next to me and follows my gaze. "A security guard found him unconscious with mystyl tentacles still clutched in his hands." He shakes his head grimly. "Bastard gave them a hell of a time before the toxin knocked him down."

"Is there an antidote or something for the venom?" I ask, almost afraid of the answer. I knew from my attack before the answer was no, but I clung to the hope that maybe they'd had time to find something new.

Dr. Rajesh's face is grim. "It's not like a snake where we can get anti-venom. From what we can tell, the injuries from a mystyl act much like severe chemical burns, and a high enough exposure will cause paralysis or with extensive tissue damage could even kill."

I shudder, a phantom of pain radiating through me from my ankle. I knew all too well how painful those burns could be. I couldn't imagine a person's entire body covered in them. The agony had to be unbearable.

Another anguished groan comes from the cot beside us, and Dr. Rajesh rushes to tend to him. The man's face is swollen and blistered, so much so that his features are nearly unrecognizable. A vice clamps down on my heart as I realize it's one of the groundskeepers.

Rajesh gently lifts the oxygen mask to allow him a sip of water through cracked, bleeding lips.

"Hurts..." the man rasps out, his eyes wild with pain even through the morphine haze.

"I know, I know," Rajesh murmurs. "You're receiving the strongest pain medication we have. There's nothing else I can give you. I'll check on that transfer to Leviler General."

He replaces the mask and adjusts the intravenous drip, and the man's body stills, although his breaths are still labored. I take a step closer, the faint scent of antiseptic mingling with the sharper, saltier tang of sweat and blood. My stomach churns at the sight.

Red, angry welts streak his arms and legs. His breath hitches, and I squint at the wounds, trying to understand the extent of the damage.

"Until we know more, we're treating the injuries like jellyfish burns," he offers.

"Is it working?"

He sighs, wiping his brow with the kerchief from his tux pocket. "Well enough, considering. We're using all the equipment and medicine we have on hand. It's not perfect, but it's keeping them stable. We've sent samples of the tissue to the lab in Uncy'lia to analyze and see if they can come up with a better anti-toxin," he explains. "It'll take several days, but it's our best hope."

Absorbing the information, I chew my bottom lip when a groan from the next cot draws my attention. Another victim groans, his skin mottled with the same red welts. The medics move quickly, but I see their uncertainty and fear. They are doing their best. However, judging by the hushed side conversations and exchanged looks with the doctor, this is beyond their scope.

These creatures are supposed to be dead. Mythological monsters used to scare children into behaving. The war had wiped from existence centuries ago.

Why would Sharice bring them back and then let them loose here? She'd known I was here. Wasn't she worried I'd be killed too?

Just as I'm getting ready to leave, the clinic door bursts open, and Carla rushes in. "There you are!" she exclaims, making a beeline towards me. "Thank god you're okay." Without hesitation, she wraps me in a tight embrace, and I instinctively lean into her, savoring the warmth and comfort of her presence.

We've grown close over the past few weeks, bonding

through the challenges of putting together the gala. I cling to her, grateful for her safety as well.

"I was so worried," Carla whispers, her voice trembling. "I'd heard the rebels took you during the attack." She pulls back, her eyes searching mine for reassurance.

My heart plummets at the doubt I see reflected there. She wasn't worried about me being hurt; she was afraid I was part of the attack and the rebels. How far does her doubt go? Does she think I stole the egg, too? Would she have already called the police if she knew Sharice was my sister?

A wave of hurt and disbelief engulfs me, cutting deeper than any physical injury ever could. I swallow the lump in my throat. "I'm okay," I say, mustering a faint smile. "Just shaken up."

Carla seems to relax at my words, but the seed of mistrust has been planted. "How on earth did you escape them?" she says. "You must've been so scared."

I press my lips together. I can't tell her the truth, one because she'd never believe me, and two because it would only lead to more questions—questions I don't have the answers to. I narrow my brows. I've been holding it together, keeping the fear buried, but now I let my guard down, and it rushes to the surface raw and real. "I've never been more terrified." My voice cracks. "It was a nightmare, and I must have a guardian angel because a police shuttle came right on time and shot at them. When they were distracted, I ran."

Intrigued by my story, Carla's dark eyebrows inch higher. "Wow, you escaped, and you *saved* the egg?"

I shrug sheepishly, lowering my eyes to my hands. "Yeah. One at least."

As if sensing my mood, Carla's hand squeezes my arm. "You did your best, sweetie. No way could you have been prepared for that. No one is going to blame you for the egg breaking, I promise." Tears sting my eyes. "Is there anything you need?" she asks. "Anything at all?"

"No, I'm okay." I sniff and look back up at her.

"Comms are working again if you need to contact anyone. Family? Friends?" she asks. "Or I can reach out to one of the station therapists we contract with and—"

I shake my head, cutting her off. "I'll message my mom and call everyone later. Right now, I'm hungry and could use a nap."

Carla flashes me a smile and nods. "Of course. I understand. Well, somehow, your cottage was undamaged, so once you get the all-clear from the doctor, you're free to go rest."

The clinic doors swing open again with a creak, and Carter strides in. He's changed from his formal coat and pants he'd worn at the gala into loose shorts, and a Meridian station logoed t-shirt.

He's all golden-tanned muscles and tousled sandy-blonde hair. How can he look so good right now when I feel like something a trawler dragged out of a tox zone?

Carla's eyes light up, and she greets him. "Sounds like you and the others had quite a ride last night."

"You heard right," he says, grinning. "Hell of a ride."

Carla watches us intently, and I wonder if she's picking up on some of the tension between Carter and me.

"Well, thank the tides, it wasn't as bad as it could've been," Carla says.

Carter's expression sombers. "True. We didn't lose any druadans, and there were just a few injuries among the riders, but a shuttle pilot was caught in the explosion, and we had to send Joe Cochin, one of our hosts, to Delford General for surgery."

The list of names I'd written for invitations flutters in my mind's eye. Every one of them I'd personally hand selected and invited. And every one of them had been put in danger because of it. "And the guests?" I say, finding my voice.

The muscles in his jaw tighten. "Four casualties. Three from mystyl venom, and one was trampled to death in the hall."

My stomach twists as I picture the panicked people crushed underfoot. As soon as I suspected I saw her, I'd chased after Sharice and so I hadn't been in the hall when the real attack had begun. The highest of Venovian society was the farthest from equipped to handle that kind of situation. They must've been terrified.

Meridian will need a good lawyer, and my job just got a lot harder.

Restoring a business's reputation after something like this will take months if not years.

"What happens now?" I ask.

"Circuit will compensate all the families," Carter says. "They'll probably need you guys to help with a public statement.

"No way we can keep a lid on this," Carla says, "but if it's going to be out there, Heath will want it done right." She pauses, glancing down at her comm. "Oh dear." She looks to Carter. "Elena's team heard yelling in the hall, and they need a hand."

"Someone's still alive in there?" I ask.

"Yes," Carla says excitedly. "It's a miracle, given the state of that place."

Carter looks at me.

I tilt my head and nudge him. "I'll be fine. You go be a hero."

"I'll swing by the cottage to check on you later, okay?" He gives my shoulder a reassuring squeeze, and the two of them exit the clinic.

I hang around another hour, volunteering to organize medicines or change sheets. Sweat runs down my back and I move to the window fan to cool off. I touch the bracelet on my wrist, the sapphire stone resting against my skin. Sharice's gift. *"To match your eyes, Brigid,"* she had said. I take in the clinic, looking at the bloody bandages, dripping IVs, and injured people in cots. Now, I can't reconcile the memory at all. Sharice was never the warm or overly kind type, but she was far from cruel.

And yet, looking at this scene, no one in their right mind could deny this is the definition of cruelty.

Six

LOGAN

Jamming my hands into my pockets, I leave the clinic, letting the door slam closed. I lean into the bond, pushing into the fear until sweat forms on my brow. Galaxian's emotional turbulence from the last twenty-four hours clouds the connection, and I'm forced to stop walking and close my eyes to sense what direction my stallion is in.

He's to the Southeast, not in pain but is super fucking pissed off.

Heading to my bike, I follow the path around the back of the medical building but pause when I see two Circuit police heading my way from the south gate.

I beeline it to my bike.

One holds up a hand when I'm a few feet away. "Master Rider McCelroy?"

I ignore them and take my helmet off the seat.

"We've been given orders to bring you into custody."

"Good for you." I swing my leg over the bike.

"You're the rider of a rogue druadan and are considered a responsible party in the active investigation of the scientist's death."

"Fuck off. I've got somewhere I need to be."

The first officer grabs my right arm, and I snap my eyes up, leveling him with a glare. "You don't want to do this."

The man doesn't flinch. Either he's got balls, or he's an idiot.

"We have specific orders from Ewensen not to let you leave the premises."

I shrug off his arm. "Then you'll have to stop me."

They both draw their guns from their hips and step back. A thrill runs through me as my instincts engage, calculating the odds of starting the bike and speeding away before they get a shot off.

They're low. But not impossible. Redhead has his safety on, and ol' mustache looks days away from retirement.

Galaxian has gone rogue, refusing to submit, so why should I? Anger fuels my movements as I mount the bike and start it.

They shoot, streaks of light whizzing past, and I duck over the handlebars, twisting the throttle. Tires skid on the paved sidewalk as I round the corner, leaning hard to the right until my knee grazes the ground.

The dry air slams at my face, tugging tears from the corners of my eyes. Once around the edge, I straighten the bike and send it at full speed to the open gate. Circuit police dart in front of me, forming a wall, and I gun the engine. The roar slices the air, and several officers break rank, scattering like dune beetles under a flashlight, while others bellow at them to hold their ground.

I brace myself, preparing to ram into them, but then a sharp tug, like a strap cinching around my heart, pulls at me from the left. I snap my head to the side, and the sight that greets me is a knife between my ribs.

Galaxian is down, looking like a large brown carcass on the gravel driveway. With a curse, I slam on the brakes. The motorcycle obeys, tires screeching in protest as they skid. I wrench the handlebars and drop my feet.

Galaxian's teal tail swishes slowly on the ground, and he is unable to lift his head under the weight of the steel mesh net that glitters in the sunlight.

Phase-suppressing nets are expensive as hell, and the realization that they'd brought one here turns my blood to ice. They had their opportunity to kill him but chose not to. Their true intention had always been to capture him. But why?

Before I can dwell on it, though, my temper flares at the six tranquilizer guns aimed at him. One dart has already found its mark lodged in his neck, and his movements are sluggish, desperate attempts to fight off the drugs. The sight ignites a fury within me, a raging inferno that consumes all rational thought.

"Let him GO!" My voice is low and filled with the promise of violence.

The officers hesitate, their faces hidden behind half-masks. "We can't do that, sir, we have orders," one says, but neither move. They might not know who I am, but they know *what* I am.

A druadan rider whose bonded stallion is threatened.

For a moment, the officers, Galaxian, the steel net—it all crystallizes into a singular point of focus.

My stallion gnashes his teeth, attempting to bite at the netting as his legs thrash and the air hums with his voice. "*Fight. Logan. Need egg. Run.*"

He's fighting against the tranquilizer, against the net, against the betrayal of his own body. But it's a battle he's losing.

The bond snaps tight as a fresh surge of Galaxian's anger washes over me.

Two ready their tranq guns, getting set to hit him with another dose. *Enough of this bullshit.* I lurch for the closest one, wrenching the pistol from his hand, but he holds tight and yanks it back. Pain explodes in the back of my skull as someone else hits me with the butt of their gun, and I lose my footing, falling forward onto the first one.

He pulls the trigger, and a laser blast crackles in the air.

Seven

CARTER

The worst way to live is without a penis.

Alright, so I'm not so shallow to think that a man without a penis is no less a man, but for me personally, I can't imagine a worse fate.

A shuttle is still a shuttle even if it can't fly.

Shit, never mind. Maybe *having* a penis that works but not being able to use it would be worse.

Yeah. That would be pretty damn terrible.

It's these thoughts that cloud my mind as I help Carla in the exhibition hall. When we arrive, they're pulling out an injured guest. I didn't know his name, but a pillar had fallen on him, trapping him, and I overheard the medic say something about his dick needing to be amputated.

Poor man.

I help two of the security team lift the pillar, freeing him, and then he's carried on a stretcher to the clinic.

I make my way further into the exhibition hall with Carla while memories of the party turned nightmare replay in my mind.

The inside is a wreck. Overturned banquet tables, torn white tablecloths, and trays of hors d'oeuvres littered the floor, crushed and forgotten during the panic to escape.

A dead mystyl lies sprawled among the debris. I pause, staring at the spot where the laser blast tore through its translucent skin. Six slimy tendrils are splayed out in a pool of inky black blood.

How many times had I fought these fuckers during training exercises? Hundreds? Thousands? And yet, when I actually faced them, I was caught with my pants down.

We all had.

Helping in the hall is taking me longer than I'd assumed, and every time I try to leave, someone else calls for a hand.

It's going to take days to clean all of this up.

Finally, when I get a free moment, I duck out of the hall. Heath was a real asshole when it came to being punctual. He will be waiting for me, and he will be pissed.

While the hall is a disaster, the main house is mostly intact. A few missing shingles lie on the ground, and there's a jagged crack in one of the basement windows like someone had tried to break in. I climb up the stairs to the front porch and pull open the large front door.

"I know, I know," I say.

Heath doesn't say anything but starts walking once I'm at the top. He turns left while we continue down the hallway. The sight of Tim's empty room hits me hard, anger bubbling up. Tim was a good guy, funny as hell, and the guests loved him.

It'll be hard to replace him.

I swallow down the emotion and follow Heath.

"Your leg's bleeding," I say, keeping my eyes forward.

Heath glances down at the spreading red stain on his riding pants. "Damn."

"Why don't you go to the clinic," I say, "And I'll meet her."

Heath squints at me skeptically. "I think it's best if I'm here when Ewensen arrives."

I scoff. "You don't trust me to be alone with a woman for ten minutes?"

"No," he says, without an ounce of sarcasm.

I'm left confused about whether to take that as an insult or a compliment.

I'll take it as the latter.

"I'll call Dr. Rajesh," he says. "See if he can spare a medic, and please, during the meeting, behave yourself. This is serious."

I shrug and mock salute him. "Aye, aye, captain."

Heath frowns, but there is a glint of humor in his eyes.

He loves me. Everyone does.

As we move into the meeting room adjoining his office, I slide into one of the armchairs and put my feet up on the table.

Heath barely has time to glare at me before his wrist-comm chimes with a message.

"Jess?" I offer.

He nods. "Safe in Grouseway."

"That's good. Her parents?"

"With her at the penthouse. They'll be there for a while to recover."

"Makes sense. Coffee?"

Heath nods, and I get up, moving to the machine on the counter.

As the coffee maker whirs, heating the water, I open myself

to the bond, catching glimpses of his mood. He's tired as hell, like me, and worry muddies the edges of the connection. There's also a tinge of red. Pain.

His leg's bothering him more than he's admitting. I swipe my comm, messaging Rajesh to send a medic to where we are.

"Ewensen got held up," he says, wiping a finger over his wrist.

"Great," I say, handing him a cup of coffee and then returning to my chair. I take a long sip of the bitter liquid and then tip my head back and close my eyes.

"Wake me when she gets here."

Heath laughs dryly.

I've only dozed off when there's a knock. I pry open an eye as a medic tech, a young woman with a no-nonsense demeanor, carefully tends to the gash on his thigh. He's in his boxers, and the pants he'd worn last night lie in a heap on the floor. They're torn, and even though the fabric is dark, I can see they're stained with his blood. My stomach tightens, but I don't turn away. I don't want to forget this. These people did this to him, to *us*.

I'll never forgive them.

Heath's face is a mask even as she applies the pink gel. "This might sting a bit, but it'll help numb the skin while I close it," she warns, and then tears open the paper-wrapped tray and carefully begins stitching the wound.

As the medic works, my mind drifts back to the events of last night. The rebels' attack, the screams, the desperate struggle to protect the egg—it all feels like a blur, a surreal nightmare from which I have yet to fully awaken.

"How's it looking?" I ask.

"Should heal up nicely," she replies. "You're lucky it didn't hit the femoral artery, but you should still try to take it easy for a few days."

Sighing, Heath says, "*Easy* isn't really on my agenda right now."

I grin at him as he lowers his leg from where he'd propped it on a chair. "I'll make sure you do even if I have to tie you to the bed myself, and you know how much I enjoy doing that."

"If that isn't encouragement to heal fast," he says, smoothing the taped bandage on his leg. "I don't know what is."

Heath smirks as I press a hand to my chest, mocking hurt. It's the first time I've seen him smile since the attack, and it's like the sun is finally fucking out again.

The medic finishes her work, snipping the excess thread with a pair of scissors. "All done. Take these for the pain," she instructs, handing him a small bottle of pills.

He pops two capsules into his mouth, crushing them between his teeth with a scowl, then washes it down with coffee.

How is it we can genetically modify horses to bond with us telepathically, but we can't make pills taste better?

Deputy Ewensen passes the medic as she opens the door and joins us in the meeting room.

Her gaze immediately fixes on me before moving to Heath.

"Master Rider Lockwood, I was hoping this would be a private conversation?"

"Whatever you need to tell me, you can say in front of Master Rider James."

Her nostrils flare, but she gives a slight nod, moving to one of the end chairs.

"Most of the rebels managed to escape on a boat to Nelworth," she starts, "and from there, they paid off a shuttle driver to take them to Leviler, but our officers found the port empty. They've gone underground and covered their tracks." Ewensen's lips form a thin line. "We'll find them," she assures us. "But first, we need to focus on securing this station."

"I agree," Heath says. "I've interviewed other witnesses but would like your opinion on the rebels' motives." Ewensen prompts.

She saw me carry the egg to the barn but didn't say anything, which meant she either didn't know what it was or was playing dumb to get us to tell her more about it.

"Why are you asking us?" I say.

"Don't play coy, Master Rider James. It's clear they targeted this station for a reason. You must have an idea why."

I glance at Heath, struggling to stand with his one good leg. "We believe the attack was a distraction," Heath says.

She furrows her brow. "Go on."

Heath repositions himself to half sit on the edge of the table and lays his hand on his thigh. "A year ago, a druadan egg was stolen from here."

Ewensen's lips part, and since I've met her, she appears genuinely surprised. "I never heard of this. Was it reported? Who handled the investigation?"

He looks squarely at Ewensen. A tiny trickle of worry eases from him, but it's whisked away with his usual steady confidence. We all knew this day would come. "I made the call to keep the investigation private, keeping it internal to the station."

Her eyes tighten, wrinkling the skin on her temples. "So, it was never formally reported?"

"No," Heath says, "I understand how you may see things differently, but I decided what I felt was best to protect the station."

"To protect the station or to protect *you*?"

Heath's eyes narrow, and I force myself to sit still as the silent battle goes down between him and Ewensen. He's a

Lockwood and a rider, and even with her shiny badge, she knows better than to push him too far. "I can assure you," Heath says slowly, "my actions were done with the station's best interest at heart."

She pins him with a stern look. I had concerns about Heath making the call to keep the egg's disappearance a secret, although I had never voiced them. He was smarter than me, and even if I hadn't fully understood it, Logan and I had backed him up.

Besides, it was only a druadan egg. Yeah, they were valuable and rare, but it wasn't like drugs or a bomb. And up until twelve hours ago, we didn't even think the eggs were capable of hatching. So, what if a fossil was stolen? It wasn't like they could do anything with it.

Heath also reasoned that if we told the police, the investigation would do more harm than good. They'd shut down the station and potentially scare off anyone involved, causing the trail to evaporate along with the hope of finding the egg.

Control freak that he was, Heath would rather die than let someone else clean up his mistakes.

"All right," she says, "There will be repercussions for your decisions. However, that will be dealt with at a future time by your superiors." She pauses, wandering over to the coffee pot. She picks up the bag of coffee and sniffs. "Right now, let's discuss what happened before the attack. We followed up on the reports of the caves you and the Lannett scientists searched. It was determined the mystyl had been living there for some time in crates with timed-release locks."

Crates? Do I remember crates? I squeeze my eyes shut, trying to pull the details from the fog of my memory. But all I get is Ember's pain, ripping through me, tearing my skull apart. God, it was agony. I never want to feel that again.

"It seems," Ewensen continues, "that one opened early,

whether intentionally or a faulty timer on the latch, we don't know, but either way, those were the ones that escaped first, and you sent samples off to Lannett to process. The crates looked to have been there for some time, and many creatures were dead inside, appearing to have starved to death."

I press my tongue to the roof of my mouth, trying to focus on everything she's saying.

"How long can they go without food?" Heath asks.

Ewensen punches the start button, and a second later, the room smells of freshly brewed coffee. "Lannett is trying to figure that out as we speak since that will give us a timeline for how long the crates were there and how they got onto the island in the first place."

A big part of Logan and the security team's job was to chase trespassers off the island. Was there a chance they could have seen or even spoken to the people that snuck the mystyl into that cave?

"Now," she says, dropping a spoon of honey into her coffee. "What I want to know is how you believe these two things, the release of the mystyl and the attack, are connected?"

"We believe," Heath starts, "the mystyl were released as a distraction, allowing them access to the other two eggs. During the confusion at the gala, both were taken, proving our theory, and we witnessed them loaded on a truck." Heath continues to explain how we'd grabbed our stallions to chase down the truck but leaves out the bit about being able to sense the mystyl while mounted.

I still didn't completely understand it, and honestly, I was glad he'd left that out. Druadan secrets were meant to be kept in the stations. The less the outside world knew—or thought they knew—about us, the better. The mystery of druadans was part of their appeal, sure, but it was also about security. We couldn't risk people thinking they could force a bond or, even worse, discover where the feed came from and find a way to poison it. It's like how celebrities don't share their addresses or send their kids to public schools—there are too many dangers and too many people who might cross the line.

When Heath finishes, Ewensen sips her coffee as if mulling over everything. "Well then," she says. "Seems like I owe you an apology."

Heath shifts his weight to his good leg while I keep my eyes pinned on her back. She's toying with us; I know it.

Ewensen sets the coffee down. "I accused you of abandoning the station to save a woman, but you actually saved something of greater value."

Not sure I agree with that, but I keep my mouth shut.

"There's more regarding the egg now," Heath says. "It's hatching."

Her stoic facade slips. She reaches for her coffee but grasps air. "Interesting. I was under the impression it was for display only and not viable."

"As were we," Heath replies.

She taps a few words on her tablet. "Do we know how long the hatching will take?"

Heath shakes his head.

She lifts the cup and blows the steam from it. "ITM has proved difficult to monitor. However, now we know what their target is, even if we're unsure of their ultimate goal. But to maintain this advantage and everyone's safety, we can't let the word spread that it's survived and is hatching."

ITM? Is that who they're thinking is behind this? I remember seeing their booths at Circuit-sponsored conventions. The Inherited Terra Movement was an environmentalist group trying to encourage people to appreciate the little land we had left. And from everything I'd heard, they were peaceful, nothing more than planting trees in town and weekend nature walks. What has happened over the past two years to transform them into terrorists?

Oh. Oh Shit.

Sharice. Sharice is what happened.

"Of that, we agree," Heath says and I nearly jolt out of my seat, thinking he read my mind. He gives me a quick, curious look before returning his eyes to Ewensen. "Keeping the egg's hatching a secret will be difficult, but we'll do what we can."

Ewensen taps her comm as if reading a note. "We're monitoring Nelworth, especially around the docks. We counted ten of theirs dead."

"None injured?" I ask. "I know I hit at least one."

She sniffs and taps her comm screen closed before lowering it. "Two were found with mild injuries, but it seems they didn't want to be caught alive."

My stomach rolls with the undercurrent of her words.

"They'll take time to regroup," Ewensen continues. "We don't know why they want the egg, but whatever reasons are behind it, it's clear they're not afraid to use extreme measures to get it."

"Like bringing back the mystyl," I add.

Ewensen picks up one of the plastic stirrers and starts chewing it. "Exactly."

Heath and I remain silent while she paces to the opposite end of the table.

"I've been cleared by my superior to share information we feel might assist in the security of the station; however, I must have your assurances you will not share this information until I give the go-ahead. Are we clear?"

"Yes," Heath says as I nod. She's still suspicious we're connected, but her tone is lighter, as if she's starting to see us on the same side and not as suspects.

She straightens, moving the flattened straw to the other

side of her mouth. "Before the attack, we picked up chatter on one of our Network sites regarding a weapon of some sort, biological or chemical." She pauses. "Meridian was mentioned."

I twist my mouth. "You think the egg is a weapon?"

"I'm not in the business of guessing, but it is a possibility," she says. "I'll relay everything you've told me to our Nelworth field office to see if they can look into it further. However, this is encouraging me to make the call I know you don't want to hear. Everyone here at the station, riders, staff, and all the druadans, are in danger. Ashburn Island and Meridian are too isolated for us to protect."

"The isolation is what gives it protection," Heath defends, "ask any of the station managers; we always have the lowest number of incidents."

"While that might have been the case before, we believe the isolation is what led to this catastrophe in the first place. It's abundantly clear the eggs should've never remained here. They should've been kept somewhere more secure, and that was a mistake on everyone's behalf that we are now paying the consequences for."

The egg that broke, I think to myself, and my stomach turns with guilt. Fuck, maybe she was right. Maybe I should've pressured Heath to go to them when the first one went missing cause now...

"You're shutting us down?" I ask.

"Understand that this decision was not made lightly. We have to prioritize the safety of both the staff and the druadans. We are particularly fortunate that none of the stallions were lost. However, four people were killed, and many staff members were injured. This was devastating, and I don't want to risk the next attack being even worse."

I swivel my gaze to Heath. "And you're okay with this?"

Heath's mouth twitches, but he nods. "I don't want to leave either, but it is a wise decision. We need to start planning how we're going to pack up the station."

You've got to be shitting me. Just like that, he folded? I stare at him dubiously, but he doesn't look my way, instead maintaining eye contact with Ewensen. His poker face is legendary, so I'm left to glean from the bond any clue as to what he's feeling.

A minty coolness drifts wisp-like to me.

Resignation.

He's already made peace with this. It's like he *knew* this was going to happen.

Heath rubs his leg. "Whatever you need, just let me know."

"I'll speak with Carla and the rest of the staff."

"Very good," she says and leaves.

WE LINGER IN THE MEETING ROOM AFTER EWENSEN LEAVES, discussing the transition of everything. I bite my tongue, even though I want to accuse him of caving like a bed at a cheap hotel.

It'd be pointless. Guilt trickles from him like a leaky faucet. He's torn up about it, and my comments would only make him feel worse. He's the manager, and I'm just a rider. I'll do whatever he says. However, he has his work cut out for him with the rest of the station, Logan, especially. Not for the first time in my life, I'm thankful he's the one in charge.

Shortly after we've coordinated what needs to be prioritized with packing and what can be boxed and sent to storage, we retreat to our rooms to change.

I pull on a pair of shorts, a T-shirt, and tennis shoes, and Heath wears something similar. Then, together, we spend the remainder of the afternoon checking on staff. Shattered windows litter the floors, curtains flapping in the desert breeze. Maintenance is already hard at work, boarding up the broken panes and sweeping up shards of glass.

The grounds crew also has their hands full, ripping out the burned sections of the shuttle pad and scooping the twisted metal and debris from the destroyed shuttle. I sent Circuit a purchase order requesting approval of new siding and windows, fencing materials, and heavy equipment to assist with the repairs.

As we turn the corner of the largest of the guest houses, a laser gun cracks from somewhere nearby, and then a woman shouts. "Master Rider, remove yourself from my officer this instant."

Heath and I exchange a look. "Logan," we say simultaneously and race toward the sound.

Eight

LOGAN

"If you don't cooperate," Ewensen says, "we have more of those tranquilizers, and I have no qualms about using them on you as well."

I open my mouth, ready to tell her to go to hell when Heath and Carter appear. Eyes fixed on me, they flank her.

Fuck me.

"What is the meaning of this?" Heath shouts.

"Master Rider Lockwood, we've sedated a rogue stallion as per Circuit druadan protocol section 612-5, and Master Rider McCelroy seems to think he can interfere with our procedures."

"I see," Heath says, keeping his voice neutral. "There must be a misunderstanding. We're all quite weary from the attack last night. However, I can assure you Logan is a smart man and was reacting as any rider in his position would."

His gaze drifts from Galaxian and lands squarely on mine. "He *will* cooperate."

I clamp my jaw but say nothing, even as fury continues to seep into my veins.

"Very well then," Ewensen says, looking at me as well. "Since that is settled, I believe your expertise will be invaluable for this transition, and we will not pursue this insolent behavior further. Master Rider McCelroy will be allowed to move around freely on the station over the next twenty-four hours to ensure all security items are handled with care until the time we depart."

Depart? I give a quick "What the fuck is she talking about?" look,' to Heath, and he replies with a slight shake of his head.

Don't.

Ewensen rests her hands on her hips. "Do you understand what we're telling you, Master Rider McCelroy?"

"No," I say through gritted teeth. "I really don't have a clue. Maybe if you pulled that —"

"We're closing Meridian Station," she says before I can finish telling her what to do with the stick firmly clenched between her ass cheeks.

I blink. "You're..." I trail off. "Heath, they can't." I stammer and take a step toward her. Two officers close in as if they can stop me. I'll be damned if I don't stare the person in the eye who is shutting down the place I've devoted the last two years of my life to. The one place I'd ever felt like I belonged. However, she waves them off before they reach me, and soon I'm face to face with her.

I snarl. "How dare you think you can fucking waltz in here and shut us down?"

"Logan," Heath says, his voice passive. "It's done."

My chest heaves, and through the haze of anger, it takes a second for his words to register. "What the hell, Heath?" I redirect my rage on him, pinning him with a glare even as the first undercurrent of betrayal slices through me.

The bond shivers, and his dark eyes meet mine.

He presses his hands together. "Please understand, we did not make this decision lightly. The assault on the station put us in a difficult position, and we based it on what's best for the staff and druadans here."

"Don't tell me you're good with this?" I ask Carter.

He folds his arms over his chest. "We have to follow Heath's orders."

"Oh, what a good little soldier you are."

Carter doesn't flinch, but his eyes blaze at the insult.

As I open my mouth, Galaxian's voice drifts to me, weakened by the effect of the drugs. *"No More fight. Take Egg Where Safe."*

Fuck me.

Shithead is right. The egg should be the priority, and if Heath thinks it'll be safer somewhere else, then I have to go with it.

I pivot and direct a hard look at the deputy. "If any of your badge-wearing asshats so much as breathes in my stallion's direction, I'll take that fancy firearm of yours and use it to rearrange your faces so your mom won't even recognize you."

"Master Rider McCelroy, the threat of a Circuit official is a top-tier violation of Venovian law section—"

I move closer before she finishes. I'm a good foot taller than her, and a quiver of fear flickers in her gaze. Her throat bobs as she swallows. "I can understand your concern," she says, with only the slightest tremor in her voice. "You have my word that I will oversee Galaxian's safety and security personally until we relocate him."

My eyes search hers. She's telling the truth. A fucking feat if I've ever seen one coming from a Circuit lackey.

She presses her lips into a thin line. "Rest assured, we are on your side."

I ease a step back. "We'll see. Where are we going?"

"Blackhawk," Heath says. "We're moving everyone to Blackhawk station."

Nine

BRIGID

My bones themselves feel as if someone has poured molten lead into the marrow, and I can hardly lift my feet as I make my way to my cottage. The last traces of adrenaline have abandoned me, replaced by exhaustion and numbness.

After getting pain meds and an all-clear from Dr. Rajesh, as well as being told for the fourth time, in increasingly stronger terms, that they have enough medical staff to help and I'll only be in the way if I stay to lend a hand, I left the clinic.

A smile touches my lips as I round the corner. Carter, Heath, and Logan are waiting for me in front of my cottage like three of the hottest male solicitors. The old me would've handed over all my credits for those discount shuttle tickets or the steaks that turned out to be beef-flavored chicken.

This me knew better. Sure, I'd still buy, but I'd make them work for it.

"Hey," I say, coming up to them. "What's going on? I assumed I wouldn't see you guys for the rest of the day."

Heath's eyes lock with mine, and I notice the bags under his eyes and the sallowness of his cheeks. He's overextended himself and looks like he's about to fall face-first into the window box of flowers. "We're done for now," he says, "and wanted to check in on you."

"Yeah, and you got anything to eat?" Logan asks. "Circuit set up at my place, and assholes ate all my food."

I laugh. "Come in. I'm starving, too." I unlock the door and wave them into the cozy space. As they make their way in, I rummage through the cabinets, pulling out a random assortment of crackers, dried apricots, and a stack of sliced chicken breast from the fridge. I assemble a basic sandwich from the meager supplies and set it on the table. The others situate themselves in chairs around it, and over the next ten minutes, the four of us eat in heavy silence as an air of exhaustion hangs over us like a shroud.

This is *the* daze, I realize.

The part of shock no one talks about. That eerie calm after the storm where you're left alone with your darkest thoughts and no way to make them go away. Nothing to do but sit on your hands and wait. Wait for what, though? For the disorientation to pass and normality to return? Is that something time alone can accomplish? There are limits to how much mental stress a person can endure, and I'm pretty sure we've tested them.

Carter breaks the silence. "I never want to relive a night like that again."

"Indeed," Heath confesses.

The room falls silent as all eyes turn toward me. I inhale, steeling myself for the words I'm about to speak—words that have remained secret for far too long.

"When I was younger, living in Uncy'lia, I had to defend myself once," I begin, my voice thick with emotion. "It was an accident, but there was a boy... he didn't make it."

The weight of those words hangs heavy in the air, and I'm grateful for the stillness that envelops the room. No one interrupts, allowing me the space to gather my thoughts and continue.

"That's why I was sent to a private school in Delford," I explain, my gaze distant as the memories flood back. "I haven't returned to Uncy'lia since. It's been years, but I still can't shake the image of him from my mind."

Carter shifts closer, his hand finding mine. Heath leans forward, dark hair swishing across his forehead. Cool air flutters my hair from the fan in the window. It's already over a hundred degrees out there, and it feels so good to be inside and out of the heat.

I look between the three of them, feeling a connection that transcends mere words. "I've never told anyone this before," I admit, my voice hovering above a whisper. It's hard to believe that after all this time, it really happened.

Carter gives my hand a reassuring squeeze, his warm presence grounding me. "I'm sorry you were forced to make that choice." He smooths the hair from my face, and his green eyes bore into mine. "But I'm glad you did. It's okay to let yourself feel it," he continues as his thumb slowly circles the inside of my wrist. "You can feel sadness for the family, but don't you dare feel guilty for protecting yourself."

My shoulders lighten, and I offer a small, grateful smile

before the unease from all the attention makes me shift my gaze to Logan.

Logan's gaze is fixed on the floor between his boots. After a beat, he looks up, his expression unreadable. "Remember those two poachers we caught stealing fuel from the shed last fall?"

Carter's sandy brown hair falls over his forehead as he nods. "The ones you said fell off the cliff into the ocean?"

Logan shrugs, a flicker of something haunted crossing his features. "They were never going to leave unless I made them."

A chill runs down my spine at the implication, but deep down, I'm not surprised. Logan's security would undoubtedly entail having to 'secure' the station with force. A burden he doesn't seem to complain about, now that I think about it.

My words appear to resonate with Logan, and he meets my gaze, a silent understanding passing between us. The four of us have been forced to make impossible choices, thrust onto the treacherous path between right and wrong, life and death.

"You're right," Carter affirms, his grip on my hand tightening. "Last night, we did things we're not proud of. But where others had died, together we survived."

The four of us stare at the empty platter of food in the center of the table, lost in our thoughts. He's right. As unfathomable as this situation is, we'd come out the other side closer.

And as messed up as bonding over trauma sounds, this quiet moment with them is nice. Peaceful. Like easing into a warm bath after trudging through a blizzard.

I let the realization wash over me and rub my face. The backs of my eyes feel like sandpaper, and I fear I'm going to pass out if I don't get up. Since I don't trust Circuit to move the egg without telling us, I don't want to be away from it for too long.

The damn shower is broken, so I can only brush the sand out

of my hair and change into my own clothes. If I have time, I'll try to grab a quick nap before I fall over. I let out a weary sigh, my body aching from the strain, both physical and emotional.

Reluctantly, I let go of Carter's hand, and he rouses from his half-dozing state, mumbling a complaint as I stand. I yawn, feet swaying slightly before steadying myself.

"I'm going to change into my pajamas," I say.

"We'll wait here," Heath says, his chocolate brown eyes holding mine as a thousand unspoken words pass between us. The ramifications of the kiss we'd shared.

How my feelings for the three of them had only grown when they'd risked their lives to find me in the desert. The way my entire world felt like it'd tilted on its axis since my sister had reentered my life, only to disappear again.

If I'd felt like I was chasing a ghost before, it was so much worse now. Ghosts can't hurt you. She had. And not just the way she'd let her friends roughly handle me, but in the way she'd stared at me.

Like an enemy.

No worse, like a stranger.

Emotion clogs my throat as I stagger to the bathroom. I shut the door behind me and my clumsy fingers struggle to take the plain t-shirt and drawstring pants off.

I rub my hands over my face, still refusing to cry. When I open them, my naked body reflects to me in the waist-high mirror. My hands and arms are covered in scratches, and green and purple bruises stain the insides of my thighs. Limp curls and frizzy pale hairs around my face are all that remains of the elegant style I'd put it in last night.

One by one, I take out the gold clips, setting them on the vanity, before reaching for my hairbrush.

"Dammit," I shout as the brush gets stuck in my hair. A sob tears from my throat as I throw the brush into the sink.

"Dammit, dammit, dammit," I mutter the word over and over again, burying my face in my hands. What am I doing? What is the point of all this? Suddenly, there's a gust of wind as the door is pushed open, and warm arms wrap around me.

"It's okay," a man's voice says.

It's Carter.

His voice is low and soothing, and I latch onto it instantly like an anchor, pressing my head against his chest as the dam bursts and the tears fall.

"You're okay," he murmurs. "I'm right here."

"My hair," I stammer. "It's dirty and tangled, and I just want to take a shower," I choke on the last word as I continue to cry.

Still holding me with one arm, he reaches in and turns on the shower, adjusting the temperature to the right warmth.

My heart skips a beat and blinks up at him. "There's *water?*"

He beams at me. "Pump is back on, which means it's shower time."

I'm so overcome by the knowledge that I'll get to bathe that I completely forget that I'm standing naked in front of him. And in a surprisingly gentleman-like manner, his eyes grip mine, never wavering as he pulls off his shirt and steps out of his shorts.

Unlike him, I can't resist the urge to look — correction: gawk — as his shirt falls to the floor. His god-like body draws my gaze, accentuating the hard-lined muscles of his chest, arms, and toned abs that flood my core with desire. God, how I want to run my hands over him and feel the muscles under his skin. My eyes trace the intricate lines of the horseshoe-shaped tattoo adorning his right pectoral muscle, the flame design surrounding denoting him as a rider of the Inferno line.

My eyes then drift upwards, taking in tattoos of three

stripes that wrap around the sides of his neck. The vibrant green of the ink compliments the rugged angles of his jaw and the intensity of his matching green gaze.

Supporting my elbow, he gently guides me over the threshold. I tip my head back, letting the warm water cascade over my face and hair. He carefully lathers soap on a sponge and starts to wash my shoulders, his touch gentle and soothing. As he moves down my back, I can feel the tension and pain melt away.

Even though we showered before after the dust storm, this time, it's different.

For one thing, we both have our clothes *off*.

For another, it's less rushed, less frenzied. Each touch is deliberate, and without speaking a word, we both act as if we have all the time in the world.

With light fingers, he shampoos my hair and uses a cloth to clean my body before I do the same for him. It's a considerate dance we each partake in. As his calming presence and the warm water relax me, the flashbacks creep in, and I let my tears mix with the flowing water. Carter's arms wrap around behind me, and in silence, we stand in the shower. Sadness and anger slough off of me and are swallowed by the drain.

Through hooded lids, he peers down at me. "Ticklish?" he murmurs.

I smile cheekily. "Maybe."

He lifts my right arm and kisses the scrapes on my knuckles, then the bruise on my wrist, and works his way up my arm. I giggle when he reaches the crook of my elbow.

"Knew it," he says, holding my arm as I try to pull away. Before I can protest more, he's moved upward, his mouth working its way across my collarbone, up my neck, and then finally to my lips. His kiss is gentle yet full of desire, mimicking my own. Lips firmly pressed against mine, a fire ignites. I didn't know I still had the energy for it.

His tongue playfully works along my lower lip, and I arch my back, pressing my breasts against his hard chest. He breaks away, his soft lips brushing against mine as he speaks. "I've never been more scared in all my life than I was last night. I want to make you mine, Brigid. I need *you* to be mine."

My heart races at his words. A rider could have their pick of any woman or man in Venovia to share their bed. Carter James was no exception. He had a fan club and modeling contracts, and during my first week here, I'd worked with Carla to file a cease and desist against a toy maker making an inspired replica of the highly sought-after accessory between his legs.

And yet, here he was, telling me he wanted *me*.

It's all too much to comprehend, so instead of answering, I press my lips to his, wrapping my arms around his neck. His hands cup my face, deepening the kiss, and I pull him closer as if we could merge into one being.

I squeeze my legs together as desire heats my core but wince at the soreness of my inner thighs.

Carter pulls back, and green eyes search mine. "What is it?"

"Just a little sore from my first druadan ride, is all."

He frowns and lowers his hand. Soft fingers caress my inner thighs, applying only enough pressure to ease the tension from my muscles. I let out a small sigh and lay my forehead on his shoulder as he continued to work his magic, soothing and arousing me at the same time.

"How's this?"

"*Good*," I moan.

His lips form a smug smile. His hand drifts higher, his knuckles brushing against my core. "How about this?" his voice husky. My body tenses at first but then relaxes as he increases the pressure around my clit. "Good," I repeat. As he rubs me with one hand, his other hand reaches up to cup my breast. "And this?"

The sensations are overwhelming, and I can feel myself growing wetter by the second. Before I know it, I'm on the brink of release. Carter's skilled fingers push me over the edge, and I pant as waves of pleasure wash over me. The pleasure consumes me as I ride out my orgasm, my body trembling in Carter's grasp.

He continues to gently rub me through the aftershocks. Carter's graveled voice whispers in my ear, "You're so goddamn beautiful when you come undone."

At his words, a flurry of butterflies takes flight inside me. I gaze up at him, and his eyes are dark with desire. He brings his fingers to his mouth and licks them clean. It's erotic as hell, and I can't help but watch in awe as he savors my taste.

Then, his attention shifts downward again, this time towards his own arousal. His erection is impressive, thick, and long, and I whimper with want as he strokes himself.

I need him inside me, like *now*. "I want you," I breathe.

He laughs a deep, rich sound. "Don't worry, I haven't forgotten your promise, and while I want more than anything to cash in, I don't want it now, not like this." His eyes dance between mine. "When I fuck you, Brigid, I want to fuck you so hard you see stars. I want you to scream my name while you forget your own. I don't want to hold back, don't want to restrain myself."

His words settle over me, and while I see the reasoning, it doesn't mean I have to like it. As he continues to stroke himself, I reach out to feel him, too, wanting to give him pleasure as he gave it to me. Our hands intertwine around his hard cock, and we move together in harmony. Carter's touch is electric, sending shivers down my spine as I stroke him. His moans mix with mine as we kiss, our bodies moving in perfect rhythm. I can feel the intense heat radiating off him, his desire for me evident in every touch.

Our moans become louder and more desperate as his release builds. Our tongues tangling together in a frenzy of craving and yearning. With one final thrust in my hand, he finds his climax.

Only when the water begins to turn cold do we finally break apart. My lips are swollen and sore from the kissing, and we do a final rinse-off before Carter helps me out of the shower. He wraps a towel around me, then takes another from the rack for his waist.

He takes my hand, leading me into my bedroom. Sitting on the edge of the bed, he pulls me down next to him and wraps his arm around my shoulders.

"Thank you," I whisper, relishing his presence.

"You have nothing to thank me for," he says.

Tears well up again in the corner of my eyes, but this time, they're not tears of sadness or fear. They're tears of gratitude for having someone like Carter know what I needed. Saying what I should hear then silent when I wanted to speak. "I don't know what would have happened if you hadn't found me," I admit, my voice shaking with emotion as I realize it goes so much deeper than finding me with the egg.

On my first day at Meridian for the interview, I was lost in a place I didn't understand, surrounded by strangers I didn't trust. But Carter had been his charming self—kind and welcoming, even stepping in to defend me when Logan accused me of working with my sister.

Carter tightens his hold on my hand. "No matter where you go," he whispers into my hair. "I'll always find you."

I offer him a small smile, even as a dozen butterflies have set flight in my stomach.

He releases me and stands. "Get some rest. I'll check on the egg."

I fall onto my side on the bed and tuck my knees underneath me. Within seconds of my head hitting the pillow, sleep overtakes me.

Ten

CARTER

I emerge from the bedroom, slowly pulling the door closed behind me to avoid waking Brigid. While I wish I could've stayed in there with her tucked safely in my arms, Heath and Logan are waiting for me.

"How is she?" Heath asks from where he stands behind the wingback chair. He's made a pot of coffee and is sipping from one of Brigid's ridiculous mugs. This one has yellow rubber duckies parading around the rim and I wonder if Heath even noticed.

"Better now," I say. "She's finally asleep."

"A+ work, James," Logan says from where he's watching out the window. "Looks like that cock is good for something besides dangling between your legs."

"I do my best."

An uneasy silence stretches between us. Logan shifts his weight from one foot to the other, a muscle twitching in his jaw as he seems to wrestle with something internally.

Finally, I let out a heavy sigh. "For fuck's sake. Why do I have to be the one to say it?"

"Say what?" Logan growls.

I point to Brigid's room, then sweep in front of me before patting my chest. "*This*. I feel her. This connection to her, and I know you two do as well."

Logan scoffs. "It's your bond fucking with your head. Ember's stress is getting under your skin, making you feel things that aren't there. She's just a woman."

"Like hell, she is," I snap. The bitterness wafting from him via the bond is so thick I can chew it. He's trying to mask it, but he's lying through his goddamn teeth. "When you were on the motorcycle, you were seconds away from pulling over, ripping off her clothes, and fucking her right there in the sand. Don't deny it. It was all over you."

I shift my gaze to Heath. His face remains neutral, but the muscles in his jaw flex. "Carter is right. I sensed it too, and so did Shadowmane."

"Fuck you both," Logan says, folding his arms.

Neither of us reply.

It's a familiar position, Heath and I being on the same page while Logan hasn't even cracked open the book. His defiance is his strength and his curse. No one pushes Logan to do anything. Even us. So, when he's dug his heels in, we've learned to be patient.

I wander to the kitchen and pour myself a cup of coffee. Only when I return and sit on the chair next to Heath, Logan finally has had enough time to mull it over. "All right," he says, sounding resigned. "So, I want to fuck her. Big deal? That doesn't mean I have a connection with her."

My shoulders bristle, but not out of jealousy. Brigid was hot as hell. Of course, he'd want her, and so long as he shared with me, that was okay in my book. No, I'm annoyed at myself because I knew better than to try to convince him. I don't know what I'd been thinking. Logan was the kid who stayed up at night to catch his parents' hiding gifts under the tree.

The tie between him and Galaxian was as far as his imagination allowed, and still, he'd made a paranoid comment once in a while that perhaps the bite had caused a long-term infection, and we were all high and hallucinating that we were talking to our stallions.

He needed concrete evidence to believe something. I run a hand over the side of my head and pace behind the couch. "Okay, fine, so how about you pretend for a minute that you *do* believe what I'm saying? Imagine that something is different, like something has changed since she got here. What could have caused it?"

"I don't know. Are you sure it's not just your cock talking? Maybe you've formed a special bond with that pussy of hers."

I growl, a guttural, primal sound I didn't know I was capable of.

"For Tide's sake, Logan," Heath says.

Logan holds up his hands. "I'm just saying what we're all thinking."

The world around me blurs, furniture fading into the periphery as a haze of red descends. All I can focus on is that infuriating smirk and the desperate need to wipe it from his face.

Without a second thought, I close the distance between us and clock Logan with a powerful punch that makes him stumble backward, but not as far as I'd hoped. The agile bastard regains his footing, the stubborn smile remaining even as he rubs the side of his jaw. Steel-colored eyes glint, daring me to try it again. "You get one."

"Are you sure about that?" I ball my fists, readying to hit him.

"Carter..." Heath says, his voice a low warning.

But it's too late.

In one fluid motion, Logan launches himself at me, and before I can react, his arm snakes around my neck in a vice-like headlock. I struggle to break free, throwing myself against him as instinct takes over. His arms cinches tighter, starting to cut off my air supply.

I spit and curse while trying to pry his meaty arms free.

"That's fucking enough!" Heath shouts. The two of us freeze.

Heath rarely curses.

"We're all exhausted," Heath says, having gained our attention. "What we should be doing is resting, not this nonsense."

With a huff, Logan releases me from his grip, and I stumble away, lungs burning from the exertion. Unable to shake the lingering tension, I stalk towards the kitchen, desperate to put some distance between us.

Anger still simmering, I yank open the cabinet door with enough force to rattle the dishes. How dare he reduce the intense feelings I have for Brigid to just lust? No way was Logan right. This driving, relentless need is about more than carnal desire. It has to be. Why or how? I didn't have a clue, but it was.

I try to push the thought aside, but it clings to me like a parasite, burrowing deeper.

I continue searching the cabinets as confusion swirls within me, each a wave of clashing emotions. Even with the thousand other things happening, she consumed my every waking thought. How can I deny what I felt?

I find a bottle, take it down, and slam the door closed.

"Be quiet," Heath hisses. "Are you trying to wake her?"

I glance at the door of her bedroom. Dammit. Shame heats my cheeks as I grab a bottle of wine, uncork it, and take a long, defiant swig straight from the bottle. It's a sweet dessert wine, but it'll do the trick.

The alcohol sears my veins, and I only stop when the bottle is empty. I set it down, intentionally gently. I wipe my face, glaring at Logan, still standing guard by the window.

"Better?" Heath says. When I don't respond, he continues, "If the two of you are done acting like children. We need to discuss this. It's clear Carter has concerns, and since our bonds are especially sensitive to each other, they should be addressed before they fester."

Logan scoffs, but Heath levels him with a pointed look. "I'll be the first to admit, there's something odd about the connection I feel to Brigid. It's not anything I've experienced before, but I don't sense any threat from it."

"You're both fucking nuts," Logan grumbles, flopping onto the couch. "We've been up all night, tired as shit, and you lost a lot of blood from that gunshot wound to your leg, but fine, I'll keep my mouth shut and listen."

"Regardless of the nature of these connections," Heath says, sipping his coffee, "or feelings, or whatever they are, we can all agree that Brigid protected the egg, putting herself in great danger. If we want her risk to be worth it, we need to work together."

Logan exhales a heavy sigh, some of the fight draining from his posture. "Well, shit. People think the rider's bonds are all fairytale shit too. So, while I don't understand what's happening, I'll try." The tension dissipates ever so slightly as Logan lets out a weary sigh and turns to me. "Fuck it, fine."

I hold his gaze. It's the closest thing I'll ever get to an apology.

"There, was that so hard?" Heath says. "Now, Carter, how about you take the first sleep shift? Logan will check on the egg, and I'll stay up in case anyone needs something.

I look at the couch, thinking about joining Brigid in the bedroom. Last week, I'd held her in my arms when she'd been recovering in Heath's bed. I want that again, to feel her close and protect her.

But I don't want to risk waking her up more than I already had. She needs rest. We all do. With a sigh, I kick off my boots and stretch out on the couch. I pull the faded throw blanket over me as exhaustion takes over. The worn couch cushions mold around me as I turn over. With my eyes closed, I start to drift off, faintly aware of Heath drawing the blinds and settling into the armchair. My eyelids grow heavier, and right before sleep takes over, a pair of piercing blue eyes and silver hair fills my mind.

Eleven

BRIGID

I feel *amazing*.

As I awaken, I smile to myself and rub the sleep from my eyes. Images of Carter and me in the shower last night flit through my mind while echoes of the sensations skitter across my skin where he'd touched me with his hands, his lips, and his tongue. I shiver at the memory.

I'm still naked, and glancing around the room, I see someone has hung up my towel, and my loaner scrubs are neatly folded on a chair. Wrapping a sheet around me, I get up and get dressed for whatever is left of the afternoon.

I slip into a pair of soft blue leggings and a pale gray long-sleeved button-up shirt. After everything that happened today, I'm opting for comfort. Once dressed, I make my way to the bathroom to brush my teeth and run a comb through my wild bedhead hair. I fell asleep with it wet, so it's wavier than usual, the pale strands catching the light and looking like molten silver. When I'd been born, my hair had been as dark as Sharice's, but then, over time, had lightened to where it was now. Mom never mentioned anyone in our family having a similar hair color. Of course, she never talked about distant relatives much at all.

I dab on lip gloss, mascara, and some blush and begin to feel more human again.

A murmur of voices drifts in from the living room, and I recognize Heath, Carter, and Logan. Knowing they'd stuck around sets my heart fluttering with a warmth I can't quite explain. They must have a hundred other things they needed to do, and yet here they were.

A girl could get used to this kind of attention.

After one last glance in the mirror, seeing surprisingly bright eyes for only a four-hour nap, I head out to the living room. They go silent as I enter, and I scan their faces. Logan's sporting his usual grim look, while Heath's face is unreadable. Carter's expression, however, looks undeniably guilty.

"Okay," I say. "Care to share with the class what's going on?"

Logan and Carter both look to Heath, who then leans forward, resting his elbows on his knees. Worry furrows the skin between his brows, and I can't miss the fact that he's hating what he's going to tell me.

I think back to the warm, fluffy blankets I'd been cocooned in.

I should have stayed in bed.

"I know you're still recovering from last night, but there's something we need to discuss."

I move to the kitchen to fetch a glass of water. I rest it and my hands on the kitchen table, steeling myself for the question that seems to have gotten all three on edge. "I'm listening."

"You came here looking for your sister, and while I'm sure you're shocked by how you found her, you now know she's alive and somewhere in Venovia." He pauses, and Logan and Carter lean closer to him. "So, now that you do, you are welcome to leave your position here. None of us would blame you if you wanted to. In fact, I've had two employees already send me their resignations."

My tongue sweeps the insides of my molars as my mind circles the question. "What are you saying? If you're trying to scare me into leaving, it's not going to work."

Carter laughs. "Scare you? Never. What Heath's trying to say is no job is worth this risk, especially one that we all know you took for certain reasons."

"While I appreciate your offer," I say. "You can't ask me to go back to my old life. Not now. Not after everything I've seen."

"We only want what's best for you, including your safety," Heath says.

I want to tell him he's wrong. That everything has changed, and the only way I'll be safe is if I'm here with them. They can sense the mystyl better than any Circuit police or security. In fact, in all of Venovia, the safest place for anyone right now is surrounded by druadans and their riders.

"To be clear, we don't want you to go," Heath adds quickly. "You are..." he trails off, and it's surprising to see this confident man's words falter. "You are wanted here."

When I'd first arrived here, I'd missed Delford terribly, but now it feels more like a home than Uncy'lia or my apartment ever did. My heart belonged here. With a passion for history, this place is a dream come true. Sure, I'd taken this job initially as a chance to find my sister, but since then, I'd discovered that I'm actually kind of good at it. My instincts for reading people and knowing what they want work to my advantage.

Since riding Galaxian and finding the egg, I'd developed only more questions, and a druadan station was the best place to get the answers unless I found Sharice and asked her, which wouldn't happen anytime soon, if ever.

I don't want to go back to Delford. I don't want to return to that old life in the city with the noise and the aggressive climbing of the corporate ladder where your coworkers become your enemies.

Carter's green gaze softens. "All we're saying is we want you to stay here because you want to, not because we're forcing you."

"Great," I say. "Then it's settled. I'm staying." I move over to the couch and prop my feet on the coffee table. Running a hand through my tangled locks, I find one of my hair ties among the pile of empty glasses and disposable soup cups — the boys had helped themselves to my cupboards while I slept — and begin braiding it down the side.

"About you staying *here*," Carter says.

"Meridian is closing," Heath says. "Temporarily, so we've been ordered to move to Blackhawk."

"Blackhawk? Like up north?"

Heath nods.

"Why there? There have to be other stations closer?"

"Blackhawk is the largest and has room to accommodate us. Circuit believes Meridian's isolation is a safety hazard. Blackhawk has more resources and is better fortified."

I lick my lips, a gesture that gains both Heath and Carter's attention. "And I will keep my job there, too?"

"If you wish, yes."

From the first day I arrived here, Carla and the rest of the staff had been lovely. And just because you survived a traumatic incident didn't mean life stopped. I still needed a paycheck.

Life went on.

Any mental wounds I needed to see a therapist about would have to take a back seat.

"All right," I say, clapping my hands together. "So, how do we move a druadan station?"

OVER THE COURSE OF THE DAY, I HELP PACK BOXES, CHECK OFF LISTS, and label crates. By noon the following day, Meridian's primary staff and the riders are stepping up the ramps of two transport shuttles. One police shuttle remained, and Ewensen said they'd do another last sweep before reporting to Nelworth. She'd also promised when it was safe, we'd return.

I could only hope she was telling the truth.

They load the druadans last after receiving light sedation from Dr. Gideon. Metal-barred transport stalls line the back cargo hold and allow them to peer out but not nip at each other, although they still try through the narrow bars.

A tense silence fills the cabin as we all take our seats.

"We'll come back someday," Carla mumbles to no one in particular. Her voice is barely louder than the engine's hum as the pilot guides the shuttle up into the air. Across the aisle, the partially cracked egg snoozes peacefully in the padded crate, totally oblivious to all the chaos happening outside its little world.

A strange tingling spreads across my skin, and I fidget in my chair, trying to shake off the uneasy feeling running through me. *New place jitters,* I tell myself, recalling how I'd vomited in the lecture hall bathroom before my first day at DU.

Carter takes my hand, his warm fingers intertwining with

mine. "I'm glad you decided to stay," he whispers, his words calming my frazzled nerves.

Ever since the shower, he'd been inhabiting my thoughts, often turning them into vivid sensations at the most inappropriate of times.

But it wasn't just the way he kissed me or touched me. It was the way he looked at me like he was trying to say something more. What were we to each other? Friends? Friends with benefits? A tryst to heal a traumatic experience? If that was all this was, a short-term fling, then what had he meant by 'I'll always find you'? Carter might have a reputation for being a playboy, but I still didn't imagine he told that to every woman he slept with.

I have to believe there is something more between us. I glance at the other two as they scroll through the list of supplies on the tablet.

Logan is a hot-tempered jerk, but he'd protected me from the mystyl when they'd swarmed me. What if he had been acting on instinct, though? He is security here. Wouldn't he have done the same for anyone else?

Then there's Heath. Mr. Formal is off-limits, and yet I have to be blind not to see the way he is staring at me when he doesn't think I'm looking.

In the past twenty-four hours, I haven't had a chance to catch my breath, let alone contemplate the increasingly complex relationship dynamic I have with these three men.

I don't know what I want from them.

To be their friend? Good friend? Okay, that's a lie. I totally wanted more, but that'll work for now. What I do know is they make me feel safe and needed. I like this version of myself — confident and free to be myself — when I'm around them.

The shuttle's interior is the largest I've ever seen, built for cargo—wide and utilitarian, with fold-down chairs and tables bolted to the floor. Harnesses and straps dangle from the ceiling, clattering against the metal walls with every jolt. The hum of the old props fills the space, a constant roar, but they've tossed in pillows and blankets to soften the hard, worn-out seats. The staff have scattered throughout, each taking what space they can find in the noisy cabin.

My eyes drift to the closest wall monitor displaying our flight path. Our little pip is currently soaring over Tox Zone Beta, and I press my face against the window to get a better look at the land below.

The last time I'd flown over a tox zone was five years ago when I'd been seventeen and was shipped to Delford to finish my last year of school. It was at night, so I'd only been told about it after I'd woken up.

Now, during the light of day, I have a chance to glimpse at the poisoned land.

Low-hanging gray clouds, streaked with hints of green and purple, drift ominously over the ground thousands of feet below us. Through the thinner patches, I glimpse rolling brown hills and scattered bushes. From up here, the landscape looks no different from any other—far from dangerous. But within those borders lie countless invisible dangers—lethal bacteria, cancer-causing radiation, toxic spores, and deadly wild animals.

Every child in Venovia goes through a phase where they're fascinated by the tox zones. Class projects are often based around the history and formation of these contaminated areas as well as Circuit's efforts to contain them. *"Prevent the spread, prevent the dead."*

In between spelling tests and whatever defrosted soup the Uncy'lia school room provided us—we learned about the horrific mutations, birth defects, and the slow, agonizing deaths caused by exposure. Despite the danger, kids would still make bold promises they'd adventure into one someday or skip college altogether and become a daredevil trawler.

From his seat across from me, Heath taps open his comm and sighs. "Deputy Ewensen sent another list of questions for us to fill out."

"For you or all of us?" I ask.

"When we spoke before, she said she'd prefer all of us."

I nod, clasping my hands together on my lap. "Okay, shoot."

"Ewensen specifically was interested in what Sharice said to you before Galaxian intervened."

A pang of unease twists inside me as the memory resurfaces, my muscles tensing with the rush of emotions I had felt. I'd been so relieved, so thrilled to see my sister alive, only to be shattered by the cold, distant look in her eyes and the revelation she was a member of the rebel group. Some parts are a blur as I strain to remember. She'd barely spoken to me, more focused on giving orders to the others. But then something she said flashes back — something I almost forgot. "She said she'd needed me," I say.

"Needed you?" Carter echoes, "What the hell does that mean?"

I shake my head. "I wish I knew. I swear I've thought about it since then and still don't have a clue."

"She probably meant she needed you as leverage," Logan offers, "like as a hostage so they could escape on the boat without the police blowing it up."

"It's possible," Heath says, tapping it on the screen. "I'll make a note of it and pass it to Ewensen for her to figure out." Heath swipes his finger to move to a new document. "As far as the rest of what Ewensen wanted, I think we should take a step back and think about what we *do* know. We know Sharice attacked the station when we would be at our most vulnerable, and the wealthiest and most connected families would be there. That can't be a coincidence. She knew that this was an important event, and the media would definitely sit up and pay attention if a threat was made to these people most of all."

There had never been a doubt in my mind that Sharice had timed this attack precisely. Still, there was another thing that bugged me. "What doesn't make sense is the recording on her comm bracelet. She'd said she was in danger and claimed someone was threatening my mom and me to force her to steal this egg. Was she lying then?"

"I believe so," Heath says. "I think she left the recording as a way to distract us, or a way to cover up her true intentions."

I frown, his words only confirming my fears. "Okay, but what if she was coerced in the beginning, and then once she'd stolen the egg and met with the rebel group, she realized she *was* on their side?" Once I've said it, the questions pour out of me. "What if they lied to her and somehow convinced her that what they were doing was right? What if she was tricked into joining?" I pause, my eyes scanning their intent gazes. Sharice is far from a pushover and wickedly smart. If she was being manipulated, whoever it was that convinced her must've had one hell of a good pitch they gave her.

I ball my fists by my side before continuing. "I want to believe that she is still a good person even though she's made bad choices."

"Bad choices," Logan huffs. "Fucking understatement of the century." He earns a glare from Carter and Heath.

His words strike me, and I can't ignore the guilt that coats my tongue. If only I had said something to her *before* the rebel group had sunk their claws into her. If only I had discouraged her from taking the job at Meridian. If only I had kept in closer contact with her and continued calling even when she didn't pick up. If I had asked more questions about her life, maybe then she wouldn't have joined them.

Maybe none of this would've happened, and those people who died at Meridian would still be alive.

But dwelling on the past never changes anything. The only thing left for me to do is move forward and accept the reality of the here and now.

"My sister is smart," I press on. "There's a reason why she felt the need to do this. I need you all to trust me that my sister isn't evil. Good people do bad things all the time, thinking that they're justified." My throat clenches. Was I really being that naïve? When I'd confronted her, I'd barely recognized her. She was so angry, so cruel and cold.

Further, Sharice had come back for the other two eggs. Why would she do that? Maybe it hadn't hatched, or maybe it had, but she, or whoever oversaw her group, felt she needed the other ones, too. There were so many questions left unanswered. What purpose could this egg possibly provide to the rebels? Selling it for money? Holding hostage for bribery? Or was there less to it and it had been a random act of violence to get Circuit's attention? That didn't seem like Sharice.

Once, when she'd flunked an organic chemistry report in seventh grade, she'd gotten a lecture from mom, but the teacher had allowed her extra lab time to redo it.

It was only weeks later she'd told me she'd failed the report on purpose. It'd been her plan all along. She'd wanted more time in the lab to continue testing her hypothesis of starfish limb regrowth with a custom gel bandage.

Sharice *always* had a purpose.

"No one would ever argue she isn't smart," Heath replies to me. "Bringing back the extinct mystyl, coordinating an attack on a secure druadan station, all of that requires serious dedication and planning. But we're smart too *and* have an advantage." He leans closer and lowers his voice, although the hum of the engines makes it impossible for the staff members surrounding us to hear. "No one outside the station knows the egg is hatching. We must keep this secret as long as possible. If word gets out, it could provoke the rebels to attack again."

"Agreed," Carter says.

"And as of right now," Heath continues, "she's a fugitive, and unfortunately, I don't think that's going to be changing." His face tightens. "Even if you insist she was manipulated, Circuit is going to want proof, too, and all we have is the security camera footage at Meridian and her comm videos. Neither of which is much to stand on to prove her innocence."

Logan murmurs an assent. "I've seen the footage, and it's pretty damning."

"I know she's your sister," Heath says, "but I don't want your feelings for her clouding your judgment. She is an enemy of Circuit. Innocent people were injured and even killed because of what her group did at Meridian. She has their blood on her hands. And you need to come to terms with the best possible way this ends is with her in jail."

"Fuck jail," Logan snaps before I can reply. "She signed her death sentence the second she let the mystyl loose. And for you to tell me putting her in jail is her punishment is bullshit. If I ever see her again, one of us won't be walking away."

As the words leave Logan's mouth, it feels as though a dagger has been plunged between my ribs. I know he means it. And if it comes down to it, he will do whatever it takes to stop her. I can only pray it doesn't come to that.

I've always looked up to my big sister. Idolized her resourcefulness and intelligence. My family is small — just me, her, and my mom. But no matter what she has done or what choices she's made, she will always be my sister.

And despite everything that has happened, I still cling to a sliver of hope that there was some good left in her and that maybe, just maybe, she could be redeemed. "I won't give up on her," I say stubbornly, looking directly into his steel-colored eyes.

Logan's jaw flexes. "And *I* won't let you risk your life for someone who doesn't deserve it."

"Fine," I say with a heavy sigh. "She's done bad things, but she should have a fair trial and justice."

Logan sneers. "Listen here, Blondie. The only justice that psycho deserves is one between the eyes."

My reaction is instant as I unbuckle and shoot up from my seat. I close the distance between us until I'm glaring up at him. "Screw you. How dare you criticize my sister while you have blood on your own hands? Someone died because you couldn't control your stallion."

The second the words leave my mouth, I know I've gone too far.

Shit.

Logan's massive form goes rigid. "You're right," he says, his voice eerily calm. For a fleeting moment, I think he might back down and let it go. But then his steel gaze cools, all pretense of restraint shattering like glass. "I almost forgot." Instantly, my feet are dragged across the floor as he grabs me by the neck and slams me against the wall.

His right hand clamps down around my throat, cutting off most of my air supply. I gasped, feeling the first heady wave of panic as his eyes bore into mine.

From the first time we'd met, he'd frightened me. His massive frame was pure muscle, with shoulders and arms so huge you couldn't help but be intimidated.

"Easy," Heath says. "Think about this, Logan." He and Carter rise from their seats.

"Don't you fucking hurt her," Carter says, voice low, but neither moves any closer.

My pulse pounds in my ears. What are they doing? *Why aren't they stopping him?* I want to shout at them, calling them cowards, but I can't inhale deep enough to speak. The rest of the staff is either asleep or in the front compartment eating lunch.

If I want to escape, I'll need to do it myself. "Logan," I gasp. "Stop." I reach up, gritting my teeth as I sink my nails into his forearm.

"You need to..." I manage to say. "Stop."

He remains a statue, eyes locked with mine. With his hand clamped around my throat, I kick helplessly, continuing to claw and scratch his arm.

I'm seconds away from blacking out and am rapidly losing the strength to keep fighting.

"No, stop." I think the words tumble from my mouth, but the voice isn't mine. It's deep and menacing and makes Logan's eyes widen, as if waking up from a daze, and the pressure around my neck eases and then is gone.

I collapse to the floor, coughing, clutching my throat as I gulp in long, ragged breaths.

Logan takes a step back, staring down at me.

Heath steps between us, putting his face inches from Logan's. "What the hell were you thinking?"

Carter races over to me and helps lift me to my feet. "Are you okay?" he asks gently, even as anger seers the edges of his voice.

I nod, still catching my breath, and he eases me over to a chair. As soon as I'm seated, he moves to Heath's right, eyes pinned on Logan. "What the actual fuck, man? You could've hurt her!" He shoves him, and, to my surprise, Logan is pushed back into a stack of crates and has to catch himself before falling. Logan is the biggest of the three, but all riders are wildly strong and athletic. And, not for the first time, I wonder if they have something more, an advantage from the bond regular men don't have.

As Logan regains his footing, it's like the three of them are balancing on a knife's edge, the slightest shift threatening to plunge them over the precipice into an all-out conflict.

To my relief, Logan shakes his head as if clearing it, and like a switch being flipped, the fight drains out of him. His shoulders sag, and the heat is gone from his gaze as he turns, walking to the empty chairs behind us. He ducks into one of the fold-out cots, lies back, and closes his eyes.

"What an asshole," I curse and tuck my legs under me. I know I should be more pissed than I am, but I'm shocked more than anything.

He could've killed me, crushed my windpipe with one hard squeeze.

And yet, he hadn't.

The realization dawns on me. Maybe he never intended to kill me at all?

Perhaps it was a dominance thing or a warning not to test his patience.

Is that why Heath and Carter hadn't stopped him? Could they sense he'd restrain himself? Maybe they'd detected a hesitancy in him I couldn't?

Confusion muddies my thoughts, and I resist the urge to rub the tender skin on my neck, instead resorting to stuffing my hands under my legs. It had been two days since my unplanned ride on Galaxian, and thankfully, the soreness in my inner thighs had finally faded.

Carter and Heath give each other a silent glance, then join me at the table, an uneasy quiet settling over the room.

"I'm deeply sorry, Ms. Corsair. That was inexcusable, and I

will have a strong word with him," Heath says, his voice clipped.

"Like it'll do any good," I say, more than loud enough for Logan to hear.

Heath exchanges a tense look with Carter, then says, "There's something you should know."

I raise my brows. "Oh, about what? How he needs an anger management class?"

Carter smiles and scoots himself a little closer to me so he can rest an arm over the back of my chair. "You're not wrong, but there's something else."

"Riders share more than a bond," Heath says. "We share everything. We have to. Most of what we do in the arena is dangerous. We're pushing our stallions and our abilities in order to demonstrate difficult maneuvers performed during the war. Trust is a must for our safety, and that only comes from being open and honest with one another. However, one limit exists that every rider must respect. A line they must never cross." He pauses, letting me process his words before continuing. "The worst thing a rider can do is to ride another's stallion."

A walnut-sized lump forms in the back of my throat as I sense the direction of the conversation.

"It's not only a big no no," Carter says. "It's forbidden for a reason."

"I... I'm sorry. I had no idea," I whisper.

"How could you?" Carter says. "It was a life or death situation, and you couldn't have ridden Galaxian if he hadn't allowed you. But to Logan, it doesn't matter. You broke a sacred rule."

A knot of anxiety coils in my chest. Without even realizing it, I'd committed a cardinal sin, treading into territory I didn't fully understand. My ignorance of druadans was dangerous, like wandering through a minefield with no map.

How could I be more careful when I didn't even know what I was up against? Being connected to these riders meant I was bound to be near druadans, and yet I felt vulnerable like I was playing a game without a rule book. The thought of it makes the hair on my neck stand on end. How could I avoid missteps when the very ground beneath me seemed to shift with every new revelation?

I draw in a steadying breath. "Can I ask why?"

"There are stories told at Vanguard," Heath says, face grim, "rumors of novices riding bonded druadans as dares or pranks and the stallion phasing and leaving them behind."

"Behind? Behind *where*?"

Heath's jaw ticks. "The nowhere. The dark place in between."

Worry clouds Carter's eyes. "We probably shouldn't be telling her this."

"I think it's time she knows," Heath replies before switching his gaze back to me. "No one knows what the nowhere is. It's been theorized that it's another dimension or space between versions of our world. While some believe that a phase bends time around it and that rider and stallion aren't really moving at all, it's actually the passage of time being warped so the earth moves under *them*."

"Wow," I say, widening my eyes. "Can't say that really clears things up." I purse my lips, earning a smirk from Carter.

"Don't think about it too hard," he says, "Trust me. Some big-brained scientists don't even understand it."

"Think he's cooled off?" Carter asks.

"Doubt it," Heath replies, "but we should go anyway before he decides to blow off steam with one of the novices." Heath turns to me before leaving. "There are blankets in the crate over there if you want some rest."

I thank him, and they walk over to where Logan lies on the cot. They sit on the cot next to him, their muffled voices occasionally reaching me.

I give up trying to eavesdrop, a nearly impossible task with the drone of the shuttle's engines, and let my thoughts drift as I stare out at the stretching landscape dotted with snow-peaked mountains and glittering lakes and rivers. My sister could be hiding anywhere down there.

Carter and Heath rejoin me, and we silently eat the lunch brought to us by an attendant. Full of vegetable soup and bread, I doze, surrendering to fatigue and resting my head against Carter's shoulder. His warmth seeps into me, and there are snippets of time when I forget we're on a shuttle. Forget we're leaving Meridian. Forget that while I'd come there seeking answers, and I'm leaving with more questions than when I'd arrived.

Inhaling Carter's comforting scent of pine and musk, fragmented memories cut through the haze of my half-dreams. Mystyl attacking me flashes in my mind — then I'm surrounded by my sister and her group, their eyes cold with their drawn guns. I'd been completely at their mercy. The image shuffles to Logan's angry, looming face in my mind and the feel of his hand around my neck.

Every time, it ends the same. It's a pattern I can't seem to break, no matter how hard I try to think of something else. Each time, I'm back in the dark memories, left waiting for someone to pull me out of the fire.

Struck by an idea, I shrug off the drowsiness and get out of my chair, trying not to rouse Carter or Heath.

"Where are you going?" Carter says, cracking one eye open.

"It's okay," I whisper. "Just the bathroom. Go back to sleep."

His lips form a tight line and I see the question hovering behind his one open green eye, but then it shuts, and he repositions his head on the blanket he'd wadded into a pillow.

I have no idea what the staff and rider situation is going to be like at Blackhawk, and the odds are good. We won't be as cozy as we were at Meridian. When we land, there's a high probability Logan will disappear to the riders' quarters, and I'll never get a chance again with him alone to clear the air.

Logan has moved from the cot, and sits on one of the passenger chairs hunched over, head hung heavily, with his elbows braced on his knees. He doesn't look up as I draw nearer.

I take the seat next to him. The last person who used it had adjusted to be at a recline to allow them to sleep. The adjustment button is on the other side of Logan's chair, and I'd rather stick my hand in a blender than ask him to push it. So, with no other option, I sit, and my feet swing freely like a small child, and the confidence I'd proudly brought with me disappears.

"If you're telling me to go to hell," he says, "believe me, I'm already there. I should never have done that."

I'm taken aback by the regret saturating his words. He feels bad. I don't know what to say. I never expected him actually to apologize.

"I'm not here to start a fight," I reply. "In fact, I want to do the opposite."

He runs a hand over the short bristles of his tawny hair but refuses to look at me. "Carter and Heath told me about how I shouldn't have ridden Galaxian."

"Good for them."

"So, while I did it because I had to, I understand why you felt you needed to react like you did."

He tilts his head. Hard gray eyes briefly meet mine before he stares down at his hands. "You have no fucking idea how I feel. What it's like to be constantly on edge, to hold everything in, day after day, because losing control isn't an option. And then, in one moment, to slip up... to lose that control, even for a second."

His words hit me harder than I expected. He's talking about Galaxian that day and the moment everything went wrong.

"I didn't realize," I say softly, almost to myself, the words feeling inadequate. I want to reach out to offer some kind of comfort, but I don't know how. He's not the type to accept pity, and I know that if I show even a hint of it, he'll shut down completely.

"What do you want, Blondie?"

I inhale through my nose, choosing my words carefully. "It's become clear," I say, picking at a bandage on my wrist, "that I need a way to protect myself. I need someone to teach me self-defense. I can't always rely on others to keep me safe. And with my sister still out there, there's a good chance I'll end up in dangerous situations again."

Logan sighs, wiping his hands on his pants and sits up. "No."

"No?" I echo him. "Why not?"

"Go ask Carter."

I stare at him. "I don't want Carter to teach me. I want *you*."

"Why?"

"You know why."

He's silent for a moment, then laughs, a deep rumbling sound. "You're afraid James will go easy on you."

I give him a half-smile and nod. "I know he will. And he's..." I hesitate, trying to form the words. "Easily distracted." Sure, I'm easily distracted by him as well, but this is serious, and if all we end up doing is getting naked instead of him teaching me, I'd never learn to protect myself.

"Fine. Ask Heath, then. He's a deadeye with a gun."

I shift in my seat, feeling ever increasingly that I'm being dismissed. I'm not going to back down. "I will ask him when I want to use a gun, but first, I want to defend myself without one. I want to learn how to throw a punch without breaking my hand. How to find someone's weak points. How to use my smaller size against someone bigger than me." I pause as a shuttle attendant walks by carrying a basket of packaged snacks.

"Care for crackers or dried fruit?"

"Fuck off," Logan says before I get a chance to answer.

The attendant's face blanches, and they hurry away. Once they're out of earshot, I continue. "You oversaw security at Meridian. I saw you fight off mystyl. You saw them before I did, and you knew what to do."

"The answer is no."

"At least tell me why?"

"No."

I grind my teeth together, annoyed at myself for thinking this was a good idea. "Well fuck you, then."

"Fuck you right back, Blondie."

I leap to my feet and tromp back to where Heath and Carter are rousing from their nap.

Carter sees me first. "Everything okay?"

"Yeah." I fold my arms and collapse into the seat. "He really is the world's biggest jerk. When he showers tonight, I hope he gets shampoo in his eyes."

Carter laughs and even Heath cracks a smile.

"No argument there," Carter says. "You want to talk about it?"

I eye the two snack bags lying on the table, untouched by

Heath and Carter. "Do you mind?" I ask.

Carter's eyebrow arches as he nods. I snag one, tear it open, and shove the mix of almonds and dried cranberries in my mouth. Logan's refusal only strengthens the resolve that burns brighter than ever within me. I refuse to be the one in need of saving. I will find a way to defend myself.

No more damsel in distress.

Sharice certainly wasn't.

At some point, I finally dozed off and awoke to the stomach-flipping sensation of turbulence as we descended. Meridian had been so warm and bright, but here, so far north, our shuttle drifts in and out of gray clouds, and a mist has formed on the windows. Most of the shades have been pulled closed, but faint sunlight shines through those that are open.

"There's Blackhawk Village," Heath explains, pointing to the clusters of buildings and houses out the window to our left. I'd been to the village twice before, but both times, I'd flown in at night, so it was nice to see it during the day. Instead of wide open spaces and cozy homes like my cottage, the town has sharp rooflines and cramped brick buildings. It was as if the builders had wanted to save on materials by making each structure share a wall. The streets are narrow and winding, and I make out only a handful of cars driving lazily along them.

"That's where there's shopping and restaurants," Heath continues, "and some station workers live there and commute daily."

"We'll have to take you to Blink," Carter says. "It's the bar all the riders go to. They have the best specialty drinks, but the Raging Stallion is my favorite. It's basically shuttle fuel mixed with lime juice. It's wicked shit, but it works wonders if you're brimming." He flicks a quick glance at Heath, who is tracing the outline of the scar on his hand. Carter had mentioned earlier that Heath was struggling with the lingering side effects of brimming. But looking at him now, he seems fine.

I grin at Carter. "Not that I'll ever have that problem, but I'll try anything once."

"Damn right, you will." Carter nudges me playfully. I stifle a laugh, pressing my lips together.

Up and down both sides of the shuttle, other station workers press against the glass, eager to see their new— hopefully temporary— home.

I'm no different. I peer back out the window, seeing a broken stone bridge partially spanning a rushing river. Hundreds of feet below it, the water froths and churns, kicking up a fine spray that forms foaming eddies among the jagged rocks and broken pieces that had once been the remaining part of the bridge.

The North Bay bridge had been broken for as long as I can remember and I'd always found it interesting they'd never rebuilt it so people could drive up the hill to the station. Perhaps they didn't think it was worth investing in or wanted to limit the traffic that came to Blackhawk.

But from a marketing perspective, it made perfect sense. The cable car was installed by one of the wealthiest families in the area, and over time, it had become iconic to Blackhawk Station. Rebuilding the bridge would mean fewer people using the cable car, diminishing its allure.

As if on cue, I watch the sleek black gondola with gleaming gold trim glide effortlessly along a pair of suspended steel cables, its reflection a dark shimmering shadow on the ground below. It's not only a mode of transport; it's a symbol of the station's charm and exclusivity.

As we approach, my pulse quickens as I get my first

glimpse of Blackhawk Station. If Meridian had felt old, this place felt ancient. Our shuttle passes between two towering black-bricked watchtowers standing sentinel at the end of the bridge.

Giant walls and parapets soar hundreds of feet into the air, reminding me of the castles from the history books I'd devoured as a child. This place is a massive fortress of black and gray stone, and disorientation washes over me as I realize I can't see all of it, even from the height of the shuttle.

The broad-topped hill extends out to the left, where rows of perfectly aligned trees stretch into the western horizon. It's an orchard or tree farm, which would make sense considering the food needs of such a large population.

The shuttle lands with a soft thud, rattling the straps securing the moving crates to the floor and I'm forced to grab to the back of a seat to steady myself. After the shuttle settles, I casually place a hand on the crates next to the one with the egg, trying not to appear too eager. I know they'll never let me carry it, but I can't help it. I'd risked my life for it. I won't let some clumsy-handed attendant break it now.

Meridian staff unbuckle themselves from their benches and begin to stretch and gather their bags. Their faces are drawn, exhausted—mimicking the way I feel.

"Attention, passengers," the pilot's voice crackles over the intercom. "Check that you have all of your belongings. General staff, please use the side ramp for disembarking. Riders secure your druadans, and cargo personnel will assist with supplies, then proceed to the rear ramp."

The side ramp descends with a hydraulic hiss, and I lay eyes on the inside of Blackhawk Station for the first time through the opening. The shuttle had put us down in the center of a large courtyard. A light drizzle is falling, casting a glistening sheen over the obsidian stonework.

Drawing in a deep breath, I clutch my bag tighter and step out onto the ramp, the misting rain instantly dampening my face. "Ah, a true North Bay greeting," a nearby attendant in a black jumpsuit says, "Welcome to Blackhawk. Hope you brought a raincoat."

Twelve

LOGAN

Tall stone walls surround me, hiding anything beyond.

Even with my memory, it's disorienting to not be able to see anything beyond. Unlike Meridian's horizon wide onto the lake or the desert, the world here ends at the damp, moss-covered stones that border the square courtyard that doubles as a shuttle pad.

The shuttle's doors hiss open, releasing a gust of steam into the evening air. Rain pelts us, coming down in steady sheets and turning Blackhawk's cobblestone courtyard into slick rivers. The streams wind their way through the cracks and eventually drain through grates set in the base of the walls.

The rush of cool air caresses my face, and I smell the slight tinge of ozone from the filtration center I'd seen a mile back as we'd flown over it. A wave of nostalgia hits me, and I shove it aside, slinging my bag over my shoulder.

Centuries ago, they'd built Blackhawk Fortress as one of the last bastions during the mystyl wars. The enormous blocks of dark gray granite that make up the walls are what give it its name since they darken to black from the rain.

If it weren't for the open gate and lack of guards, this place could be a prison.

Galaxian is still groggy from the drugs, so he only half-heartedly tugs against my hold as I lead him down the ramp extending from the side of the shuttle. He shifts restlessly beneath his TTU blanket. A specialized blanket, made from a high-tech fabric I can't pronounce, that was designed to insulate his body for transfers like this. Without it, the shuttle cabin would struggle to keep cool and rapidly overheat with a dozen druadans inside it, whose body temperatures rival that of an oven.

To the rest of the riders, moving to Blackhawk means nothing more than packing a bag and changing an address.

To me, it's the end. It's where Galaxian will be killed, and I will be shunted off to some place off the continent. I shove down the cold reality that I'm in deep shit, *alone*. It's a familiar feeling, one I've carried since Vanguard. No family name, no connections, just grit and never fucking backing down.

I survived then, and I'll survive now.

"Help unload the druadans," a voice calls out over the sound of rain and hooves clicking on stone. As we lead our stallions out of the shuttle, I'm acutely aware of the attention we're attracting. Everyone's heard about the rogue druadan by now. As rare as they are, they're practically myths.

Yet, we're proof that it's real. I square my shoulders and ignore the gawkers.

Let them fucking stare.

Outside the passenger door, a tall woman with purple lipstick, short brown hair, and pale skin greets Blondie and

Carla and leads them to the metal door to the left while I follow the other riders straight to the large double doors that have been propped open.

Inside, the transition from gray evening sunlight to artificial bright light is abrupt. Tracks of small bulbs line the ceiling, casting harsh shadows on the sloping floor below. The grooves cut into the stone are damp with moisture but provide enough grip for boots or hooves not to slip as they descend underground. Galaxian snorts, his breath forming misty plumes in the cool air as we make our way lower into the bowels of the fortress.

At Vanguard, there was a saying that once you go to Blackhawk, you'll never see the sun again. At the time, I thought it was because it was always raining, but now I understand. The stone fortress above was the tip of the very large iceberg of passages and structures underneath.

The stone underfoot eventually gives way to dirt, and the tunnel's low ceiling just clears our heads. The sound of hooves is muffled by the earthy ground.

"Stalls are that way," a man in a Blackhawk jumpsuit of gray and white directs, his finger pointing lazily over his shoulder. "After you've secured your stallion, head to the barracks for your bunk, uniform, and badge."

I fall into line behind Carter and Ember, but the man motions for me to stop. "Master Rider McCelroy?"

I grunt a reply.

Nearby riders pretend not to stare. They are all thinking the same fucking thing. This is it? The rogue stallion and his rider are going to snap.

"You and your stallion are going to be in the west wing, an isolation stall." He thumbs to the arched opening to the right of where the others are going. "Standard protocol until your trial."

Just fucking peachy. It's not like Galaxian is a social butterfly, but in isolation, he won't be able to see or hear the others. I grind my teeth, wanting to tell him to shove the protocol up his ass, but Galaxian jerks forward, startled by a bump from another rider's stallion. "Shit, Logan, sorry," Ben apologizes, maneuvering Ravenvein out of the way.

"We're like goddamn sardines in here," I grumble, directing Galaxian away from the group and under the archway leading to the right.

The path narrows, stone walls closing in until they're only wide enough for a single file. We pass by open stalls with fresh bedding and I pick one and lead him in.

"It's only temporary," I tell him, patting him on the neck. *"And I'll be down here twice a day to visit."*

"Where is egg?"

"I'm not sure where they're putting it, but I can find out."

"Good."

I remove his blanket and then, squatting, unsnap the protective legwear he'd worn to keep from hurting himself on the shuttle ride. Galaxy lines have heavier bones than the others. While not as dense as the Obsidian or Raven stallions, Galaxian's legs are strong and covered in feathered hair above the hooves, unlike Ember's more finely boned ones. I toss the boots over the stall door, then unbuckle his muzzle and halter. Fucking pointless. He knows better than to bite me. He immediately dips his head low and scratches his face on his front legs.

While he paces around the space, smelling the corners and walls, I search for a water spigot. Finding one near the corner, I fill the metal pail, and Galaxian hums from his stall.

"Egg. Safe. Happy."

"Yeah, it is," I mutter, watching his ears prick up at the sound of my voice. He raises his head, nostrils flaring as he catches the scents of the other druadans further down the other corridor.

The metal door slides open with a loud clang, and I step inside, hooking the bucket on the wall. He flips his lips over the water, splashing and earning a smile from me. Then, satisfied it's only water, he begins to drink deeply from the bucket. His tail swishes, and for a moment, I envy his simple contentment.

Life for him was so damn easy— running, sleeping, getting brushed and pampered with his biggest worry being how long until dinner.

I've never known that kind of peace. Even as a kid, I didn't have it.

At the filtration plant, they put us to work as soon as we could lift a broom, half our days spent sweeping vents, the other half at school, learning just enough so we wouldn't be totally useless as adults. In my twenty-three years, I could count on one hand the days I'd slept in.

I lean against the stall door, waiting until he's settled. I'd told him about the trial and the hellish mess we were in, but I wasn't sure he grasped the extent of it. These easy days for him might be coming to an end quickly. Once I'm sure he's not going to try anything stupid like escape, I step outside to grab my bag from where I left it. Then, I head back to the barracks.

I re-enter the center of the barn and take a right passing through the North wing, which contains the rest of the stallions. It's double the stalls here from Meridian's fifteen, and all but the end two are full. There's also a south wing for unbonded druadans or overflow, should they need it for transfers or visiting riders. Overall, Blackhawk could house eighty stallions at total capacity.

At the end of the aisleway, the heavy wooden door groans as I push it open and step into the brightly lit rider barracks. It smells like you'd expect an underground barracks to. Musty,

Earthy, with a tinge of body odor. But it's clean, and floorboard heaters take the chill off. It's not my private cabin at Meridian, but I've slept in worse.

Row after row of double bunks line the space, each one accompanied by a simple trunk, nightstand, and lamp. The sleeping quarters are positioned in order of ranking. Novices nearest the barn, riders in the middle, then Master Riders closest to the rec room and showers.

Sturdy cobblestone walls line the room, and polished granite covers the floor. As a remnant of an ancient army base, it has undergone multiple upgrades and renovations. Tiny rectangular windows sit above the bunks. Their frames are reinforced with iron bars and they cast striped shadows across the rectangular room.

Eyes watch me haul my duffel bag full of clothes and gear to the end of the row. I heave my bag onto the lower bunk beneath Carter's.

With one leg dangling off the side, he swipes through his comm as if we're at summer camp.

"Hey," a voice says, "You're new riders from Meridian, huh?"

I turn, and Carter sits up, taking note of the man who'd spoken.

A brown, patchy beard covers his chin, and he has a scar over his left eye. His stance is casual, but his light brown eyes are laser-focused on us, measuring us.

"That's right. I'm Master Rider James, and this is Master Rider McCelroy."

A grin flickers across his face as he steps closer. "Rolan," he introduces himself. "But unless you're one of the starting twelve for the show, you ain't no master rider anymore. New station, new ranking."

Fucking fantastic. "Is that so?" I say.

"Sure is. Blackhawk doesn't care much for past glories but by proving it where it counts," Rolan continues. "Everyone is equal in the arena. At least at the beginning. There's a scoreboard that records all your points for training. Those with the highest scores by mid-winter get selected for starting positions."

My blood heats with the challenge. I'm a damn good rider. They just don't know it yet.

"Oh, and Chief Lugsen doesn't allow for mess in here," Rolan says behind me. "Make sure your shit is picked up and the bed is made, and you'll be fine."

"Thanks for the heads up," Carter says.

He tosses his duffel on his bunk, and a mild resentment lingers between us. What I'd done to Blondie might have been excessive, but it was necessary.

She couldn't have known about the one rider, one stallion rule, so it'd been up to me to teach her. Scaring her had been for her own good. It was dangerous as hell riding a bonded stallion. Galaxian could've phased anytime during their ride, leaving the egg in the nowhere, or worse, returning with only half of her. My jaw tightens so hard I think my teeth are going to crack. Two, now three times, he'd defied me to protect her. He was my stallion. He should be loyal only to me.

Why was he so hellbent on guarding her?

I meant it only as a warning and not to hurt her, but Galaxian couldn't tell the difference. He'd told me to stop, and so I had.

I was going to anyway... eventually.

Respect went both ways in our bond, and if Galaxian wanted me to rely on him again, I needed to show him that he could trust me. Pulling that stunt with Blondie probably wasn't the best way to start.

I turn away from him and unzip my bag to unpack. I'd

snagged a bottle of Delford gold from one of the crates when no one was looking and so now tuck it between two pairs of rolled-up fatigue jumpsuits in the bottom drawer. Next are my clothes. Three pairs of Khaki cargo pants, black t-shirts, workout gear, and my riding pants and carbon fiber jacket. There's a rod to hang my formal jacket on, and I spend a minute rubbing the wrinkles from the blue velvet and carbon fiber fabric. I don't know the next time I'll get to wear it again *if* I ever get to. I shove away the dark thought.

Hushed voices murmur from around the room, and I overhear my name.

"What the fuck was Marshal thinking letting a rogue rider come here?" one says.

Then another replies, *"I'm surprised they let him in here without a muzzle."*

A group of riders have gathered around one of the bunks further down, all with stupid smirks on their faces.

"Let it go," Carter says, keeping his voice low so they won't hear.

My eyes narrow as I return to my task, trying to tune them out.

But then another voice pipes up. "I'm surprised they're still wasting feed on that stallion. They should've left it there on the island to fend for itself. If it wants to be wild, then why stop it?"

I stiffen, my grip tightening on the strap of my duffel bag.

No one insults my stallion. Ever.

Ignoring Carter's murmured protest, I stalk toward him, boots thudding against the wooden floor. The group of riders falls silent as I approach. "Do we have a problem?" I say, glaring at the one who'd opened his stupid fucking mouth.

He blinks as if taken aback by my sudden appearance. "Uh, no, I was saying —"

I don't give him a chance to finish. Lunging forward, I shove him up against the nearest wall, pinning him there with my forearm pressed against his throat.

"I'd think about your next words *very* carefully," I growl, my face so close to his I can smell the beer on his breath.

His eyes are wide with fear. "Hey man, I didn't mean anything. Everyone's nervous after the attack, okay?" he stammers. "Please."

Carter's boots thump on the floor as he hops off the bunk. "Look at you, already making friends," he says dryly, grabbing my arm and easing me off the terrified rider.

I reluctantly release my grip, and the guy slumps down, scurrying out of the room.

Carter steers me back to our bunks. "What the hell do you think you're doing?" he hisses under his breath.

I shrug, returning to unpacking my bag. "The guy was talking shit. You know I can't stand that."

Carter sighs, shaking his head. "Look, I get it, but you gotta learn to pick your battles, man. We just got here and are going to be stuck here for a while, so try to play nice, okay?"

I grudgingly nod as he tells me he's going to check out the mess hall. "Heath had to run to a meeting but should be down in a bit."

He leaves, and the murmured chatter of the other riders continues, and more than once, I hear my name. I glance back at the group, all of whom are now eyeing me warily, including the one I'd pinned against the wall.

That's fucking right, you better be worried.

I drop my empty duffel bag into the top drawer, then finally take a minute to eye my new surroundings. My eyes snag on the table in the center of the room.

Between the showers and a rec room is a large bowl filled with the most vibrant, delicious-looking apples I've ever seen.

I must physically restrain myself from gasping out loud. Real, fresh apples — something I haven't tasted in years, not since...

My mouth waters at the sight, and I start for them.

But before I can take a single step, a pair of medics in white jumpsuits materialize in front of us. "New rider physical," the first, a woman with curly black hair, says. "Please follow us."

Glaring at the apples, I follow her to a table with scales set up at the end of the barracks, where the other riders, including Carter, are being examined.

"Name?" she asks.

"Logan McCelroy."

Her eyes scan the digital tablet. "Ah, there you are." Her tone gives nothing away, but there is a slight tremor in her hand as she passes me the small cup. "Urine sample, please." She motions to the bathrooms, where a line of other riders holding cups has formed.

I unzip my pants and pull out my dick.

"Sir, please," she says, blocking her face with the tablet.

"I got shit to do, lady," I say, ignoring her. A few seconds later, I set the full cup on the metal table and zip up my pants.

She lowers the tablet, her face as red as the apple I'd been drooling over. "Uh, okay. Well, thank you. Let's get you weighed." I step on the scale, and she jots down a number with a nod.

"Allergies?" she asks.

"Bees."

She makes a hmm sound and keys it in. It's a worthless allergy since bees are pretty much extinct at this point. But there had been a wild hive in one of the filtration plant's water towers and we'd dared each other to climb up to get it. I was eight and had no fucking clue what bees were, but I'd be dammed if it wasn't me that claimed it.

Five stings and the biggest shot of an anti-histamine later, I'd survived and learned real quick that bees and I didn't mix.

Next, she makes me sit in a chair while she takes two vials of blood from my arm.

She waves me forward into another line where a short man with an eye patch is handing out pills. As I wait, I hear the word 'rogue,' whispered along with 'that's him.' There's too much other chatter, so it's hard to tell if it's the riders or medics.

They can all whisper about me all they want. Maybe they'll steer clear of me, and I won't have to make small talk in the mess hall.

An attendant hands me a cup with two yellow pills.

"What are these?"

"Vitamin D and B12," he replies. "Everyone gets them weekly since we don't get a lot of sun."

I swallow them with a glass of apple juice they hand me. God damn, that's so good. I snatch another even as a medic gives me the side eye.

Carter— holding a small bandage on his arm— steps up next to me. "We're definitely not at Meridian anymore," he murmurs, sipping his own juice.

Ain't that the fucking truth.

Thirteen

BRIGID

Walls whisper the secrets of the past.

My history professor, Stanley Elliot, had told me that once while waxing poetic about pre-flood architecture. "These buildings," he'd said, "are survivors and have voices if we only know how to listen." The remnants of PF design were everywhere in Blackhawk: from the shapes of the rooflines and the stained-glass windows to the iron hinges supporting century-old doors.

Carrying my shoulder bag and one suitcase, I stand on the landing at the fourth-floor residence hall. A dark-skinned woman, appearing to be around my age, leans out of an open doorway. "Hey there, looking for your room?"

I click the map closed on my comm. "Is it that obvious I'm lost?"

"Just a little," she says, "Luckily you found me. I'm Sadie Benson." She's cute, reminding me a little of Laura with her sparkly purple eyeshadow and pink headband as if subtly objecting to the drab gray uniforms. "I manage the staff apartments. If you run out of toilet paper or your heater isn't working, I'm the one you ask."

"Nice to meet you," I say, smiling. "I'm Brigid Corsair."

"Admin, right? So, you work with Carla?"

"I do. Mostly public relations, but also some marketing."

"Ah, well, welcome," she says. "Sorry to hear about Meridian. We're all glad you're here, even if some act otherwise."

"Let me show you to your room. This place can be a maze, so," she points to the plaque on the wall, "As I'm sure you gathered, this is floor four, north wing, which is rooms ten through twenty. If you get turned around, the lowest numbers are starting here, so you can work your way backward until you reach yours."

I follow Sadie down the hallway, marveling like a gawking tourist at how the old army base has been transformed into a modern apartment building. Where boot-clad feet once marched, there's now a quiet elegance—electric sconces on the walls, a faded yellow and black patterned rug underfoot.

When Sharice had done her internship here, I'd begged her for details about everything, but she'd been tight-lipped, brushing me off with a shrug. *"It's just an old building with people who refuse to see beyond their own noses,"* she'd said. "Everyone's closed-minded, stuck in the past. I could barely get them to consider anything outside their usual box for marketing."

I remember how frustrated she'd sounded, how her voice had grown sharp whenever she talked about this place. Now, walking these halls, I see what she meant. The walls may be dressed up in new fixtures, but there's still an air of the old clinging to everything, like a stubborn grime that won't wipe away. No wonder Sharice didn't last long here as an intern.

But unlike my sister, I've always loved history and while I'd only been here a few hours, Blackhawk already captivated me.

The contrast between the sleek, modern fixtures and the rough old walls is striking, and I can't help but notice the irony. It's like Meridian all over again—I'm a newcomer stepping into a world heavy with history and tradition. But this time, new place jitters mix with excitement. I'm walking through hallways I've only ever read about at DU. The thrill of being here, where so much has happened, is almost enough to drown out the nerves. Almost. I can't deny there's something exhilarating about standing where soldiers once stood, feeling the weight of the past beneath my feet.

We pass by a pair of Blackhawk security, and they give me a momentary look of recognition. Their gazes grate against my nerves. Ewensen might've let me off the hook, but it's clear I'm still considered a "person of interest."

Or maybe that's how they looked at everyone from Meridian? Like we were tainted and bringing bad luck here.

Sadie halts before a nondescript wooden door with a painted 17B on it. I wonder if these rooms once housed officers or enlisted men. I know it had been transformed into a hospital, too, for a time. The morbid thoughts of the people who had died here creep into my brain, and I push them aside.

She hands me a brass key and waits for me to unlock it. She lets me go first and then follows me inside. It's spacious, and motes of dust dance in the shaft of sunlight spilling through the circular room's solitary window. Wood-framed paintings line the stone walls, and the air carries a faint mustiness overlaid with hints of citrus oil. It's clean, if a bit sparse — the floors swept, the ironwork polished to a dull gleam.

"So, this is your room. You can decorate it however you want." Sadie's words pull me back to the present, but I'm overwhelmed by the echo of memory—Carla telling me the same thing just two weeks ago. Another room, another place to call home, and yet I'm still trying to find somewhere to settle.

"It's a standard single," Sadie continues. "We didn't have much time to shuffle everyone around with the short notice." She gives me an appraising look, eyes scanning like she's trying to size me up. "It'll be yours unless you snag yourself a rider." She shows me a gold band with a pear-shaped diamond on her ring finger. "The double is definitely an upgrade, trust me."

I'm stunned by the enormous rock. Riders make good money, and her husband certainly had put it to good use. "You married a rider?"

She beams. "Sure did. Three years last June. There's about a ten-to-one ratio of men to women here, so you'll have all the choices if you want to pick one, too."

I feel a heat bloom in my cheeks, but before I can formulate a response, Sadie's eyes widen with delight. "Oh, my mistake. You already have! Look at you go." She lets out a small laugh. "Any chance you'd give a girl a hint?"

I open my mouth, then close it again, unsure how to respond to this unexpected turn in the conversation. How am I supposed to reply? *Yeah, there's this rider. Well, actually, there are three, so it's a little complicated.*

Yeah. I've known this woman for a handful of minutes. Probably best to hold off.

Caution wins out, and I offer a noncommittal shrug, letting her interpret my reactions as she will.

She raises her eyebrows, a lop-sided smile forming on her face. "Shy, are we? Well, no matter. I'll find out soon enough.

This station is bigger than Meridian, but it's still a tight-knit community, and though the walls are thick, the boundaries between riders are thin. Secrets don't last long here."

I skim over the neatly made bed and the ancient washbasin with its chipped enamel. Even the claw-footed tub looks centuries old.

Wandering back into the bedroom, I go to the window and look out at the sweeping vista. Blackhawk is perched on a hill, and the broken stone bridge partially spanning the North Bay River

is visible down below through the evening mist shrouding the distant village. Beyond that, I can make out the steel cables of the aerial red and gold gondola lazily ferrying passengers between here and the village.

I'd seen pictures on Network of the Northern Cliffs. Steep rock faces plunge sharply into the restless ocean, the cliff sides far too rugged and the waters far too frigid for any chance of swimming. Not at all like the gently lapping waves and warm, sandy shores of Uncy'lia's beaches. This place has a quietness to it, like I'm almost afraid to speak above anything but a whisper, and yet there is a coziness inside. The radiant heaters provide warmth, as do the rugs.

"The clothes bin is taken once a week by our housekeeping staff when they come in to clean and vacuum. If you need something washed sooner, there's an on-site laundry room on the first floor. Meals are in the mess hall between 6 am and 9 am unless you request in advance to have it delivered to your room, which I don't recommend except when you're desperate, as it's always cold when they make it up here."

Sadie goes on to explain where the staff offices are, meeting schedules, and amenities, such as our workout facility that isn't for the riders, as well as a theater room and pool.

"Unless they're married, riders live in the barracks." She

drums her thumb over the metal footboard to a tune I don't recognize. "Hookups don't count. They have to be committed under the law and approved by Marshal before they can live here."

Hearing the word barracks conjures up the sight of stacked cots and windowless rooms. "I thought riders would get preferential treatment?"

Sadie scoffs. "Don't let the name barracks fool you. They're not that bad, but we've outgrown the main estate, and they've found riders and druadans do better if they're housed closer together." She pauses, and her face grows serious. "Oh, and so you know, the barracks are strictly off-limits from us unless Fiaro or Lugsen give you permission. If you want a rider to visit, they must come here." She pats the bed playfully and laughs. "Pun intended."

A wicked giggle escapes me. Okay, so it's confirmed.

Sadie and I are going to be the best of friends.

We exchange comm numbers and she says she'll meet me at dinner to go over any more questions I have.

"The rest of the staff from Meridian?" I ask.

"All admins, like you, are on the fourth, while maintenance, grooms, and guides will be on the first."

"Which room is Carla's?"

Sadie taps her comm. "She and her boyfriend Mack are four rooms down in 13A. Since he's IT, the whole 'have to be married' rule doesn't apply."

"Thanks," I say, relieved that a familiar face won't be too far away. But I still wonder why they're so strict with the riders but not the general staff. Maybe it has to do with the bond—Heath always said riders share everything and that every feeling and emotion is amplified. Jealousy, heartbreak... if one rider is going through it, it could ripple through the whole group, and mess with their performance. Or maybe it's one of the old rules Sharice had been meaning. Riders did have egos, and Logan couldn't be the only one with a short fuse, so maybe the better accommodations were encouragement for them to be tied down and avoid bad choices.

Sadie opens the door to leave. "Get settled. Kaeden and I eat around seven, so we'll save you a seat at dinner tonight."

I turn back to the room once she's gone, taking it all in—the unfamiliar space, the soft hum of the heater, and the patter of rain against the window.

Catching my breath, I close my eyes and remind myself that this is where I'm supposed to be. The egg is protected here. I am protected here. Sure, it's new and overwhelming, but Blackhawk offers more possibilities for advancing my career and learning how a larger station functions.

I open my eyes and sit up straight, looking at the dozens of comm messages awaiting me regarding the move, press releases, and meeting schedules.

Two hours until dinner. If I'm determined to do this right, I better get started.

Fourteen

HEATH

I wake up in the bottom bunk, and it takes me a second to acclimate myself to the fact that I'm in the barracks and not in my room. It's still dark, but I can make out Carter in the top bunk next to me, his comm casting a faint glow as he scrolls, new Dragonfly City songs playing softly. It's a far cry from my bedroom at Meridian—clean, neat, with everything in its place. I miss the quiet, the sense of order. Here, it's cramped and noisy, reminding me of Vanguard's dormitories.

I stretch, feeling the tightness in my neck and back ease. The mattress isn't the problem; it's the smallness of it compared to the expanse of my king bed.

The majority of the other riders are still asleep, and I wonder how anyone gets any decent rest with the constant drone of the druadan's voices echoing off the walls. All night, it had sounded like a freight train running under the floor, although judging by the schedule of the practice routine here we'd had sent to our comms, we'd be so exhausted by the end of the day, the noise wouldn't matter.

The long ride and exposure to Shadowmane the day of the attack had reset my brimming, and I felt for the first time in a long time, clear-headed. The dull ache of arousal is still there, of course, and I rub my straining erection.

I'm overcome by the need to use it.

But if I call Jess now, it'd take her hours to get here. While she permitted me to be with other women, so long as I was discreet, it was something my consciousness wrestled with until it became a life-or-death matter, and I'd have no choice but to relent and make a call from Carter's list.

But now, there's only one woman I'm drawn to, and the idea of anyone else doesn't even cross my mind. Brigid has a hold on me, a connection as Carter had sensed, and it's one I can't shake and find I don't want to.

I frown as I sit up and stretch, preparing to head to the showers before anyone else and relieve this built-up... tension.

Dammit. I *need* a release.

I climb off the bunk, hurriedly gathering my clothes and soap, when my comm rings.

It's Jess. It's early, and since only a few other riders are stirring, I make my way to the rec room to answer.

"Good morning," I say, my voice groggy. "This is an early call from you. Is everything alright?"

"Sorry," she says, "I didn't realize the time."

"I assume you and your family have increased security at the gate to the Northshore estate?"

"Of course, Heath. We're not idiots."

I center myself with an inhale. "Might I ask what this is

about?"

"Our parents want to have dinner tonight."

"Dinner?"

"Yes, you know where people sit down and eat a meal."

"I know what dinner is. Can I ask why?"

"To talk about the wedding. Since you're no longer at Meridian, it's a shorter flight for you from Delford to Blackhawk. There are final details we need you to be a part of."

"We've only just settled," I argue. "and they need me to help modify the schedules for the mess hall and drill practices. Not to mention the orders of supplies being redirected. Are you sure you really need me to be there?"

I hear her sigh and know she's doing that thing where she pinches the bridge of her nose. It'd be cute if it weren't always because of her annoyance with me. "You are the groom, Heath. You are kind of important. So, whatever you think you need to do, have someone else do it."

"It's not that easy."

Jess scoffs, "Oh, and planning a wedding with a rider *is*?"

I let out a weary sigh, already imagining the hours-long conversation about napkin colors. But if it'll only get worse the longer I put it off, and if I think Jess is persistent, she's a mild breeze compared to the storm that is my mother. "Fine, I'll come to dinner."

"Thank you," Jess says with a hint of relief in her voice. "7 PM at Orchid Terrace."

I end the call and look down at my flagging erection.

Breakfast first, shower later.

The barrack's dining hall door is propped open, and I move into the large oval-shaped room. An expansive countertop dominates the space, adorned with an array of instant food options—packets of noodles and dehydrated oatmeal. However, it's the heated display that grabs my attention.

The aroma of cured pork products permeates the air—both bacon and sausages. A tower of perfectly formed pancakes stands alongside a selection of eggs prepared to various specifications.

I find myself pleasantly surprised by the quality and variety. We'd been forced to rely on imported fruits and vegetables at Meridian, and the on-site agricultural facilities lend Blackhawk a culinary advantage.

I select a plate, contemplating my choices with genuine appreciation, and add four strips of bacon, freshly sliced pears, a bowl of oatmeal, and a hard-boiled egg from the fridge. I carry my tray to one of the metal-backed booths. And once I sit, a mess hall attendant in a gray and white jumpsuit comes over and offers me coffee.

I gratefully take it, then add two spoonfuls of artificial sweetener and goat's milk. As I sip, I scan through Network news updates. There have been no new rebel attacks, and it appears that the curated information we had casually shared with the media about Meridian's termite infestation and the need for temporary relocation had worked. I can only imagine the amount of hush money they'd had to spend to keep the guests from talking. And knowing my family, it wouldn't be enough. Eventually, they'd slip or come back asking for more.

It was too big of a disaster to be kept quiet forever. People had died. People who had loved ones who wouldn't be persuaded by money alone. They'd want their pound of flesh and Circuit would eventually have to issue a formal statement, retracting on the termite one.

But that was a problem for a future day. As I eat, other riders trickle in, chatting quietly or laughing over jokes.

It's Vanguard all over again, with me sitting alone at a table like some leper. Being associated with a Lockwood might earn you a few points in the real world, but in the rider world, I'm just another guy in a long coat with a scar on his hand.

As I chew on my oatmeal, my comm buzzes with notifications from Circuit and other rider groups, reminding me of upcoming meetings and training sessions.

Carter and Logan finally arrive inside, wearing the dark gray uniform with the badge on their right shoulder: a horse's head with two wings spreading out behind it. Instead of the golden Meridian crest, it's black with 'Blackhawk' emblazoned beneath in bold lettering. Their jumpsuits are short-sleeved, with panels on the inside of the thighs and calves for protection and grip.

Carter wears a white ribbed tank top and has his jumpsuit unzipped and tied around his waist.

As they get their food trays, the other riders part like water, letting Logan pass. It's hard to tell if this annoys him since he's wearing his usual grim expression. I lean into the bond, subtly trying to sense how he is and find nothing but the general annoyance undertone. Carter's happiness wafts to me in waves, and I instantly feel the tension in my shoulders relax.

They set their trays on the table and sit across from me. Immediately, Carter starts digging into his food, and I watch him for a moment, and he notices.

"What?" he asks through a mouthful of scrambled eggs.

"Nothing," I reply, cupping my cup of coffee. "Just glad to see at least one of us is settling in here."

Logan has never been one for breakfasts, but the pile of bacon on his plate proves otherwise. His gaze flicks between Carter and me before pinning me with a questioning look. "Don't fucking start."

I shrug and sip my coffee.

"There's a hatch date and time prediction pool if you want to buy in?" Carter says. "I've got next Friday at 6 pm."

"No way it'll take that long," Logan says.

"Oh yeah? And who makes you an expert?"

"Never said I am. Just saw the size of that crack, and that baby has three days, tops before it's out."

I'd heard Dr. Gideon had talked to the druadan vets from North Crimela and Oak Hill stations, but it's anyone's guess when it'll hatch. Still, I was never one to pass up a bet. "I'll take Tuesday at noon then," I say, putting down some credits on the table.

Carter slides the nickel-plated discs across the table and into his hand. "Looks like we've got ourselves a little competition here."

Once we finish our breakfast, Carter and I head to our stallions while Logan retreats to the barracks. Since he's on probation, he's been relegated to the gym, weapons training, and laundry duty.

He murmurs something about hanging Chief Lugsen with a towel before veering off to the showers and barrack laundry. I hate seeing him like this, stripped of his security position and demoted to just a rider. It's like the fire has been snuffed out, but there's nothing I can do about it. Galaxian killed someone, and Logan must pay the consequences. Hopefully, however, not forever. Or, for the Chief's sake, not for long.

We stop at the viewing window outside the grooming stall, which has four overhead infrared lights that are typically used to dry bathed druadans, but, in this case, are being used to keep the egg warm.

The egg — nestled comfortably in the hay — appears unremarkable.

All this. The attack, the death, the closing and moving of Meridian, all of it for this one egg.

I inhale sharply, unable to ignore the churn of my stomach, warning me this is only the beginning.

Fifteen

Carter

"**B**y the time spring rolls around," Chief Lugsen announces, "only ten of you will be in the exhibition. Look at the faces beside you. Those are the ones standing between you and that spot."

Ten out of sixty riders. Damn. This isn't going to be easy.

I shift in my saddle as my eyes drift over the other riders. They land on the oldest one here, Rolan—the guy who introduced himself to Logan and me on our first day. His stallion, a dark chestnut, is the only other Inferno clone in the group. But he's got nothing on Ember. My boy is smart *and* fast—a prime example of the Inferno line. If anyone's got a shot at showing off what these red horses can do, it's us. Rolan might have years on me, but I've got the better ride.

Because Blackhawk is bigger, they not only have Lorenzo Fiaro as station manager and Marshal as head Master Rider but also a barrack supervisor, Chief Lugsen. He's balding and grumpy and isn't even a rider, yet Heath never fails to mention how he's managed to keep Blackhawk running smoothly for over twenty years.

Lugsen's stern gaze sweeps across us as we stand in the arena, sizing each of us up like we're livestock at auction. "Everyone line up on this wall here. Since there are more of you, we'll start with groups of eight running through basic drills, then move on to the next group. The first round of auditions is in six weeks, then the final round at mid-winter. Anyone not chosen for starting positions will be required to continue practicing the routine as an understudy or for matinee performances."

At Meridian, it was different. Heath was a friend and the station manager, and the place was smaller. I was practically guaranteed a starting position just by showing up. But here, it's a whole new game. No friends in high places, no small pond where I'm the big fish. Just me, Ember, and sixty other riders hungry for the same prize.

As Lugsen calls out the first group, the clatter of hooves echoes through the halls, and Marshal enters the arena, notably late. He's astride his dappled gray stallion, Nightshade, splashed with black on his hindquarters and face. Unlike the rest of us in our jackets and chest protectors, he's dressed casually in a hooded sweatshirt and riding pants.

The guy is a legend.

At thirty-two, he's outlived every rider ever.

And while most people would've milked the privilege that comes with his position, Marshal never acts like he's better than us. He doesn't throw his weight around or look down on anyone. He treats us like equals, faces the same challenges, and works just as hard.

And damn, was he hilarious when he drank. More than once, the four of us had shut down Blink when an impromptu post-rider meeting drink had turned into an all-nighter. He'd even convinced Logan to do karaoke.

I've still got the video on my comm that I'll treasure forever.

His light blue eyes scan the arena until finding mine and a wide grin replaces his questioning look as he approaches. We both hop off our stallions. He pulls me into a firm hug, clapping me on the back before doing the same to Heath. "Sorry, I missed the gala and..." he pauses, frowning, "and for everything else. Really fucking shitty."

"Appreciate it," Heath says.

"I still can't wrap my head around it," Marshal says. "But I'd be lying if I didn't say I'm happy you're here. The novices will benefit from seeing other styles of riding from other stations."

"Heard you were off the continent," I say. "Where was it again?"

Marshal glances over at the other riders mounting up. "Canna Canna, a small island, way north. Cold as shit."

"Was it station related?" Heath asks.

"Nah," he says, shrugging. "I just needed a vacation, that's all."

Without the risk of brimming, the man has no idea how good he's got it. On a whim, he can travel anywhere for any length of time.

"We'll have to grab drinks later and catch up," Carter says.

"You bet," Marshal replies. "Swing by anytime you want a break from barrack boredom."

We mount again, and Marshal calls us to group up, and

soon after, we're out running drills on our stallions. He barks out orders, calling for different formations and serpentines, as well as shoulder-ins and shoulder-outs for stretching.

Sweat beads on my brow as I concentrate, muscles straining with the effort as these are new, and I'm unable to rely on my muscle memory. Every station has unique routines and drills, and Blackhawk has apparently chosen the one listed next to torture in the riding handbook.

A Blackhawk rider bumps into Shadowmane, and he kicks out, narrowly missing the other stallion's chin.

"Too long behind the desk, Lockwood," the other rider says. "Or did you forget how to ride?"

"Cavan," Marshal shouts from the front of the line. "Shut it!"

Heath lowers his eyes under his helmet, navigating Shadowmane back into formation.

Anger flares within me, and my protective instincts kick in. Just as I'm about to react, Heath catches my eye, and the cooling sensation seeps into our bond, overpowering the other riders.

It's a war of emotions, ripping at me, but ultimately, Heath's wins, probably because it's loudest, and it's enough for me to keep my mouth shut.

I heed the silent warning, reining in my temper and spurring Ember into a fast trot. But at the next corner, the same rider overtakes Nelson. Gemindusk is young and not as patient as Shadowmane. He snakes his neck back and forth, snapping his pointed teeth at the spotted bay belonging to the other rider.

Nelson shortens the reins and pushes his stallion to the side, which he obeys but throws a defiant kick.

"Pick a speed, rookie!" Cavan bellows, and Nelson's face pales.

That's the final fucking straw.

Digging my heels into Ember's sides, I urge him forward, charging toward the rider.

"I'm healed. I'm strong. Fighting is a good time." A smile curls my lips as Ember hums with excitement.

I pull him next to the rider. "Get your stallion under control, or I will." It's the worst threat a rider can give, but if Marshal won't step in, then I will.

They should be damn thankful it's me and not Logan right now.

He wouldn't have warned them.

"Shove it up your ass," he says, turning his stallion away.

Quick as a dune snake, Ember lunges at him and sinks his teeth into the stallion's flank just behind the back of the saddle.

The stallion kicks out as Ember rears, dodging the flying hooves, and my world tilts violently as my saddle slides. Suddenly, I'm airborne. The wind knocked from my chest in a harsh wheeze as I hit the ground hard, jarring every bone in my body. A ragged groan tears from my throat as I curl in on myself, dazed from the impact. Chaos explodes around me— the scream of terrified horses, the crash of bodies colliding. I scramble to my feet, head spinning, as a towering figure slams into my back. I stagger, whirling to face my attacker.

It's Cavan. The beefy redhead's eyes are wild, and his mottled face is twisted into a feral snarl.

"Meridian assholes!" Cavan spits. Adrenaline jolts through my system as I dodge his clumsy blow and counter with a vicious jab that snaps his head backward.

The coppery tang of blood bursts over my tongue as his fist connects with my mouth a heartbeat later. Pain blossoms, hot and immediate, but I blink away the tears, blurring my vision to land another solid hit to his ribs.

Out of the corner of my eye, I see Heath grappling furiously with another rider, a towering Blackhawk twice his size. Heart pounding, I launch myself into the melee without hesitation, bulldozing into the giant with my shoulder. He staggers back a step, allowing Heath to break free and swing a wild haymaker at his face.

Riders clash, druadans attacking each other in a flurry of fists and curses.

It's an all-out brawl. Meridian versus Blackhawk.

Our matching uniforms make it difficult to single out friend from foe, and more than once, I find I've grabbed hold of Nelson or Ve'Loth before shoving them away and spinning to find a Blackhawk rider.

I'm swept up in the fray, adrenaline pouring into my veins as I leap for one, kicking him, then pivot and box in the ears of another. The air whooshes from my lungs as a punch lands on my side. In between blows, druadan's limbs flail, and I duck, narrowly avoiding a kick to the head. Spitting curses, I whirl, dodging two stallions that have squared off and are preparing to lunge. Everywhere, druadans turn on each other, some still mounted, and iron-shod hooves glint in the lights.

Fuck. I need to find Ember.

The air thunders with the chatter of druadans, and I struggle to listen for my stallion, but before I can, a body slams into me, and I ricochet off a solid chest, ears ringing.

As I stagger upright, my vision clears, and Ember looms before me, his massive chestnut head tossing in panic and dragging his broken set of reins behind him like a deadly, snapping whip. His rolling eyes are twin pools of liquid terror as he rears.

"*Come. Easy.*" I mouth the words, feeling the vibrations low in my chest.

Ember's nose flares even as his legs stay firmly planted

where they are. *"Fight."* He replies, excitement licking through the bond toward me. The redheaded shit is eating this up.

"Need to stop. Someone hurt." I close the distance to him and reach for the reins just when we're buffeted by the piercing shriek of feedback from the arena's sound system.

All around me, everyone drops to the ground, covering their ears. The fighting stops, except for one stallion who does a final snap of the air before lowering his head above his rider, laying facedown in the dirt.

"Practice is over. Everyone back to your barracks."

"My arm!" someone shouts.

"Those that are hurt can drag your sorry asses to the clinic. The rest of you better be prepared for a long night. Cause we're running."

"Running?" I ask, chest still heaving.

Heath glances at Marshal walking Nightshade over to us.

"Fuck me, that was fun," Marshal says. His sweatshirt is spattered with dust and blood, and his lower lip is busted open.

Heath swipes the side of his face, but I don't miss the glint in his eyes. Mr. all-business enjoyed getting that out of his system, too.

He can deny it all he wants. Sparring is in our nature. Druadans were created to be warriors, and even though time has passed, the bond still pushes us toward violence.

We are typically able to control it, but it's hovering under the surface, and all it needs is a tiny spark, like today.

"If I catch any of you fighting again," Lugsen continues, "there will be more than just running for consequences. Those that instigated it will be transferred to another station, and your druadans with you." He glares at all of us, staring at us one at a time. "Therefore, I suggest you all get your acts together and learn to play nice." His words hang heavy in the air. A lump forms in my throat as I realize just how different things will be here compared to Meridian.

My shoulders bristle with irritation. "Put your stallions away and change. I expect every one of you on the wall running in ten minutes. Twenty laps, gentlemen."

The riders groan in protest.

All except me. An hour of running to show the other riders they don't fuck with Meridian?

No problem.

It was so worth it.

Sixteen

LOGAN

I'm scrubbing the last of the sweat and grime off my skin when I hear a group of riders complaining about rain and blisters come in.

Typical. I keep to my shower, letting the hot water do its work and soak into my tight shoulder muscles. Lugsen had assigned me stall cleaning, insisting that every new rider gets rotated through, but it was all bullshit.

The other riders had bitched, and they needed to show I was being punished.

Carter and Heath sidle up, taking the showers next to mine. "Logan, you missed it." Carter is practically vibrating and grinning like a jackass. "Liam bumped Shadowmane, and then another stallion charged him. I jumped off and then," Carter pauses, letting the water run over his face before shaking it off. Heath remains silent, lathering his chest with the bar of soap.

Carter spits on the ground before plowing on. "Fuck,

Heath's wicked right hook nearly knocked out the one guy, but then his twin brother Luke, I think his name is, jumped him from behind. But I jumped off by then. Shit, man, you should've been there!"

"Hell yeah. Sounds like a blast." Damn, it would've felt good to blow off steam with them, but instead, I'd been shoveling shit from the stalls like a novice.

Carter catches himself. "Oh, fuck, sorry. If it balances out, Lugsen had us run wall laps. I'm pretty sure I have a sore where my balls kept slapping my legs."

We switch off the showers and then grab towels from the hanging rack.

I sigh as I wrap a towel around my waist. As the cool air hits our damp skin, steam rolls off of us, and within seconds, the entire bathroom is engulfed in mist.

Danner steps into the empty shower stall, clutching a towel around his waist. Roberts' voice cuts through the sounds of splashing water. "Wait a damn minute, boys. What's that on you there?"

All eyes swivel to Danner, wearing a shit-eating grin. He peels back the edge of the plastic covering his new tattoo, revealing the horseshoe-shaped U on the right side of his chest. The skin around it is angry and red, but the design itself is striking—all dark gray, like swirling storm clouds, representing Wraithwind's Ghost lineage.

"Got it done in the village last night."

Carter and other riders crowd around, admiring the ink. They take turns fist-bumping Danner, congratulating him, but when he turns to me, holding out his fist expectantly, I wave him off.

It'll be a cold day in hell before I fist-bump a naked man.

Danner shrugs, unfazed by my rejection, and moves on to Heath, who gives him a hearty pat on the shoulder that makes him beam even brighter.

As I towel off, I catch a glimpse of my same 'U'- shaped tattoo but dark blue with stars. It was sick as hell, and I'd never get it removed, even if I were dismissed as a rider.

Marshal's voice booms through the locker room, interrupting my thoughts. "James, Lockwood, McCelroy." All three of us look in the direction of his voice by the exit.

"If you're done slapping each other's asses, get dressed and come with me."

Carter and I wear black jumpsuits with white T-shirts, while Heath wears navy slacks and a polo shirt.

We catch a few sideways looks as we stride out of the room and follow Marshal out of the barracks and to the first-floor foyer. Marshal leads us to the right, across the stone floor, and into a corner office with a glass door etched with the words 'Station Manager' in fancy lettering.

Lorenzo Fiaro is in his mid-sixties, with a long gray beard and the sides of his head shaved. A black tattoo of a galloping druadan stands out on his right wrist above the faded silver scar. His druadan died years ago, and he never re-bonded, so he ended up here instead.

His office makes my bunk look pristine. Stacks of food trays, ledgers, and crates of unopened packages balance on every horizontal surface. My eyes catch the names of riders scrawled across the boxes.

Fan mail.

Fiaro eyes us from behind his cluttered desk as we enter, and he strokes his beard. "Close the door, Marshal," he says gruffly. "The rest of you come in. We need to talk."

"This pertains particularly to McCelroy's situation with his stallion, but as you all are master riders at Meridian, I felt it wise to include all of you in the discussions. I've conversed with other managers in similar situations, and we've decided to help manage Galaxian's energy and limit your brimming with private riding in the training arena."

"Fuck yes," I blurt, and Carter punches my shoulder excitedly.

"However," Fiaro says slowly, "there are strict conditions. These sessions must be scheduled in advance so as to not interfere with regular practice, and either Marshal or Lockwood must be present at all times."

I should keep my mouth shut and be thanking him for letting me ride Galaxian, but I can't. "Why not James?"

Fiaro shakes his head. "His involvement with Ember had been the root of Galaxian's alleged aggression. Your stallion's instinct to protect Ember led us to this mess. We can't risk further incidents."

"Don't worry about me," Carter whispers from the side of his mouth, nudging me. "This is the part where you say 'thank you.'"

The words rumble from my chest. "Thank you."

Seventeen

JESS

I rap my knuckles on the door twice and then wait for any sounds coming from inside. Sadie had told me that I'd needed permission from the station manager, a Master Rider named Marshal Clemmons, and where I could find his office. When I hear nothing inside, I knock again, my impatience beginning to bleed into the suspicion that I was being ignored.

I frown and call out through the door.

"Excuse me, Master Rider Clemmons? This is Jessica Drakeford. Sadie said you'd be in. I need to speak with you." Silence. I inhale and add, "Please, it's a rather urgent matter."

Lovely, I've resorted to pleading.

When there's no response, I jiggle the handle, concluding that I am indeed being ignored, which I will not tolerate.

It's unlocked, and turn the knob and enter. The room is pitch black, and it takes a moment for my eyes to adjust. I take in the cramped office space. A round desk sits in the corner, with two wooden chairs next to it and a larger wingback behind it. Shelves line the walls overflowing with knick-knacks, riding medals, and dust.

I notice the shadow of a figure in a chair. His back is to me, and his hand is moving on his lap in a way that makes me uncomfortable. I wrinkle my nose in disgust. Is this why he has been ignoring me?

Damn, these riders and their appetites.

"Excuse me," I say loudly.

His arm stops moving, and his elbow comes to rest on the arm of the chair.

"The door was unlocked," I forge on. "and I need to speak with you."

"I'm busy," he says, his voice low. "Come back later."

"I will do no such thing," I snap. "I flew in from Delford this morning and demand you make time to listen to my request. That is your job, isn't it? Running a station. Or is there someone higher up I should speak to?"

The chair slowly pivots. I suck in a sharp breath, my eyes immediately lowering to his lap. His right-hand fidgets with the cover of a book.

He'd been reading.

I exhale with relief. The movements of his hands weren't satisfying urges but simply turning pages. His arms are bare, and he wears a cut-off hooded sweatshirt and sweats. The dim light of the room, combined with the hood, cloaks his eyes and face in shadow.

He sets the book face-down on the table, careful not to lose his place. I cringe at the crease in the spine. It's too dark to make out the title, but judging by the linen binding and number of pages, it's likely a history book or biography.

"How can I help you," he says, annoyance tinging his words, "Heath Lockwood's fiancée?"

I purse my lips. "I'm sure you're well aware our wedding is in four weeks, and the commute between Delford and here is taxing for both Heath and I. Your floor manager, Sadie, told me I must speak with you to request accommodations."

"Riders can't live with their partners until they're married," Marshal says bluntly,

"I understand," I continue, "I have read the guidelines. However, there have been some extenuating circumstances as of late, wouldn't you agree?"

"I do, and those extenuating circumstances have led to the fourth floor reaching capacity." He rubs a knuckle over the stubble on his chin and stands.

Heath is a dedicated athlete and monitors his diet as well as I do, and yet Marshal's muscled arms and shoulders demand my attention.

His sweatshirt is only half-zipped, revealing the upper right side of his toned chest and a white 'U' tattoo, just like Heath's.

Heath had spoken at length and always in awe of Marshal Clemmons. Words like 'survivor' and 'miracle' would circulate whenever he was mentioned.

The little I'd paid attention to, I knew him to be in his early thirties, and judging from the scars on his body and the faint lines around his eyes, he'd experienced much more living outside than in this dim, dingy room he calls home.

He leans forward, and his hood slips back, revealing a strong jaw, well-defined brow ridge, and pale blue eyes.

I work my tongue in my suddenly parched mouth. Tides, he's handsome.

Eyes never leaving mine, he takes a cigarette from a

container on the desk and lets it hang on his lower lip. He swipes the lighter from a drawer and flicks it off and on.

My gut tightens, my eyes fixed on the motion of his thumb sliding back and forth on the metal wheel. It's an innocuous gesture, and yet, combined with the intensity of his eyes and the deliberate way his fingers move, I have to forcefully pull my gaze back to his.

"Please," I say, my voice cracking. "I was there at Meridian during the gala. I can't sleep without nightmares. I... I don't want to be alone at night. If I stayed here with Heath, I'd feel safe."

Doubt flickers in his eyes. He doesn't know me, but Heath is his friend. He'll do this for him. It's manipulative, but I don't care. If he'd answered the door instead of ignoring me, maybe I'd feel guilty. But he hadn't, so I don't. The part about the nightmares is true. However, the meds mostly keep them at bay. Mostly.

"I'm sorry," he says, sounding sincere. "But we're full. Why don't you check with the property managers in the village to see if there are any vacancies."

Frustration heats my chest, and I grip the strap of my purse a little tighter. "I understand riders often don't involve themselves in business or financial news, but feel I should inform you that my family owns more property in Blackhawk Village than the other top three companies combined."

He looks at me coolly. "Then it should be no problem at all for you to find somewhere to stay until you and Lockwood are hitched."

Taking a stronger stance, I pull my shoulders back. "I don't think you're listening. I don't want to live in the Village. I've walked the fourth floor. There are two empty doubles, and Sadie confirmed there are no names in the register attached to them. I wouldn't be interfering with any married couples should me and Heath take it."

His face shifts to pensive, and a deep V forms between his brows. As he rests his chin on his fingers, mulling over my words, I'm momentarily distracted by how good it smells in here. Cedar, cloves, and something else I can't name but equally intoxicating.

A hint of a smile plays on his lips. They're fuller than Heath's, with a subtle Cupid's bow giving it a slight curve. "Heath said you're impossible to win an argument against, but figured I'd give a shot."

Damn him. He did know who I was. So, what had this all been, some game to him? A test? "You have to understand if I start handing out rooms without following the rules we'd have chaos. However, as you did most of my work for me, perhaps we can come to an arrangement?"

My temper flares. "Now, listen here. I'm a Drakeford and will not—"

"Do you like dogs?" he says before I can finish.

"What?"

"It's a simple question. Do you like dogs, yes or no?"

"I, uh..." I stammer. I'd been around my father's hounds for duck hunting, but they were kenneled outside and never allowed to play. Only when they were arthritic and close to retiring would he let them inside, and by then, they wanted to do nothing else but sleep. "I don't know. Yes, I guess. Why?"

"Great." He slaps his hands on the desk and stands. Long legs carry him to the door on his right, and he pushes it open.

A massive black dog with brown-tipped ears and paws comes barreling from the other room with a navy blue sock lodged in his mouth.

I stiffen as the dog trots up to me and sniffs my shoes. A

string of drool dangles from his chin, dangerously close to the vegan suede.

"Meet Finn," Marshal says, smiling. He pats the dog on the head and retrieves the sock from his mouth. It's soaked in slobber, and the toe is torn. "Finny-boy here isn't liking my new schedule and lately has been getting bored and my sock supply can't take much more of this." He eyes me up and down, and my stomach tenses as I'm appraised. "You seem like you're a jogger. You can take him."

Oh shit. "I don't think you understand I'm not—"

"Do you want to stay on the fourth floor or not?"

"Yes, of course, that's why I'm here, but I'm really not good with animals."

Marshal tilts his head. "Well, that's the deal."

Finn wanders the room, circling me, before staring up eagerly at the tattered sock in Marshal's hand. I can't believe I'm actually considering this. Dogs are smelly, dirty, shed-prone, and that's the well-behaved ones. But staying here with Heath is important and Marshal isn't wrong; I do enjoy running. And if I'm stuck here, away from the office and the city, it would be good exercise and a way to burn off the restlessness. "Fine," I say firmly and hold out my hand. A smirk plays with the corners of his lips as he takes it, and we shake.

"Glad we could work something out." Eyes never leaving mine, he taps his comm twice. "Sadie."

"Yes, Marshal," she replies.

"Come to my office. I've got a new resident that needs a room."

Eighteen

BRIGID

The variety of sandwiches, soups, and salads had been overwhelming, and I was stuffed before I had a chance to sample everything. Balancing a cloth napkin with freshly baked fig cookies, I spot Sadie waiting for me.

She's carrying a plastic basket with bags of nuts, paper sleeves of crackers, and parchment-wrapped wedges of goat cheese. "Hey! I was just going to leave this by your door. How was your first day?"

More food. I mean, normally, I'd be thrilled, but I'm already bursting, and at this rate, I'm going to need a whole new wardrobe if I keep eating like this.

"Not too bad," I say. "The icebreakers at the meeting were interesting."

That's an understatement. They were unbelievably cringy, but I couldn't deny they'd helped me feel more at ease.

Sadie wrinkles her nose. "Oh, I should've warned you. Fiaro's kink is tormenting the staff with embarrassing 'get to know you' games."

The both of us laugh as a pretty woman with a designer purse strides down the hallway and begins unlocking the door directly across from my room.

Ice seeps into my veins.

This is Jess Drakeford. Heath's fiancée.

Everything about her screams old Venovia money. The set of her jaw and the slight downturn of her lips give her a look of perpetual disapproval.

Still, she's obscenely perfect.

Manicured nails adorn long fingers, and her unblemished white sneakers add to her whole 'this is my casual outfit' intent. However, the heart-shaped emblem on her shoes is designer, and the gold-linked bracelet is a rare vintage brand you can't find in stores anymore. I'd only met her once in person before, but it was common to see her on Network news reports, usually lurking in the shadows behind her parents as they cut the ribbon of some new building or presented a large check to a charity.

Until that damn interview before the gala, I hadn't even known Heath was engaged, and everything had been nearly a whirlwind since then. He'd told me almost nothing about her afterward, so what I did know I'd learned from Carla. She attended Haverstone Prep before transferring to DU and runs the real estate portion of her family's company, Drakeford Industries.

I'd been tempted to spend more time looking her up on

Network but quickly dismissed it since I didn't like the icky feeling that I was scoping the competition. It was clear I'd made the right choice.

There was no competition.

Jess watches Sadie with an air of cool detachment. She's my age, with jet-black hair framing a face that could be a makeup model's, with high cheekbones and frost-colored eyes.

"Oh, hello again," Sadie says, then turns to me. "I forgot to introduce you two before. Meet your new neighbor, Brigid."

"We've met," she says, lips thinning.

"At the gala," I finish, plastering a smile on my face, even as I'm dying inside. Why is she here? Why hadn't Heath told me? Are they living together? I thought you had to be married to do that. I clutch the door handle, not trusting my legs to give out. Oh shit, what if they'd moved the wedding up or married in secret? Heath wouldn't keep that secret from me, would he?

"Yes," Jess says. "Lovely event. Heath often gets nervous at those functions, but whatever you did took the pressure off." My insides squirm. If she only knew. She adjusts her earring as if gathering her thoughts. "Too bad it all went to hell after with those dreadful creatures."

"I know. I still can't believe it. It was awful," I reply, unsure of what else to say. "We were lucky there were only two casualties."

"I heard. Well, count yourselves fortunate it was no one from my family, or none of you would have jobs anymore."

The cold steel knob digs into my palm. Carla had warned me Jess was "a true Delford elite," but she'd apparently forgotten to mention the part about her being a class-A bitch. I bristle at the implication. Having connections to a wealthy family doesn't make someone's death less tragic.

A defensive remark rests on the tip of my tongue, but I bite it back. This is Heath's soon-to-be wife, which means if I wish to keep any sort of relationship with him, which I most definitely do, I have to behave.

"Well, looks like we were lucky in more ways than one," I say, keeping my tone light.

"How are you? Heath told me you and your family were staying on the coast."

"We were. But plans changed."

Changed? Changed how? I watch her face carefully, noting how she gives nothing away.

"Well, we're glad you're here," Sadie says, picking up on the tension. "Do you need me anything?"

Jess swivels her hawkish gaze to Sadie. "The rest of my bags arrived today. They're on the first floor." Sadie bobs her head. "Oh, and I put in an order for a Cobb salad with grilled chicken, but it hasn't arrived yet. Lemongrass dressing on the side, and if I spy a single crouton, it'll be on you. Understand?"

Sadie's face blanches. "I, uh... I will see what I can do." She hands me the basket. "See you later, Brigid." She hurries down the stairs, leaving me alone with Jess.

At the end of the hallway, a male attendant in a uniform lugs two giant suitcases in our direction. The man stops in front of Jess, his face red from exertion.

Jess holds open the door and frowns at him when he doesn't immediately understand that he should carry them inside.

"Any time," she grinds out.

The attendant drops his gaze and drags the bags into her room.

Seeing the overloaded suitcases, a question dawns on me.

"So, how long are you planning on visiting Heath?"

The man stops in front of her, his face red from exertion from climbing the four flights of stairs with those overloaded bags.

She holds open the door, and frowns at him when he doesn't immediately understand she intends for him to carry them inside. When he finally does, she looks at me. "Not a visit. I'm living here. Wedding preparation is tedious."

Then, without saying goodbye, she let the door slam shut. I lurk in the hallway, hearing her muffled scolding to the attendant for making her wait so long.

I let out an exasperated sigh and slink back into my room. With the door closed, I press my back to it and sink to the floor. Great. Just great.

On the bright side, Heath's risk of brimming or flaring out will be less. That's good, right?

So why did it feel like I was some jealous kid on the playground watching my crush pass notes with another girl?

Because I am.

Because her being here means that nothing more could ever come between Heath and me.

Because whatever I may feel for him needs to end. Once and for all.

I need something to drink.

I set the welcome basket on the kitchen counter, immediately taking the mini-bottle of chardonnay nestled among the snacks. The kitchenette is small but usable, with a sink, a two-burner cooktop, and a modest fridge. As I rummage for a corkscrew, I notice the digital display on the wall to the right of the refrigerator.

It's so packed that the black words nearly blot out the blue background. There are meal menus, events, training agendas, staff meetings, and gondola schedules—and that's just for today. I click a button and go cross-eyed as the week is displayed.

I switch it back to the day, then turn, sighing as I stare into the sitting area with its plush couches, stone coffee table, and stained glass lamps, wondering how much time I'll actually have to use it.

The stone walls are all covered in a thin coating of gray plaster, and round pillars in the corners support a high ceiling. The floor, too, is stone, although patterned thick rugs help reduce the sounds of my footsteps and keep my toes from freezing.

My comm dings with an alert. My message inbox is overflowing. Unpacking can wait.

I pour a glass of wine and a bag of dried nuts and fruit from the welcome basket and open the hardbacked tote to take out my portable computer. Watching as the screen lights up, I tear open the bag and cram a handful of walnuts and dried cherries in my mouth.

I log in to Blackhawk's local Network. Looks like a packed schedule tomorrow: all staff meeting in the morning and then breaking into smaller teams in the afternoon. On the PR list, I read the names Don and Kimmy. I'm eager to meet them finally and connect the faces to the names I've seen in my inbox since I started at Meridian.

There's a new message thread brainstorming a PR package for Venovia. It's a step removed from propaganda. The Venovian army is strong, and the mighty druadans show Circuit's authority, unity, strength, and security. There are suggestions to gather riders for the promo videos and have Circuit officers with them.

I scroll to the next set of messages addressed only to me. Blackhawk has its own slew of onboarding paperwork. I skim through the orientation for emergency protocols and another non-disclosure like the one I'd signed before. The NDA states everything I see here related to the handling, training, and riding of druadans was under proprietary law and owned by

Circuit. Meaning I couldn't learn everything from the station and take it out into the world and start my private one.

Which, to be fair, was a load of shit since druadan were all cloned, and there was no way I could get access to a young one. Save for stealing an egg like Sharice had. The most likely option would be stealing an unbonded from a station, but it'd be risky as hell. I knew all too well how unpredictable and dangerous they could be.

I look over the map of Blackhawk in my new employee folder. It'd been a lifesaver, and more than once since, I'd referred to it when I'd gotten lost down a corridor or found myself in a storage closet when I'd been looking for a meeting room.

However, even with the warm greetings in my message box, Blackhawk feels different. Colder.

And not just cause it's literally colder here — like I'm going to need three more sweaters colder — it's more than that.

It's the people. Everyone is so professional and disciplined, not like the laid-back air at Meridian, which now I realize was closer to a summer beach club than a station.

Had Meridian been the exception, and all stations were like this? I'd overheard on the shuttle that the riders have barracks and bunk all together with little privacy, but since I am an admin and not a rider, I lucked out with a private room in the upper-floor apartments.

It's a perk I'm particularly grateful for.

Well, that and still having a job here. I suspect Heath had a hand in my staying on, but I know I couldn't prove it.

Thinking about the meetings tomorrow, I take another sip of my wine.

A soft knock comes from the door. My mind flits with who it could be, and an eagerness carries me to the door when I hope it's one of my riders.

My riders.

I laugh to myself. Did I really just think that?

They're far from mine. Although Carter had given the impression, he felt that way, and it had a nice ring to it. There's another knock. "Coming," I say.

I open the door, and an unfamiliar man in a brown suit and tie stands in the hallway.

"Can I help you?" I ask.

He raises his chin in an unmistakable display of authority. "Ms. Corsair?"

"Yes."

He flashes me a Circuit Security Unit badge. "I'm Agent Zane with CSU. We're here doing a follow-up on the incident at Meridian. May I come in?"

I'd clock him in his mid-thirties, with tan hair and a broad nose. His cold, dark brown eyes sweep over me with thinly veiled disdain. Even if he hadn't told me he worked for CSU, he might as well had it stamped on his forehead.

I lean against the door. "What's this about?"

His eyes dart to the left and the right. "It's a rather sensitive discussion."

I purse my lips. I'd seen his badge, but old habits die hard. My stint living solo in Delford before moving in with Laura and Vince had left its mark. Those months alone had ingrained a wariness of strangers at my door, badge or no badge.

"I've spoken with Lorenzo Fiaro, and he's allowed CSU to meet with and question the staff as it pertains to an ongoing investigation."

I frown, knowing I don't have a choice. Fiaro's station, Fiaro's rules.

I step back, letting him enter.

Once inside, he moves further into the room, his eyes scanning the interior. There are socks and shoes abandoned by the couch, as well as several dirty dishes on the table. I normally wasn't this messy, but every one of the meetings today had run over.

Agent Zane taps on his comm. "I've reviewed the report from Deputy Ewensen, and there are just a few details we need to clarify."

My mouth turns to ash. We'd been so thorough and honest. What other details could he possibly want?

"We know you're using your mother's maiden name," he says, "for what reason we will determine. However, we know Sharice Harlow is your sister. Is this correct?" He lifts his eyes from the comm to mine.

"Yes," I say. "Sharice is my sister." It was in the report. No need to hide it anymore.

He nods. "We also know from your report that they took you hostage for a brief time." He pauses, his mouth falling into a frown. "Now I understand the stress of the situation might make memories difficult to recall, so I want you to think hard. What specifically did Sharice say to you?" Irritation scratches the base of my skull. I'd told Heath this. He'd put all of it in the report to Ewensen, so either he hadn't read it in its entirety or had and was trying to catch me lying. I've done nothing wrong. I'm innocent. My pulse drums in my ears as I realize I'm in over my head. My fingers fidget with each other as I try to think how Heath would handle this. He'd be calm and rational and claim some law I wasn't aware of that would force Zane to back off.

I'd studied history, not law.

Okay, then, what about Carter? He'd have a joke to deflect the answers, but quick, clever comebacks aren't my strong suit.

Then there's Logan. Yeah, that's a *big* no.

Guess it's up to me. Inhaling, I say, "I swear, everything she said to me is in that report. Yes, she is my sister, and yes, she talked to me, but before the night of the attack, we hadn't spoken in years."

Zane picks the inside of his ear with his pinky, then wipes it on his pants. "Ah yes, I did read that part. And I quote. "She and the other group members surrounded me as I held onto the egg. Sharice told me she 'needed me." He looks up from the screen. "Care to elaborate on what that could mean?"

"I don't know," I say through clenched teeth. "I swear. She didn't say anything else." He doesn't buy it.

"Odd phrase, though, isn't it? Need you. Not miss you or love you. Need. You were surrounded. You were at their mercy, so what in the hell could she have possibly thought you could give her?

"Please," I say, my voice breaking. "I don't know anything." It's the truth. I don't have money or connections. And although I couldn't ignore how absurd it was that Galaxian had saved me or that the egg had shielded me afterward, she couldn't have predicted that. Galaxian was a rogue druadan—his unpredictability was the only thing that made sense. And as for the egg, I knew nothing about druadan eggs, their power or lack of it. No one did.

Even if, by some impossible twist of fate, she had known, what difference would it have made? How could she have stopped it? Shooting Galaxian or me would have put the egg in danger—something she seemed to focus on more than anything else. Is that why she didn't shoot me? Was it fear of hurting the egg that held her back? I want to believe it wasn't the case, that she still cares about me at least enough to hesitate. We're still sisters, even when it feels like we're standing on opposite sides of a chasm.

He cracks his neck, then steps closer, peering down at me. "While that may be, we have reason to believe she may have attempted to contact you since you arrived."

My face is a mask of indifference, even as my heart feels like it's going to beat right out of my chest. "Well, your information is wrong. She hasn't."

"Are you sure? It could be a note or some secret code?"

I shake my head. I'd been here a day; I hadn't even unpacked. There very well could be any kind of note tucked under the cushion or stuffed behind a picture, for all I knew.

No. Sharice would never leave something so obvious. She's clever as hell. Hence, her not being caught yet. Not only that, how would she have known I would be assigned to this room unless she did something to their internal network and set my name to match this room?

Shit. No way she had that kind of reach, did she?

"Well," he continues, even as my mind reels from the possibility that my sister's influence has followed me here. "Since we made the trip here from Delford, you won't mind if we do a quick search around your room, will you?" He holds his hands to the side.

Do I have a choice? "Uh yeah, sure." I look at my open computer and empty cup of tea.

He goes to the door, and two Circuit police follow him inside.

"We'll be quick," he assures me and the three divide. One going to my bedroom, another to the kitchen behind me, and Agent Zane to the living room.

They flip cushions, slide chairs, and scan the floor. A second one opens cupboards in the kitchen and runs a hand under the edge of the countertop. Sweat prickles my scalp. What if they do find something? Some note or letter? It won't matter how much I claim I'm innocent. I'll be arrested as a terrorist. Cold anger seers my veins, crystallizing into resentment towards my sister. *Please don't find anything.* I think to myself.

One of the officers emerges from my room, carrying my shoulder bag, and hands it to Zane.

"Hey, what are you doing?" I protest. "There's nothing in there. That's mine!"

My breath catches in my throat as Zane takes the bag and upends its contents onto a nearby table—clothes, lotion, hair tie, a half-eaten bag of nuts, and Sharice's comm.

"No, please!" I lunge forward on instinct, but the second officer blocks my path with his arm.

Oh no. No, no, no. In my mad dash to pack my belongings at Meridian, I'd completely forgotten about it.

Agent Zane scoops up Sharice's comm and cocks his head as he turns it over in his hands. Sharice's name pops ups as the locked screen flashes on. "Interesting. I don't recall any mention of a comm in the report. Care to mention why this might've slipped your mind?"

Before I can answer, the sharp, cold bite of cuffs digs into my wrists as the officer from the kitchen takes my arms and places them behind me. I don't struggle. It's no use. I'm so screwed. Dammit, why had I kept that stupid comm? I should have tossed it out of the shuttle on the way over. Panic claws at my throat as they strip my own comm off my wrist. "Stop, please. Just let me explain."

"Brigid Corsair-Harlow," he says. "You're under arrest. For suspicion of assault on a druadan station and cooperation with an extremist group conspiring against Circuit."

Without warning, I'm shuffled out of my apartment and down the hall. I bow my head, praying no one sees me like this. I've only started working here, and now I'm being escorted in handcuffs. I've spent my entire life trying to avoid trouble. I pay my taxes. I attend my annual medical check-ups even though I hate needles. I thought staying on the straight and narrow would protect me, but now, all of that carefulness seems pointless. It's done me no good, and here I am, paraded down the hallway like a criminal. All for what? Because I'd gone looking for my sister?

Rage bubbles up, a bitter taste in my mouth. I'm humiliated. Frustrated by the unfairness of it all, I grow angrier with every step. We descend two flights of stairs, and then I'm maneuvered into a small office.

The officer sets me in the chair with my hands behind me and then leaves, sidestepping Agent Zane, standing in the doorway with a sadistic grin on his face.

"Wait!" I call after them, desperation edging my voice. "Please!" As Zane shuts the door, the bang swallows my words into an oppressive silence. I flinch at the sound, my heart pounding in my ears. I'm alone, with nothing but the lingering scent of recycled air and a hollow ache in the pit of my stomach.

I'd thought they'd brought me here on good terms. I'd thought that I would resume my job, and although there would be a transition period to adjust to this new station, very little would change. But I'd been wrong. They'd tricked me. They'd claimed the move here to be an evacuation, but in actuality, they'd wanted us all here to interrogate. They don't want the truth as much as they want to pin the blame on someone.

The minutes drag. I try to itch my elbow, and cold metal bites into the skin of my wrists where my hands are manacled together on top of the desk, but I growl in frustration when I can't. After stewing for what feels like an eternity, I snap my eyes to the door when I hear it creak open again.

Agent Zane strides in, carrying a steaming mug. Aromas of peppermint and clove drift toward me. "Now that you've had some time to cool off, where shall we begin?"

I chew the inside of my cheek, glaring at him.

"Let's start with some simple questions regarding your

sister." He sets down a tablet with my sister's photo on it. "She's been quite the live-wire for some time." I study the image. It's an older one of her since her hair was longer, and she's captured mid-shout surrounded by other college students at the Delford University protest.

So, they have old pictures of her protesting, big deal. "Last I heard, free speech was still legal."

"Oh, it is, which is why you're going to speak oh so freely for me." He swipes a finger over the screen, revealing another photo of her. This one is of the side and is taken from a distance as if pulled from a security camera. She's clutching a bag to her chest and wearing a dark black hooded sweatshirt, and her eyes are to the side as if looking at something out of frame. "This was taken eight months ago. Ewensen reported another egg was stolen from Meridian before you started there. Is this that other egg?"

My insides curl. "I don't know."

"Are you sure? Look closer."

I stare at the image. It's grainy and dark. Whatever she's holding, she's made sure to keep it concealed. "It could be? I don't know."

He cycles through three more images, asking me the same questions. The images show Sharice at a different angle or pose. One with her riding in a shuttle, another her face partially obscured as she waits to cross a road, and a third of her from the back walking along a dike with a group of people.

I'd seen her at Meridian, alive. The initial shock had worn off, but the full weight of what it meant hadn't truly sunk in until now. This whole past year, while I'd been desperately searching for her, she'd been out there, living her life. Breathing, laughing, and existing in the same world as me. Of course, she had. And was still, even now. A tidal wave of hurt crashes over me, and I blink, willing the tears not to fall.

"Now you've seen the photos, care to speculate on what she is planning?"

I shake my head. "I already told you. I don't know where she is or what she's doing."

He slides the tablet away. "Very well, then let's return to the subject regarding the name change. You applied to Meridian station with your mother's maiden name. Why?"

I bristle at his accusatory tone but remain silent. I should have a lawyer. I should demand one now. But it could take hours for one to come to the station, and they'd keep me in here until then. It's no use. I need to tell him what he wants to hear so he'll let me go.

"I don't know what you want me to say," I reply carefully. "My sister and I use different names. That's all."

He arches an eyebrow. "Is it? Why don't I give you some time to think about that," he says, turning on his heel and exiting the room.

The cuffs jingle as I cradle my head in my hands. Dammit. Why are they treating me like a criminal? I'd done nothing wrong. They had Sharice's comm. What else did they want?

I shift minutely, the harsh screech of chair legs against the floor grating on my already frayed nerves. My gaze darts towards the solitary window, little more than a slit in the concrete. Where are Heath and the others? Do they know I'm here? No way they would allow me to be here if they had any say? My stomach sinks. What if they'd done the same to them? Separated us into different rooms so they could grill us for inconsistencies in our stories.

An hour passes before he enters again. Zane circles the table in a slow, appraising orbit as I resist the urge to squirm beneath his gaze. He makes my skin crawl.

"I've read the report from Meridian, including your statements, but there's just something that doesn't sit right with me." He pauses, letting the weighted silence stretch unbearably taut before continuing. "You claim you're an innocent bystander caught up in this unfortunate mess, and your relation to Sharice Harlow is purely coincidence?"

He seems convinced and I doubt anything I say will convince him, but I have to try.

"Agent Zane," I begin, striving to keep my tone measured. "Whatever you may think you know, it's wrong. I got the job at Meridian to look for her. I've done nothing illegal, and I was simply—"

"Save your bullshit," he cuts me off with a curt slice of his hand. I cringe at the sudden shift in his mood. "The sooner you tell me the truth, the sooner you get out of here and can return to your pretty little life prancing around in your tight skirts and heels."

A tremor skates down my spine at the unspoken threat lacing his words. I swallow hard against the lump forming in my suddenly dry throat. Is that what he really thinks? That I'm working here just to get a rider husband?

Well, fuck him. I clamp my teeth shut, refusing to say anything else.

He notices my attitude change, and his eyes narrow. "Fine, you don't want to answer? Then listen." He pauses, letting the silence stretch, then continues, "ITM. Inherited Terra Movement. We know your sister is connected to it, whether directly or indirectly." He taps the tablet still on the table, revealing a half-naked person lying on the sidewalk, their body covered in red welts. "This was taken last night. Three mystyl were released in a bus station bathroom. Two people died, and three were injured."

I try to look away, but he won't let me.

"Look." He shoves the tablet closer. "Matthew Walker. He was on his way to his sister's funeral when they attacked." He swipes the tablet, revealing other images from inside the bus station. Overturned benches, people huddled with blankets, and paramedics knelt next to an older woman.

My blood turns to ice. It's like Meridian all over again.

"ITM has already taken credit. Protect her all you want. I can promise you we will excise them like the malignancy they've proven themselves to be."

His hawkish glare pins me like a specimen laid out for an examination. "Anyone found collaborating with these extremists will be tried to the full extent of the law. No mercy, no exceptions."

For a moment, I can only gape at him in stunned silence. When I find my voice once more, it's nothing but a hoarse rasp laced with desperation.

"What's that?" he says, leaning close enough I can smell the tea on his breath.

"I said *fuck you*."

His left eye twitches, and he retreats to the far side of the room.

Maybe I'd written Logan off too soon.

He starts pacing, pulling Sharice's comm from his pocket as he moves. He twirls the metallic bracelet on his finger. "I don't suppose you're going to make our lives a little easier and tell us the code?"

I don't move.

He shrugs. "Worth a try. No bother, we'll have one of the tech team crack it."

He disappears behind me, and my shoulders stiffen, feeling like I'm back in that dust storm with Wraithwind stalking me. His fingers land on my shoulders, squeezing them, and I wince. "You can act all tough. Pretend like you're immune 'cause you work here." His touch starts light and perfunctory but then grows harder until his fingers dig painfully into the space between my collarbone and shoulder.

I have to fight back the need to cry out even as tears prick the corners of my eyes. What is happening? My throat tightens, and I swallow against the pain. "Because I assure you," he continues, "The truth will emerge one way or another. So it would behoove you to do yourself a favor and disclose any..." His hand drifts up to caress the nape of my neck in a disturbingly intimate gesture, "... pertinent details." His last words are little more than an insidious hiss against my ear, and I shudder violently, bile burning in the back of my throat.

The grind of the hinges on the doors draws both of our attention. The pressure on my shoulder ceases as Zane abruptly drops his hand.

Deputy Ewensen's imposing figure strides into the room. Relief washes over me at the sight of her familiar face, but it quickly fades as worry sets in. She's on Zane's side. She might not be the savior I think she is.

She's changed out of the Circuit jumpsuit she'd worn at Meridian and into navy slacks and a blazer with her name tag. "Agent Zane," she says, lips thinning. "Please explain to me what is happening here?" A disapproving scowl rests on her lips, and Agent Zane shrinks slightly, signaling to me that she pulls rank.

Thank the tides.

Agent Zane clears his throat. "Ms. Corsair here was just telling me about how she planned the attack with her sister."

"No," I blurt. "No. He's lying. Please, I haven't talked to my sister in months. I didn't know Sharice was—"

He starts to argue but is interrupted by her. "Agent Zane, you are dismissed."

"What?" he says, swiveling his gaze to her. "You know she's the key to—"

"Don't make me repeat myself. I will call you when you're needed. Now, please, leave."

He gives me a final glare that turns my blood to ice.

With a huff, he scoops the tablet off the table and clicks off the screen. He strides out of the room, and only when the door clicks does Ewensen face me.

She moves closer to the table and slips a hand into her pocket before revealing a tiny key.

"I've spoken with riders McCelroy, James, and Lockwood, along with my superiors. Their stories all check out, so, Ms. Corsair, you're free to go." She unlocks my handcuffs and the pressure from the cuffs releases. I draw my hands to my lap, rubbing the tender skin. "But let me be clear," she continues, standing upright. "This is an ongoing investigation, and there is a chance we will need you to remain available for more questioning." "Understood?"

I glance up at her and nod. The skin around her mouth and eyes is etched with wrinkles, and a light aroma of cigarette smoke radiates from her clothes. Tobacco is hard to grow in the Venovian climate, but apparently, her Circuit salary is enough to support the expensive habit.

"Thank you, ma'am," I murmur.

"Now, I will escort you to your room and make sure Agent Zane doesn't bother you anymore."

I let out a shuddering breath, feeling like I'd just dodged a bullet. What would've happened if she'd been a minute later? I can still feel his hand on my shoulder, the way his thumb had dug into my collarbone like he'd wanted me to fight back.

Agent Zane might've been a CSU agent, but he was also a fucking asshole.

Nineteen

Heath

The chatter around the restaurant table fades that evening as my mind drifts back to the arena. It'd felt wrong, fighting the other riders, but hell if the stallions didn't enjoy it.

I often wondered how much we shackled our stallions. They were bred, not created for war, and here we were, parading them around like circus animals.

I glance at Jess, seated next to me. Her black hair is loosely curled, and her perfume permeates the space. After I'd already agreed to this dinner, she'd blindsided me with her surprise move to Blackhawk.

The idea of living together had always been this distant,

theoretical concept—something we'd deal with eventually, not now.

This is practical. I tell myself. Just another step forward. But it felt like she'd crossed an invisible line, stepping into a space I hadn't even realized I'd been guarding.

I still can't believe she convinced Marshal to let her stay without us being married. She wouldn't tell me how she did it, and I wondered what sort of deal she'd made.

Jess always got what she wanted. I'd give her that.

She was like Brigid in that way.

Between the busy schedule and the vastness of the compound that literally separated us, it'd been days since we'd spoken.

Tides, how I missed her.

And now, my first free evening, I'm spending it here at dinner with Jess and our parents.

"It's so drafty in the station's hallways," Jess tells her parents at dinner, her voice pulling me back to the present. "If it weren't for my cashmere sweaters, I'd be shivering like a tourist at a Gaergan street market."

"You'd think with the amount of money we send them," her mother replies, "they could afford more heating."

"The clouds block out solar panels, Elise," her father, Preston, says. "They're doing the best they can with the aging windmills."

I watch Jess toy with the edge of her silk napkin, a sign she's growing impatient. My gaze drifts over the elegant dining room, noting the warm glow from the chandelier above the polished driftwood table. The venue is quiet, just the soft clatter of cookware from the kitchen and the shuffle of the wait staff.

My parents, Arthur and Margaret, occupy the seats across from us, while Jess's parents sit to her left. She forces a smile, but I sense the tension between us, the distance that's grown since the attack at the station. She's upset, and I can't blame her.

"Six weeks seems like such a short time," Elise says, steering the conversation toward the wedding. "But everything is falling into place beautifully. The florists have outdone themselves, and the cake sampling will be in two weeks."

Mother tilts her head with mild interest. "I'm sure it will be a lovely affair." She picks up the wine list and adjusts her glasses. "Horrendous."

Jess stifles a sigh as Mother complains about the wine for the umpteenth time. It's her ritual, a way to assert status since she'd married money, not been born into it.

The servers hover, alert to her displeasure. "Is there an issue with the wine list, madam?" one server asks politely.

"The choices are quite limited," she says, waving her hand dismissively. "I was hoping for something more refined, or is it so much to ask for a decent varietal?"

The server leans in slightly. "A terrorist group stole one of our shipment shuttles, and unfortunately, some of our finer selections were among the cargo. We filed a report with the police and have issued a rush order for the replacement."

My father shakes his head. "Those rebels are becoming a real thorn in Venovia's side. It's about time Circuit took offensive action instead of defensive."

Jess's father murmurs in agreement. "What more do they need to incite a courageous response? The assault on Meridian left Margaret and me pretty shaken. We've been seeing a therapist for the trauma."

I clench my jaw, recalling the mayhem of that day. Jess and her family had hidden in the basement while I'd been running around the station with Carter and the security team, trying to protect it.

They'd been safe and had escaped unharmed, and I was grateful they hadn't witnessed the violence. Father had taken me hunting many times in my youth, and while I could never place a person as equal to an animal, I was no stranger to blood and death.

At Vanguard, I'd been a top marksman, and when a stray wolf had kept harassing the school's chicken coop, they'd called me to dispatch it.

I'd only needed one good shot.

I feel Jess' eyes on me, sensing her thoughts also returning to the attack at Meridian, but I keep my gaze fixed on the table, avoiding any more conversation.

Mother finally selects a bottle of sparkling red, and the server fills our glasses. Jess reaches for hers, sipping slowly, composure returning.

"Elise," my mother says, "how many guests are we expecting now?"

"Around two hundred," Jess's mother replies. "Mostly family and close friends. We want to keep it intimate."

"Intimate? At two hundred?" Preston chuckles, a hoarse sound that devolves into a cough.

"Easy, dear," Elise says, patting his hand. "Did you take your pills?"

He waves her off, and she frowns, her painted lips turning to my mother instead. They dive into discussions of dietary restrictions and the choice between a live band or a string quartet.

Jess flashes me a strained smile. Neither of us wants to be here right now, but she's putting on a show, so I should at least try.

"So, Heath," her father says, looking at me, "how are things at Blackhawk? Did they reassign you as a manager?"

I straighten, even though I'd anticipated the question.

"No. Lorenzo Fiaro retains the position, and Marshal Clemmons is his secondary. I will only hold the status of a Master Rider."

Arthur grumbles. "It's ludicrous to demote you. You can be sure I'll let them know my disapproval at the next quarterly budget hearing."

I give him a tight smile. "There's no need. I am satisfied as a rider."

"Nonsense," Arthur bellows. "Lockwoods are leaders. Captains of ships, not deckhands. I will see this oversight is corrected."

My jaw tightens, frustration simmering beneath my calm facade. I'm on the verge of walking out, a familiar impulse.

The server returns. "Are we ready, then?"

"The fried urchin and artichokes, please. Lemon and butter on the side," Jess says, handing over the menu. She glances at me, and I realize I haven't decided.

"He'll have the same," she says, saving me.

"And to drink?" the server asks, eyes flicking between us.

Jess laces her fingers in her lap, and I feel her eyes on me. "Do you want your usual whiskey, darling, or something else?"

I nod absently. "Oh yeah, whiskey is fine."

Our parents' eyes are on us, expectant. Jess meets their gazes with a reassuring smile. "Heath's developed a taste for the Leviler aged," she says. The others look at me, waiting for me to speak.

I clear my throat. "Yes, um, it is quite complex, and I'm glad Jess introduced me to it."

Jess beams and pats my hand on the table. "Since Heath rarely gets to travel, it's my duty to bring the tastes of Venovia to him."

Our parents nod, and then my father's comm dings, and he swipes it open, earning a disapproving look from mother.

"Finally, some good news. Says here they caught one terrorist fleeing Nelworth."

"'Bout damn time," Jess's dad replies, waving his empty glass. The server hurries over to refill it.

I listen half-heartedly as the conversation shifts to business that, being a rider, I'm not involved in. Guilt coats the roof of my mouth, and I work my tongue, trying to smother it.

I still hadn't told them. Between the attack and the egg, there hadn't been a good time.

Further, they'd been so distraught. Mother, especially, had been fragile since the attack, and telling her I was infertile would only send her into a full spiral.

I would tell Jess soon, and then together, we could decide how to break the news to our parents.

As dessert is served, I force myself to engage, offering clipped responses to questions about the station and the wedding. But my thoughts are elsewhere, preoccupied with a future that feels more like a burden than a promise.

The night drags on, a blur of forced smiles and polite conversation. Finally, it's time to leave, and relief washes over me.

We exchange goodbyes with our parents, and Jess and I head to the private car that will take us back to Blackhawk.

"Thank you for humoring me at dinner," she says once we're seated in the backseat of the Towncar. "I know how hard it is for you to get away from the station, so I appreciate your effort."

The passing streetlights illuminate her profile. She's beautiful, like a pristine statue, not a hair out of place, and yet, I feel nothing more than a mild kinship for her, one created from a childhood of our families summering together and our arranged engagement.

"I know how dull you find the wedding planning, but we'll

be married soon, and with any luck, this time next year, I'll be pregnant." She folds her hand on her lap, looking wistfully out the window. "I will try to make this work if you are willing to."

Her mention of pregnancy twists the dagger of deceit painfully into my side.

This can't wait any longer. It's time.

I take a deep breath, steeling myself for what I'm about to say. "Jess," I say, my voice coming out softer than I intended. "I need to tell you something that I should have done a long time ago."

I watch as she furrows her brows, confusion evident on her face.

Sighing, I press a hand to my head before meeting her gaze. "Riders can't have children."

She lifts her brows. "What are you talking about?"

"We...," I mutter, gathering my thoughts. "Because of the bond. It affects us. We are infertile."

A small laugh escapes her lips. "No. You're wrong. There was that couple at North Crimela station a while back. They had twins, remember?"

My heart sinks as I realize she doesn't believe me. I look at her grimly, hating what I'm about to say. "They weren't his. The wife admitted later she'd had an affair with his brother,"

Jess blinks rapidly, her eyes widening, and the moment it hits her, the color drains from her face. "This whole time," she finally stammers, her shock visibly turning to anger. "This whole time, *you* lied to me?"

"I know it was wrong. I should have told you sooner, but I didn't think—"

"Didn't think what?" she interrupts, her voice rising to where I worry the driver will overhear even through the glass barrier separating us. "That we'd make it this far? That you'd actually have to go through with the wedding? Well, surprise, asshole. We did."

Jess crosses her arms, her face becoming unreadable as she stares out the window at the passing buildings. A sharp pang of regret tears through my insides, clawing at my heart. I curse myself for waiting to reveal the truth, and a deep well of frustration bubbles within me as I watch her shut down and bury her emotions. I'd been prepared for her to lash out, scream, and berate me, but the silence was so much worse.

The car drops us off at the private port gate, and I collect my thoughts as we board.

As the shuttle lifts off, carrying us above the twinkling lights of the city, Jess asks, "Do you think cookies with locks painted on them would be too cliche for wedding favors?"

"Jess," I say.

She peers down at her engagement ring, adjusting the diamond so it's centered on her finger. "What? They'd be fun if they had matching keys, sort of play off the romance —"

"Please, Jess. Talk to me."

The shiny metal doors open, and we move inside. The accent lighting in the elevator makes her features look sharper than usual. "I thought that's what we were doing?"

Running my hands through my hair, I blow out a long breath. "God dammit. Don't do that."

"Do what?" she says, her voice sickly sweet.

I jab a hand at her. "*That.* You're pretending like what I told you meant nothing."

Her nostrils flare, and she lowers her hands to her side. "While unfortunate, it is a minor setback, and we must carry on. So we'll never have children. We'll find other ways to fill our time. You have your stallion anyway, and I will continue with my property management." She purses her lips. "I dabbled with watercolors my senior year. Perhaps I'll pick that up again."

My jaw ticks as I watch her casually scroll her comm. "I'm sorry, Jess. Truly, I am. But I can't be what you want me to be."

Cold eyes glare up at me. "You can and you will."

"I'm sorry I hurt you," I say, and something in my tone seems to push her over the edge, and her carefully controlled expression crumbles.

"Hurt me?" she says, scoffing. "Do you think I'm not angry and hurt every day that I'm tied to a man who will leave me widowed before I'm thirty?" Tears form in the corners of her eyes, but she blinks them away quickly. "You know *nothing* of hurt. How I've prayed for your stallion to die so your bond breaks and you'll be free to love me. How many days I've spent lying in empty hotel rooms when you'd been unable to see me for the weekend? The excuses I've been forced to tell our friends and family when you'd ghosted me, yet again, because your 'duty calls.'"

I remain silent, unsure how to respond to her outburst.

"I didn't choose this life," I eventually say after a moment.

"And you think I did? People like us don't get to choose our futures. Before we were born, our parents had it all mapped out for us. Yours means you'll die young, which is why I've been infinitely patient with you. Understanding the times you can't leave the station, forgiving your *indiscretions*. But it's time you started giving back to me."

I press my lips together, unsure how to respond.

The shuttle sets down in Blackhawk courtyard, and we make our way to one of the main entrances. Out of habit, I turn left, but Jess' hand on my arm redirects me to the right.

No barracks. Not anymore.

We ascend the stairs and then down the carpeted hallway to what is now *our* apartment. Jess turns to me, her smile cold and cruel. "I'm exhausted, so I'd prefer if you sleep on the couch tonight." Then, without waiting for me to reply, she moves into the bedroom and closes the door behind her.

I watch the door click shut, her words still hanging in the air. The temptation to follow her is strong, almost instinctual. But I know it would be wrong, a lie. It'd be unfair to her to give her false hope, pretending that I could somehow be the husband she might want. My father's voice echoes in my mind, telling me to assume my role, to push open that door and demand my place beside her. It's what he would do—what he'd expect of me.

But I'm not that kind of man and as much as I want to fake it, to play the part, I can't. Not tonight. Not ever.

The couch it is.

In the living room, I loosen my tie and unbutton my shirt. Wearing only my boxers, I flip off the lamp and tug the throw blanket over me. Resting my head on my arms, I stare up at the mortar and stone ceiling.

I'd justified keeping this secret by telling myself I was protecting her, that I was ensuring our families' alliance would be secured through our marriage. But now, facing her hurt and anger, I saw through my own lies. The real reason was far more pathetic: I wasn't man enough to watch her break. I couldn't bear to see the pain in her eyes, to witness the moment she realized her dreams of a family with me were impossible.

In trying to shield myself from that pain, I'd only magnified it, letting it fester and grow until this moment of brutal revelation. I'd believed myself noble, but in reality, I was a coward hiding behind pretenses of duty and protection.

I could call Logan the selfish asshole, but the cold truth is I'm the one who deserves that title. The crown of selfishness has always been mine.

Twenty

BRIGID

I'm free.

Well, sort of.

It's not so free that I can run away, hop on a shuttle to Gaergen Island, and live in a cabin in the woods.

But at least I'm out from the stuffy room — and from Agent Zane, the creep.

As I ascend the stairs back to my apartment, my mind reeled with everything that happened. Ewensen's words ring in my head, reminding me that this is no longer just about finding Sharice. Now, it's about proving my innocence and keeping my nose clean until my sister is found.

I'm relieved to see the stairwells empty, and my nerves remain frazzled from the whole encounter as I return to my room. Once inside, I consider brewing some tea, but then remembering the smell from Agent Zane's turns my stomach. I slam the kettle back into the cabinet.

Damn him for ruining tea for me.

Rifling through the fridge, I find a bottle of apple juice. I crack open the lid, take two large gulps, and then wipe my mouth. The sugar hits my veins like a truck, and I'm nearly giddy from the receding adrenaline.

My eyes go to the spilled contents of my shoulder bag, and I grind my teeth as I clean it up.

White-hot resentment boils in my veins. They have her comm now, and they will watch the videos and very likely call me in for more questioning. I hope I have time before then to call a lawyer or, even better, they catch her.

Once picked up, I looked at where I'd left my luggage in the bedroom.

Unpacking it feels daunting, and I'm so emotionally drained I want to collapse under my covers. However, I consider the simple task might be a way to calm my nerves.

Control in the face of the uncontrollable.

Convince them I am in no way connected to my sister and the attack?

Nope.

Make sure my shirts are free of wrinkles and hanging in the closet?

That I can do.

Once my clothes are put away in the dresser, my two sets of shoes are set on the bench — a pair of work boots and slip-on flats. I stow my toiletries in the single drawer in the bathroom.

I shove the two empty suitcases under my bed.

The effort has left me sweaty, and the clawfoot tub and the basket of pretty scented soaps are calling my name.

Breath exhales from me as I sink into the sudsy water.

Vanilla and lavender fill my nostrils as I breathe deeply, letting my whole body relax.

I could so get used to this.

My fingers scoop out some of the sugar scrub from the little container and I work it into my arms and legs before rinsing it off.

Then I lean my head back and close my eyes, letting the warm water seep into me.

Yet, try as I might to clear my head, his questions shook something loose in my brain that I couldn't shove away.

I didn't have a clue where my sister was. That was a fact.

But did I even want to find her?

Yes. Of course. She was a terrorist.

She should be caught and charged for what she'd done. People had died. Innocent people who'd done nothing wrong than working at a station.

And while she might've been my sister by blood, she wasn't the same person I'd spent a childhood with. Something had changed in her. A bitterness, a hatred with an origin I didn't know. She was an adult. She made her own choices, but I could not *not* care about her. Even as much as I tried to ignore it, worry tugged at the edges of my mind. While I was here soaking in an oversized tub with fancy soaps and shampoos, where was she? What was she doing?

My bracelet slips down on my wrist as I wring out the washcloth over my legs. The same question echoes over and over again in my head: ITM was all about equal land rights and the protection of wildlife habitats, so why did they want a druadan egg? Agent Zane had slipped and revealed that mystyl had been reported at other stations and, thankfully, leading to only mild injuries. But why? If the mystyl had been used as a distraction at Meridian in order to steal the eggs, why target other stations?

Meridian was the only one with eggs.

I splash water over my shoulders as a pit forms in my stomach.

Heath and the others wouldn't lie to me about that, would they? No. They had to be telling the truth. However, secrets clung to the druadan stations like frost on shuttle fuel tanks, and perhaps they were just as ignorant as I was. Perhaps there were other eggs out there, tucked away in storage closets or locked in basements of stations.

If that were the case, and ITM truly was trying to get them, then someone more powerful than Heath as a station manager had been and was connected to all the stations and was leaking the information. The realization shudders through me.

Only when the water turns cold do I haul myself out of the tub. I towel off, then take my time sniffing the collection of lotions before applying them to my face, neck, and body. Then I turn to brushing my hair until it gleams in the dim light. Since I'd been in the sun at Meridian, the sun had left highlights of white streaks to appear among the silver-gray strands. I put it in a ponytail, leaving loose strands to frame my face.

I pull on a green halter-topped sundress that reaches just above my knee. The fabric is recycled linen but the store I'd got it from washes them in this special chemical to make it as soft as cotton. It hadn't been cheap — I twist, getting a better view of my backside in the full-length mirror hanging in my closet —but damn if it didn't make my ass look good.

Dressed and with the afternoon off, I contemplate going for a walk to get a better feel of the station, but as I move into the living room, there's a knock at my door.

My throat cinches shut.

What if Agent Zane or Ewensen have returned with an 'Oops, just kidding, you actually are going to jail.'

The air in my lungs freezes, but I shove down the panic and pad across the rug to the door.

There's no peephole like my apartment in Delford, so I have no option but to open it.

A whoosh of relief floods through me as I see Carter's muscular, tall form standing there. He's leaning on the door-jamb like he could wait all day. Just seeing his hazel-green eyes soothes me, like taking a deep breath after holding it too long.

"Carter," I exclaim, my voice bright with surprise. "What brings you by?"

"I heard the good news and thought you might be in the mood to celebrate since I heard Circuit is letting you go and not pressing any charges." His black jumpsuit is unzipped, the sleeves tied around his waist, and his white V-neck T-shirt reveals the shadow of the horseshoe-shaped tattoo underneath.

"Good news travels fast, huh?" I sigh. "Want to come in?"

He steps away from the door jamb and adjusts his shoulder bag, which is weighed by something I can only guess at.

I move out of the way and close the door behind him.

As we walk to the living room, he says, "So what did you say?"

"The truth. I'm *not* my sister, and I have no connection to her whatsoever." He settles into the armchair, and I move to the couch next to him. "I'm glad you came by because I wanted to thank you. They said that your statement, along with Logan's, Heath's, and Carla's, was enough to convince them that I was telling the truth."

Carter leans back, resting his arms on the sides of the chair. "I can be *very* convincing. In fact, I'm about to convince you right now to come with me so we can *really* celebrate."

A grin edges up the corner of my mouth. "Is that so?"

He opens his shoulder bag and produces a bottle of champagne proudly. His face lights up with the signature smile that makes my knees weak, and I consider jumping on his lap right then and there. "Swiped this from the locked storage room," he says. "The mess hall really needs to come up with harder passcodes. Care to join me for a picnic?"

I look toward the window blurred with rain. "Are you serious? Have you looked outside?"

"I know, but you have to trust me. You won't get wet, I promise." A devilish smirk appears on his face, and my heart skips a beat. "Never mind, I can't promise that."

I roll my eyes. "Let me grab my sweater."

I slip on a pair of boots, preparing myself for the puddles forming outside. The rain has been beating against my window all day, and I've seen very few people scurrying about in the courtyard down below. Most have umbrellas or hoods pulled up and drawn against the battering rain.

I follow him out the doorway, and in the hallway, he tucks his arm into mine. As we walk, another resident stares at us. They're wondering if we're together.

If they asked, what would I say? Yeah, kinda? I do care about him, and I know he cares about me, but is there anything more? He's not exactly the poster boy for monogamy, and yet I hadn't heard he'd shared his bunk with any other girls.

Sadie had been right. Gossip spread like wildfire here. Everyone knew who was screwing who, how often, and when.

You couldn't sit through one meal in the hall without overhearing the latest drama from either staff members or riders.

We go down the stairs that spiral to the bottom floor and then out one of the side doors that leads into the back part of the courtyard. To the right are the basement windows looking into the druadan barn. Everything is subterranean here and hidden so it's protected by the elements and any possible attack.

Outside, that cold mist douses my face. It's been off and on some version of rain since we got here, and I doubt I'll ever see the sun again at this point.

We pass through the courtyard gate, and he leads me down the steep path to the right, away from the old road that connects to the broken bridge. There is another gravel trail that runs parallel to the fortress wall, and a trio of riders wearing sweatsuits jog along it.

Stepping carefully on the slick rocks, we make our way down to where several outbuildings sit next to the orchard. I'd glimpsed them when we first arrived, but I hadn't had a chance to go out here since between the egg-hatching and the interrogation by Agent Asshole.

I grind my teeth, trying to suppress the annoyance. It was over and done with and now I'm out here on some mysterious journey with Carter.

I'm tempted to ask where we're going, but his footsteps don't slow, and I bite my tongue, trusting that he has a plan. I can't deny the butterflies that are swooping in my stomach.

This feels like a date.

I hadn't been on a date in, well...a long time, and even though he was fun to be around, I suddenly felt awkward.

My foot catches on one of the rocks, and I'm grateful his arm steadies me. He shoots me a quick, concerned look. "Is everything all right?"

"Yeah," I lie. "Just slippery, is all."

He smiles, convinced, and the path flattens until we follow the paved walkway that leads us to the edge of the trees. One of the maintenance staff is standing there with a tablet, assessing a monitor under a covered shelter. Carter approaches him, and they exchange a few words before he returns. "We've got an hour."

"An hour to do what?"

"Whatever we want," he says, smugly.

"Why do I feel like I'm not the first woman you've done this with?"

He flashes me a shy smile.

"Are you serious?"

"I've never been here more than a day," he says, shrugging, "and they were always for long-ass meetings."

"Well, you're very smooth, you know. How did you pay off that security guard?"

"I didn't pay him off."

"Then what was that —"

"He owed me a favor."

"What kind of favor?"

A wry grin appears on his face.

"I regret asking." It's something dirty.

Carter continues anyway. "The day before his daughter's graduation, he — "

"Never mind, I don't want to know." I wave a dismissive hand.

"You didn't let me finish."

The rain continues to fall from the gray sky and I pull up my hood, trying to keep my hair from getting drenched. "Sorry, go on."

"At the graduation," Carter continues, "there was a guy in her class she'd liked for the whole time in high school but never once looked her way. I showed up as a date. He got jealous cause it's me, obviously," he gestures to his body, "and the jealousy got the better of him, and he sought her out." He plucks a leaf from a nearby branch and twirls it in his fingers.

"What happened after?"

He tosses the leaf, and it flutters to the ground in a slow spiral. "While he was chatting her up, I got called away for rider business. Last I heard, they dated for a while, but he ended up being a prick. She's going to be an English teacher."

"So what you're saying is I should feel special you cashed in your favor on me?"

"You are special, Brigid."

A nervous laughter bubbles from me, and I suddenly feel warm all over. How am I supposed to reply to that? I mumble 'thanks' and step into one of the clearings between the rows, hoping he doesn't pick up on my unease.

But he doesn't seem to care because he takes my hand, leading me further into the orchard, where an invisible laser field shimmers between two stone pillars.

"It's all right," Carter says when I hesitate. "Leroy deactivated it."

As if to prove his point, Carter moves through it first, then when no sirens or alarms go off, tugs me through.

As we stroll under the canopy of leaves, the rain stops.

The rain eases to where only an occasional drop hits my hand or cheek. I hold out my hand and let out a surprised giggle. I crane my neck to look up, fascinated at how this is happening.

"Pretty wild, isn't it?" Carter says.

Every tree is an identical, a symmetrical clone of the next, hundreds of canopied branches align like puzzle pieces, blocking out the rain like a natural roof. Lowering my gaze, the ground beneath is nearly as dry as Meridian, save for a few stray clusters of yellow grass.

"But don't the roots need the water?" I ask.

Carter points between the trunks. "They run pipes underground with rainwater caught on the roof. That way, they can filter it and add fertilizer to it."

Trees are only found in parks in Delford, and the ones that do exist are typically ornamental maple or pine. These are fruit-bearing and apple trees, by the looks of it. They're loaded with ripe fruit. Every color and variety: reds, greens, yellows, pink.

"What do you want to do first?" he asks.

I look up at the nearest apple tree. "How about this?" I say, reaching for one of the glossy-skinned fruits.

Carter laughs, taking out the bottle of champagne and popping the cork. "It's fine, as long as we don't take too many." He takes a swig from it and passes it to me.

I raise my eyebrows. "Forgot glasses," he confesses, shrugging.

I press the bottle to my lips, feeling like I'm committing a dozen egregious sins of etiquette by drinking something that costs a week's salary.

The bubbles dance across my tongue, honeysuckle, lemon, and sunshine. Fuck me, it's good.

I pass the bottle back to him and survey our surroundings. There must be hundreds of trees covered in ripe apples. How would they ever know if any were missing?

I take one of the apples, plucking it from the branch, and stare at the perfect fruit. I press it to my face, inhaling the scent before taking a bite. The skin snaps with my teeth, and the juice pours down my chin. A giggle escapes me. "It's delicious."

I reach for a shiny red one with yellow stripes. Even in the gray cast of light from the sky, his green eyes sparkle.

In between bites, I say, "Thank you. It has been a pretty shitty few days, and this is nice."

"It is, isn't it?" he says, setting the bottle down. "Although I can think of a way to make it better."

There's a heat in his voice that wasn't there before, and it causes my heart to flutter in my chest. He moves closer still, and I hear him drop the core of his apple into the basket.

He cups the side of my cheek, and his warmth makes me

gasp. "All I want is to make you happy, Brigid. Every moment of every day, I want to see you smile and hear you laugh."

"Carter, I—"

"I'm telling you I love you. More than I've loved anything. I'm telling you I want you, and I need to kiss you right now."

I gaze up at him, losing myself in his touch and his piercing green eyes. "Then what are you waiting—?"

Instantly, his lips crash against mine, his hands gripping my arms as he pulls me hard against him. The apple core slips from my fingers, forgotten as his bonded rider heat overwhelms me, leaving me breathless. His mouth moves against mine with a fierce hunger, and without breaking the kiss, he undoes the buttons of my sweater. Desperate to have less clothing separating us, I peel it off and let it fall to the ground. He guides me backward, my steps faltering until my shoulders press against the rough bark of the tree. He doesn't stop.

If anything, his movements intensify, spurred on by my inability to retreat. His hands are in my hair as I grip his strong forearms. His firm body presses against mine, claiming every inch of space between us, leaving no room to think—only feel. The roughness of the bark rubs on my bare shoulders, but I don't care. I never want this kiss to end, and he does, breaking the kiss just long enough to curse under his breath.

"What is it?" I breathe, staring up at him.

His green eyes swirl with desire. "I can't wait any longer. Take off your dress before I rip it off."

The space between my legs throbs with longing as he gives a simple command. Ignoring the anxiety that we're outside and could be seen by any passerby, I eagerly agree and undo the tie behind my neck, and the dress falls from me.

I resist the urge to cover myself as I face him, wearing only my bra, a thong, and my ankle boots. The cool breeze wafts over the bare skin of my ass and the growing wetness between my legs even as goosebumps coat my skin.

He appraises me slowly from head to toe before settling on my face again, "Good," he says, his voice low and commanding. "Now turn around and put your hands on the tree."

Oh my god. I'm outside, half-naked, standing in an orchard. *Is this actually happening?* I barely hesitate before I obey.

I hear him shuffle behind me as he lowers his pants. "Spread your legs a little more."

I shift my feet wider.

Deft fingers pull my panties to the side, and grabbing my hips with one hand, he positions himself with the other and presses lightly into my entrance. "Ready?" he whispers into my ear.

Looking over my shoulder, I bite my lip.

"Tell me."

"I'm ready," I whimper.

I gasp as he enters me, savoring the delicious stretch and fullness as he seats himself. God, how long have I wanted this? To feel this closeness, this euphoria. Slowly, he works himself in and out. He releases my left hip and reaches his free hand to the front, his fingers softly encircling my clit. It's a slow, glorious rhythm and feels so freaking good. I react immediately, arching my hips into him.

Carter's breath warms my cheek. "See the trees with the red ribbons on their trunks?"

I search for the line of trees down the row about a hundred feet away.

"A gardener is going to be there soon to prune one, and while he's there, I want you to come."

I stiffen. "What? I—" My words dissolve into a moan as he lazily pushes into me.

"We can always go back to your apartment," he offers.

"No. This is *fine*," I whisper, arching my back, wishing he'd go faster. His teeth graze my neck, and a flood of heat pours into me. The gardener appears just as Carter said he would and begins lopping away at the lower branches. Carter's fingers brush against my clit, and I inhale sharply as my orgasm builds. At any second, the worker could turn toward us, and there'd be us — me with Carter deep inside me.

There was kinky, and then there was *this*.

This is dirty in so many ways. But the timid version of myself that would be appalled by this behavior is nowhere to be found. At this moment, I am reckless, Brigid, consumed by the here and now and the myriad of sensations this man is summoning from me.

My body buzzes with electricity, my stomach tightening with anticipation. "You're so goddamn wet," he breathes into my hair, sending shivers down my spine. His fingers speed up, tracing delicate patterns over the bundle of nerves.

His rhythm becomes more urgent, matching my cresting wave.

My knees buckle, but firm hands grip my waist.

"Not yet," he whispers huskily in my ear before pulling away abruptly. I whine in protest as he flips me around, pressing my back and shoulders against the bark of the tree. Hands grab my thighs and lift me. I wrap my legs around his waist, and immediately, he's thrusting inside me. A hungry moan flutters from my lips, and Carter shakes his head playfully as he presses a finger to his lips. I bite my lip, stifling the whimpers of pleasure his movement induces, and he regains his hold on my ass.

He drills into me harder and harder, and with a muffled gasp, I cascade over the pinnacle I was poised on. Wave after wave of pleasure rushes over me. My legs tremble as he maintains his hold, keeping himself buried inside me as he finds his release with a sharp curse.

He pulls back, and his eyes dart to the space behind me.

"He's gone."

Trembling from the aftershocks of the orgasm, he lowers me gently to the ground. The cool earth seeps into my back and shoulders through the blanket of grass as I stare at the overcast sky filtering through the leaves. He repositions himself above me, and now that we're alone, I sense all hesitancy is over as he plunges into me with unbridled abandon.

I arch my back. Still slick from his first release, he easily enters me again as I spread my legs wider. The sensation is overwhelming as the length of him fills me completely, stretching, pressing against every inch of me. My body tightens around him, my pleasure pulsing with his every movement.

With each deep thrust, I feel my climax building again. I dig my nails into his back, and he drives deeper, faster, harder. Ecstasy sweeps me away again, and with a growl in my ear, Carter's body tenses as he spills into me again.

For a long while, he tenderly kisses my lips before finally lowering himself to his side. He props his head on his left hand, elbow pressed firmly into the ground as his right traces the lines of my neck and collarbone.

Even though the sky is covered in clouds, Carter's skin seems to be bathed in a soft light. The shimmering effect is barely perceptible, yet it lends him an almost otherworldly aura, highlighting his face and sculpted shoulders that make my breath catch.

Damn. That post-sex glow sure looks good on him.

My heartbeat flutters in my ears as I stare, taking him in, when a faint beep chimes from somewhere far off to the left.

Carter's hand drifts to my breast, tugging down my bra, and his thumb coaxes my sensitive nipple to harden. He shifts, pressing his insistent erection against my thigh, warming my cheeks, as I can't help but marvel at his persistent arousal.

Beep.

I sit up on my elbows and search the trees. "Did you hear that?"

"I don't hear anything," he breathes over my breast, evoking a surprisingly needy shiver between my legs.

Beep, beep, beep. "Carter. Wait, listen," I say, tapping him on his bare shoulders.

Carter's arm falls onto my lap.

"Dammit," he mutters, "Time's up."

He tugs on his underwear and then pants. My eyes dip down, noticing the still present bulge. I clamp my teeth, suppressing the moan that nearly escapes me.

"We need to go," he says, helping me up. I hurry into my dress as he takes the bottle of champagne and my hand. "But so we're clear. I'm far from done with you today."

As we hurry out of the orchard, the rain has eased, but still dark clouds circle overhead.

He's holding my hand as we make our way up to the fourth floor. We pass a giggling Sadie and her husband, Kaeden, and pause to greet them.

Sadie's face is aflame as they quickly hurry past, muttering a mumbled excuse as to why they can't stay and visit. At the base of the stairs, I glance over my shoulder, and Kaeden and Sadie are wrapped in each other's arms, making out like two horny teenagers. They separate just long enough to scurry into one of the storage closets.

"Guess we're not the only ones enjoying the afternoon off," Carter says as we start climbing, and I laugh.

We reach the fourth-floor landing when his footsteps falter, and I hear him curse.

"What is it?" I say.

"A headache."

Near Sadie's office, a woman stands in a beige Circuit uniform with so many medals and ribbons on her left breast pocket. I'm shocked she can keep her shoulders as straight as they are.

"Who's that?"

"That's my mom," he says hurriedly.

My eyes widen at the sight of the highly-ranked Brigadier General Allison James. She's middle-aged, with reddish brown hair with streaks of gray around her temples. Her eyes are darker than Carter's, although still the same green with more specks of brown, and her nose and lips are full. She's actually quite pretty, but her somber demeanor induces a hollow pang in my stomach. Somehow, I knew I'd never amount to her standard. Even though women were equal in the military, the competition to gain rank was fierce. Every director on Circuit's council had been spring boarded by their military career.

"This is Brigid Corsair," Carter says, then quickly adds. "My friend."

I give a small wave. "Hi, nice to meet you."

Ignoring me, she levels him with a cool gaze. "You're late for our meeting."

Carter's throat bobs as he tilts his chin upward.

The tense looks between them speak volumes. Our date obviously has ended. I release his hand. "I should go," I say, hurriedly scooting by.

"Yes, you should," she says, her eyes never leaving Carter's.

I step down to the end of the hall, then briefly take in Carter's apologetic face, and slip inside my apartment.

Twenty-One

CARTER

"Carter Alexander James," my mom says. "I will not tolerate you slinking about with this week's latest whore."

"Don't call her that. She's not—" I retort, still standing in the hallway. God, I hope the doors are thick here so Brigid can't hear us.

"No? Then what is she? Who is she to you so much that you're willing to risk your reputation for?"

Her question is like a slap to the face. "*My* reputation, or do you mean yours?"

I can't put a name on what there is between us. Fuck labels. They're meaningless. "She means more to me than the others."

She huffs a breath. "Carter, don't be ridiculous. What kind

of life can you offer her? A cot in the barracks? Fighting off fans as they come knocking on your door at all hours? Not to mention, your bond with that stallion takes all your attention?"

"I don't care about any of that. It doesn't matter."

"Oh, Carter, I don't have time for this."

Without waiting for me, she marches down the hallway, turning at the stairs and then, once on the first floor, into a meeting room.

Someone has set up a pitcher of water and two glasses, along with bread rolls and butter on the table. She closes the door behind me as I reach for a roll, famished from vigorous workout in the orchard.

"Please sit," she says, "I have a shuttle leaving in an hour, and we have much to discuss."

I plop into one of the chairs and lean back. My teeth dig into the warm bread, and melted butter coats my fingers.

"How are you?" she says. It sounds forced coming from her, as if she's going through the motions of a caring mother.

"Happy as a clam," I say, meaning it as the orchard activities have left me high as a fucking kite even now.

"Good. I commend you for your quick thinking during the attack. I read the reports, and it appears you assisted in the defense efforts. Nice work."

I cram the rest of the roll into my mouth. "Thanks."

Mom scowls but continues. "In regard to our meeting, I have been in discussions with the other managers and what threats they're currently facing. We have all come to a consensus that more of the rebels and those mystyl creatures are out there, and we should be fully prepared to up our security at each of the Circuit bases, including this one."

"Great idea," I say, rocking my chair forward. "Glad we had this little chat." I get to my feet. This is a waste of my time.

"Wait, Carter. I'm not finished."

Sighing, I stop before reaching the door and turn to her.

"I see how the fans praise you," she says, resting her hands on the back of the chair at the head of the table. "Telling you accolades for performing tricks on your druadan. But you didn't earn this celebrity status. You have some athletic skill, I'll not deny you that, but you were handed this life. The second you gained a spot at a station and bonded, you became famous. But famous for what? For being an overrated cowboy gymnast? What did you do that changed the world for the better besides bed every woman you could?"

I lift my chin. *Tell me that's not a noble endeavor.*

"You found a gun and defended the station when others ran," she continues. "You are a James. The instincts of five generations of Venovian soldiers run in your veins."

The dark memories of that night claw through the fragile barriers I'd constructed to keep them at bay. I've tried my best to bury them, but they still manage to resurface when I least expect them to.

Like now.

Heath and Logan had mentioned nothing. So, why was I the one waking up in a cold sweat in my bunk with the echoes of screams and the lingering scent of burning flesh still haunting me?

They'd go away in time.

I hoped.

"Don't you see?" she presses. "This is your chance to contribute to your country. To have Carter James be more in the history books than a small footnote about a Master Rider. Here is the opportunity to do more. Be more."

"But what if I don't want to be more than a rider?"

"Then I'll have you tried for treason."

"Seriously?"

"I'm always serious when it comes to national security. If you refuse to lead this task force, you'll be defying the order of a Circuit officer in a time of crisis." Her lips thin as she continues to stare out the window.

Time of crisis? It can't be that bad, can it?

"I understand your hesitancy, so what I'm about to tell you is not to leave this room. Understood?"

"Yes, ma'am," I say stiffly.

"From our informants in the cities, there are the rumblings of a revolution."

I snort. "So? There have always been anti-Circuit nut jobs protesting and spamming Network with bullshit."

"True. But those have been disjointed and disorganized. These are different. More calculated. Releasing the mystyl was only the latest. For weeks, they've been knocking out power to Lannett labs, crashing shuttles into storage facilities, and even a few scientists have disappeared."

My mind starts to race as I consider the implications of these events. This is more than just some disgruntled citizens causing chaos. Someone is trying to sabotage the Circuit.

"What exactly do you want me to do?" I ask, keeping my voice measured.

"I want you to put together a team of druadan riders capable of fighting alongside Circuit's army should the need arise. Ten, to be exact."

My breath catches in my chest at the request. "What? Why me? Why not someone more qualified?"

She leans forward, her eyes boring into mine. "Because you're already in a position of influence and power. You have connections with other riders and can gather information that others may not be able to uncover. Plus, your reputation as a womanizer will help you blend in with the crowds and gain intel."

I swallow hard at her words. I'm no leader, and I have no desire to be. Give me the perks of fame and fortune that came with being a rider, and I'm good.

"I don't know. What about Marshal or Heath?"

She shakes her head. "Believe me, it crossed my mind. However, they have other duties here. You don't."

An astonished laugh escapes me. "That's it then because I'm just a regular rider with no other responsibilities. You're picking me?"

"In all honesty, yes. And because you're my son, and I know you are capable of so much more than you let yourself do."

"No," I say, "I don't want this."

"You don't have a choice," she responds curtly. "This is bigger than any personal preferences or doubts you may have about yourself. Lives are at stake here, both within the station and outside of it."

She sets a portable electronic tablet on the table.

"This has all the information I can provide regarding the station's attacks, the intel we've collected from rebel interrogations, and mystyl dissection reports. Read it. Then, discreetly select ten other riders to be on your team. I don't care how you pick them; draw them out of a hat for all I care. Just make sure they're good. If what we fear will happen happens, they're going to be the ones watching your back."

I clench my fists, eyeing the tablet with a golden interwoven wreath on it, representing Circuit. "I'll be back in a week, and we'll proceed with the next steps to getting you all properly equipped and what additional combat training you will need."

Defensiveness bleeds into my veins. It wasn't even a discussion. It's a command.

I've spent all my effort avoiding Circuit military bullshit, trying to enjoy the brief life I have left, and here it is, dumped on me.

"Ten names. One week," she says, striding to the door. She pauses and rests a hand on my arm. "This is important. Please don't disappoint me."

Twenty-Two

JESS

While this apartment was not the Delford Grand, not by a long shot, it was quiet, and the mattress had been unexpectedly comfortable. Though still shaken from our argument, I'd fallen asleep nearly instantly.

I flip off the covers and ready myself for the day.

As I'm applying my face creams, my comm dings from where it's charging on the counter.

I glare at it, reading the alert I'd set to walk Finn at noon, and grumble to myself.

This is temporary. Soon, we'll be married and officially have the apartment, and Marshal can find someone else to assign his demeaning tasks.

I despised that he'd coerced me into this arrangement.

It wasn't supposed to be this way. I was a Drakeford, a

descendent of a long line of legendary and ruthless negotiators.

And I'd been bested by a rider.

I nearly gag in disgust as I unzip my carry-on to begin unpacking.

As the hour passes, I attend to work-related messages. I frown at the declined offer on a property with a South Sea vista I'd had my heart set on. Ocean views had only recently returned to popularity as most people saw the ocean as a symbol of destruction. The reason our world was a fragmented series of islands instead of giant land masses.

It'd been the tides after all that had nearly wiped out humanity.

Up until a hundred years ago, mountains and valleys had been all the rage, with seaside houses going for next to nothing.

However, with the population growth and more people wanting to work and live near the cities, beachfront property values have been on a steady incline.

One which I was eager to snatch a piece of.

I reply graciously and ask to be put on a waiting list should any other similar properties arise. I'd overindulged on the wine last night, and it'd left me with a dull throb in my temple. I pop two aspirin from my purse and open one of the glass bottles of filtered water.

Sipping from the bottle, I wander around the room, considering which pieces of art I'll have sent from my penthouse.

I'd told Heath I needed time to process the reality we'd never have children, but the more I thought about it, the more I realized it was probably for the best.

I could focus more on expanding my interests, and he'd never feel torn between his family and the station.

If there's one thing I hate more than anything, it's putting off the inevitable. I tap on my comm, messaging him, "We need to talk." It's mid-morning, so there's a chance he's free between drills and lunch.

Over the course of an hour, I mull over what our new, childless future will look like as I organize my clothes. Formal dresses in the back of the closet, jackets in front, and t-shirts folded in the dresser. Once satisfied, I move on to the two crates of shoes I'd brought, arranging and rearranging them on the shelf.

I've just placed my last pair of heels when I hear the door open.

"Heath, is that you?" I call out. "I'm in here."

He enters the bedroom as I emerge from the closet. As usual, he looks incredibly handsome, wearing his monogrammed black t-shirt with the BH on the left sleeve, canvas riding breeches, and knee-high boots. A white fur clings to the thighs of his pants, and I look at the dark upholstered furniture about to be shed upon.

"I'm glad you messaged me. How are you?"

I paste a tight-lipped smile onto my face. "Fine." I lie. "Sit, please?"

"I should change," he says, glancing toward the hallway that leads to the master bathroom.

I shake my head. "There's no need."

Indecision flickers in his eyes, but then he moves to the padded bench at the foot of the bed. I bristle as he sits, already seeing the druadan hair on his pants cling to the crushed velvet upholstery. A station like this must be prepared to handle such a mess, but I make a mental note anyway to request slipcovers for the furniture. Sadie informed me they clean once a week, and I don't think I can stand plucking dirt and hair off the furniture every day.

"Since last night, I've had some time to think," I begin,

taking the seat beside him. I place my hands on my lap and stare down at them. "I feel we should clear the air, put everything out in the open regarding us."

"I agree." He crosses his legs, letting his boot dangle. He keeps them cleaner than most, but a fragment of dried manure clings to his heel.

"While our inability to expand our family will pose an issue in the future, we have more present problems to consider."

"Go on."

I draw in an emboldening breath. "Rumors have reached the Drakeford's board that our relationship is tenuous, and there is fear from shareholders that the merger negotiations between our families won't proceed." I rise from my seat and begin pacing. "It's in part why I chose to move here ahead of the wedding as an effort to show at least a pretense of us being a happy couple."

His jaw twitches as he considers my words.

When Heath and I make love — usually once a month when he's on the verge of his condition going too far — it's quick and passionless. I'm treated to a handful of minutes where I forget this is all orchestrated and fantasize about sharing my body with someone who actually cares about me.

Despite everything, I don't hate him.

Shocking, I know.

It's not entirely his fault he's this way. Our upbringings molded us into keeping our emotions in check, rarely showing fear or doubt, but underneath his restrained, controlling nature, he is still just a man.

And it'd been ignorant of me to see him as anything else.

I'm not naïve. I know that love isn't a requirement in a marriage. Take my parents, for example. Thirty years, two kids, and millions of acres of land later, they're better than ever.

Happiness is relative. By abiding by my grandparent's wishes when they were young, they now get to choose the courses of their lives — where to eat, where to vacation, and if they're lonely, with whom they want to spend time.

I'd toured the filtration plants owned by Heath's family and walked through the oppressive underground hallways, smelled the foul stench of body odor and natural gas. Entire generations were born, lived, and died in houses that could fit into the closet here.

Our lives weren't perfect, but it could be so much worse.

"All right." He leans back. "What do you want me to do?"

I clear my throat and straighten my shoulders. "I will live here for the time being and commute to Delford when work requires. We will continue with the motions of wedding preparations like we've been doing, and I'll even make some noise about purchasing a house in the village. But for all intents and purposes, you and I are through."

"And then?"

"And then, in two weeks, the merger should be completed, and once the ink is dry and if you still wish to do so, we can call off the marriage."

"That's it?" he says, arching a brow. It's reasonable that he's skeptical.

I would be.

I nod. "That's it. I'll pack my things, move back to Delford, and you'll never have to see me again."

Heath gets to his feet and turns away, but not before I catch the visible relief on his face. A heavy weight anchors in the pit of my stomach, and once again, I wish I could turn off my feelings for him. I'd rationalized that it was some part of my subconscious wanting something I could never have, which in my world was such a rarity it made it even more valuable.

Finally, Heath looks at me again. "I am sorry," he says softly.

"Me too."

"I'll be back late, so don't wait up." He offers me a reassuring smile, then strides out of the room.

As the door clicks shut, a silence envelops me, mirroring the uncertainty that now clouds my thoughts. Convincing Heath to end the engagement was easy; now, I needed to prepare myself for our parents to come to terms with the fact that they would never get a grandchild.

I look at the empty bar cart in the living room and message the mess hall.

"Sixteen B needs wine."

Twenty-Three

BRIGID

The clink of glasses and the murmur of conversation envelop me as I make my way across the crowded restaurant. In the corner, Laura and Vince await me at a table and wave me over. As if by magic, their warm and welcoming smiles ease some of the stress I've carried for days.

This is the first time I've been away from the station and the egg, and the nagging fear that it will hatch while I'm gone is undeniable. But deep down, I know I *need* this break. A single day of normalcy away from terrorist groups and riders to center me and remember who I am.

Or at least who I was.

Carter had messaged me an apology after his mom had met us on our way back to my apartment two days before.

Later, he'd told me it was a family thing, and I shouldn't worry. When I hadn't replied right away, he sent a shirtless selfie of himself lounging in his bunk.

I'd saved it immediately to my favorites file. On the shuttle ride over, I thought of this and messaged Heath and Logan, asking for pictures, too, using the excuse that I could identify them quicker in my comm.

Heath replied ten minutes later with the professional headshot used on Meridian's Network page and another ten minutes after that. To my surprise, Logan sent me a blurry reflection in a mirror, flipping me off.

So, we hadn't exactly made up. He'd been a jerk, and I refused to apologize for doing something that saved my life, but it was a start.

"Brigid!" Laura calls out as I approach her. The subtle scent of her floral perfume wafts over me as she pulls me into a tight hug. Then it's Vince's turn, and he greets me with his wide smile and caramel brown eyes.

"It's so good to see you! It's been like forever," he says, releasing me.

Laura steps back, gesturing to a chair. "How have you been, B?"

I slide into the chair next to her as Vince pours me a glass of wine from the bottle on the table. "Good," I say, taking the glass from him. How can I summarize everything that has happened? I can't. "You know. Settling in at Blackhawk has been interesting."

Worry tinges Laura's voice, and she frowns. "Hey, it's us, remember? Seriously. How are you really holding up?"

I ball my hands in my lap, staving off the insecure doubt that assaults me. My sister, my ability to ride Galaxian, the feelings I have for Carter, Heath, and Logan, not to mention the connection I felt to the egg. Lately, it feels like I'm grasping at loose strands of threads, pulling me in every direction, trying to force them into a bundle that forms *me*.

Why is being me suddenly so hard?

"I'm still processing, to be honest."

"The others? How are they coping after the attack?" Vince's question pulls me back, his voice laced with genuine worry.

"The staff have really pulled together. Everyone is patient and supportive." I pause. "It's been crazy for sure, but the riders and security team really are something. During the attack, they helped rescue all the people, and many even fought."

"It's a miracle you're alive," Laura says, taking my hand.

"I know," I say. "I still can't believe it myself."

"Most people would've gotten their asses out of there," Vince says. "God knows I would've. And yet you chose to stay?"

"Vince is right. Why are you still there? You said you were looking for Sharice, and since you didn't find her, so why stay? No way the pay is *that* good, and even if it is, Tritan would match it. I know for a fact they'd have you back in a heartbeat."

"Besides, you still have your room, and our lease isn't up for a year," Vince adds.

I take another sip of the wine, buying time to think about how to reply. A day after the attack, Heath had asked me the very same question. Even though I'd expected this, I falter, trying to come up with an answer. It's not like I was going to pin a Venovian flag outside my room and tattoo "Circuit Lover" on my chest, but I didn't have to be a staunch patriot to respect our government.

Circuit did a lot of really great things: free healthcare, free college, and retirement at sixty. However, I could pretend all I wanted was that I liked the salary and old buildings at the druadan stations, but secretly, I stayed for selfish reasons.

Carter had confessed his love to me, and while I hadn't said it back, he occupied my thoughts and dreams often. And while I suspected there was something between Heath and me, his own barriers and his fiancée would never allow us to be more. Still, there remained the longing to break down his walls and see what mysterious creature lay beneath.

Then there was Logan. Tides, he was insufferable. But he'd risked his life to save me.

Twice.

And if that wasn't enough to snag a girl's attention, I didn't know what was.

Of course, I couldn't come right out and say my complicated love life was why, so, once again, I'm left fumbling with an excuse that is believable enough that they won't question me. "They need me," I finally say. "Admin does, I mean. Public relations is more important than ever, and I like the team I'm working with. It is surprisingly challenging and rewarding." I finish with a timid smile. "Plus, the food there. Oh my god, everything is so fresh."

"There it is," Laura laughs, pointing a finger at me. "They have an orchard there, right? Please tell me you've eaten the fruit there."

Heat creeps its way up my neck to my cheeks. "Yep. I sure have."

"And? Come on," she presses. "I've never had any fruit outside of canned or dried before. Give me all the juicy details."

Juicy. *Well, that was one way to put it.* "I've had fresh apples, and they're so sweet and crisp, better than I ever imagined."

"I bet," she says, more than a little wistfully.

Our conversation meanders away from what I'd sampled in the orchard, which is appreciated since the longer I think about Carter and me getting busy, the more I regret not bringing a change of underwear.

Vince unknowingly distracts me with pictures of his newly

adopted cat, and Laura tells me about her recent promotion at Tritan and how she's seeing the new guy from IT.

"He's upping the company's security, and they're watching everyone's Network activity searches."

"Circuit police are like everywhere now," Vince says.

"Arresting anyone they suspect has anti-Circuit opinions. Even places like this," she whispers, glancing around the room.

Vince nods, his face somber. "I swear, every day it's getting worse. You look around, wondering if the person next to you might be a terrorist."

I shiver at the thought, remembering how I had been the one on the other side of the interrogation table. It seems the fear and paranoia were spreading beyond the druadan stations.

"I have to admit, we've missed you, Brigid," Laura says.

"Blackhawk's only a couple of hours from here. When they start up exhibitions in the spring, you should come and see it."

Laura barks a laugh. "Even with everything going on, the country is literally ready to combust, they're still going to hold exhibitions?"

I shrug. "They've tightened security and background checks of ticket holders, but they think it helps to keep a sense of order in the country to continue with them."

"And do you agree with them?" Vince asks.

"I do," I say, my voice firm. "I believe if Circuit makes it appear business as usual, it keeps people from overreacting."

Vince skewers me with a skeptical gaze identical to the ones Sharice often gave me when I'd tried convincing her to loan me her allowance for clothes when, in actuality, it had been for the chocolate bars from the vending machine. "I hope you're right. I'd love that to be true. Just promise me while you're there you'll be careful?"

I nod. "Promise."

Our meal ends, and we make our way down the overhead-lit streets back to what is technically still my apartment.

Once inside the second-story loft, Laura pops open a bottle of wine, pouring generous glasses for each of us as we settle on the couch in front of the projection monitor. She's selected a rerun of a documentary about Gaergan's first settlers that she knows is one of my favorites.

Vince flips open his comm to show me an image of him and a handsome brown-skinned man posing beside a fountain in one of Delford's parks.

"His name is Jasper," he says proudly. "It's nothing serious, and only been a month, but I like him."

"Don't forget the best part," Laura says.

A mischievous twinkle appears in Vince's eyes. "He's a police officer."

"I've already told him he needs to show him his handcuffs," Laura comments.

I laugh as Vince's face reddens, and he tosses a pillow across the room at her, jostling the bowl of popcorn on her lap, making her exclaim.

"Well, I, for one, am happy for you," I say, clutching my glass of wine. As we continue to watch the film, my mind wanders to the station. I check my comm for any updates from Heath or Carter about the egg.

Nothing.

On the screen, archeologists tour the inside of a giant wooden building with rusted metal gambling machines and a swimming pool with a broken yellow plastic diving board collapsed into it.

The credits have just started rolling when there's a knock at the door.

"Who would be here this late?" Laura says, setting the popcorn aside. As Vince goes to the door, Laura scoops up the bat I'd insisted we keep for protection and positions herself behind him.

"Who is it?" Vince asks.

"It's me, Vince. Jasper."

I rise to my feet from where I'd been on the sofa as Vince and Laura exchange a bewildered look.

"Jasper?" Vince sputters, unlocking the door and opening it. "What are you doing here?"

I recognize the Latino man from Vince's photo with long sideburns and an officer's uniform standing on the threshold. "Sorry it's so late, but I'm working. I've received a call for a pick up. Is there a Brigid Corsair here?"

"Yeah, I'm here." I stand on somewhat shaky legs from the wine and brush off the bits of popcorn from my lap. "That's me."

"What's this about?" Vince asks, and Laura slowly lowers the bat.

"We aren't at liberty to discuss." His gaze shifts to me as I move to pick up my coat. "Ms. Corsair. I'm Officer Fredrickson. You need to come with me."

I turn to Laura, her eyes full of worry. "It's okay," I say with a reassuring smile. "I'll see what's going on, and then I'll catch a ride back here."

"I'm going with you," Vince insists, taking his jacket from the nearby rack.

"I'm sorry you can't," Jasper says. "We've been instructed to escort Ms. Corsair to drive. She is to return to Blackhawk station immediately."

My breath comes in rapid succession. Oh shit. Am I in danger? I'd requested the day off and the shuttle pass. What if Sharice had found out I was here and was trying to track me down?

"It's okay," I say again, more to myself than my friends.

Laura squeezes me with a tight hug. "Please be safe," she murmurs in my ear before letting me go.

I quickly hug Vince too, then picking up my shoulder bag, I follow Officer Fredrickson down the narrow stairwell and out the backdoor.

In the alleyway, we meet another officer, who opens the side door to a van with black tinted windows.

Yep, totally not creepy at all. If Jasper hadn't been Vince's boyfriend, this would be the part where I'm screaming my head off that I'm being kidnapped.

"What's going on?" I ask as he leads me to the van. My mind whirs with the possibility that there's been another attack, only this time at Blackhawk. "Did something happen?"

"Watch your head," Officer Fredrickson says, ignoring me and guiding me into the dark interior.

Two others are already seated inside. One is an older man I vaguely recognize from repairing lights around Blackhawk. His eyes are closed, and he rests his head against the headrest. The other passenger I recognize is Kaeden, Sadie's husband.

I climb into one of the empty seats, setting my overnight bag in the space next to me. I barely have time to strap on my seatbelt before the van is moving.

"You got nabbed too, huh?" Kaeden says, flashing me a toothy grin. His red hair pokes out from under a crooked baseball cap, and his eyes have that telltale glassy look that he's been drinking.

"Yeah." I laugh. "Do you know what's going on?"

Kaeden shakes his head. "My guess would be it's a security thing, and they're calling us all back to the station."

I scowl, looking through the tinted windows.

"What were you doing in town?" he asks.

"Visiting friends. You?"

"Brother's birthday," Kaeden slurs, showing the stamp on

his hand. The black smudge is hard to read, especially with the scar distorting it, but it's an R and maybe an S? "Party at the Sagebrush saloon. He's the baby in my family and is turning eighteen."

The van turns right and then picks up speed as we hit the highway to the shuttle ports on the edge of town.

I peer out the window at the dark landscape passing by. The last time I'd left Delford, it'd been to go to Meridian to look for my sister. How blissfully ignorant had I been then with my padded résumé, pencil skirt, and a misbelief that I'd be able to keep my identity a secret?

"It was a whole weekend thing," Kaeden continues. "My parents insisted we make it a big deal since he's moving off the continent soon once he enlists."

The inside of the van is dark, but I still look in his direction. "Circuit local or national?"

"National. He has his sights set on being a shuttle pilot to work on natural disasters."

"How long did he sign up for?"

"Two years." He slurs the 'S' and then sucks in a deep breath as if preparing to say more.

But when he doesn't, I attempt to fill in the awkward silence. "Well, if he's half as determined a rider as you, he'll do great." I want him to keep talking. Anything to distract me from the irritation of my trip being cut short and the possibility of not being able to see my friends again anytime soon.

Silence.

I squint, unable to see more than the shadowy outlines of him. Perhaps he's fallen asleep or reached the stage of intoxication where depression seeps in, and he's reflecting on his younger brother growing up. Shit, if I hadn't been there before. Sadness is a sneaky bitch, taking advantage when your inhibitions are at their weakest.

When a minute has gone by, a passing car's headlights illuminate the interior, and I glimpse his face.

Terror clamps my throat shut, and my mouth falls open.

Kaeden's eyes are gone, replaced only by the whites as they've rolled back so far into his head. He clenches his hands into twitching fists, and drool dribbles from the side of his mouth.

Something is terribly wrong.

"Kaeden?" I shout and tap him on the shoulder. No response. "Kaeden," I say again with more urgency. Nothing.

"Stop the car," I shout. "Please! Something is wrong with him. I think he's having a seizure."

Fredrickson looks in the rearview mirror. "What?"

"Please!" I scream.

"There's nowhere to pull over. Is he breathing? Any obvious wounds? Bleeding?"

The momentary illumination is gone, and we're plunged back into darkness. "I don't know! I don't think so." Icy claws of fear slither into my chest. "Something is happening. I think he needs a doctor."

Someone clicks on an overhead light. "He's flaring," the old man says, leaning over and placing a hand on the back of Kaeden's forehead. "It's a bad one. Call a medic."

The driver taps on his comm. "This is Lieutenant Officer Jasper Fredrickson en route on Highway eleven. We need a medical team at shuttle port Bay Seven. My passenger is having a medical emergency."

"Copy." There is a brief pause, then. "Is it a rider?"

"Yes." The car slows as he takes the exit ramp.

Another pause. "Copy that. We'll have a team on standby."

Panic bubbles inside me as I stare helplessly at Kaeden's unconscious body.

The old man looks at me. "Help me elevate his feet."

I unstrap my seatbelt and, as he shifts to, lie sideways on the seat. Both station orientations covered what brimming was and how, if left untreated, it could progress into flaring, but while the pages of text and diagrams talked about signs and symptoms, I'd never actually witnessed it.

And had hoped I never would. I rifle through my memory, willing myself to remember what they'd said. Early symptoms included fatigue, deliriousness, and slurring of speech. Treatment included being moved to proximity to the rider's bonded druadan, with secondary treatment being that of limited medical intervention.

With his stallion hundreds of miles away, his only chance at survival is getting him to a doctor.

A sheen of sweat glistens on his forehead, and his breathing is ragged. I wish there was something I could do for him, some way I could comfort him, but all I can do is hold his feet to keep the speed bumps from jostling him. Even through the fabric of his pants, he feels like he's on fire. "Hurry! He's burning up!"

Kaeden's body convulses violently, and the acrid stench of sickness hangs heavily in the air, making my stomach churn. The old man holds him steady, murmuring soothing words.

Kaeden is slipping away, and there is nothing we can do to stop it.

Officer Fredrickson honks the horn as we crawl painfully through the grid-locked traffic.

A crowd of protesters comes into view, filling the street ahead of us and blocking the road. They wave signs and chant angrily about the plant worker's rights.

"*Circuit is lying to us! Filtration doesn't work!*" they chant in unison.

A rock collides with a thud against the rear window with a

deafening crack. I scream, ducking instinctively as panic rises in my throat, and I realize how vulnerable we are.

"Go, go, go!" I yell as two more thuds hit the side of our van. "We have to get out of here!"

"Hold on!" Fredrickson shouts back. He curses in Spanish, slamming his palm against the steering wheel.

The van lurches forward, weaving dangerously close through the throng of protesters. Some bang on the sides of the vehicle, their faces twisted with fury, and he honks the horn.

I grit my teeth as Kaeden lets out a weak moan, his body trembling.

I'm powerless to do anything but watch.

His fever-glazed eyes fix on me, and he reaches up with a shaking hand to touch my face. "Sadie," he says hoarsely, and I can hardly hear him over the yelling protesters. "I'm so sorry. I thought we had more time."

My heart clenches at the tenderness in his voice. I blink back tears, swallowing hard against the lump in my chest. "It's going to be okay, Kaeden," I lie. "We're almost there."

Finally, there's a break in the crowd, and Fredrickson seizes the opening, swerving around them, and then takes the next right.

Fredrickson guns the engine as we drop onto the large parking area where roads to each landing bay jut off.

We're not going to make it in time.

We zoom by an illuminated sign alerting us that bay seven's shuttle departure is in ten minutes. Two ambulances sit in front of the awaiting shuttle, and Fredrickson stops the van next to it.

The van door slides open, and two green-clad paramedics appear, eyes searching the van's interior.

"Please help him," I say, even as they're already reaching to take his body out. I take a deep, shuddering breath as one carries his head and the other his feet, and together, they move him to the back of the awaiting ambulance.

I press my hands to my mouth. "I thought he was drunk. Please. Please help him. You have to save him."

They lay Kaeden on a stretcher, working quickly, administering injections, and packing ice around his body in a desperate attempt to lower his dangerously high temperature. He shakes violently, gasping for air as they fit an oxygen mask over his face.

I watch in horror, my mind refusing to accept the reality unfolding before me.

This can't be happening. I want to rush to his side, to hold his hand and tell him it'll be okay, but I'm frozen.

Tears stream down my cheeks as the seconds tick by. Finally, their bodies still as they drop their hands.

"No, no, no," the words tear from my throat as they exchange defeated looks with each other. "Please, no." I stumble forward, but Fredrickson grabs my shoulders, holding me back.

The world blurs, the sounds muffled as if I'm underwater. The medics strip off their gloves and cover him with a blanket. I can't pull my eyes away from Kaeden's lifeless form as it disappears behind the ambulance's doors.

Kaeden is... dead.

The word refuses to solidify in my mind. It's not possible. Minutes ago, he'd been alive, talking to me about his brother's birthday, and now he's...*gone*.

A wave of hot fury crashes over me at the protesters who blocked our path. If only they hadn't been there, Kaeden would still be alive.

I want to scream at them, to unleash the anguish and rage that's clawing at my insides. But the words stick in my throat, replaced by a strangled sob.

Fredrickson's grip on my shoulders tightens. "I'm sorry, but we need to go. Delford has been raised to level three for terrorist activity, and they're going to ground all shuttles after this."

Mind reeling, I reluctantly turn from the ambulance as he gently guides me towards the idling shuttle.

The engine's rumbling mixed with the relentless buzzing filling my ears, and by the time we reach the shuttle, my face is streaked with tears.

I'm ushered onto the shuttle, and an attendant directs me to a seat. As she hands me a blanket, I cast one last anguished look back at the flashing lights of the ambulance fading in the distance.

Twenty-Four

MARSHAL

"Ready for another go?" Heath asks me, tugging on the rope tethered to my waist.

The air smells of chalk and the sour tang of the sweaty bodies. The rhythmic thuds of feet hitting the floor, the muted grunts of exertion, and the background hum of music from the speakers fill the room. Heath stands beside me, adjusting the safety elastics attached to my sides.

"Hit it," I reply through gritted teeth, and the elastic rope propels me upward. I arch my back, flipping in the air. As Heath lowers it, I land a little too far on my right, causing me to stumble.

I spit a string of curses.

"Careful, old man," Carter shouts from the sparring mats. "Charlie will have your ass if you roll an ankle without her here."

Our physiologist, Charlie, is on maternity leave. Regardless,

I can still hear her instructions on repeat in my ear about focusing on nailing the landing. The padded mats in the gym are one thing, whereas in the arena, high on adrenaline and the roar of the crowd is another altogether. This maneuver we've been drilling is a variation of another one we've used in the past, where we leap off our druadan's backs and then vault back on. It requires precision and flexibility, and it's anything but easy.

But the audience demands it. Each season has to be fresher, shinier, and ultimately more dangerous.

Other riders around us practice their routines—some doing choreographed weapon drills like Carter and Logan, while others stretch or lift weights.

"Let's go again." Heath gives me a nod, and I take a deep breath, feeling the tension in the elastics tug at the harness under my legs. I leap up and launch myself backward. The world spins, and for a moment, everything is a blur of motion. I pop my head up and straighten my shoulders, and this time, my feet contact the mat evenly.

"Better," Heath says. "But you need to tighten your legs in the spin."

"If I tighten anymore, I'm going to rip the ass out of my pants."

"I doubt anyone in the audience would mind," Heath says, shaking his head. "In fact, they'll probably love it."

Someone yells from across the gym, "Hey, change the song!"

Guess not everyone appreciates my taste in music.

I roll my eyes. The southern Uncy'lia rock band is what most consider classics as the group is well into their nineties now, but the simple rhythm and catchy lyrics keep me amped during training. "Don't you fucking dare," I shout back and grip the ropes by my side.

I'm the most senior rider, so until I leave, no one touches that goddamn speaker.

As I prepare for another attempt, Heath steps back, tightening the ropes. The song fades, and I spin, ready to lie into whoever thought they could go against me, but immediately, there's a shift in the atmosphere in the gym.

I open myself to the bonds of the other riders, and wariness saturates it. The chatter dies down by the main door as Chief Lugsen enters.

My stomach knots. Something's wrong.

As usual, Chief Lugsen's deep-set eyes and stern mouth make his expression unreadable. "Marshal," he says. "Something's happened."

I swallow hard, dread curling in my gut. My first thought is of the egg that it had been stillborn or stopped continuing to crack. I search his face for any clues about what's happened, drawing on the years we've known each other, but it reveals little.

"Tell me."

Subtly, he glances over his shoulder at the other riders staring at us.

They're too far to hear, but it won't matter. Mine and Heath's bonds will reveal our emotions. Whatever it is, they'll know soon enough, at least the severity of it. Chief Lugsen clears his throat and, keeping his voice muted, says, "Kaeden Benson flared out while in Delford."

"Damn," Heath curses next to me.

The words hit me like a blow to the gut. This isn't right. Kaeden was a fourth year.

I glance over at Rolan, who is doing one-handed push-ups with another rider on his back, laughing. He's well into his ninth; he's the one that should've been next. We'd all mentally prepared for it. He'd even set up a will for his assets to return to his family. And as morbid as it was, he'd even picked the niche in the catacombs for his urn next to his best friend's.

I force myself to focus. "Does Sadie know?" I ask, already knowing the answer.

Chief Lugsen shakes his head. "We haven't told her yet. Station protocols for a flare are—"

My hands unsnap the buckles at my waist, and I angrily toss them onto the ground. "Fuck protocol. She needs to know. They were shopping for a vacation house, for Christ's sake."

"Marshal, I know you're upset," Chief Lugsen says. "but these rules exist for a reason. If we show preferential treatment for one rider, it could disrupt the entire system. We can't go against protocol."

"Out of respect for our years together, I'm going to ask you to politely move the fuck out of my way."

"Marshal," Heath says, resting a hand on my arm. "Just think about this, please."

"I already have." I swipe my hooded sweatshirt from the stack of mats and pull it on before looking at Lugsen again. "Where's his body?"

He lets out an exasperated sigh. "Medical office B." He knows better than to argue. Even if he is station chief, he's not a rider, so if push came to shove, I technically outrank him.

Not that it mattered.

Rank or no, he still couldn't touch me. I was the 'miracle,' the 'defiant one,' and the 'shining star' of all the druadan stations.

"I'll come with you," Heath offers.

"Thanks," I say, and it comes out more clipped than I'd intended. Heath is a friend, but there are still remnants of that station manager's ego. He'd been demoted, and no doubt, there was a small part of him that was annoyed as hell at having lost his powers.

Lugsen leaves for a meeting with Fiaro and Heath, and I head out of the gym.

Together, we enter the clinic, the sterile smell of antiseptic hitting me immediately.

Kaeden is lying flat on an examination table, still wearing pants and a shirt, but his feet are bare. I steel myself and step closer, feeling Heath's presence behind me. He looks peaceful, as if he's sleeping, but the sallow skin tells a different story.

While the specifics of each flare are different, some stroke out, and some develop high fevers that induce a lethal seizure. The details of how he flared don't matter, just that the rider was alive one second, and the next, they're gone. Over and over again, it's the same story. Beyond the death of your druadan, there's no escaping your fate.

The bond always takes you in the end.

I close my eyes, trying to gather my thoughts. The memories flood me, cycling through like a macabre Network show. How many times have I stood here, staring down at the still body of a friend, feeling the void in our connection?

Twenty-seven, no, twenty-eight.

Twenty-eight riders I'd seen lay on this metal table. Twenty-eight souls departed this world while I remained. Angrily, I shove away the question that threatens to crawl into my skull, the question I have no answer to.

And probably never will.

When I open them again, I ask one attendant looking over their digital tablet who found him.

"He was in a car on his way back to the shuttle port, and Ben Livingston from maintenance and Brigid Corsair from public relations were with him."

Ben has worked here for years, but the name Brigid Corsair triggers something at the back of my mind. We'd had so many new faces come in from Meridian, and even in the few days they'd been here, and I hadn't learned all their names. Heath stiffens next to me, and I feel something tense, almost unease, filter to me.

"Ms. Corsair, do you know her?" I ask, glancing at him.

"I do," he replies, his voice tight. "I hired her at Meridian for PR. She was the one who saved the egg."

Ah, that's where I recognize the name. I'll have to make time to talk to her and thank her.

Save for the soft hum of the lights above, the room is quiet. I reach out and gently touch Kaeden's shoulder, a gesture of farewell. "May your burning end and your bond be freed."

Heath repeats the saying in a murmured whisper.

"He was too young," I say, the words feeling hollow.

Heath doesn't reply.

Taking a blanket from the foot of the table, I pull it up and over his head.

That's it. The last time anyone will ever see him.

The reality of Kaeden's death settles over us like a shroud as we leave the clinic.

"Want me to go with you?" Heath asks once we're in the hallway.

I shake my head. "Go tell the others and reserve the banquet room at Blink for his party."

Heath nods and, with a pat on my shoulder, turns and leaves.

Thoughts like swirling dark clouds, I head toward Sadie's office.

I wish I could say this is easier since I've done this before. Countless times, I've walked these hallways to break the news that someone's brother, son, or husband was dead — but it doesn't.

There's no good way to tell someone that their loved one is gone. That their life has been irrevocably changed. Sure, they've been prepared. Read the brochures and watched the videos on what to expect when your loved one is a rider, but none of it can really prepare you.

I reach her door and inhale deeply before knocking. After a moment, the door opens, and Sadie stands there, her face lighting up with a smile that quickly fades when she sees my expression.

"Marshal, what's wrong?" she asks, her voice a little breathless. I rarely step foot on the fourth floor and can already see the confusion swirling in her eyes.

"It's Kaeden," I begin.

She pales, her hand flying to her mouth. "No, no, no," she sobs. "God, no, please." She collapses onto the threshold.

"I'm so sorry." I kneel and place a hand on her shoulder. "He flared out. He's gone."

Sobs wracked her body as she rested her head against me. I hold her, trying to offer what little comfort I can.

"It wasn't enough time," she cries. "I want more. I need him. I —" her voice breaks off as sorrow clogs her throat.

Biting down hard on the inside of my cheek, I taste copper as she clings to me, her grief raw and unfiltered. We stay like that for some time until, eventually, I help her inside and sit her on the couch. I make her a cup of tea and bring it to her, which she tearfully accepts.

I tug a knitted blanket off the back of the couch and cover her shoulders.

Eyes red and swollen, she sniffs, holding a tissue to her nose. "What happens now?"

"We'll arrange for a proper farewell," I say gently. "And we'll support you in any way we can. Is there family or friends I can call for you?"

"My mother and sister live in Leviler." She reaches for the cup, and as she takes a shaky sip, I key in the shuttle request in my comm to bring her family here. Rules dictate visiting family and friends are allowed a one-week bereavement stay at the station, but I've never been one to be a strict enforcer of it so long as they don't turn into squatters.

"Thank you, Marshal."

She doesn't ask about herself remaining there. Since she works here, she'll have her room downgraded to a single but will remain at the station. If she weren't, she'd have one week to collect her belongings and leave.

Rider's death packages are quite generous, and most spouses are set for quite some time with no need for other employment.

Once she falls asleep on the couch, I leave Sadie's quarters, my heart feeling like it's pinned in a vice that won't release.

I'd silenced my comm when I'd been with Sadie, and checking it out now see three unread messages from Heath. Geminesta, Kaeden's mount, is not doing well.

I rush to the barn, meeting Dr. Gideon, who's already gone ahead and sedated him. The seal brown stallion's eyes are half-closed, and his head droops low.

We're not sure how druadans sense their rider's death, but it's likely from the absence of the bond, similar to the riders I've known who lost their stallions. A silence where there was once sound.

The rest of the day blurs by. I cancel practice and double-check that the novices are prepared for when Geminesta recovers and calls to one of them. A new bonding will likely take several weeks, though I've seen it happen in just days.

Heath must have told the others because every rider I pass radiates a quiet sadness, except the novices who buzz with nervous energy.

Nightshade's bite on my hand tingles, triggered by my

emotions. It happens so rarely that I almost don't notice it until I'm back alone inside my room.

I stare at the faint silver scar, tracing the crescent shape left by my stallion's teeth. Twelve years have passed since that day. Nearly triple what Kaeden got.

The cupboard door bangs as I open it, pulling down a bottle of rum. I fill a glass and drain it, savoring the delicious burn of the alcohol as it sears my throat.

A screeching alarm comes from my comm. I tap it on and an urgent message from Dr. Gideon in all red projects on the tiny screen.

> COME TO THE STABLES. THE EGG IS HATCHING.

Twenty-Five

BRIGID

Something is happening.
At first, I'd thought it was the lingering heartbreak from watching Kaeden die, but now I'm unsure.

There's something more. A current of underlying restless anxiety that I can't place.

Finally, alone, I lean back against the wall, letting out a long, shaky breath as the heaviness of everything that happened yesterday weighs down on me.

It'd been so good to see Laura and Vince until the jarring arrival of the police officers and the nightmarish drive to the shuttle.

Once again, I'm seething with anger at the protestors who'd selfishly blocked the road.

I'd barely recognized the Delford I knew, with tranquil parks and bustling sidewalks with people going about their day, shopping, working, or just enjoying the city.

Instead, Delford had felt like a tinderbox ready to erupt into flames of violence at any moment.

Pushing those haunting images aside, I move to my bathroom. I peel off my sweat-damp pajamas and let them fall to the floor. The scalding shower water pelts my skin like tiny bullets, but it can't erase the disturbing visions burned into my mind. The froth spilling from Kaeden's mouth. The whites of his eyes rolling back in agony. The memory of how he had looked at me with desperate confusion, mistaking me for his beloved wife, is seared into my soul.

No matter how long I stand under the hot water, I can't wash away that moment. I grab the bar of soap as tears flow down my cheeks, and I let them merge with the water. My heart aches for Sadie. Her future with Kaeden has been stolen from her, and I'm consumed with anger and resentment once again at the life these riders are forced to face.

Heath had heard from Marshal that I was with Kaeden when it happened. After my debrief with Lugsen last night, he pulled me aside. He was gentle, offering to set me up with a grief counselor if I wanted. I probably should talk to someone, but if I'm going to be around these riders and live this life at these stations, I need to toughen up. Their short lifespans are just part of the deal. Still, it was sweet of Heath to check-in.

After drying off, I pull on one of my favorite wool sweaters and jeans. The familiar fabric brushes my bare arms as I slip it over my head.

I'm tempted to dive into work early. God knows I have plenty to catch up on since my day off, and perhaps the mundane will help quiet the noise. I start by reviewing memos from the station, scrolling through mock-up photos for the network website, and plans for the balcony seating renovations next season. A half-hour passes, and I rub my forehead as the words and images begin to blur together meaninglessly.

All of a sudden, my whole body shudders hard as an intense, electrifying awareness sparks through my nerves. I squeeze my eyes shut as a downpour of overlapping voices and scattered phrases tangle like dense brambles in my head. Sight, smell, sound, taste, every sense is bombarded as if I'd been shoved into one of the funhouses at a carnival.

They're relentless.

Chest heaving, I resist the mental assault.

Go to the barn.

The urge takes root rapidly, an undeniable compulsion winding through me with chilling power. Just like at Meridian, when I'd been drawn to the stables, but even stronger this time - a ferocious magnetic force violently pulling me like a black hole's gravitational grip.

Sweat beads on my skin as I pant, my muscles instinctively tensing against the summons. With shaking hands, I grab my comm and punch in Carter's number.

"Where are you?" I rasp out desperately. I brace myself, body vibrating with rising panic for which there was no origin.

Carter's face appears on the screen. "In the barracks." His lips curve into a cheeky grin. "Do you want me to bring you breakfast?"

"No. I need to get to the barn. I know I'm not allowed, but can you meet me anyway?"

His face sobers. "Meet me at the South door."

I slip on my boots and race to the door, the impulse growing more intense even as part of me recoils in fear.

What is happening to me? Am I losing my mind? The urges feel so viscerally real yet make no rational sense.

As I rush to the barn, every cell in my body is screaming for me to run faster.

Twenty-Six

ORIANA

Everything is so bright.
   Is it always this bright? And louddddd. Why is it so LOUD?
I am hungry. Why is no one bringing me something to eat?
I can't see. I can't hear over all this noise.
Where is my warrior? I smell her. I know she's here...
There she is.

Twenty-Seven

BRIGID

Six days and four hours after it first cracked, the egg finally splits in half.

When I started looking for my sister, never in a million years could I have imagined everything that happened since. All of it has led to this moment, this chance to witness history being reborn.

Carter had met me at the side entrance, and I'd hidden in one of my hooded sweatshirts as he'd ushered me into the barn like smuggled cargo.

Riders were gathered in the aisleway, and I spotted Heath and Logan on the far end.

Marshal stood near the stall's entrance and gave us a disapproving frown as we tiptoed into the barn. However, the excitement of the event is too much as he returns his attention to the inside of the stall, clearly letting the indiscretion slide.

I breathe a relieved sigh and shuffle myself into the group. I perch on my toes, trying to get a better look. Why did all the riders have to be so freaking tall?

I can just make out the edge of the egg and let out a soft gasp as the shell falls to the ground. Iridescent but clear liquid spills onto the straw, unlike the dark, inky fluid that oozed from the one that hadn't made it after the truck flipped.

Maybe the other egg had been dead all along, the embryo never developing, and rotted centuries ago. I take a small comfort in the thought, reassuring myself that the life I didn't save was never really there to begin with.

The cracking shell reveals two small fluffy ears and a delicate body, leaving everyone in silent awe. I'd never seen a newborn druadan before, but since it'd started cracking, I admit I'd daydreamed more than once when I should've been paying attention during a staff meeting, imagining what it'd look like. Would it be tiny? Would its coat be solid colored or spotted? What would the nubs on its face look like? Well-defined like Shadowmane's or flatter like Embers.

However, not even my wildest fantasies could've prepared me for this.

The foal's fur is a beautiful light golden shade, and its eyes are violet like the horizon just before sunset.

It's breathtaking.

Minutes old, the druadan struggles to stand on its spindly legs, wobbling as it attempts to find its footing. After a few adorably shaky steps, the foal finds balance and lifts its head high. I marvel at its grace and poise, especially for such a young creature. It pauses as if taking in its new surroundings for the first time. Its large eyes dart around, curious and alert, taking in the crowd of onlookers.

Suddenly, it lets out a gentle whinny, a high-pitched call that seems to reverberate through the air as if a declaration of its arrival. I feel a surge of protectiveness wash over me. This tiny, impossible creature is here.

The other druadans in the barn respond to the call with snorts and stomps in their stalls. The foal stands its ground, unafraid, its gaze steady and unwavering even as the air hums with the voices of the neighboring stallions

A novice hands Dr. Gideon a plastic shipping crate, and he moves from where he's in the corner, carefully collecting the broken shell pieces. "We'll get these shipped to the breeding lab in Pyrnia," he says to whoever is listening. "They'll be eager to analyze the membrane for any genetic anomalies or defects, as well as confirm the bloodline."

Dr. Gideon maneuvers closer to the foal and slowly examines it. A confused smile spreads on his face. "Well, I'll be damned." He shakes his head, and a dry laugh escapes him. "It's a female."

Audible gasps fill the space, and I blink in surprise, wondering if I'd misheard him. I must not be the only one because Marshal says, "There must be a mistake. Check again, Gideon."

Dr. Gideon sighs and rests his hands on his thighs. "Don't believe me? Fine. Check it yourself."

Marshal confidently steps into the stall. As he squats down, studying the druadan, she bats her long white eyelashes and swivels her fuzzy ears toward him.

Several riders, including Carter, laugh. "Confused which end there, Marshal?"

Marshal grumbles and gets to his feet. Everyone falls silent, all eyes fixed on him and the baby druadan. "He's right. This little one is a female. A druanera."

Druanera.

The word concretes itself in my mind.

In my years of history classes, I'd never come across it before. The exhilarating tingle of newfound knowledge lights a spark in me. Pages and pages of notes, tests, and Network programs, and still, there remained parts of Venovia's past I didn't know about. This was why I'd pursued history, even when Sharice had belittled me and encouraged me otherwise.

A murmur of surprise ripples through the group. As the others gather around the foal, inspecting it with a mixture of awe and uncertainty, I push my way closer.

"It's a miracle this thing even hatched," someone says.

"Indeed," Gideon says. "It goes against everything we know about druadan egg viability."

The foal, with its violet-colored eyes and long, envy-inducing lashes, peers at me from behind the bars. The breath whooshes from my lungs.

As impossible as it sounds, there's a fleeting glimmer of recognition.

I grip the bars, overcome by the desire to trade places with Marshal and run my hands over her fur. "She's beautiful," I murmur to no one in particular.

"You've got your work cut out for you," Heath says by my shoulder.

I shoot him a sideways look, and he nods to the foal. "Now she's born, we'll need to work extra hard keeping this quiet. Circuit will know soon enough, but we have to control this before it gets out to the public."

I nod in agreement before, out of nowhere, I'm hit with a wave of exhaustion. I cover my mouth, yawning. I thought I'd slept fine last night, but maybe I was coming down with something? Squinting through half-closed lids, I catch the briefest glimpse of ribbons of light swirling in the stall. I rub my eyes, and when I open them, they're gone, just motes of dust drifting above the foal, nuzzling one of the feed bowls.

Maybe staring at my comm all day had damaged my retinas.

I make a mental note to get my eyes checked.

"Do we get to name her?" I ask.

Marshal stands up and places his hands on his hips, staring down at her. "Druadans are named after their lineage. Since this one descends from the Solara line, we'll have to check the records, but it'll be named something connected to that."

A soft buzz vibrates through the air, and all the riders look down the hall to their stallions. I feel the hum, too, deep in my bones. "What is it? What are they saying?"

Heath exchanges a look with Carter and Logan before settling his brown eyes on me. "Apparently, she's named herself?" he says, voice edged with disbelief. "Shadowmane says they're all saying the same thing. Oriana. Her name is Oriana."

Twenty-Eight

HEATH

"What the hell is the meaning of this?" Deputy Lugsen barks, causing everyone gathered around the stall to jump.

My head swivels as the rest of the riders scurry to the side, revealing a very red-faced and very angry Deputy Lugsen clutching a towel around his waist.

He pins a glare on one of Blackhawk's riders. "Taylor, I had strict orders for you to find me when the egg hatched, and yet here, I see the lot of you gathered around like it topless night at Mickey's."

Taylor blanches, adjusting the square-framed glasses on his nose. "Sorry, sir, you were in the shower, so I thought I'd wait—"

"You thought wrong." He adjusts his towel under his rotund belly and then looks at Brigid. "You. General staff can't be down here. Who let you down here?"

Carter steps forward. "I invited her, sir."

"James? I should have known." He grumbles. "Please see that she returns to her quarters, and we'll discuss your punishment later."

"Sir, with all due respect," I say before I can stop myself. "This foal wouldn't be here if it weren't for her."

Lugsen adjusts the towel on his hips. "Oh, I'm well aware. However, now is not the time to bend the rules. Having non-riders in the barn poses any number of safety risks, and I won't have a newborn druadan endangered because of our failure to abide by the rules."

"But Oriana isn't a druadan," Brigid blurts. "She's a *druanera*."

Lugsen's eyes widen, letting the mask slip briefly until he regains his composure. For a long moment, he says nothing as every single pair of eyes watches him. Finally, he clears his throat and tightens the towel, straining under his fingers.

"Then this is all the more reason why you should not be here. Every rider at my station has completed the certified safety classes for handling druadans. You have no formal training and therefore remain a liability not only to yourself but to this foal's wellbeing."

"By what? Standing here?"

"You're being unreasonable, Miss Corsair. And if you continue this outburst, I will have no choice but to call security, and I guarantee that will put your employment here in jeopardy."

Brigid's eyes flicker with defiance. I can see she's ready to argue, but Lugsen's stare is unyielding. Even in just a towel, his twenty years of experience give him an undeniable air of authority.

I hold my breath, half-expecting her to continue, but instead, she shakes her head. "Fine. Screw you and your outdated traditions." She turns and shoves her way through the cluster of people.

Carter starts after her, but I stop him with a firm hand on his shoulder. "Let her go," I tell him.

"Now," Lugsen says, a little calmer. "Party is over. All of you have drills or chores to get to, so let Dr. Gideon continue his work." The group of riders disbands, and Carter and I move to where Logan reclines with a foot up against a stall where he'd watched the whole scene play out.

"I thought Blondie was about to have a throw down with ol' Lugsen," Logan comments.

"It was my fault," Carter says. "When she called me, I should have told her no."

"What's done is done," I say, trying to sound neutral as a small pang of jealousy burns my chest. It was a bold move—no doubt about that but it'd also been foolish. It'd nearly cost her a job. But Carter never thought about stuff like that. Never thought ahead.

Still, it'd been Carter she trusted enough to sneak her into the barn.

I glance at Carter, who's still looking guilty, his eyes avoiding mine. He's got that easy way about him, the kind that draws people in and makes them feel comfortable. It's no wonder she trusts him.

I wish she saw me that way, more than just her boss, more than the guy enforcing the rules. But that's the problem, isn't it? The stigma of being her superior is a wall that's hard to tear down, even if, on paper, I'm not the manager anymore.

Logan slaps Carter on the back. "Could've been worse. At least Lugsen kept his towel on."

As if hearing his name, Lugsen hobbles over to us. "I'm going to get dressed, god dammit, and then I want you three in my office."

He exchanges a few words with Marshal, then disappears out of the barn.

Marshal joins us as we head to his office, that's situated on the far side of the rider's mess hall. The space shares a doorway with his small, one-bedroom apartment. He was married once, but his wife caught pneumonia and never recovered, dying ten years ago, leaving him alone with no children. His job was all he had now, and the encroaching retirement.

Inside, Lugsen, now dressed, gestures for us to sit. "A druanera." He curses under his breath. "Tides all mighty. As if I didn't have to deal with enough." He sighs into his chair behind the desk. "I've notified Fiaro, but he's held up in the Village, so we can't expect him until later. Until then, protocol dictates I inform the other station managers; however, since this egg came from Meridian," he says, looking at me. "I'll give you the opportunity to have a say in what happens next after we discuss what risk this newborn will pose for Blackhawk. There are reasons stations take yearlings, and a newborn could aggravate the stallions."

Marshal leans forward. "I'll be honest, sir. I've felt only excitement from Nightshade."

"Shadowmane as well," I add.

Lugsen laces his fingers on his protruding belly. "Good. Let me know if anything changes."

"I trust Dr. Gideon," I say, "and would like to be looped in with any updates regarding the foal."

Lugsen nods. "I agree. This is unfamiliar territory, riders, and I fear we will have to take this day by day as the foal grows."

"And she bonds with a rider," Logan finishes for him.

Lugsen's nostrils flare as he glares at Logan standing in the corner. "Perhaps. But that is a very distant problem, I assure you."

"Is it?" Logan presses as tension thickens the stale air.

"It is no longer up for discussion. Moving on." His eyes scan the room, his expression hardening. "Now, beyond our blonde friend being down here, I would like to keep the general staff's knowledge to a minimum." He swivels his gaze on Carter. "I never want to see her down here again without my explicit permission. Are we clear?"

"Yes, sir," Carter responds.

Lugsen stands, dismissing us. "I believe you have a feed delivery that needs unloaded, McCelroy."

We vacate Lugsen's office and make our way to the barracks to change into our riding clothes while Logan continues to the barn.

"Lugsen might not want to talk about it," Carter says, taking out his riding pants and long sleeve shirt. "but it's what everyone is thinking, right? How fast she'll grow and whether she'll ever bond with a rider?"

"Every druadan is capable of bonding," Marshal says as we halt at our bunks. He's already changed into his riding gear but sits on an empty bed to finish lacing his boots.

"Capable, yes," I say, "but initiating a bonding is something entirely else. Not a year passes that we haven't had at least one stallion refuse to bond."

Marshal murmurs in agreement.

"So, what do you suggest we do?" Carter says.

Marshal takes a helmet from the stack on the shelf. "Learn more. Lugsen has a full plate to begin with, so if we want to find out more about druanera and how they bond, it'll be up to us. You all know we have one hell of a log archive in the basement. If there's anything about druanera growing or bonding, it'd be there."

"Reading?" Carter nods his chin in my direction. "Looks like you're up, Lockwood."

I scrub my hand over my face, irritated by the casual way Carter assigns the task to me as if it's a given. Unfortunately, he's not wrong. I do enjoy reading, and if someone's going to dig through those archives, it might as well be me. At least then, I'll know it'll be thorough and done right. No cut corners.

I take a breath, forcing the annoyance to dissipate. "Sure, why not," I say, keeping my tone even. "I'll handle it."

Marshal tosses the helmet from one hand to the other. "Good. The more information we have, the better."

I pull on my black riding pants with the carbon fiber shell, securing the knee-high leather boots. The black polo shirt and protective vest fit snugly, and I adjust the black helmet and gloves before leaving to get Shadowmane.

Back in the barn, a novice had already saddled my gray stallion, and I led him to the practice arena, trying to focus on the patterns, but my mind kept drifting back to the foal.

If this were my station, I would've postponed practice. Everyone will be distracted today, including the stallions. But it's not my station, and I'm just another rider.

"Let's go, boy," I murmur, patting Shadowmane's neck and spurring him forward.

Once I've finished drills for the day, hit the gym, and eaten lunch, I end up wandering the archives. I trace my finger along the spines of books, savoring the stillness and scent of ancient parchment.

Wide blue eyes and silver hair invade my thoughts. Days

had passed since our kiss, and yet I could so readily recall the way she'd tasted, the softness of her mouth against mine...

I linger in front of an especially thick volume discussing west coast geologic surveys and an idea seizes me. Quickly, I slide it back on the shelf and retreat from the library. Resolve burns in my gut, fueling each step closer to her room.

My hand hovers over the panel for a moment before knocking.

"Oh, Heath," Brigid says when she answers a minute later. Her eyes widen slightly, and she looks flustered. "Is everything all right?"

She's wearing a soft white robe that falls just above her knees. Her hair is down, flowing over like ashen waves around her shoulders.

"Apologies, Ms. Corsair, I see I am interrupting your—" I start to back away.

She reaches out, and her fingers encircle my wrist. "No, no. Yeah, I was going to take a bath, but it can wait."

"I wouldn't want to intrude on your evening."

She rolls her eyes. "Seriously, Heath. Come in."

Reluctantly, I follow her into the room and take a seat on the couch as she disappears into her bathroom. I hear her turn off the running water.

Brigid emerges, still in her robe and barefoot. Her long, slender legs snag my attention, and I dig my nails into the arm of the chair. My word, she's a gorgeous creature. "You want tea or something?" she asks, lingering by the kitchen island.

"Yes," I croak. "Tea would be great."

She fills the kettle with water before plugging it in.

"I should start by apologizing for Lugsen, and I'm sorry you had to go through that."

Brigid shakes her head as she takes tea from the jar. "Honestly? I'm over it. I get he was just doing his job and trying to make Oriana safe." After pouring two mugs, she brings them over and hands one to me before taking a seat on the sofa. She crosses her legs, and the hem of her robe rides up, exposing her thigh.

She notices my stare and gently adjusts it. "Speaking of which, how is she doing?"

I shift my gaze back to hers. "Good, last I heard. She's hitting the milestones she should have, and Dr. Gideon is pleased with her development."

There's a long pause as we both sip our tea. It's a floral one I've never had before, with rose hips and violets.

"So," she says, setting her mug down. "What brings you by? Is everything all right?"

"In truth, I came to ask you to help me with something, Ms. Corsair."

She shrugs her shoulders. "Anything."

The way she says it, with such quiet certainty, stirs something deep inside me—something I hadn't expected, hadn't prepared for.

It's not just the word, but the way she looks at me, her blue eyes steady, as if she means it with every fiber of her being. The epiphany shudders the foundations I'd carefully constructed, and my hand tightens on the chair.

I've built my life around discipline, around keeping everything in check—emotions, thoughts, desires—all boxed away, neat and orderly. But now, with just one word, she's blown it all apart.

I swallow, suddenly aware of how close we are and the lavender scent drifting from her. "I...I wanted to ask you to join me in researching the druanera. With your history background, I think you'd be an invaluable asset."

Her pale eyebrows lift an inch higher. "You're serious?"

I nod. "Indeed. In fact, I'm free now if you'd care to join me?"

Brigid cocks her head to the side. "Tonight? Now?"

A small laugh rumbles in my chest. "Yes."

Her eyes light up with elation, but then she quickly tries to subdue it by straightening her face. "Oh, okay. Uh, of course. Let me get dressed."

I stand outside Brigid's room, listening to the faint rustling of fabric as she changes. My heart beats a little faster, a mix of anticipation and something else I can't quite name. I'd known about Blackhawk's archives but had never had time to explore them, and the idea of diving into the texts excites me more than I care to admit. But there's more to it than just the prospect of research making my heartbeat quicken.

It's the thought of spending time with her. Alone.

No one would doubt my decision to bring her on board. Brigid's history degree makes her the perfect partner for this task. She'll see connections I might miss, ask the right questions, and offer a unique perspective.

It's both logical and wise.

And feels like a rare and unexpected gift.

Just the two of us working side by side as we sift through the texts stirs something in me. I'm not sure I want to fight.

When she finally emerges, she's wearing a burgundy sweater dress with black buttons on the shoulders.

Together, we exit her bedroom, and I lead her down to the first floor's west wing, past the amphitheater, where sometimes they'll hold larger meetings or the occasional award ceremony. The archives are tucked away at the end of the hall, guarded by an elderly Asian man at a desk. "Yuto," I nod in greeting.

He makes us sign in, his weathered hands pushing the

ledger towards us. "I can guide you to what you're looking for," he offers.

Before I can respond, Brigid blurts out, "Oldest books first." Her eagerness is contagious, and I can't help but smile.

Yuto leads us into the library proper, a vast room filled with shelves and boxes. "Some were sent from other stations that shut down," he explains, gesturing to a stack of crates. "Others from antique auctions. I've been trying to catalog them all, but..." He trails off with a rueful shrug.

We start our research, pulling out a book on Blackhawk's first manager. Brigid finds another on druadan biology, though it's thin and seems to focus more on horse evolution and shared traits for medical purposes.

As we settle at a table, a comfortable silence falls between us. And I consider how different this is from Jess. She'd be complaining about the quiet, insisting we go out to a restaurant or go shopping. But here, with Brigid, the silence feels natural, peaceful even.

My mind drifts back to my days at Haverstone Prep before the Vanguard. While the other boys were out playing rugby or tennis, I was always studying, losing myself in books and research. My father had called me a 'loner' to my mom behind my back, and the disappointment had only grown further when she'd learned she couldn't have any more children.

I was it. My father's legacy would be sent to Vanguard.

"I keep forgetting to ask you, how are your parents?" Brigid says.

"They're well. Shaken like most, but resilient."

"Do they have any other family to stay with? Brothers, sisters?"

I shake my head. "No. I'm an only child."

"That had to have been lonely?"

"It was, I suppose, but I didn't know anything different."

And after I went to Vanguard, I considered Logan and Carter my brothers.

"I used to be close with Sharice when I was younger." She twists her head sideways to look at me while resting her hands on her knees. "But after I was sent to private school, it was like a crack formed between us, and we were never able to patch it. Eventually, our paths just went different ways."

I watch her from across the table. "I'm not saying I'm happy your sister chose the life she did, but if there's one good thing that came from it, it's you ending up in my office that day for an interview."

She sighs, offering me a warm smile. "I sure nailed it too, didn't I?"

"The applicant pool was limited," I tease.

She throws her head back, her laughter ringing out like the purest melody, and in that moment, she's more than just beautiful—she's breathtaking. The way her eyes light up, the way her whole face transforms, glowing with unrestrained joy. It's as if the world pauses, holding its breath to savor the sight.

The sound stirs my soul, so much so it's almost painful. Every ounce of my will is focused on staying in my seat, on resisting the overpowering urge to climb over the table, take her in my arms, and feel her laughter reverberate through me as I kiss her.

Finally, her laughter subsides, and she wipes a tear from her eyes. "You really know how to charm a girl, don't you?"

Our eyes meet, and a charge forms in the air.

Across the table, my gaze burns into hers. Her smile falters and then fades. The playfulness is gone, replaced by something that's been building between us, unspoken but undeniable.

"Heath," she breathes my name as if she's afraid saying it aloud might shatter the fragile moment we're sharing.

I lean in, my chest bumping against the edge of the table,

every muscle in my body drawn toward her. Just this moment, raw and real, and the overwhelming realization that whatever this is, it's not something I can ignore anymore.

Her eyes flicker down to my lips for the briefest second before returning to my eyes, and I know she feels it, too. The pull, the inevitability of what's happening between us. It's in the way her hand trembles as she lowers it from her face, in the way her lips part as if she's about to say something.

"Who wants hot chocolate?" Yuto's voice breaks the moment, materializing from the stacks with a tray of steaming mugs.

We both jump, the charged air between us snapping apart. My jaw tightens, irritation flaring. For a second, I wish I had Logan's lack of restraint—could just tell him to fuck off—but years of etiquette training won't let me. I swallow the words, forcing a tight smile. Brigid's cheeks flush, and she looks away, embarrassed, as the moment slips out of reach.

"Uh, me, please," Brigid says hurriedly, her eyes darting from mine as she stands.

"I had a feeling you might be thirsty," he says as he hands her a mug. Brigid's eyes light up, and she thanks him profusely. As he leaves, she eagerly takes one of the mugs and holds it up in a mock toast before sipping it.

"*Real* chocolate," she coos. "You riders have no idea how good you have it."

I take the other one and wrap my hands around the warm mug, inhaling the rich aroma. "Believe me, we do." Chocolate wasn't only expensive, it was extremely seasonal. Even growing up, with access to all the grocers, my family had reserved it only for special occasions.

THE IDEA OF SPENDING MORE EVENINGS LIKE THIS FILLS ME WITH SUCH contentment I'm at a loss as to how to absorb it. It's like rediscovering a part of myself I'd forgotten or perhaps never fully appreciated. Unscheduled time had been a luxury when I'd been station manager, and now I had an abundance of it.

"Find anything interesting?" I ask, blowing on the steaming mug.

Brigid licks the chocolate off her lips, and yet some remains on her cheek.

I'm overcome by the urge, and without thinking, I lean over and wipe it away with my thumb. She giggles, a soft, melodious sound in the room's stillness. "Thanks."

The feel of her soft skin, coupled with the intensity in her eyes, makes my breath quicken, and the crotch of my pants tighten.

"Maybe," she says, answering my question. "Look at this..." She slides the book over.

"It's a collection of journals, memoirs really from riders during the peak of the war. The first one is dated 352 AR, which is like thirty years before the gas bombs were dropped."

My eyes scan the handwritten pages so thin they're almost like tissue paper. With exceedingly delicate care, I turn to the next entry. I recognize none of the names of the riders but catch bits of words like 'phasing' or bloodlines, like Inferno and Ghost.

"From what I've found, it's about riding drills, mystyl battle tactics which could be handy, and weapon care." She pauses, ensuring I have her full attention. "But here's the interesting part: I'm only halfway through, but there's no mention of flaring anywhere."

I squint at her. "What? That can't be right?"

She bobs her head. "And there's no mention of brimming, either. Odd, right?"

"Very." I scratch the side of my chin, re-reading the passages on the page. She is right. Not once is the word brimming or flaring, nor are symptoms written anywhere.

"Perhaps they used another word for it?" I suggest.

She nods. "Maybe?" She reaches back, sliding the book to her. "I'll keep reading, just thought you'd like to know."

"Indeed. You have a keen eye."

"Well, if you haven't noticed already," she says, puffing up her chest. "I've been told I'm an excellent student."

"I can see that," I say, a smile tugging at the corner of my mouth.

The books stack up beside us as we continue to dig through them. When Yuto has retrieved our empty cups, Brigid leans back and yawns.

"I need a break." She stretches her arms and stands. "So, tell me, what do you do for fun?"

I close the book I'm reading about druadan saddle making. "Fun?"

"Yeah? You know, *fun*?"

"What are we doing right now?"

She laughs. "Okay, besides this. You know things that *don't* involve riding or the station?"

"You've been spending too much time with Carter."

The tops of her cheeks turn a lovely rosy pink. "Maybe, but I already know what he does for fun. I'm asking *you*."

I purse my lips in thought. "I don't have a lot of free time for fun, but I do like reading and listening to jazz."

"Really? Who's your favorite artist?"

"Etta Langston. Jess dislikes them, says they're too slow, and puts her to sleep."

"I've never heard of them. Maybe you could show me some recordings sometime?"

"I'd like that," I reply.

She beams as if I'd just promised her a membership to Barnaby's on 9th. I rise from my chair and move closer to her. "I've been thinking about that night at Meridian."

"And?" she says timidly.

"And," I say, taking her hands in mine, and, to my delight, she doesn't flinch from the touch. "And *this* has never happened to me before, not with Jess, not with anyone. And until now, I didn't think it ever would."

"What are you saying?" she breathes.

I look down at our joined hands, feeling a surge of electricity pass between us at her touch. "My life was orderly. Perfect. Everything laid out and planned. I knew my future. My purpose. But *now*... now I know nothing."

"Heath, I...I don't understand. You and Jess–"

"On a break."

"But you're living together?"

"It's all for show."

"And the wedding?"

"Not going to happen." I pause, searching her eyes. "There are reasons, but I promise you." I inch closer. "I am all yours."

"What about Carter?" she asks.

"I don't care. You're my ruin. You're my undoing. I'll gladly share you if it means you're mine, too."

Her mouth falls open, blue eyes searching mine for the truth I know is there. "Heath," she whispers my name like a prayer.

"I...I want you, Brigid. No words could ever capture my need for you. It is beyond reason or restraint. You are all I crave. Ever since that night, you're all I think about. I want you to be mine. Ours."

Before she can answer, I'm kissing her like a man starved. I've never tasted anything so sweet, so delicious. Her rear collides with the desk, and it slides back, dragging on the floor with a loud screech.

She pulls back from the kiss. "Shhh," she whispers, pressing a finger to her lips. "This is a *library*."

"I don't want to be quiet."

She reaches up, slipping her fingers into the hair at the nape of my neck. I lay her back on the table, positioning myself between her legs, which she willingly parts for me. My erection digs so hard into my pants that I swear it's going to rip the seams. As I rub it against her, I reach down, caressing the inside of her thigh, and find she's not wearing underwear.

"Ms. Corsair," I growl, as I'm instantly fully aroused and a surge of desire floods my veins.

"Sorry," she murmurs. "It's laundry day."

I stiffen and narrow my eyes at the illustration that caught my attention. "It can't be."

"What?" she says, confusion clouding her blue eyes.

"This picture...it's you."

She pivots in my arms to look up at the full-page color illustration in the book that had fallen open. A beautiful woman with long, pale blonde hair cascading over her shoulders peers up from the pages, her fierce blue-eyed gaze commanding attention. But the most shocking detail isn't her beauty or the sky-blue rider's jacket with gold buttons—it's that she sits astride a pristine white druadan, its golden eyes gleaming.

"You," the words leave me, "She looks like you."

Twenty-Nine

BRIGID

Why is there a picture of a woman who looks like me in an old book? And more than that—how is she riding a druadan?

My mind stumbles, still tangled in the lingering heat of the moment with Heath. The sudden shift jars me, and I press a hand to my forehead, trying to shake off the haze and focus. Memories of those few art classes I took in college flicker weakly, but they don't explain what I'm seeing.

Heath appears just as confused as I am. They said antique stores shipped books here. Perhaps this is a forgery? A book made to look old, but it really wasn't. Someone had found out we were going to be down here and slipped a modified photo of me in it as a prank or hazing ritual.

I squint, trying to notice the small details.

Okay, so she isn't me. Not exactly. Her nose is rounder, and her eyes are darker than my teal blue.

But her hair is the same ashy-gray blonde as mine. Of course, she could've dyed it, but that wouldn't explain the rest. The lift of her eyes and the shape of her chin, too, was the same.

I look at the artist's signature in the corner.

L. Moacher

I key in the name on my portable computer, and a single hit appears.

"Lionel Moacher," I read aloud as Heath continues to study the painting, "was born around 2410 PF and was a member of a freelance artist group. He also taught art classes at the Levilier recreation center until his disappearance in 2448."

Heath turns at that. "Disappearance?"

I gesture to the computer. "That's what it says. It goes on to say they never found him but found what they believed to be his personal ID, coat, and painting kit near the perimeter of one of the tox zones."

"He died during the bombings."

"That's their conclusion."

"So, how did this painting survive?"

"No idea."

Heath rubs his chin. "Make a note of that name. I have some friends in the antique art community, I can ask."

I straighten and gaze up at him. "Heath, I—"

But before I can finish, he retreats into the stacks of books, murmuring something about mystyl biology.

My hand goes to my lips, still burning from our passionate kiss. I guess we're not going to discuss how he'd confessed his feelings for me.

I'd been so surprised I'd barely had time to respond before he saw the picture of the woman rider who looked like me.

Now, it's like his emotional wall is back up, shutting me out again.

Maybe this was how it was going to be with us.

This tango of desire and restraint.

I twist my fingers together. I care about him deeply, but until he got over whatever *this* was, which didn't take a leap to guess it involved his engagement, I'd have to make peace with the whiplash.

Minutes later, he emerges from the bookshelves with three more thick, linen-bound books on biology, including one related to post-rise marine life and the evolution of certain species in the warmer oceans.

He sets the book on the table and flips it open. A small round metal disk slips loose from the pages.

"Hell yeah," I exclaim. "They don't make these anymore."

Heath nods. "I'll ask Yuto if they have a disk reader somewhere in storage that still works."

He strides away, leaving me alone to skim through some of the driest texts on Uncy'lia archeology sites. And I should know since I'd read some in college that doctors could've prescribed to help people with sleep disorders.

I know all of this already. The pictographs, the caves, and the shells of metal buildings are now infested with birds and flowering vines. I'd visited them many times as a child on field trips for school.

My favorite had been the boat ride out to the monument of rusted metal that had once been a mile-long highway lined with antique vehicles. You can barely tell what they are anymore, but they have artists reimagine what it had looked like. Thousands of people were trapped in their vehicles as they tried to flee.

But the over-saturated ground had collapsed, and hundreds of cars had plunged into the sinkhole. Within seconds, the water had filled in, drowning all of them. The shifting currents had left the water shallower, and the rusted shells were like carcasses under the glass-bottom boat. One girl had even cried when a boy joked he could see the skeleton of a dead person still seated in there.

It had been fascinating and haunting, and I'm sure attributed to my pursuit of a history degree.

However, this book reads like a guide to assembling a toilet.

I flip to the front to determine which author I'll vow never to read again when Heath returns carrying a metal box.

"Yuto told me it's a digital record from before the bombs." He sets the box in front of me and hits the triangle to play. My heartbeat quickens as holograms of mystyl appear, hovering an inch above the screen.

A disembodied male voice says: "The mystyl is a type of cephalopod, similar to squids. Being nocturnal, they seek moist, dark places and avoid heat and direct sunlight. They are experts at camouflage, but their numbers are their greatest strength, and they can easily overwhelm creatures many times their size. A translucent skin reveals their organs and circulatory system.

While unsure of the origin, they appeared shortly after the rising of the seas. Some scientists believe they were microorganisms far below the surface of the ocean and then, with the warming of the planet, mutated into larger creatures that could thrive on the land. Others hypothesize they were of an alien origin that traveled on a meteor that crashed into the ocean. However, to date, no mystyl has ever been found in aquatic areas. Although they can swim, it does not appear that they need to be near water to reproduce or to eat. When genetic mapping was performed, a fascinating discovery was made — " The hologram freezes, and the narrator's abruptly cut off.

We stare at the hologram showing strands of DNA. My mind spins with what it could mean, what discovery lay just out of reach. "You've got to be kidding me," I stammer. Frustration bubbles up, hot and sharp. I yank open the player and pull out the disc, turning it over to inspect the damage. A jagged scratch runs across the bottom third. Of course. I curse under my breath.

"Damn," Heath says. "That was still a good find and tells me there might be more like it here." He rests a hand on my shoulder. "Why don't we go for a walk and take a break?"

I huff a sigh, causing the loose strands of hair near my face to flutter. "All right."

"I passed something I think you'll like when I went to get the disk reader." I tilt my head to the side. "More books?"

"Better."

I laugh. "What can be better than books?"

Heath's brown eyes brighten, and he smiles that perfect smile of his. My mind goes blank.

Holy shit, was he handsome when he was happy.

"Come on," he says, in that gentle way he'd spoken to me when he'd given me a tour during my interview. Unlike before, he uses his hand to guide my arm, and as soon as his fingers touch my skin, a tingling sensation spreads, creating a wave of goosebumps.

Carter's touch does this too, a spark that ignites a fire deep inside me — but Heath's touch is so... unexpected. My heart stutters, unsure how to process the sensation. It's disorienting. I glance at the side of his face, searching his face for any indication he felt it too, but per usual, Mr. Show No Emotion, gives nothing away. His eyes remain directly ahead as he guides me away from the table and between the bookcases.

But instead of taking a right to the exit and Yuto's desk, we go left. Under my shoes, the floor changes from a dark gray stone to a mosaic tile. The intricate swirling design decorates the ground, and my eyes trace the patterns. Heath nudges me gently, and as my gaze drifts up, the sight causes my jaw to drop.

Stretching as far as the eye can see, dark wooden bookshelves line the walls of a massive arched hallway built underground. Thick beams, resembling entire tree trunks, support the ceiling.

Dust particles dance in the beams of light emanating from electrical sconces adjacent to each bookshelf, reminding me of the evening walks back from the DU library in winter under street lights while snowflakes drifted down and coated the ground. And while the floor here is rectangular granite tiles, it is nearly as cold as those late-night walks through campus. Busts of riders sitting atop their mounts flanked the walls. Each is captured in a dramatic pose, rearing or prancing, with arched necks and hooves raised as if they could trot right off their marble podiums.

I pause to read the names as if I would recognize any. My knowledge of famous riders extends only to the limit of my life span and the names that cross Network news.

Every so often, there are exposés on novices from well-known families who have bonded or riders who have been selected for that year's exhibition first string lineup. Images abound of riders dining at cafes. Riders shopping in designer clothing stores. Or riders lounging on the south coastline, chiseled abs and rugged good looks on full display, and always with one or two leggy models in bikinis tanning next to them.

Heath gestures to one further ahead. It's darker than the

others, with gold and brown veins lacing through the man's face and the horse's body. The druadans all look the same except this one. It's different in that the stallion's mane reaches past his shoulder and has a braided tail.

"Joaquin and Twilight," Heath tells me. "He's one of Shadowmane's ancestors. They named a maneuver after him, called it the 'Twilight breach.' It's hard to explain. When they open up training again for staff to watch, I'll show you. The Shade line is exceptionally good at it."

And there it is. Another tiny morsel of druadan lore he so casually drops. Since starting at a station, I'd learned of the eight original stallions and their lineages, but only recently had I discovered each had a special knack for maneuvers. Some were faster, some stronger, some could phase easier, others were overall just more graceful.

"Speaking of training," I ask. "how is it going?"

"There's been some growing pains, " he says. "Chief Lugsen is strict and has tightened the schedule, but he's fair. I assume his grip will loosen before long once the hierarchy is established."

He says hierarchy like they're a bunch of wolves instead of men. I'd seen the other riders limping through the halls, sporting black eyes, so it was clear to me that the "growing pains, as Heath had referred to them, were far more brutal than that. I'm thankful I didn't have to be in the barracks with them.

"I'd heard there'd been a few disagreements," I say, "Marshal said they were having to put more limitations on leisure time and enlisted more security to patrol the gym and barracks."

Heath leans back and rubs the back of his neck. "Combining this many riders in the off-season was a foolish idea, and I'd foreseen there would be adjustments. I'm managing Meridian's riders, and if Lugsen and Marshal can keep a handle on theirs, things should improve once rankings are listed. Then, when the exhibition starts next spring, there won't be Meridian or Blackhawk anymore, just riders."

Heath retakes my arm, and I resist the temptation to slip my hand into his. That would certainly send him running for the hills, and I'm enjoying this quiet tour. It's the first time I've felt like I'm in my element since arriving here.

Between Oriana, Sharice, and my increasingly complicated love life, it felt like I was drowning. But here, among the books and statues, I felt like I could finally tread water and wasn't being swept away downstream.

We make our way almost to the end of the corridor, and Heath stops me in front of the enormous map pinned to the wall.

From what I'd seen in college, maps of the world showed gigantic continents of land. Paintings and antique paper pictures showed landscape vistas with mountains and or miles of flat expanses of land.

However, since the flood was so sudden and so many buildings were destroyed, most records were lost.

Except this map is different. It's unlike any I've ever seen.

New coastlines blurred state borders, and the names meant nothing with the old government gone. I move closer, craning my neck to study the three-foot by three-foot map.

"Holy shit," the words spill from me. Someone has taken a red pen and sketched a border on a map of the prehistoric continent of North America. In the center of what was once Montana, Idaho, and Wyoming are the words VENOVIA in old red letters.

"I thought you'd like that."

"Heath." My vision blurs as tears cloud my eyes. "This is...I can't believe they have this here. Why isn't this printed into copies and uploaded to Network? People should see this!"

"You're probably right."

"So, then, why is it down here in some dusty basement instead of out there for everyone to see?"

"Why do you think?"

"Circuit."

Heath smiles gently. "All you see here belongs to them, and it is through their generosity and our sworn secrecy that what is here remains here."

Sharice's words from all those years ago echo mockingly in my ears. *"We only know what Circuit wants us to know."*

He must read the worry on my face because he hastily adds. "If it's any consolation, think what difference it'd make if people knew. Ancient borders of states that are no longer relevant. How would that benefit people? It's fascinating. I agree with you there, but that's the extent of it. It won't create jobs, won't make more land, or reduce food shortages. It's just trivial information."

I chew my bottom lip and return my eyes to the map. Heath is a smart guy and extremely educated, but this is the first wrong thing I've ever heard him say. And it's proof that he's been born without ever having to worry about his next meal or how to afford clothes. Dismissing information because it's not important to you doesn't mean it's not important.

Information is everything, and in the right hands, with the right people, it's *power*.

Thirty

LOGAN

"Don't get your dick in a twist," I tell Carter. "It's set to stun."

He glares at me. "I know, but I'd still like to use my right arm for the rest of the day."

I wave the training sword at his crotch. "Afraid Blondie won't like playing nurse until you recover?" We've been sparring for twenty minutes in the gym and the blood pumping in my muscles has me feeling better than I have in days.

Carter takes a step back on the mat. "She's busy."

"There's a lunch break, isn't there? You don't need more than what, five, six minutes?"

"I'm serious, Logan. Turn the stun off. I have a meeting after this."

"Since when?"

"Since..." he begins, then his throat moves as he swallows. "My mom, General James, saw me when she visited here."

"Yeah, I know," I say. "The whole station was in a damn tizzy as if the devil himself was visiting."

Carter laughs dryly. "She has that effect on people."

I rock my weight to the balls of my feet. "Byron said she met the security team to check what measures we had in place."

"That was part of the reason why she was here," Carter says. "But there was another reason." He pauses, pursing his lips together. "She was here to see me, and it wasn't just a social call. She told me some things that I'm not supposed to share."

Carter glances over at me. Anxiety permeates the bond, thin and slippery like an oil but with a weight that clings. It's adjacent to fear but stickier, harder to shake, and is only amplified since we're near the stables.

"Just fucking spit it out already," I bark. I hate seeing him this way. All spun up like he's hopped up on orange striker powder other athletes put in their drinks so they don't feel the pain from tough workouts. I'd tried the stuff once at Vanguard, and the benefits weren't worth it.

Sure, I'd felt like the King of the Mountain for a day, but the comedown was a motherfucker. My jaw wouldn't stop clenching, and it felt like every joint in my body had ground glass between it.

"She said that the rebels are more of a threat than they're letting the public know. She knows that druadans are the one advantage we have over the mystyl. She's worried about other attacks happening and wants a group of riders to be trained as soldiers."

"Fuck me. That's the first good idea I've ever heard from Circuit."

"Yeah, it is, but there's more," Carter says. "She wants me to pick out the best of the riders here, form that team, and then wants me to lead it."

Carter's eyes narrow as he gives me a pained look.

"So, she wants us to fight with Circuit military?"

"Eventually, yes, I think that's the idea."

"Well, that's bullshit."

"It is. But the worst part isn't just being away from the station on these missions. It's knowing I'll be responsible for the other riders with their lives in my hands."

"You better not fuck it up."

Carter shakes his head. "Goddammit, Logan, I'm telling you I want *you* on the team."

My mouth grows dry. Even I could see how rough things had been between us, but no matter how much we argued, he knew I had his back.

But that didn't mean I'd make it easy for him.

"Screw Circuit," I snarl. "Those greedy bastards might pay our checks, but the truth is they don't give two shits about us. And now they're asking us to put *our* lives on the line. Fuck that."

Carter shakes his head. "Would you just listen, please? I'm trying to tell you I'm freaked out of my mind. I can't do this without you. I can play the crowd until they're frothing at the mouth, but I'm not trained to kill. I wasn't born a fighter like you."

I slide the blade into the holster on my back. "No one is born a fighter. There are those that survive and those that don't. You're never prepared to kill, but you do it because if you don't, you and everyone else next to you will die."

Carter tilts his head, his eyes narrowing as he takes in *my* words. "All right, all right." Carter rests a hand on his hip. "Is that a yes, then? You'll join me in doing this?"

Fuck, first Brigid and now Carter. Against my better judgment, I was making promises faster than Galaxian shit on fresh straw. The thought of my stallion causes his plea to echo in my mind. He'd been going stir-crazy in that stall, and I'd felt like a total ass telling him no. And with Heath and Marshal always busy...

"Fine," I grumble, and immediately his face lights up. "Yes, I'll join your little team. On one condition."

He raises his right eyebrow and crosses his arms. "What?"

"I need to ride."

Carter frowns. "You know I can't be in the arena with you."

"That's the offer. Take it or leave it."

Carter's mouth twists as he mulls over the proposition. Fiaro's rule was a bullshit power play. Galaxian had reacted in defense of Ember, who had been away from the station in a new place. The training arena was the safest place we could be.

"Galaxian is practically chewing through his bars, and my scar's been scratching all day." It's a lie. I'm nowhere close to brimming. I flex my hand, feeling my glove rub against the scars. It's been suspiciously quiet since I've been here, without an ounce of brimming. I even turned down a blow job from one of the cafeteria ladies.

I mean, I could've for the hell of it, but the fact that I didn't *need* to was a surprise.

My hearing is in four days.

If these are my last days as a rider, then I will be on his fucking back every chance I get.

Carter curses under his breath and stares at the floor. "Thirty minutes. I'll give you thirty minutes in the arena, but if anyone shows up, I'm not taking the fall."

"Like anyone would think *you* made me."

Carter rolls his eyes. "Let me get Ember saddled."

∼

A half-hour later, we're both mounted on our stallions, wearing our riding gear.

Carter scratches Ember's withers right under his coppery mane. The faint smell of burning leather drifts to me as his stallion's hide singes his glove.

"Now, where were we?" Carter says, tapping his chin as if thinking. "Oh yeah, we were about to wipe your asses."

He taps his comm, setting the hologram target program, and we spend the next thirty minutes chasing down imaginary monsters and swiping at them with our swords. Carter scores two points on me, but it's because I'm off my game. Gritting my teeth, I pull Galaxian to a halt, even as the next hologram appears at the west end of the arena. I can't get the hearing out of my fucking mind.

Carter stops Ember next to us and runs a hand over the back of his neck just under the helmet and I know he's sensing my agitation.

If Galaxian is euthanized, I won't bond again, and if I'm not a rider, I don't want to be here.

I'd be like a bird with clipped wings, staring at the others soaring over the canyon walls.

I'd rather die.

So, I'll leave. Where? Hell, I don't know, but somewhere. A twinge of discomfort twists in my gut as I think about it. I bury it down deep before it lingers long enough in the bond for Carter to feel.

I should tell my parents at least a goodbye before I don't have the chance or the nerve.

However, they won't even miss me. It's the thousand credits I send every month they'll miss.

The holograms fade as the program times out, and Carter drops his eyes to his comm to reset it.

I swing my sword at his leg.

"Fuck you — " he starts to say but is cut off as Ember phases. The red stallion and him disappear from the arena for several seconds and I seize it, repositioning me and Galaxian to where I think they'll reappear. There's no way to know for sure, but there are tricks and techniques to guess.

Right-handed riders tend to appear to the right side of where they disappeared. Left, more left. Timid riders will stay closer to where they started, while dumb shits like Carter will push the limits, trying for the farthest they can.

The distance between phases is the quickest way to spot a new rider.

There are bold claims from stations that some rider extended their phase for over a minute and then reappeared a mile away. But it's all bullshit. No one could be gone that long, or they come back a corpse.

In the in-between, there's no air, no light, nothing. And your only tether to reality is the bond.

With a soft pop, Carter and Ember reappear ten feet to my left.

"—nearly cut off my arm," he finishes his sentence. Ember tosses his head, pulling at the reins, agitated that I'd almost hit his rider.

"Then don't be so fucking slow." I press my heels into Galaxian's sides. The stallion instantly responds, charging towards the middle of the arena. The holographic mystyl hovers, eight tendril-like legs wavering as if alive, but it's all an illusion. Since I'd seen the real ones, I'd be dammed if they didn't set my teeth more on edge.

Illusion or not, they're fucking satisfying as hell to run through with my sword.

Carter and Ember take my flank, and they almost reach us, but I'm able to swipe the hologram a second before earning a point before they get a chance to. I switch hands, carrying the reins on my right and the blade on my left as I bring Galaxian around. My eyes dart around the arena, anticipating where the next hologram will appear as it's set to random.

Carter follows me to the end but instead chooses to turn right. Both of us sit, chests heaving as we wait. Galaxian jigs to the side, and I hug my left heel into him to keep him straight and focused. *"We fast. We win."* He says, eagerness in his voice.

"Two more and I win, bitch," I shout.

Carter's lip curls at the challenge, and he repositions himself in his saddle. The indoor arena here is a mix of shredded rubber and sand, so very little dust hangs in the air, unlike at Meridian, which would turn into a dust bowl if it wasn't watered often. It's also four times the size, which makes this all the more difficult. But since I'd come in last during the first trial, I needed to get the practice in and get my name on the fucking leaderboard.

I'm a master rider. I deserve to be at the very top. But since I wasn't allowed to practice with anyone other than Heath or Marshal, both of whom seem to have busier calendars than the Havershams — shuttle designers turned celebrities — I'd have to use every opportunity I could.

And what better time than the present? *Carpe fucking diem.*

A flicker of light in the corner catches my eye as a mystyl appears a foot above the ground, hovering. Waiting for me, Carter reacts, leaping out into a gallop, and Galaxian does the same. Our stallions' hooves thunder across the arena. I grip the reins in my left hand, squeezing my legs against the stallion; since this is lower, I'm going to have to bend over to reach it with the sword.

Galaxian might have a higher top speed with the distance to get there, but Ember is quicker from the line, which means they reach it before us. Carter leans over the side of the saddle and slices through it before we race up to him. I pull Galaxian back so I don't crash into the side of them, and agitation surges white-hot through the bond.

Neither of our stallions like losing.

We barely slow before another appears twenty feet from us. Since it's closer to me, I gain a split-second head start.

It's all the advantage I need.

Ember tears after it, his teeth bared, but Galaxian is out in front and I claim the kill.

Carter's comm dings with the alarm, and he climbs off Ember's back. "Productive session, McCelroy, but I'm afraid that's all of our time for today."

"But I didn't get to the part about my uncle touching me yet."

Carter chokes a laugh as he slides the reins over Ember's head. "Way above my pay grade." When I don't dismount, he peers up at me.

"He's been cramped in that stall, so I'm going to do an extra long cool down," I say. "Make sure he doesn't get stocked up."

Carter eyes me suspiciously. It's against the rules to be alone, but I don't care. I'm not ready to put Galaxian away, and judging by the swish of his tail and tossing of his head, neither is he. I gesture to the empty arena. "C'mon. No one is here. I'll be ten minutes. Tops."

He studies my face, and I flash him the sweetest smile.

He rolls his eyes. "Ten minutes," he says, then leads Ember out through the side doors and into the barn.

I click on the holograms again, and they buzz to life. Two taps on my comm ups the setting to hard mode. The wall displays the top ten list of record holders and the one at the top is fifty years old. If we beat it, it'll be like a parting fuck you gift we'll leave behind. I lean forward and whisper to Galaxian. "We gotta get fifteen in under 68 seconds. Let's go."

Galaxian rears back and charges to the first one. The timer on the wall automatically starts as I swipe through it. My hands tighten on the reins and Galaxian pivots on his hind end, spinning to face the next one at the center of the arena. He's on autopilot, and I barely have to cue him. We make it to the fourth, and the fifth shimmers in the farthest corner. There's no way we'll make it unless we phase. Galaxian feels me tense, and I mutter the command word. The world falls black, the air icy cold, and then, with a thud of his hooves, we're next to it. We've barely landed before I cut through it, and he's galloping again.

I steal a look at the timer.

Forty-two seconds.

Fuck. It's going to be close.

Standing in my stirrups, I lean over his neck, urging him faster. He misinterprets my cue and phases again, cutting off my surprised laugh.

We disappear into the inky cold.

In the nowhere, Galaxian and I become one—one heartbeat, one held breath. I can feel his pulse, each stride like the thrum of a distant drum. The air is thick with something unnamable, something old, tugging at the edges of my awareness.

He hesitates, his head turning, ears pricked. I follow his gaze, drawn by the same pull, and there, in the darkness, a figure shimmers into being. A woman—her form delicate, almost transparent, as if the dark itself is shaping her outline.

Nothing is supposed to be here. This place, this between, is empty. It's safe because it's nothing.

Yet there she stands.

"*Logan,*" a distant voice whispers, and it's so faint I almost don't believe I heard it. But before I can register what is happening, we're back—galloping into the arena, the light blinding, the thunder of his hoofbeats deafening.

"Logan!" Brigid calls.

My breath seizes in my chest as Galaxian slides to a stop, and my head swivels to where she stands, resting her arms over the arena wall.

Galaxian snorts at the same time. I shout, "You're not supposed to be down here, Blondie?"

She lifts her chin in defiance. "You're not supposed to be out here by yourself."

"Neither are you." I pull the rein on Galaxian's neck, pulling him to a stop. I'm not the only one who can still feel it, the ghost lingering in the space between. *"What was that?"* I ask, ignoring Brigid trailing along the wall following me.

"Not know. Not safe?"

I shake my head. *"I don't think it can hurt us. I will ask Marshal."*

Galaxian tosses his head, sensing my lie. He knows we're on borrowed time, and my bringing up any issues with the manager could only potentially speed up our sentence. 'Don't rock the boat' goes for double when you're already in a thunderstorm.

"We need to talk," Brigid says when she reaches us.

"How did you even get down here?" I ask.

"Sadie is dealing with Kaeden's pension stuff today and gave me her key to check the towel supply in the bathrooms nearby. She said no one was on the schedule right now, but when I heard someone riding, I came to check."

Check if it was Carter or Heath. I unsnap the strap under my helmet and rub my jaw. "I'm not in the mood."

"Too bad. I'm tired of you avoiding me. Ever since Oriana hatched, you've been even..." she trails off, "Look, Heath and

Carter are worried. They're afraid you're going to hurt yourself or —."

"I don't have time for this." I urge Galaxian away from her as the timer on the wall buzzes with the one-minute mark.

"Then *make* time," she shouts, and I can hear her footsteps trailing me. "I know you're dealing with a lot right now, but avoiding us isn't the answer. We want to help you."

Heat surges in my veins, and I spin Galaxian around. I'm sick of all this bullshit, touchy-feeling talk. "You want to help? Fine. How about you stop running around with hearts in your eyes, sneaking off to the orchard and library even though everything else is falling apart? There are mystyl loose in the world. Riots in the streets. That baby might be the first druanera born in a long time, but that's all it is right now, a fucking baby. It isn't going to change anything, at least not for a while. Only *we* can. The three of you are living in fantasy land while the rest of us are facing reality."

Her cheeks turn scarlet, and it takes her a moment to respond. "No. You're wrong. We're all trying to do what we can to keep *that* from happening."

"By doing what? Writing letters and having meetings about which rich family is going to buy box seats next year?"

"That's not fair," she says.

My chest heaves, so ready to be over with the conversation. "You want to know what's not fair? How about the filtration plants shutting down that will force my parents and brothers from their homes?"

Brigid's eyes widen. "Logan, I–I had no idea."

"Of course you didn't. You've been too busy playing house with that goddamn foal," I lash out, frustrations fueling me. What had started as a cold anger has now morphed into a white-hot flame.

She wrings her hands together, moving closer. "This isn't

about Oriana at all, is it? This is about Carter and Heath and me."

"Get out of the arena before I call Lugsen." My voice is hard and unyielding. It'll get me in trouble, too, since I'll be admitting to being in the arena unchaperoned in order to implicate her, but I don't care. I need her gone.

She lowers her hands, and her mouth twitches as her eyes search mine, but I don't falter.

Finally, she gives a resigned sigh and walks to the exit gate.

I stare at the still-ticking clock on the wall, hearing the gate slam shut behind her.

Three minutes is all it took for me to destroy the one good thing in my life.

I'd set a new personal record.

Thirty-One

BRIGID

I step out of the conference room, my mind buzzing with marketing strategies and plans for the fall quarter. Heath had been busy, but I'd convinced Yuto to let me spend an extra hour in the archives last night, right after my confrontation with Logan. God, he'd been a dick, lashing out when all I did was tell him the truth—that Heath, Carter, and I were worried about him. He looked ready to bite my head off just for caring.

Thankfully, Kaeden's memorial is at Blink tonight. And while I'm sure Logan will be there with the other riders, I hope the loud music and flashing lights will be enough to drown out my thoughts and allow me to have a good time. The busy day of meetings should have been enough to keep me focused, but my mind kept drifting back to him in the arena on Galaxian. The way he looked at me when I first walked in was like I was some ghost had caught me off guard, but I quickly reasoned it was just surprise.

I wasn't supposed to be down there after all.

However, last night, it took forever to fall asleep, my brain churning with thoughts of ancient stables, long-dead riders, and, most of all, what Heath had said to me our first time in the archives. I'd replayed the conversation over and over, trying to make sense of his surprising confession. He said he'd be willing to share me with Carter, and instead of feeling conflicted, I found myself drawn to the idea. Maybe I'm just wired differently—capable of loving them both, my heart big enough to hold space for them without needing to choose.

Carla steps beside me, and her tablet is clutched to her chest as she taps out a few final notes.

"I'll see you later at Blink for Kaeden's wake?" I ask as we pause at the base of the stairs. Although I'm playing it cool, my belly is a knot of jittery nerves, reminding me of when I'd helped plan the gala.

It has to be perfect.

Better than perfect. For Sadie and Kaeden.

"You better believe I'll be there," she says. "Rider memorials are always a blast. And by the way, if you need something to wear, you're welcome to borrow that black-and-white striped dress of mine." Carla laughs as she gestures to her stomach. "I don't think I'll be fitting in it anytime soon."

Her eyes twinkle with a secret joy that takes a moment to register. "Oh my god," I squeal, "Are you serious?"

"Yes," Carla confirms, bobbing her head. "We're waiting to announce until after Kaeden's party, but thought, what's the harm in telling a few people?"

"When are you due?" I say, feeling a rush of warmth, honored that she's sharing this exciting news with me.

"Next March. I'm three months along, and I swear I can already feel it kick," Carla continues, her free hand resting gently on the tiny bump on her stomach. "Mack and I are moving up the wedding to next month, and I'd love for you to be a part of it."

I'm flattered, and tears prickling at the corners of my eyes. Instantly, I pull Carla into a tight hug, careful not to squeeze too hard. "Of course," I murmur, my voice thick with emotion. "I'd be honored."

We're interrupted by the sound of approaching footsteps, and I quickly compose myself as Don and Kimmy walk past. I manage a professional nod, telling them we'll update the rider profiles on Blackhawk's Network site based on their suggestions. Once they're out of earshot, I turn back to Carla.

"Congrats again," I say softly. "See you later."

We part ways with another quick hug and I make my way back to my apartment. When I reach my room, I'm surprised to find a stack of books on the table, accompanied by a letter. I recognize Heath's handwriting immediately, and my curiosity is piqued. Settling into a chair, I begin to read:

Heard back from my art gallery, friend. The painting is of Rosaline Devereaux. She was a druanera rider. One of the last, she was born in 355 AR and died when the bombs dropped in 382 AR. It took some digging with Yuto, but they had her journals in storage here. There might be more, but I found three.

My heart somersaults as I run my fingers over the

leather-bound spines. The books look old, their covers worn and faded, but I know better than to judge a book by its cover.

Rosaline Devereaux.

That had been her name, so the theory that she'd been related to me definitely decreased since she didn't share my mother's maiden name or our father's Harlow. Perhaps she'd married and changed her name?

Heath's letter continues:

I've browsed them some, but you might get more from them than me. We can discuss later what you find.

I can't believe it. Actual journals from a druanera rider?

This is beyond anything I could've hoped for. My fingers tremble as I open the first journal, the leather creaking softly. The pages are yellowed with age, but the handwriting is still clear, flowing across the paper in elegant script.

The first is dated January 11th, 377 AR. Five years before the bombs were dropped over four centuries ago. A quick count on my fingers tells me that if she had been killed in the bombing like most druadan riders, she would've been twenty-seven when she died. Which means she'd written this when she was twenty-two, the same age I am now.

That can't be a coincidence. *Right?*

I read further, my eyes widening with each word. Rosaline's voice comes alive on the page, her descriptions of life as a druanera rider so vivid I can almost see it. She mentions her being taken from her family at age twelve for her 'sensitivities' and a master rider taking her to a station to become a novice. My heart aches for her. Twelve is so young. I re-read trying to learn more about what this sensitivity is, but she seems vague.

Still, it's different from how druadan riders are created now. First-born sons are sent at sixteen to Vanguard and then as novices at a station until they bond.

But based on her notes, it was different back then, at least for women. They started younger and selected them for different reasons.

As I ponder this, a thought strikes me. Could it be that I possess some kind of innate sensitivity? Perhaps it's a remnant of those older selection methods, a latent ability that's only now surfacing. It would explain why I can perceive these bonds, these auras when I'm not a rider myself.

The idea both excites and unnerves me. If I have this sensitivity, what does it mean for my future? And how deep does this ability go?

She writes about riding her druanera, Solara, with the wind in her hair and the world spread out beneath her like a tapestry. Her words convey hope and joy, masking the violence and chaos I know were unfolding during the height of the mystyl wars. She describes the bond between rider and mount, a connection so deep and profound it transcends mere partnership. It's a melding of minds, of souls.

But there's more.

Dated two days later, Rosaline writes of the responsibilities that come with being a rider, of the duty to protect and serve.

It's fascinating, wondrous, enchanting.

It's also pure and utter bullshit.

This isn't a first-hand account of a woman's life. It's propaganda. A fanciful tale used to entice people to sign up to be a rider. It made sense they'd needed to recruit more to replace those who died.

I frown as I turn the pages, hoping I can glean something

insightful from these supposed journals. The dates are random, some spread days apart, while others by months. The first book ends after a year, so I take up the second.

Chewing my thumbnail, I start on the first page. The writing is identical. Details of food served at extravagant feasts held in tents on the grassy plains. Or early crisp autumn mornings, when hundreds of druadans and their riders charged down a steep hill. I skim past the flowery prose, only pausing when she mentions Solara or a location I recognize. Finally, I flip through the last half, but a single word snags my attention.

Sentinel.

As I delve deeper into the paragraph, I lose all sense of time. The world outside my room fades away, replaced by Rosaline's words.

Holy shit.

I need to find Heath.

Thirty-Two

CARTER

Riders don't get funerals.
 There's no eulogy. No mourning. No somber words spoken over a fresh grave.
A rider's death isn't a tragedy.
It's a celebration of a life lived to the fullest. Enjoyed. Savored. Indulged.
When a rider dies, what few friends and family they have will gather at a restaurant or a bar and drink and laugh and, if the night goes right, end up in someone else's bed.
However, the party is for an essential reason. A newly unbonded druadan has an increased chance of turning rogue, and keeping the mood light throughout the collective bond encourages another, like a novice, to bond.

Minimizing the delay is a priority.

Especially now with one rogue druadan already existing at Blackhawk.

The thumping bass reverberates through my chest, and I find myself bouncing on my bar stool, wedged between Heath and Logan like the filling in a stoic sandwich. I have to take these guys out more.

Servers in sequined blue dresses weave through the crowd with trays of drinks that catch the light and identical long brunette ponytails swaying in time with their hips. My eyes drift away from following their asses to the nearby table where Brigid and Carla are sitting with Sadie.

I take another swig of my beer, savoring the hoppy taste as I watch Logan avoid looking in Brigid's direction.

I thought they'd made peace after his bullshit on the shuttle ride, but obviously not. Since we've been here, they've been avoiding each other like grade-school kids with cooties. Every time he looks at her, there's a fresh surge of annoyance and frustration from our bond.

I wish they'd just fuck or fight or whatever they need to do to get over it cause it's really killing my mood. Beside me, Heath nurses his third whiskey like he's sipping tea while the alcohol buzzes pleasantly through my veins.

I swear, the guy has a steel liver. His eyes appraise the party like he's a teacher chaperoning a school dance. It's boring as hell and definitely *not* how I'm going to spend my evening.

I glance over at the game tables and decide to change the pace. "Hey," I call, waving them over. "Prickball, anyone?"

Neither moves. "Come on," I plead. "I promise to go easy on you."

Logan and Heath eye each other, then drain their drinks and make their way over.

The table is a hybrid of ping-pong and hacky sack and is

catnip for riders for two reasons. One, it's a way to show off your dexterity and agility, and two, it's a good way to get drunk fast. The objective is to keep a small plastic ball in the air. It doesn't matter how you hit it, hands, arms, legs, head, just that it doesn't touch the ground or table. Each round has a timer and if you hold it too long, tiny spikes pop out and stick into you like rose thorns. It hurts like a bitch, so the game gets hectic as the rounds progress.

"Alright, you're with me," I ask, clapping Logan's broad shoulders.

"Shane," Heath says, calling out to the other rider, flirting with one of the pretty servers. Regretfully, he pulls himself away.

Carrying his mug of beer, he sidles up next to Heath. "Drinking rules?"

"You know it. Five rounds, and the Loser team drinks."

I take the ball from the tub of disinfectant, a bucket full of expired vodka and soured whiskey. The first round starts with Heath and Shane working at their end of the square table while Logan and I cover ours. The ball flies back and forth. Shane loses the first point, the ball sticking to his shoulder.

He winces and pulls it off, and tiny beads of blood appear on his neck. "Fuck, I always forget how bad that hurts," he mutters and taps the button on the ball to reset it. The spikes withdraw into it, and the timer resets. He tosses it into the air, and for another twenty seconds, we keep it suspended. I feel eyes watching us as we play, and even a few other riders move to closer tables.

I dive to save the ball from bouncing off Logan's shoulder but get one in the wrist. The sting shoots up my arm, but I shake it off, keeping the game going. Heath gets one next, stepping backward and knocking into a table and causing three of the women there to scold him. He apologizes to them and then scurries back with the ball clinging to the inside of his palm, face looking like a cat that stepped in a puddle.

In the third round, the pretty brunette with freckles and glasses he'd been with earlier goes to Shane and whispers in his ear. A smile materializes on his face. "This has been fun, but I gotta go," he says, draining his beer and swinging a look around. "Danner, you tap in for me." He glances at us with a cheeky grin. "It's Diane's smoke break."

The two of them rush out of the bar, giggling, leaving us to continue the game.

Danner stumbles over to take Shane's place by Heath. His cheeks are red, and his eyes look watery. *Hell yeah, this is going to be easy.*

"How's bonded life?" I ask.

Danner laughs, rubbing his eyes. "It's like I'm more awake when I'm asleep," he slurs. "Wraithwind and I phased for the first time yesterday, though."

"Congrats on not dying," Logan says, holding up his empty beer glass to a server who rushes over to exchange it with a full one. "The fun's just beginning."

Heath pats him on the back to reassure him of his hard work or to encourage him to hold up his end of the team, I'm not sure.

We start again and Logan and I dominate, our movements fluid and synchronized. Heath practically has to carry his side, as Danner is swaying more than Oriana did when she first hatched.

In the final round, Logan starts hitting the ball harder, forcing Heath and Danner to leap and dive to volley it back. I scan the bar and see Garret and Caven chatting up a petite redhead and her leggy brunette friend. Good, I hope they stay over there. Logan's competitiveness is kicking in, and I don't want to end the night breaking up a fight. The ball flies back and forth, a blur of movement. The tables next to us cheer when the ball pops off in Danner's left hand, causing him to curse in pain, and Logan and I win the match.

We watch smugly as Heath and Danner drain their glasses, foam dripping from the corners of their mouths.

Four Blackhawk riders, Darren, Taylor, and the twin brothers, Liam and Luke, take the table next to ours. Darren's the oldest and a master rider. "Since you've apparently warmed up. Winner from each table faces off?"

Darren adjusts his stance, the sleek metal of his prosthetic leg catching the light. The brother's jaw flexes under the deep brown skin of their faces.

"Game on," I challenge, looking over at them. The four of them grin, and beer sloshes over the sides of their glasses as they raise them.

Tonight's just getting started.

Thirty-Three

BRIGID

At Blink, the air hums with the strangest mixture of joy and sorrow. Everyone swore it was the norm to celebrate a rider's death like this, and yet, I couldn't shake the uneasy feeling. The laughing, the joking, even the dancing all of it felt *wrong*.

Was this survivor's guilt?

Kaeden had died right in front of me, and here I was, sipping a citrus spritz like I was out celebrating a promotion.

The club's sound system is impressive, and I can feel it vibrating under my shoes. I lean against the worn bar of what I'd heard everyone call "The Mermaid." The signage outside is lost, but hints of what this historic building was are everywhere, especially the red-bricked wall with the smiling cartoon woman with the two fishlike tails flanking her painted on it.

The tiny bathroom has chipped and stained ceramic tiles. No one remembers the original name, but we all know the legend—this was a place for coffee and tea, and now it sells wine and ales.

I smooth the hem of my dress where I'm perched on the bar stool. It's thin-strapped and black-and-white striped with sequins. Sadie and Carla are seated next to me, and the server swaps our drinks. Carla's sipping seltzer water with a lime, and Sadie doesn't seem to be any the wiser.

Since reading Rosaline's journals earlier that night, I hadn't had the chance to speak to Heath yet, and I figured that this wasn't the best time either. I felt like I was bursting to tell him.

Surrounding us is a cluster of round tables, where riders, station staff, or regular visitors are either seated or standing.

It's glaringly obvious who the riders are. The novices are dressed in torso-clinging T-shirts with the Blackhawk logo, while the master riders, like Marshal, have their formal black long coats with gold buttons, although some have taken them off, leaving them to rest on the stools. Their faces alight with laughter as they raise glasses in toasts or slap each other on the backs.

All riders share a presence, an air about them that exudes confidence. And while some might tell me it is because I'm familiar with these particular three that color my opinion, I don't think that is the case.

Not only are they the biggest of the group, with broad shoulders and long legs, but they share a sharp intensity that never fails to make me weak in the knees.

Which, if I'm being honest, is quite a lot.

Except for Logan. As of late, his stare made me want to

punch him. It felt like the more I tried to reach out to him, the more he pulled away.

So, I stopped trying.

If he wanted to fix this rift, then he needed to be the one to take the next step.

Just then, Carter catches my gaze, and a tilted smile forms on his lips. I can't help but smile back across the bar, feeling that alluring pull toward him. I grumble to myself as a group of four women moves in, blocking him from my view. Dressed in short skirts with sleek hair styled into waves, they shuffle to a half-filled table.

They grin and giggle in an effort to gain their attention. When no other riders make a move in their direction, I start to feel sorry for them.

Riders rarely visit Delford in these kinds of numbers, and when one does, they are often surrounded by photographers or fans hoping for an autograph. But here, it seems the village is used to the celebrity buffet, and whoever these women are, they are clearly the minority. Most of the patrons either politely move out of their way, letting them order first at the bar, or give up their seats for them to sit. Some even ignore them altogether.

"Kaeden would've loved this," Sadie yells over a particularly loud chorus.

"How long were you together?" I ask.

"Four wonderful years. We always knew we were living on borrowed time, and he made sure we didn't waste a moment."

I smile warmly despite a familiar fear tightening around my heart. Heath, Carter, and Logan, three riders I've grown to care for, are destined for the same fate. How long until we're having another party like this for one of them?

I swallow down the dark thought. They're not even in their third year yet.

They had time.

The music shifts, and the speakers play a more sultry tone. The song swirls around me, and Sadie leans close, her head on my shoulder. "Kaeden said something to me once I've never forgotten."

"Hmm?" I murmur, tracing my finger over the rim of my glass.

"He said the bond carved out a piece of his soul," she whispers, her voice so faint it's almost lost to the music. "I know he loved me, but Geminesta owned him, and now that he's gone, he's free."

Her words settle like snowflakes over me, stinging my skin with their chill.

Is that what will happen to Logan if Galaxian is euthanized? Perhaps it'll be shitty at first, but after some time, he will be whole again?

Even as I think it, I know it's not true. Logan might be many things, but a forgive-and-forget kind of guy isn't one of them. If Galaxian dies, Logan will vanish like my sister to some outskirts of Venovia. Maybe bunking up with the wanderers that lived along the tox zone borders.

Over the next hour, rider after rider came to pay their respects to Sadie. Over raised glasses, they share with her stories about the times Kaeden had bailed them out when they'd forgotten the choreography or the swapping of starting positions when a stallion was having an off day.

I catch Carter's eye from across the room and motion for him to come over with a tilt of my head. He raises an inquisitive eyebrow, and in three long strides, Carter's behind me, pulling me off the stool. He wraps his arms around my waist and plants a kiss on the sensitive skin just under my ear. "Hey there," he murmurs.

"You're drunk," I say, but there's no heat to my words, and playfully, I arch my back into the front of his pants.

"Sure am," he says, pressing back into me. "Want to dance?"

Sadie giggles. "You two are adorable."

"Only if you can keep up." Laughing, I let him pull me away from the safety of the bar, the cool metal leaving my back as we weave through the crowd to the dance floor. As the rhythm takes over, Carter finds a spot right in the center, his hands finding my hips like they're meant to be there. I let the music and his touch guide me, a smile playing on my lips as I move against him, the beat pulsing through us both.

Across the room, perched like watchful hawks, are Heath and Logan. Logan's face is guarded, and he appears to be more interested in the people surrounding him than in the music. Heath, though, snags my gaze, and there's a challenge there. I nod towards him, a silent invitation as Carter's hands tighten on my hips.

Heath's eyes darken. Between our packed work schedules and this memorial, I hadn't found a chance to tell Heath about what I'd discovered in Rosaline's journals. And — between the loud dance music and prying ears — now was certainly not a good time.

It'd waited hundreds of years. It could wait another day.

"Come on," I call to him, "don't let us have all the fun!"

Heath raises his drink. "I'm good over here."

"Suit yourself," I say, shrugging and shifting so I'm facing Carter as we dance. The song changes to one of my favorites, and I let myself go, feeling the music transform my body.

Three songs and a raging stallion shot later, I'm perched on a bar stool watching Carla and Mack slow dance.

I'd expected the crowd to thin as the night dragged on, but

it's only grown thicker. Sadie steps up behind me, her voice soft. "Hey, I'm ready to go. I'm tired."

I nod, taking in her glassy-eyed expression. "I'll walk you to the gondola," I offer, not liking the idea of her navigating alone in this state.

As I grab my coat, my eyes drift to Carter and Heath, talking with the other riders. They're part of a club I'll never be cool enough for. Their laughter feels distant, their discussions of private, funny stories from the barracks or arena. It's a familiar feeling, this half-belonging, one Sadie recently confirmed remains, even in marriage. I pull my coat tighter and lead her through the crowd, accepting that some things never change.

I guide Sadie out of Blink. The bar's neon lights give way to the dim, ambient glow of the village street lamps and the ominous dark form of the station on the hill in the distance.

It's a short walk to the cable car station, and as we make our way down the street to the next block, Sadie says, "I can't go back to that apartment." She sniffs and wipes her face. "I can't sleep in that empty bed tonight."

Without hesitation, I say, "You can crash on the couch at my place."

"Oh, I couldn't intrude," she says, shaking her head quickly.

I flash her a warm smile. "It's no problem at all."

There are only four seats per carriage, so I'm forced to wait the other twenty minutes for the next one. Sadie's steps are unsteady as I help her into the next carriage and whisper the code to my room.

"Thank you, Brigid," she slurs. "You're a good friend. Really."

"Good night," I say. A timid smile appears on her face before the doors close, whisking her away.

Left alone on the platform, I consider going back into Blink but decide against it as I realize I'm tired and looking forward to burying myself under the covers of my big bed. Carter, Heath, and Logan are still inside, enjoying the camaraderie of their fellow riders, and I expect them to be out all night.

The club's music echoes in my ears, replaced by the low hum of the gondola's machinery and the distant sound of shuttles coming and going over the village.

As the minutes tick by, the hairs on the nape of my neck stand up, and I suddenly feel very alone.

I shift my weight back and forth, debating about returning to Blink and seeing if Carla is ready to go, but then I see two figures step out of the shadows of the station's awning.

Recognition dawns on me as they draw nearer; their long black navy coats with brass buttons and white pants mark them as Blackhawk riders.

Their approach slows, and I shift my eyes ahead of me again. I don't know them personally, but that's not unusual since there are almost fifty at Blackhawk.

"Hey, girlie," he says. "I saw you there dancing with James. Is that an exclusive thing, or are you available for anyone?"

I tighten my hold around my waist, ignoring him and glaring at the slow-moving cable.

"Come on," he says, his voice dropping lower.

A hand lands on my right shoulder, and I cringe. "Let me show you how we stay warm up here."

I pull away, but the hand tightens, and I'm spun around to face him. Another grabs my wrist as I shout. "Stop it! Let me go!" I struggle, trying to free myself from their iron-like grips. Panic flames in my chest as the realization sinks in. I'm too weak to fend them off.

The first man moves his arm from my shoulder to the back

of my head and pulls on my ponytail hard. I wince in pain and squeeze my eyes shut. Another hand gropes my breast.

No. *This can't be happening.* My mind blazes with the memory, and suddenly, I'm seventeen again and back in the boat house.

"She said, hands off, asshole." My eyes snap open to see Logan materialize behind the guy like some shadow demon. Without waiting for the guy to respond, Logan grabs the guy by the back of the neck and yanks him backward. I'm pulled with him until Logan rams his fist into the guy's stomach, and he's forced to let go.

The other guy lunges at Logan, and suddenly, he has two on top of his back. Logan bucks to the side, freeing himself. Rage flares in his steel eyes. I stand frozen, watching as he fights like a man possessed. Again and again, he punches him, and the first guy doubles over.

The guy lifts his arms defensively, and Logan changes tactics, coming in closer and nailing him square between the eyes. Warm blood splatters my face as the guy grunts.

"Fuck," he bellows, staggering backward.

I anxiously look around us, wondering if there are any witnesses to what is rapidly transforming into a one-sided fight. Logan is on probation, and while I could testify that they'd harassed me, I can't trust that they won't still find a way to use this against him.

The second guy swings wildly, nailing Logan once in the jaw and once in the shoulder. Logan strikes him again, and the man falls to his back.

The green-painted carriage hisses to a stop at the platform, and I seize the moment, grabbing Logan's arm and tugging him toward it. "Please, we need to go!"

The two of us climb inside, and the doors shut. The wheels click along the steel cable as we leave the men crawling on the ground. The first one rises to his feet, his face red with anger. "You don't know what you've fucking done!" he shouts as the cable car carries us away.

My heart pounds a frantic rhythm against my breastbone as I stare up at a heaving Logan.

"Are you okay?" he asks.

I clutch my arms around myself.

I am so very fucking far from okay.

Thirty-Four

LOGAN

All I see is red.
    I nearly lost control.
    Again. Fuck.

The fury-fueled desire to pound my fists into the wall is barely contained as I replay the moment in my mind—their hands on her, her scream piercing the night.

I'd stepped outside Blink for fresh air, trying to clear my head, and it was fucking luck that I'd heard her when I did. If I'd been a second later if I hadn't walked out at that exact moment...

I slam my hand on the side of the wall, then instantly regret when Brigid flinches. Anger and adrenaline still blazing in my veins, I begin pacing in the small space. I would have killed them if she hadn't stopped me.

"Thank you," Brigid whispers from where she's seated on one of the benches.

"Don't mention it." I grip the handle on the wall and stare over at her, watching her shoulders hunch. She's trying to hold herself together but is more shaken than she'll admit. I want to do something—comfort her, maybe—but I've seen this before. She needs space. Touching her would only make things worse.

"What happened on the shuttle ride over...it was stupid, and I never should've done it."

She looks up at me, blinking away the tears. "Then why did you?"

I'd had days to think about this, so I don't hesitate. "To teach you to fear them," my words sharp and to the point. "Galaxian told me what he did. He did it to save you. But he's just a druadan. An animal acting on instinct. You're not his rider. You were never safe on him."

I don't soften the truth even as her face tightens, and she breaks away from my gaze. "Galaxian is..." I pause, chewing over the words before continuing. "Our bond is good, but after he killed that guy, I can't trust him like I used to. And when you rode him, it was like me handing you the grenade I just pulled the pin on." If Heath and Carter won't tell her, then I will. "You were fine *that* time, but fuck if that will always be the case."

The carriage clunks over one of the support poles, jolting us both. She rests her trembling hands on the seat, steadying herself as she stands. Her gaze locks with mine, and those full lips form into a smile that doesn't reach her eyes. "I understand now. I promise I'll never do that again." Her voice wavers as her blue irises darken. "So long as *you* never do that again."

The fire in her eyes is back. That raw, primal side I'd only glimpsed before. It catches me off guard, this sudden change from softness to steel, and I'm as intimidated as I am aroused. Something inside me awakens, and I swallow. Hard. My pants tighten as blood surges to my cock.

"I promise," I say, voice thick.

Her grin widens, like a wolf showing their fangs. "Glad we got that cleared up. Now, as to what just happened, on the long list of dumb things you've done," she says, arching an eyebrow. "I think tonight tops them all. You know that, right?"

I crane my neck, staring at the ceiling. I shift my weight, trying to ease the discomfort in my pants.

Rider's stamina.

This fucker will last the rest of the ride.

She was right about me being dumb, but not in the way she thinks. "Yeah, yeah. I'm sure it'll come back to bite me in the ass, but it never should have happened in the first place."

She lets out a short breath. "Yeah, no shit."

I shake my head. "No, I mean, I shouldn't have let it happen. You were like a goddamn beacon luring them in. It was stupid of me to think they wouldn't notice you."

"Notice me? What are you talking about?"

My mouth opens and closes as I try to think about how to respond. "Nothing. Forget it."

She steps closer. "Oh no, you don't get off that easily. Tell me. What is it that makes me so…how did you put it?" She taps her bottom lip, pretending to think.

When she doesn't say anything else, I grumble under my breath. "Like a beacon."

"Ah, yes. That's it."

"It's because that's what you are, Blondie," I say, resting a hand on the window next to her, feeling the cool air through the glass. "At Blink, in the bond from all the riders. I felt it."

Her eyes wide and alluring lock with mine, and I'd be a fucking liar if I didn't want to slam my lips against hers. My cock hardens as I imagine what it would be like to silence that sharp tongue of hers with it. Let's see her keep the attitude while she's gasping for breath.

"So, what am I supposed to do?" she says, tossing her

shoulders. "Never go out, never travel anywhere, just hide in my room forever?"

"If I had my way, yes."

Defiance dances in her eyes. "*This* is why I keep asking you to train me so I can defend myself."

"You couldn't have stopped them."

"You don't know that."

"I do."

"How?"

"Do the math, Blondie. It was three against one."

"Still, I could've tried."

I frown. "I know their type. That would've only excited them. You could have scratched and bit, and they wouldn't have stopped until they all had you."

Her mouth twitches, but she straightens her face, recovering quickly. "Alright. So, what if you're not there next time? You won't always be there."

"What if I am?"

She laughs dryly. "What, like always with me?"

"Yes."

"Sort of like what you were doing tonight?"

"I suppose so, but I'd do it more."

"I don't need a bodyguard, Logan," she retorts. "I need to be able to protect myself."

Stepping back, I cross my arms, and her gaze snags on my biceps. The one upside to having a rogue stallion was the free time to hit the gym, which I'd taken full advantage of. "Fine," I sigh. "What if you could have both?"

Her eyes light up. "Are you saying what I think you're saying? You'll teach me?"

Before I can reply, I lower my arms, and she leaps forward. She wraps her arms around me. "Thank you," she says. A hard knot forms in my throat at the embrace, and for a split second,

I don't know what to do with my arms, so I leave them to hang uselessly by my side.

"Thank you," she repeats against my chest. When she pulls back, she's grinning, but tears cloud her eyes.

She's been afraid. This whole time since the attack. Why hadn't she said anything?

She did, you idiot when she asked you to teach her to fight on the shuttle. Lately, I've been blind, too focused on my own battles — maintaining my rider status and keeping Galaxian alive — to notice hers. The realization stings, cutting through me like one of the laser swords.

"You're not a rider," I add, softening my voice. "So, I can't officially —."

"Train me," she finishes for me, making air quotes around the word 'train.' "I know."

"So, then you know if we get caught, you and I both will be in deep shit?"

A mischievous smile curls up the corner of her lips. "More than we've already been in?"

Fuck me. That sounds so much sexier than it should. "You might've been let off the hook, but I'm still blacklisted."

She shrugs. "We gotta stay positive. You've got a good chance, especially since the prosecuting attorney is friends with Marshal."

I'm glad somebody is seeing my situation through rose-colored glasses. But Marshal's friend or not, he still works for Circuit, which means if they want me done as a rider and Galaxian dead, there'd be nothing any of us could do to stop it.

"Also, they have a full PR and marketing team here," she continues, allowing me a split second to regain my focus. "They're only using me for internal communications work, and since you can't ride without a chaperone, it seems we're both left with some open time in our schedules."

She was right. Carter had done me the one favor, and I couldn't ask him for another, not with his mama General James watching him so closely now, and Heath was busy pretending he was going to have a wedding and then sneaking off with her to the library. It'd fallen on Marshal to be the only one who could meet me for riding, but with novices to work with, that time was limited.

I wasn't a total idiot. I'd seen too quickly it's been Fiaro's intention all along to keep me from riding. "The upstairs gym is empty after eight," I finally say. "So, as long as you can get there without anyone seeing you, we should be good."

"No problem," she says proudly. "And what about you?"

"I was the only one at Vanguard that could sneak out of the barracks past lights out without setting off the alarm, so here is nothing."

"*You*, sneaky?" She laughs. "You're about as subtle as a shuttle landing in downtown Delford."

"Snuck up on *you*, didn't I?"

Her pale cheeks redden as she remembers the night of the attack when I'd found her surrounded by mystyl and had saved her from being swarmed. "How do you know I didn't just let you?"

I snort. "Blondie, you were two seconds away from having tentacles wrapped around that pretty little neck of yours."

She sniffs, lifting her chin as if exposing her neck, and god, how I want to touch it, feel her pulse under my tongue. But then the gondola shudders to a halt, and the automatic door slides open.

She gathers her coat and steps out into the loading room. My knuckles ache deliciously, although the rush of adrenaline is waning as I follow her out and walk side by side down the dimly lit hallway to the main stairwell.

The silence drags between us before she finally asks.

"There's one thing that's been bugging me from before." She draws in a breath. "I know those guys are assholes, and it probably doesn't matter, but what do you think they meant by 'you don't know what you've done?'"

I toss my shoulders. "Not a clue. Dickheads like them always make empty threats."

We reach the stairs leading up to her residence hall, and I follow her.

There's no way in hell I'm letting her walk back alone.

When we reach her door, she turns to face me, her eyes shining in the dull light. "Thank you again." She pats me on the arm. Before I can react, she leans in and kisses me on the cheek. The contact sends a shock rippling down my spine, and an uneasy sensation grows in my chest.

"Goodnight," she whispers, pulling back and with that, she disappears behind her door, leaving me standing in the hallway, stunned.

Without thinking, my hand goes to the place where her lips had been on my cheek, scowling at the confusion it stirs up.

I need to get back to the barracks and take a cold shower, shake this off before it messes with my head even more.

In the basement corridor, I round the corner, and a group of riders lingers in the shadows under one of the barracks' eaves, their voices carrying down the hallway.

"There he is," one of them jeers, his words slurring. "The walking dead man."

I freeze, my fists clenching. "The fuck did you just say?"

"Looks like he's deaf now, too," one says, laughing.

As I move closer, my footsteps don't slow, even as I recognize them as the assholes who'd been harassing Blondie. They must've taken the car right after us, then hurried down here to ambush me.

Clearly, they hadn't learned their lesson. No complaints from me. "You ready for round two then?"

One rider positions himself in front of the others. His nose is swollen and crusted with dried blood. "God, you really are as dumb as they say," he sneers. "I'm Garret Peterson. My dad is President Bernard Peterson."

Thirty-Five

HEATH

Carter and I round the corner leading into the barracks, and my blood freezes.

Logan is in a standoff with two Blackhawk riders. *Dammit.* Why had I allowed Carter to talk me into staying longer at the club? I knew better. We should have left when Logan did.

Logan's fists are clenched, eyes hard as he rolls his shoulders back, preparing to fight.

"God dammit, Logan," I mutter under my breath.

Carter shoots me a worried glance, and his shared apprehension bleeds into my mind. We need to defuse this situation before it explodes.

We rush forward.

It's a Blackhawk novice, Garret, who is about my height but twice my weight, and his lean, red-headed first-year buddy, Caven.

"You're gonna regret that," Garret says, holding his face as he sneers at Logan.

My breathing quickens in response to their emotions rippling violently through the bond—anger, aggression, and a thirst for revenge. The prickling sensations scorch my nerves like white-hot pokers, and I grit my teeth against the onslaught, struggling to maintain control.

I'm stronger than this. I must be the calm in the storm.

Carter sucks in a sharp breath. "We need to stop this before it goes too far."

He's right. If our stallions pick up on the escalating tension, they could injure themselves. Galaxian is in the anti-phase blanket, but it might not be enough to keep him in his stall if he senses Logan is in danger.

Jaw clenched, I step forward, holding up my hands. "Easy, boys. Let's not do anything rash here."

"Look, Master McCelroy is sorry for—" Carter starts, but Logan cuts him off.

"Sorry?" Logan snaps. "No, I'm fucking not."

Logan's hand lashes out, smashing the guy's face.

Garrett staggers back, cursing and grabbing his nose as blood streams between his hands. "Son of a bitch, I think he broke my nose!"

A deep, rumbling laugh comes from Logan.

Garret whips his head toward his friend, eyes blazing with drunken fury. "Seriously, Caven. Are you just going to stand there?"

The redhead takes a step closer but, upon seeing the chevron on my jacket, loses some of his resolve. "Piss off. This doesn't concern you," Caven says.

"Lockwood, right?" Garrett says, his face smeared with blood. "Bet your daddy would have something to say if you started a fight with a Peterson."

Peterson. A tightness radiates across my chest. My hands ball into fists, angry at myself for not recognizing him *and* at Logan for picking a fight with the worst person possible.

This is Garret Peterson—Bernard's son.

I glare at him, keeping my face under a mask. I know precisely what my father would say. He'd say that the Lockwoods are one of the largest donors to the Peterson campaign and that if I cared at all for our legacy to remain blemish-free, then I should shut my mouth.

Carter places a restraining hand on my arm and pours a steady stream of calm into my churning emotions. The worst of the anger smoldering in my gut subsides. But Garret's smug look keeps the fire burning.

"Look," Carter says in a measured tone, "it's been a long night for all of us."

I risk a glance at Logan's face, shadowed beneath his dark hood. He remains taut as a bowstring, radiating pent-up violence.

This isn't good.

I step between Logan and the others, creating a barrier, and reach out through the bond, trying to calm Logan down. It hurts, a burning pain that sears me as painfully as any physical pain. It's a battle of the wills, and I hate the feeling that I'm suffocating him, but it's the only way.

"They're not worth it," I say, my voice strained. "Walk away."

The bond whirs with rage, no sign of it ebbing.

"Logan, stand down," Carter adds, his voice sounding as stretched thin as I feel.

Logan's eyes flicker with indecision, and I know I'll need

to change tactics. I spin on my heel, facing Garrett. "If Fiaro catches you fighting, that Peterson name will do little to protect you. You might be a big name outside these walls, but here, you're just an unbonded rider. Which means you'll be punished just like one." It's mostly a lie. Riders are told their ranking and reputation are based solely on their actions and not their surname, but preferential treatment does happen.

Look at me.

"And you're an aging novice," Carter says, picking up where I'd left off. "Do you really want to test them when they're already eyeing you for removal?"

Garret spits on the ground. "Bullshit."

"It's true," Carter says. "None of the unbonded stallions have shown any interest in you. Tick tock."

I loosen my hold on Logan, hoping he'll heed my words along with Garret and Caven. "You know what Lugsen said if any of us get caught fighting."

A muscle twitches in Garret's jaw. For a beat, the tension in the air thickens.

Then Garret snorts. "Fucking waste of my time, anyway." He turns on his heel, and his friend trails after him like a trained dog.

Logan exhales a shuddering breath, but none of the rigidity leaves his body. I approach cautiously, laying a hand on his arm. "You good?"

He nods tersely without meeting my eyes. Through our bond, the residual anger roils within him, banked yet still smoldering. There's more to this. This is more than just a drunken spat. This feels personal. But why?

"Think he'll squeal to Lugsen?" Carter asks.

"He won't. He doesn't want to draw any more attention to himself as an overdue novice."

"You gotta learn to shrug shit off, man," Carter says. "You're lucky we got here in time, otherwise —"

"I know," Logan growls. His voice is low and rough, like gravel. "I just... he gets under my skin."

Carter claps him on the shoulder, offering a small, sympathetic smile. "We've got your back, man. But you gotta be smarter than this. Don't let him bait you."

I draw in a calming breath. "Look, clearly, the barracks are out of the question for us tonight, so let's go to my room."

"What about Jess?" Carter asks.

"Gone. With friends overnight in the village."

"Sounds good to me," Carter says.

With Logan between us, the three of us work our way out of the basement and up the winding staircases to the apartments.

Inside, I take off my coat and hang it on the hook by the door. Jess left several table lamps on, and the softly lit and quiet space was a welcoming change from the loud music at Blink.

Carter tosses his coat on the back of a chair and goes to the refrigerator. "Please tell me you have something besides rosé."

He opens the door and sighs.

Apparently not.

He takes one of the bottles, pops the cork, and sniffs before taking a swig. His upper lip curls, and he shudders. "Tastes like rotten apples."

A laugh rumbles from my chest as I make my way to the couch and take off my boots.

Logan curses from the entry where he's stopped, eyes glued on his comm.

"You forgot to close your tab at Blink, didn't you?" Carter says, striding over with the bottle of wine.

Logan's gaze is dark as he looks up. "It's from my lawyer.

The prosecuting attorney is handing my case over to Frank Peterson."

I sit up on the couch as an icy prickle spreads between my shoulder blades.

Frank is Bernard's brother. Garret's uncle.

Logan's lip curls into a snarl. "This is that fucking asshole's doing. I know it."

Without warning, he grabs the vase from the entryway table and hurls it against the wall. I wince as the antique shatters into hundreds of pieces. Logan's rage spirals, storming past him, and Carter clutches his wine bottle protectively. He kicks over an end table, sending the lamp crashing to the floor. The bulb breaks and winks out, casting jagged shadows over the room. Logan charges at the window. Anger billows through the bond so intensely that the air is sucked from my chest.

I'd been unable to calm him in the barracks, but now there's no way I can cool this *rage*. It's wild, chaotic, and beyond anything I've sensed from him before.

Something really had happened. Something bad.

Logan picks up a marble paperweight shaped like a crane from the table and hurls it at the window. The glass cracks but holds.

Carter's throat bobs as he looks at me, worry flickering in his eyes. Logan moves to the window, standing dangerously close with his shoulders hunched.

Logan picks up the paperweight and hurls it again. "Logan, don't," I say, but the crack widens, splintering with a high-pitched sound before the glass finally shatters. Jagged shards fall to the floor with a loud clatter. Cool night air rushes through the opening, evaporating the sweat from my temples.

Rust clings to the iron bars from the years of rain. Several are already missing, leaving gaps wide enough for a person to fit through. Logan's waist presses against them, and I know one light push, the whole structure will collapse, falling four stories below.

The bond pulses with his fury, but I push back, sensing Carter doing the same, trying to send any semblance of calm we can force into him.

A flicker of motion catches my eye as the door opens, and Carla pokes her head in.

"I heard something break. Is everyone —" She trails off as her eyes search the room, quickly assessing the scene before locking with mine.

"Go get Brigid," I shout. "NOW!"

Carla hesitates only for a second before bolting from the doorway.

Carter's eyes lock with mine, his face confused as to why I asked for her, but our trust runs deep enough for him not to question me.

With a silent nod, he turns to Logan. "Hey, man. We'll figure this out. We need to talk about this, not destroy everything."

Logan's chest heaves, and for a moment, I think he might actually jump. The thought of losing him—one of the few people in this world I truly trust—makes my blood turn to ice. He has a temper, but I admire his boldness for acting on instincts I too often suppress.

But right now, that same fire could burn everything down. He might not know it, but I can't afford to lose him, not like this.

"Please, just think about this," I say, taking a cautious step toward him. "You need to step away from the window."

"What's the fucking point?" Logan says, his voice terrifyingly low. "Galaxian is as good as dead, and I'll be nothing."

Silver hair catches the edge of my vision, and immediately, the scent of lavender fills my nostrils. Brigid's still wearing her striped black and white dress, but she's barefoot, and her long hair is down.

Her blue eyes fill with fear as she sees Logan poised by the window. She inches closer, her feet silent on the carpet, and I turn to her. "Help him like you helped me."

A crease appears on her forehead. "What...what do you mean?"

"You know what I mean. At the gala. You did something. I can't describe it, but it did something to my bond. I felt it."

She frowns, and for a heartbeat, I'm worried she doesn't understand. I know it's a long shot, but I'm desperate. Carter and I can't reach him. Maybe she can.

Slowly, she nods, recognition appearing in her eyes as she tentatively begins walking to where Logan has braced himself against the open window.

"Logan," she says softly, her voice steady. "It's me, Brigid. You're all right."

I feel the pulsing energy in the bond steady, then ease slightly. Logan's breathing slows, but his grip on the windowsill remains tight.

"This isn't the answer," she continues, stepping closer. "It might feel like you're alone, but I promise you're not. You have people that care about you. Whatever it is, we'll fix it together. All of us." She gestures to Carter and me, but her eyes never leave Logan's.

She climbs up on the windowsill with him, her movements slow and deliberate. My whole body reacts, tensing as I worry she'll slip, too, and Carter moves closer, positioning himself behind her.

Brigid clutches the curtain with one hand then presses her hands to the side of his face. She forces him to look at her. "Look at me," she says firmly.

The upper half of his face is masked in shadow as he shifts

his eyes to her. "Good. Now take my hand, and I'm going to help you down."

Logan hesitates. The air freezes in my lungs. It's not going to work.

He's already dead. Skull cracked open, and blood splattered on the cement courtyard. Fuck. Brigid is right next to him. What if he takes her with him? Or does she slip by accident when he jumps?

My feet are moving, only slowing when I see Logan take her hand, and they climb down from the sill. The bond's tension eases further, the room filling with a tenuous calm.

As he turns to face her, she presses up on her toes and slowly, carefully kisses him.

The instant their lips meet, a shock wave explodes through the room, catapulting me back. Beside me, Carter stumbles to the side and grasps onto the back of the sofa.

I squeeze my eyes shut, trying to block out the blazing lust coursing through me. The bond ignites with desire, and instantly, I'm aroused.

But I've never felt it like this before. The *need* I've been struggling to keep it quelled consumes me, and for once, I can't extinguish it.

A groan escapes my throat as I succumb to the feeling.

I don't need to look at Carter or Logan to know what they're thinking. The bond hums, connected on a level deeper than anything we've ever experienced — one mind, one body, driven by a singular desire.

Brigid.

My eyes hone in on her, and the hunger within me turns ravenous, an insatiable force that burns through every other thought.

Without a word, the three of us descend upon her.

Thirty-Six

BRIGID

Three sets of hungry, lust-filled eyes fix upon me.
Their imposing frames block the door, leaving no room for escape.

Not that I want to.

I caused this. From whatever I'd done to calm Logan, that elevated awareness had only intensified like pouring gasoline onto a campfire.

The abrupt change in the room feels surreal like I'd been in a nightmare and then yanked from it into a fantasy.

Maybe this is a dream.

Minutes before, I'd been making up the couch at my place when Carla had pounded on my door. I arrived to find Logan seconds from killing himself, and now I'm here, stripping in front of them. The idea feels almost too wild to comprehend, but I'd be lying if I said I hadn't fantasized about this more than once, alone in the dark, my hand drifting between my legs as I imagined them. Imagined something very similar to this.

"Tell us you want this," Heath growls.

Heart slamming against my rib cage like a trapped bird, I nod.

A trio of eyes watches me as I nod my head.

"Say it," Logan says, his voice rough like sandpaper against wood.

"Yes," I whisper.

Carter quickly pulls his shirt over his head, and so do the others. "Good. Now take off that fucking dress."

I'm taken aback by the ferocity in his words, and as if someone else is guiding my movements, I obey. My fingers, steady despite the rush of emotions, slip the dress off my shoulders, letting it slide down until it rests at my feet. I suck in a shaky breath, standing before them in only my black bra and lace thong. My breathing is quick and shallow as their eyes take in every inch of me.

Heath and Logan have hooded eyes, while Carter — licking his lips like a wolf about to devour its meal — inches closer to me.

Before I can react, his lips crash against mine, his tongue demanding entry until I give in. His tongue slips past, exploring with a slow, deliberate tease that sends a spark straight down my spine. I arch my head back with a breathy moan as I sense Heath move closer. Gentle fingers touch my hair, and Carter releases me, guiding my face to Heath's. His hand on my head, he pulls me closer so his mouth can reach mine. Carter moves lower, leaving a trail of scorching kisses along my neck and the tops of my breasts.

The scent of their bodies is heady and grows stronger when Logan approaches me from the back. His hands, rough yet tender, grip my bare hips firmly and pull me back against him. I feel the hardness of his arousal press against my ass and a wave of heat floods through me. I arch my back in response, my body caught between the three of them, writhing with desire.

I'm awake. That's what this is. An awareness that I hadn't even known existed until now. I'd been blindfolded, imprisoned by ignorance, but now, even as my eyes are closed, I'm seeing them clearer than ever before.

This. Is. Everything.

A faint shimmer seems to envelop them, a gossamer aura that pulses with shared energy. An invisible cord humming with vitality. The bond resonates through me, a symphony of emotions and shared consciousness that I shouldn't be able to comprehend.

My mind reels. No. This isn't possible? This has to be their bond, but why can I suddenly sense it? The questions swirl in my head, a maelstrom of confusion and wonder.

As they continue to kiss and touch me, the sensation intensifies. The ebb and flow of their connection sense the depth of their bond in a way that defies explanation.

I'm not a rider, and yet I can *feel* the energy of the bond as clearly as I can feel their hands on my skin.

Slowly, I open my eyes, blinking as the physical world comes back into focus. But the ethereal vision doesn't fade. Carter and Heath are bathed in a soft, luminous glow, their auras bright and intertwined. It's faint, like a shimmering sheen layered over their skin, but undeniably there.

My gaze drifts to Logan at my shoulder. His aura is present, too, though dimmer. As if reluctant to reveal itself, it flickers at the edge of my vision.

Someone unclasps my bra, and Carter lowers his mouth to the rosy peak of my breast while Heath kneels in front of me. I move my hips, letting him slide my panties down. The wet sounds echo around the room as he tastes me, his tongue flitting in and out as his thumb gently caresses my clit.

I moan and lean into their touch, surrendering myself. Carter captures my lips in a searing kiss, swallowing my whimpers of pleasure. My lips part, and his tongue touches mine with deliberate intensity.

I feel another mouth on my breast and open my eyes just long to see Logan assuming Carter's place, his mouth and hand going to my nipple. From the edge of my vision, there's a movement as Carter, without breaking the kiss, holds out a fist, and Logan's lips never leave my breast as he bumps his hand against his.

I laugh into Carter's mouth, and his fingers cup around my chin, pulling me closer.

"Come for me," Carter murmurs. "I want them to see you come undone."

Without waiting for me to react, Carter lowers himself. His breath is hot, eliciting a delicious shiver even before his tongue traces the already sensitive bundle of nerves. "I can't..." I whimper.

"You will," Logan's voice commands from where he's kissing my neck and shoulders.

The heat from his voice coalesces with what Carter is doing with his mouth, and I feel Heath shift beside me, his hand slipping in from behind and his fingers working in unison with Carter's tongue. Head spinning, I gasp at their synchronized movements, each sensation building on the other until it's a tower of pleasure from which I'm balancing.

"Let yourself go, Blondie," Logan murmurs, and I leap off

the edge. An avalanche of euphoria crashes over me, and my knees buckle, but Logan's arms are firm as he lowers me gently to the armchair.

Carter rises to his feet, his lips glistening with my wetness. "Please," I beg. Greedily, my hands seek the hem of Carter and Heath's pants, and they slide off them and their boxers off, springing free their erections.

Unable to deny the urge to touch them, *feel* them any longer, I reach out, but Carter stops me with his hand. "Tonight is for you."

I drop my hand by my side, as one by one, they plunge their fingers into the wetness between my legs, then withdraw and coat their formidable lengths with my slickness.

Fuck me. I'd thought Carter's dick was big, but here the other two are equally impressive, and my stomach dips at the sight.

Eyes locked with mine, the three of them stroke themselves lazily.

My mouth turns dry. If I'd thought I'd been turned on before, nothing compared to this.

I'm a queen on a throne, with a trio of gods before me, their muscular bodies illuminated by the soft moonlight. Every movement they make is a tribute to me.

My desire.

Their smoldering gazes mirror my own, hands working over their lengths in a slow, deliberate rhythm that drives me mad with need.

I've never felt so worshipped, so utterly in control, and I find my hand slipping lower to the deliciously tender space between my legs.

All three groan, their hands moving faster, foreheads creasing with the strain of holding back.

"That's right," Carter whispers, and I notice his voice is sounding thin. "You tell us when."

Heath's jaw clenches, his breath hissing through his teeth as he struggles to maintain control. The sight of them, so strong, so close to breaking, sends a thrill through me.

I hold them in the palm of my hand, well, *their* hands and the knowledge that their release is mine to command pours a fresh rush of arousal into my core. I move my hand faster, feeling another orgasm building.

I savor the moment. The way their eyes darken with longing. The way their bodies tremble under the weight of their restraint. I could keep them like this for as long as I want. Force them to teeter on the edge, their pleasure dangling just out of reach. But I won't torture them — not tonight.

When I speak, my voice is breathy. "Now," I command, and our groans fill the room. They clutch themselves, spilling into their hands, and I tilt back my head on the chair. I cascade over, my fingers dancing over my clit as another tidal wave of pleasure ricochets through me.

I close my eyes, panting as I savor the euphoric sensations. A minute later, footsteps approach, and Heath scoops me to my feet. He carries me into the bedroom before laying me on the bed. A soft comforter is placed over me, and I snuggle into the pillow.

Carter, bare-chested but wearing his boxer shorts, appears nearby with a glass of water. I take it and gulp down the entire glass before handing it back to him. Wiping my face, I glance at a still-naked Logan hovering behind Heath. I arch an eyebrow at his very present erection, and upon catching my gaze, he proudly strokes it once with a smug nod before turning away and disappearing into the bathroom.

Carter returns to my side and lies beside me. He kisses me

softly. Then it's Heath's breath in my ear. "You are an exquisite woman, Ms. Corsair. Thank you."

And then, emotionally and physically spent, I fall into a dreamless slumber.

∽

I CAN'T BELIEVE THAT JUST HAPPENED.

I'd been with three guys at once and not just any guys.

Riders.

Laura was going to flip when I told her, which I totally am because I have to tell someone. Maybe not right away, but someday. She'd tell me how jealous she was of me and then ask for all the sordid details Sharice never would.

When the oceans rose and the floods stretched further inland, people believed it was the apocalypse. And rightfully so. Records all claimed that there had been little warning for those people along the coast. A series of earthquakes at the poles and, then boom, massive sheets of ice melting in hours rather than years.

Within a week, religious types believed God's wrath had washed away the sinners and left behind the true souls. But in reality, it had been the opposite. History books centered on the early post-rise era are filled with accounts of violence and desperation. Brothers turning on brothers. Mothers giving up children for food or water. Men and women believed to be good and honest citizens were transformed into monsters by the need to survive.

So maybe this was hell after all because of what I'd done while a fresh widow and friend slept in an empty bed next door. I was still wearing my dress from Kaeden's memorial, for shit's sake.

But damn, how I liked it. No, I didn't regret a second of it. It hadn't been wrong or sinful. It'd been the purest moment I'd ever experienced.

When I awake, my body hums with satiated bliss as I lie tangled among limbs.

My gaze drifts to the two men still sleeping soundly.

No, this isn't hell. This is heaven.

Carter's chest rises and falls under my hand, and I work an arm free from under Heath. Whatever glow I'd seen or thought I'd seen was gone. But why, after all this time, could I sense their bonds? The only plausible explanation I can think of is that when Oriana was in her egg, she somehow bonded with me, enabling me to ride Galaxian. Could that be it? I have so many questions. And debate about telling them, but what if it was only temporary and would soon fade? What if it had already disappeared?

I draw in a shuddering breath. Carter, especially, would just worry, and right now, he looks so damn relaxed. Happy. Heath too. That persistent crease between his brows is smoothed for the first time in a long time.

I'll tell them once I know more and have something concrete to say. As they doze, my fingers lightly begin tracing the defined lines of abs and sculpted shoulders and arms. A lazy smile plays across my lips at the memory of how those muscles flexed and rippled beneath my touch last night.

Logan is already gone, but Heath stirs first, carefully extricating himself from the knot of arms and legs. I watch through half-lidded eyes as he stretches languidly before padding off toward the bathroom. His toned backside offers a drool-worthy view, and a girlish giggle threatens to escape me.

Carter moves next, and his smoldering eyes roam over my body. Even after last night's marathon, that heated look induces a pulsing sensation between my legs.

"About last night..." I begin, not even sure what I intend to say. An apology? Gratitude? A plea for more?

Carter's finger presses against my lips, stemming from the flow of words. "Last night was incredible. More than incredible." His voice is a low, gravelly purr that sends tendrils of desire unfurling through my core. "And this morning promises to be even better, just you and me."

His lips slant over mine in a scorching kiss that leaves me dizzy and grateful I'm still lying down.

I'd been fully aware of my actions last night, and yet it felt like we'd been under the influence of some sort of drug. Some magic that tethered our thoughts together and blurred our wants with our inhibitions.

What had Heath said, that "I'd ruin them?"

Screw that. Look what they'd done to me.

As if reading my mind, Carter murmurs against my neck, "You're ours now." His hand traces along my ribs, over the curve of my waist, every caress igniting sparks across my skin. An invigorating shiver flutters low in my belly.

"Is that so?" I whisper.

He props himself up on one elbow, green eyes shining with an intensity that steals my breath. "You make me feel so fucking alive. Sharing this"—he gestures to the space between us—"with Heath and Logan." A look of pure reverence washes over his face. "It's heaven."

Overcome, I pull his mouth back to mine, answering with the only response that feels adequate.

"Heath and Logan have a lot to do this morning," he says when we finally break apart. "They made me promise to watch after you. Which I gladly accepted."

He eyes my body up and down, sending a glorious thrill down my back.

"So, you're okay with what happened?" I say, motioning to the general area.

"I don't mind sharing you with them," he says as his thumb caresses my chin. "They're like brothers, a part of me, and I can't deny them what they want, what makes them happy. And if it means I get you, too, it's all good by me."

I sigh, relief flooding through me. There's so much uncertainty about this whole situation, and now I've complicated things further. In the past, I'd barely kept one boyfriend for more than a few months, and now I have three.

Okay, that's a stretch. Logan would rather traipse across the courtyard in my heels than consider himself tied to a societal label like that, and even though Heath assured me he and Jess were done, she clearly hadn't gotten the memo since she was still living here.

"So, how does this work, then? What should I call you?"

Carter lowers his gaze on me with a look so intense, so fierce, I forget how to breathe. "Call me whatever you want."

I tilt my chin, struggling to inhale and will my heart to keep from fluttering from my chest. "That's not an answer."

His green eyes darken a shade until they're nearly as shadowed as Heath's. "I don't care what you call me, so long as it means I'm yours."

Under the sheets, my toes curl. "Is that what you are? Mine?"

"As long as you'll have me, yes."

I draw in a sudden breath, overwhelmed by the promise. "All right. But I want both of us to be honest. No sneaking around, no lying, okay? Either we're all in or nothing."

"Works for me, but so you know, I don't mind the details." He smirks and rests an elbow on the pillow. "Thinking about their cocks in your hands gets me just as hot as if you're holding mine." He pauses, then adds.

"Speaking of which," he presses his hard bulge against my hip.

I laugh. "Hungry?"

One very vigorous twenty minutes later, that ends with us both in the shower. I towel off, feeling thoroughly, completely satisfied. At least for a while...

After rinsing off, Carter puts on his clothes from last night. In the most adorable way imaginable, he kisses me on the forehead and then leaves for the barracks.

Fortunately for me, I have a very short walk of shame in last night's dress and heels. Back across the hallway and in my apartment, I put on my wrist comm on the charger as I blow dry my hair. I change into an oversized long-sleeve shirt and leggings. My cheeks have that rosy, post-sex glow, and so I opt for a light amount of makeup. My bed is made with a note from Sadie thanking me for letting her stay there and I plan to check in on her later today.

I make my way to the kitchen for a quick snack and spot the blinking red light on my comm. It's a message from Marshal:

> Come to my office ASAP. Something's come up regarding your physical.

My physical? Oh right. When we'd landed here, they'd gone through my health history, given me vitamins, and drawn blood. I hadn't put any thought into it beyond checking us for diseases and our general health.

I scarf down a yogurt topped with honey and dried granola, then exit my apartment and head to Marshal's.

Logan, Heath, and Carter are awaiting me inside Marshal's office. Dressed in their black riding gear and looking fine as hell. My cheeks flush, and a throbbing sensation forms between my thighs as all three turn their eyes on me. A shimmering aura flutters around Heath and Carter, like a second gold skin, but there's nothing around Logan or Marshal. It's odd, but at least reassuring I'm not losing my mind. Whatever this gift or ability is, it's still there.

At least for now.

Marshal comes around the front of his desk and leans against it. "I know it's early, and it was a long night for all of us," he pauses, resting his hands behind him. His eyes drift between us, and his mouth twitches as if he's about to speak, but he doesn't. His expression remains unreadable, giving no hint of what he's thinking. There's no way he can know what the four of us did, right? I mean, the bond isn't that direct? They sense moods and vibes and…

The knot in my gut loosens, convinced I'm in the clear, until his eyes narrow just a fraction of an inch. Heat sweeps up my neck as I realize with mortifying certainty that he knows *exactly* what happened. Okay, maybe not the sordid details, but enough for me to want to dissolve into the floor and disappear.

He clears his throat, oblivious to the fact that I'm slowly dying of embarrassment. "However, I decided this couldn't wait until later."

My thoughts sprint ahead, mulling over the dozens of things that this could be connected to. Why did he need all of us here? Maybe I was sick? Had I caught something when the mystyl had attacked me? Or some bacterial infection from the egg?

Marshal pins me with a narrow look. "Don't worry, your physical was fine. There was nothing wrong with your health or anything, but they found something odd in your blood work."

"Odd? Odd, how?" I ask.

"As you know, my rider career has been uncharacteristically long, and in an effort to find out why I've not flared out yet, they did a panel of tests on me right around my tenth anniversary. They found what they thought was a peculiar genetic anomaly. We've never come across another to share the same trait. Until now."

Me. He means me. "What? Are you sure?"

"They ran it twice to confirm," Marshal says, offering me a reassuring smile. "but the results came back the same. I'm your brother, Brigid."

Thirty-Seven

LOGAN

Holy shit.

Brigid is Marshal's sister.

It seems like every time I turn around, another surprise smacks me in the face.

For a long moment, no one says anything. Then Marshal rubs a hand over his forehead.

"I thought you should know," he says. "And while I'm not spreading this information around, there is a good chance those who know, like Dr. Rajesh or one of the other medical staff, will want to run more tests on you."

Brigid's throat bobs, her eyes blinking rapidly. "I uh... sure. Of course. Whatever they need, I can do."

"Let's give them a minute," Heath says, rising to his feet. "We can come back later to talk more."

Heath and I make our way to the door, but Carter seems hesitant to leave. He lets out a low whistle, shaking his head in disbelief. "Well, damn. Talk about a small world. Two of my favorite people are related. I couldn't have planned this better if I tried. How did we not know this sooner?"

Marshal purses his lips. "I still haven't figured that out yet myself."

"Carter," Heath says. "You're late for novice lessons."

Carter tilts his head, eyes flicking between Brigid and Marshal. "Fucking wild," he says, turning away from us and marching out the open door.

We leave Marshal's office and start down the stairs on the west wing of the barn.

Heath scrolls his comm, replying to messages and reading station schedule shit I should be reading, but my mind drifts to last night. Ever since I'd arrived here, I had been drowning in rage and despair. Still, I'd managed to control it until that bastard Garrett had tipped me over the edge, transforming the anger into a living thing, writhing beneath my skin, whispering dark promises I was ready to accept.

The world had narrowed as I teetered on the brink of oblivion. I'd been at the edge, tempted by the offer to end this suffering, until her voice had pierced the darkness, drawing me back into reality. But it had been her kiss that shattered it entirely, splintering it like shadowed glass.

Immediately after, my mind had cleared, and my rage had morphed into the need to please her. *Serve her.*

It must have seeped through to Heath and Carter because, holy hell, the bond had lit up like a thousand flares at once.

How she'd felt, tasted, and the way she'd sounded as she'd come, all of it had felt so fucking *right*. And instead of the bond fighting me, it had pushed me as if Galaxian had been approving.

I've had sex before, lots of it, but this was different.

My dick jerks to attention as the shifting images replay in my mind.

Fuck me. I hadn't fist-bumped Carter, had I? I snort, drawing surprised looks from two attendants passing by us with a crate of canned beans.

Well, shit. *They must be handing out ice skates in hell.*

At Vanguard armory training, they'd drilled into us to respect our rifles. Learn how they're built so that if they fail, we can fix them. Over and over again, we'd been forced to disable the pistol all the way down to the diode that created the laser. I'd gotten so good at it that I could do it in less than a minute, including polishing the grip and oiling the springs.

Last night, with Blondie, had been like that. When I'd kissed her, it'd been like fitting the last piece of a disassembled gun back into place.

At Meridian, I'd ignored Carter's droning on and on about our connection, thinking it was bullshit. But last night, everything changed. We are four parts of the same whole.

Soulbound.

Whether fate or a weird side effect from the bond, I'd be damned if I denied it anymore. We were linked.

And she was the anchor tethering us together.

She's mine. *They're* mine. And we're never letting go.

"Logan McCelroy?" A man asks, stepping in front of us on the bottom landing that leads into the stables.

He's older, with thinning hair and wrinkled skin, and flashes a police badge. "I'm Detective Slate from Nelworth. If you don't mind, I'd like to ask you a few questions."

"About what?" I snap, even though I know damn well what it's about.

He glances at Heath, then back at me. "Is there somewhere private we can talk?"

Heath shifts uneasily beside me. He'll come to my defense

if I ask him, but he'd already stuck his neck out for me, and his family is all twisted the fuck up with the Petersons, so I'd hate to drag him further into the mud with me.

I thrust my chin ahead of us. "An empty storage closet down there."

Detective Slate gestures for me to lead, and Heath remains behind, his eyes burning into the back of my head.

The closet has two saddle racks, four folding chairs, and a single lightbulb hanging from the ceiling. I click on the switch and sink into one of the chairs. Slate does the same, crossing his legs and folding his hands in his lap.

"So, Mr. McCelroy," he begins, his voice clipped like he despises my name, "care to explain to me what happened between you and Mr. Peterson last night?"

This is bullshit. He knows fucking well what happened.

Slate uncrosses his legs and fixes me with a pointed stare. "Well?"

My hand passes over my buzzed hair, the short strands prickling my palm as I release a deep sigh. "What do you want me to say?" My voice sounds weary. Not surprising, given the lack of sleep last night. "Garrett was running his mouth and things got a little heated, sure, but it's normal to blow off steam after a rider memorial."

He arches an eyebrow, clearly unconvinced, and taps his comm to read from it. "Garrett Peterson was admitted to the Blackhawk medical clinic last night. Wounds included a fractured nose, three bruised ribs, and lacerations to his face and hands." He pauses, swiping the screen closed. "When asked about the wounds, he named you as the attacker."

I shrug helplessly as if unable to offer any real explanation.

"Sounds like a little more than blowing off steam, don't you think?"

"I guess."

He lets out an exasperated sigh, shaking his head. "Assault charges are no laughing matter, son. If you have anything to say, I suggest you do so now."

Son? The first trickle of anger seeps into my veins as I nod. I should tell him he was getting handsy with Brigid, but Garrett will deny it. I don't know other rich people as well as Heath, but I understand them well enough to know when they're backed into a corner, they'll lie. And anything they can't lie about, they'll pay off. Blondie could testify right to their fucking faces, and somehow she'd end up looking like a slut or a woman desperate for attention.

Slate opens his mouth to speak again, but a sudden commotion outside the door catches both of our attention. The door swings open, and Chief Lugsen strides in, his expression grim.

"Logan," he says, his voice clipped as his gaze darts between me and Slate. "Marshal wants to see you in his office. *Immediately.*"

I rise from the chair.

"Excuse me," Slate stammers. "This man is a suspect in a crime, and I'm not done questioning him."

"Yes, you are," Lugsen says. He's at least five inches shorter than the detective and is forced to glare up at him. "Riders implicated in any criminal case are to be questioned with the presence of their lawyer or station manager present."

Slate blubbers. "Circuit police jurisdiction supersedes any station statutes."

"Not when the supposed incident occurs on station property."

The detective's face pales.

Two points for Lugsen.

"McCelroy is coming with me," he says. "Once Marshal briefs him, you can resume your questioning."

I don't fucking wait for permission. I stride out of the storage closet, pausing just long enough to flip the detective off. He shoots me a glare, and I leave him behind, following Lugsen back to Marshal's office.

I'm damn lucky Lugsen came when he did. Nevertheless, I can't shake the feeling I have a bullseye on my back. I'm fucking up left and right, and the post-sex high of being with Brigid is all that's keeping me from running to the stables and galloping away on Galaxian.

Lugsen knocks on Marshal's door, and I steel myself for the confrontation to come, even though I'd spoken to him minutes before.

The door opens, and he's moved behind his desk, his piercing gaze fixed on me.

Brigid is nowhere to be seen, but I'm too distracted to wonder why she'd left his office so abruptly.

The moment I catch sight of Marshal, all the fight drains out of me. He can't affect my bond as strongly as Heath and Carter can, but he doesn't need to. I respect the hell out of him, with or without the bond assisting.

Brigid should find herself fucking lucky as hell to have him as a brother.

Inhaling, I step inside.

Marshal regards me silently. "Logan," he says, his voice flat. "Come and take a seat, please."

I take the chair across from him, sensing the weight of his oppressive gaze. This is it, I think to myself. This is where everything ends.

"I don't need to explain why you're here," Marshal begins. "What the hell, man? You must be smarter than this. Your reckless actions have put us all in jeopardy."

I open my mouth to protest, but he holds up a hand, silencing me.

"The rules exist for a reason," Marshal says, his voice heavy with disappointment. "We've been patient, but Galaxian's rogue status has obviously impacted your control over yourself. When the bond is abused or mishandled, it can have consequences."

I adjust in my seat as his words hit home. I'd been a dumbass, thinking I could deny it. I'd convinced myself Galaxian's choice to kill the scientist hadn't been intentional and that it was a one-off freak event. But I'd been wrong.

He really had gone rogue.

And my bond along with him. For days, it's been lurking on the fringes of my mind, the doubt, the confusion. I'd thought it was because I hadn't been brimming that the bond had been clearer, but I was wrong about too.

It was clear because Galaxian had made it that way.

He'd lit the torch where there'd been a match, and it was forcing me to lose my cool when I normally could walk away. Its power, its influence, was affecting my behavior in ways I can't understand or control. However, even as I sit there, head bowed in submission, I can't help but feel a flicker of defiance burning within me.

Fine. It's poisoned, but that doesn't mean I can't fix it.

"Until you can learn to control yourself," Marshal continues, "Your temper and the rogue effect in your bond, you are suspended from all riding drills training and cannot see your stallion without me or Lugsen present."

I snort in disbelief. "You're kidding, right?"

Marshal's eyes bore into mine, and I'm ten again, facing my dad's pissed-off face after I'd snuck out after curfew to explore the plant's restricted zones, only to be dragged back by a patrol.

"No, Logan. I'm not," Marshal says. "This is serious. Am I making myself clear?"

"Fucking crystal."

"Good," he says, the tension fading from his face. "Now, I need you to tell me everything that happened last night between you and Garret Peterson so I can try to keep your ass out of jail."

Once I've finished recounting last night's events, I retreat to the barracks. I'd kept the part about Brigid from Slate but decided to loop Marshal in because I trusted him but also cause he'd sense I was hiding something. If Brigid was pissed that I told him, so be it. She was always pissed at me for something.

Marshal listened intently as I'd explained, his focus sharpening when Brigid's name came up. Of course, he wouldn't say anything in front of Lugsen since the whole brother and sister thing they were keeping secret, but between his grip tightening on the pen and the muscle flexing in his jaw, he was glad I did it.

After a moment, he said quietly, "Thank you."

Muted anger rippled in the air between us, a shared frustration and protective impulse. Damn, how I liked knowing Marshal had Brigid's back too.

Even though I'd been drunk, my security training had saved me as I recounted near-perfect details, seeing them groping Brigid at the cable car station and then them waiting for me outside the barracks.

Marshal had interjected at that point and said it seemed like it was self-defense. He'd clear things up with Slate but told me to steer clear of Garrett for a while.

No shit.

In the barn, I avoid going to the right to where Galaxian is kept. My bond is too jacked right now, and seeing him might tip me over the edge. I need to confront him, but only with a cool head.

Most of the riders are at weapons training, but as I walk down the aisleway, I see Carter leaning over Oriana's stall.

He hears me coming and glances at me as I approach. The smile on his face falters. "How bad?"

"Nothing I can't handle," I reply and rest my elbows on the stall next to him. Heath obviously had told him about Slate.

Dr. Gideon is standing inside her stall, wearing the protective jumpsuit and holding a metal pail. "Picky little thing, isn't she?" Carter says.

"I don't know what else to do." Gideon blows air from his lips and adjusts his glasses with his free hand. "The druadan nursery tech from Lannett suggested soaking the protein pellets in a milk replacement." He holds up a metal pail filled with a thick, greenish slurry triumphantly.

I wrinkle my nose. "It smells like—"

"I know what it smells like," he says, waving me off as he walks to the stall. "But if we don't get her to eat, they're going to have to insert a feeding tube, and that opens up a whole mess of complications I want to avoid."

"Here. You try?" He thrusts the pail at me.

"What? Hell no." I shove it back at him.

"Come on, Logan," Carter pleads. "Are you just going to watch it starve?"

Taking the pail back, I sidestep into the stall. I hold the pail out. "Here. Food."

Oriana lifts her head from something she'd been looking at in the corner and tilts her head to me. I shake the pale, and the terrible aroma fills my nostrils. "This smells like shit."

"According to Dr. Sanchez," Gideon says, stepping out of the stall, "most hatchlings can't get enough of this stuff."

The foal cranes her neck, gives the bucket a sniff, and then recoils, letting out a disgruntled snort. "Yeah, well, he's wrong."

I stand upright as Oriana clumsily scratches her ear with its tiny hind hoof.

Refusing to let this little creature defy me, I scoop up a spoonful and extend it with my hand. "Don't make me force-feed you. Just try a bite."

But Oriana is having none of it. She darts behind Gideon's legs, peeking out and leveling me with a defiant glare. With an exasperated sigh, I hand the bucket to Carter.

For the next few minutes, they try every gentle coaxing method to entice Oriana while the druanera bobs and weaves, evading them with devilish delight. At one point, she kicks at the pail, sending mush splattering over the floor and on Gideon's boots. Then there's a 'pop' as she phases, only to appear behind him, taunting him and chirping in what I can only assume is her version of a curse word.

Carter glances down as Oriana darts playfully between his legs. "Is she just toying with us?"

"Sure as hell looks like it," I say.

Gideon huffs out a breath. "She's smarter than the typical foal, that's for sure. But she'll have to eat, eventually."

I edge closer to Carter. "You were right, you know."

"Oh yeah," he casually says, as if he isn't secretly getting off on it. "About what?"

"About Blondie. There *is* something there."

He sighs, plucking a piece of straw from between the wooden slats of the stall. "Welcome to the club. Took you long enough."

"I ain't part of no club. Just because of what happened last night doesn't mean I've bought into the whole we're written in the stars, bullshit. But I do believe this isn't fucking normal."

Carter snorts and shakes his head. "What does that mean?"

"It means..." I grit my teeth. "I'm open to seeing what happens next."

"Hell yeah." He slaps me on the back. "Well, next time, we should plan it better. *You* get on your knees first, and then I'll stand behind so my hands —"

Dr. Gideon clears his throat. "Well, uh," he stammers, "since she's clearly not wanting this, I'm going to make some more calls. See if I can't try another recipe." He maneuvers himself through the stall door, forcing us to take a step back before quickly retreating down the aisle.

Carter bursts into laughter, and I crack a smile.

I could only imagine the dirty shit Gideon had heard over the years, and yet Carter had done the impossible. He'd embarrassed a druadan vet.

"Nice fucking job, dumbass," I say, smacking him over the back of the head. "Now, we're stuck with babysitting duty."

Carter flashes me a toothy grin. "You can be Mama McCelroy, and I'll be Daddy James."

"I don't think so. If anyone is going to be daddy, it's me."

Thirty-Eight

JESS

"We need to talk," Heath says. "I've tried. Damn tides, how I've tried, but this can't go on anymore. I can't do this anymore. To hell with the merger. I need this to be over."

My breath hitches in my chest. He'd told me we needed to discuss things once I'd returned from staying in the village last night. I'd found our apartment with plastic sheeting over a broken window and shards of my favorite vase in the trash bin.

Heath told me Logan had one of his fits, and I hadn't pressed him for details. I'd never understand riders and their explosive emotions, especially that brute.

"It's her, isn't it?" I say, willing my voice to remain calm. On the gondola ride back, I'd anticipated this would be the conversation we'd be having. "Brianna, right? The PR girl?"

Heath drops his gaze to the floor, the muscles under his smooth jaw flexing. "Her name is Brigid, and yes."

I stare at him coolly. "Does she feel the same way about you, too?"

"I don't know. I think so."

"Very well."

His eyes return to mine, confusion swirling in their brown depths. "That's it?"

"What do you want me to do? Throw a tantrum and shout desperately to beg for you to stay? You never did that, so why would you expect the same from me?"

Hurt stings his eyes, and I'd be lying if I wasn't enjoying it.

"Besides, you and I both know that's not my style. I'm not the type of girl who needs to beg. However, you do know what this means?"

I mean, for our families, the merger. He will suffer the most, but I'm beyond caring.

His face is somber as he nods.

"Knowing you, you've thought long and hard about this, so I don't need to ask if you're sure." I lift my chin. "Still, it'd be comforting to know you at least found this decision difficult."

"I did."

"Then that is it. We are done. I'll inform my parents and the venue. I will leave Blackhawk at once, and neither of us will ever need to see each other again."

"Thank you," he says, barely above a whisper.

For a long moment, neither of us says anything, and then, without another word, he turns and leaves the room, his long coat billowing out behind him. I watch him go, a hollow ache in my chest. Subconsciously, I'd been preparing for this ever since the dinner with our parents, but it still stings to have my future crumble so completely.

As the door closes behind him, I feel the slightest hint of relief, like I'd been holding my breath this whole time and can finally exhale. My shoulders slump as I bring a shaky hand to my forehead, brushing back stray strands of hair.

"It's over," I murmur to the empty room. "Really, truly over."

My gaze drifts to the wilted bouquet of roses on the entry table, which had been in the vase Logan had broken.

I'd be packing soon, but this was still my apartment for the time being. I'd be damned if I didn't have a bouquet perfuming the space. Rotating my comm on my wrist, I tap out a message to Sadie.

> I need some fresh flowers for my room.

Sadie replies a minute later.

> I'll order some tomorrow, but it'll be three days before they arrive. Sorry!"

Scowling, I tuck my comm away and return my eyes to the once vibrant crimson petals shriveled and lying in a pathetic heap. Broken vase or not, these should have lasted a week if they'd come from a reputable florist. I'd only gotten these the day before yesterday. It was unacceptable. I collect them, careful not to prick myself with the thorns, and then toss them into the paper bag. Sadie was a sweet girl, but if she didn't want to be pushed around by whoever their distributor was, she needed to arm herself better to fight them.

This was proof that they were providing an inferior product.

I'll take them to her now.

I leave the apartment and head down to her office, but see the door is closed. It is late, so not surprising. Still, I don't trust these won't get picked up by a janitor, so I'll return with them to my room. The smell of fresh bread drifts up the stairwell from the mess hall, and my stomach grumbles, halting my return to my apartment.

For so long, I had been depriving myself, both physically and emotionally, in pursuit of a future that clearly wasn't meant for me. But now I had broken the shackles and was determined to rediscover the woman I had locked up tight behind gilded bars of obligation.

Tides, I was famished.

Since it's late, the mess hall is all but empty. Only two station workers preparing for their late shift sit in a booth at the far end, watching one of the basketball games.

I hook the paper sack over my arm and take one of the trays to slide it along the railing. I prepare a late dinner of cod, creamed potatoes, sauteed apples, and deep-fried and breaded zucchini. Smiling to myself, I scoot past the salads and to the dessert table. Tiny bowls of the sorbet I love so much in assorted fruity hues line it, and I grab one of each color.

I'm so very *done* with my wedding diet.

Moving to the window, I look out onto the courtyard and the twinkling lights of the village far down below. This dreary cafeteria is about as far from the upscale restaurants and posh eateries I'm accustomed to as one could get, but I'm too hungry and depressed to care.

I pivot to the other side of the buffet table when I spot it — a solitary bowl of butterscotch custard glistening under the hanging lights. I make a beeline for the prize, only to freeze as another hand reaches in to take it.

"Hey, excuse me," I snap, bristling, and pull back, ready to scold whatever rude individual this is.

It's Marshal. My breath freezes in my chest, stilling my tongue.

He's wearing that faded hooded sleeveless sweatshirt again, the one he should've tossed years ago, and his loose athletic shorts are hanging low on his hips. I've always been drawn to older men for their casual confidence and the way they carry themselves without fear of judgment.

And Marshal is no exception.

"You know rank has its privileges around here," he says, tone mild even as the corner of his mouth quirks upward. "But I'm feeling generous tonight since Finn came back from his outing tired and happy — so we can share."

I should tell him no. I'm *not* in the mood for his company, but I had my heart set on that custard. Wordlessly, I jerk my chin in a nod of agreement. He grins and plucks up the custard and a couple of spoons. With his free hand, he gestures toward one of the unoccupied booths lining the wall.

I grumble under my breath and begrudgingly follow. Very much aware of his looming presence seated across from me, I slide into the cracked vinyl seat. I set my tray on the table and don't wait for him before tearing into the fish with my bare fingers.

Sure enough, I can feel the weight of his stare as I lick greasy crumbs from my fingertips. Let him think I'm like one of the heathen trawlers. I don't give a single damn anymore.

"Seems like you've had one hell of a day," he observes, taking a metal flask from his pocket. "That makes two of us." He takes a swig from the flask before sliding it across the table. "Here, whatever it is, this ought to help."

"I'll pass."

"Suit yourself." He shrugs and knocks back another swig. I continue to eat as he screws the lid back on and places it in the center of the table like an offering. "So, you know, I intend to drink all of that tonight."

Damn him. "Well, if I'd known, there'd be a time limit," I say, taking it and unscrewing the lid. I tip it back, letting the strong liquor pour into my mouth. It's strong, the flavor of oranges and oak burning its way down to my stomach.

I pull it back, wincing down the burn.

"All right," he says, frost blue eyes watching me intently. "Tell me, what has the unflappable Jessica Drakeford slinging whiskey in the cafeteria well past dinnertime?"

I hadn't expected to talk to anyone tonight. The plan had been simple — gorge myself on fried foods and sweets, then retreat to a bubble bath. But now Marshal has imposed himself upon my evening. His attention is unsettling, like I'm some puzzle he's determined to solve. "Why do you care?"

"Finn has been happier than ever." He stabs a spoon into the custard. "Figured I owed you one."

I take another drink of the whiskey and scowl at the taste. It's terrible.

"Okay. Fine." I slide the nearly empty flask into the space between us. "You wouldn't know of anyone wanting a custom-made Bellezza wedding gown?"

"Not off the top of my head, no." A crease forms between his brows. "You and Lockwood have some kind of falling out?"

I laugh bitterly, surprising myself with the rawness of the sound. He's more astute than I'd given him credit for. "You could say that. We're done - just not publicly yet." I pause, pleased that the whiskey has eased the tightness in my chest. "I suppose it was inevitable, in the end. You can't force something that was never meant to be."

Marshal is silent for a long moment, digesting this. At last, he passes me the bowl of custard he'd only taken a bite of and the extra spoon.

As I eagerly dig in, savoring the creamy, buttery taste, he leans back, raking a hand through his hair. "If it's any consolation, you're handling this better than my cousin did after her husband stood her up at the altar. She climbed on the church roof in her wedding dress and demanded that someone drag him out of the dive bar where he'd passed out. It'd ended up being a big misunderstanding, but shit, I'd never seen a woman so mad."

"What's the deal with these?" he says, gesturing to the bag of wilted roses on the seat next to me.

"I'd brought them to show Sadie how they'd lasted two days and needed replacing, but she's apparently busy." I smooth back a stray lock of hair behind my ear. "Tell me. Is a *fresh*, good quality bouquet for a person's room so much to ask?" I grumble around a mouthful of food.

"Out here? Yeah." Marshal's lips quirk into a half-smile. "But that's because you're shipping them in."

My mouth twitches in annoyance. "What else am I supposed to do?"

"Come on," he says, taking my nearly empty tray, "there's something I want to show you." He slides out of the booth and gets to his feet. I eye him warily, but curiosity gets the better of me. He dumps my tray and places the empty dishes in the tub, and I follow him out of the mess hall.

We weave through the dimly lit corridors of Blackhawk, the few wall lamps casting flickering shadows on the stone walls. Marshal leads me down a quiet hallway, and I'm about to question our destination when he pushes open a heavy wooden door.

The sight that greets me sweeps my breath from my lungs. Before us stretches a vast greenhouse, its glass panes arching high overhead. The evening sky is a blanket of blue punctuated by stars.

The air is warm and humid, thick with the scents of exotic blooms. Vibrant flowers of every hue imaginable spill from hanging baskets and raised beds.

"Marshal, I..." Words fail me as I step further inside,

trailing my fingers along the velvety petals of a purple blossom. "This is incredible."

He chuckles, shoving his hands into his pockets. "This place had been empty for years. Used for storage mostly, so I had it renovated when I hit my ten-year anniversary as a rider. Not like I have anything else to spend my money on." His gaze sweeps over the lush foliage, a hint of pride in his expression.

I shake my head in disbelief, overwhelmed by the sheer beauty surrounding us. "I never expected something like *this* here."

"Most people don't," Marshal admits. "Of course, they never ask." He plucks an exceptionally bright orange flower, holding it out to me. "For you, my lady."

A soft laugh escapes me as I accept the blossom, twirling it between my fingers. "That's quite a line. I'm sure it's worked for you before, but I'm not the single-carnation type of woman."

He arches an eyebrow. "Good to know."

My heart stammers in my chest. What did that mean? And why did it feel like this was some test? Had he shown me this secret place to prove my trustworthiness?

Before I can dwell on it longer, I stride ahead, determined to meander through the greenhouse and give myself a respite from his presence.

Most of these are tropical, grown only on the southern coast or near Parnia, and I know their names by heart. Violets, daisies, roses, hyacinth, but then my eye snags on a delicate-looking orchid with two burgundy petals surrounded by a triangular-shaped buttery yellow one.

Marshal moves next to me, so close I can feel the heat radiating off of him. "Rime Marsh Orchid," he offers. "You have a good eye. This is a special one I brought back from one of my trips off the continent."

I arch an eyebrow. "There's no way *you* have been off the continent."

"I have. Why is that so hard to believe?"

My mouth fumbles with the words, the whiskey making my mind more sluggish than I'd prefer. "I just assumed a rider couldn't be gone from their stallion for that long."

He leans closer, his fingers caressing the side of the blooming orchid, and his eyes lock with mine. "I'm not like other riders."

The warmth of his breath against my skin elicits goosebumps along my arms. I can smell the faint scent of his cologne mingling with the floral fragrances around us. I turn away, trying to put some space between us. This isn't right. I'm supposed to be broken-hearted and trying not to have a nervous breakdown over the fact that I'll be breaking the news to my parents tomorrow, not in a greenhouse with one of his friends.

"It all sounds so incredible," I murmur when I compose myself. "I've never been away from Venovia."

"Really? Why not?" He voices behind me.

I pause, touching a pale yellow blossom from a shrub, and feel his eyes watching me. A rueful smile tugs at my lips. "My parents were always too worried about diseases, wild lands, or the possibility of me being taken hostage."

"Well, that's a shame," he says, shaking his head. "The world is a wondrous place. You're missing out on so much."

"I know." I lower my hands, and I sigh. "Perhaps one day, when things calm down, I'll go."

Finally, I pivot, facing him again, and his gaze holds a thoughtful gleam as he studies me. "You're not what I expected."

"Is that so?" Heat rises to my cheeks, warming them more than the liquor already has.

"Absolutely." He leans in conspiratorially. "Between you and me, I find it rather refreshing."

I can't help but laugh, the sound echoing through the greenhouse. "Oh no, you don't get to use that line on me."

He grins with the most roguish smile I've ever seen. "Is that what you think I'm doing? Using a line?"

The air stills between us, our eyes locked on each other. "Obviously?" I whisper.

Marshal steps closer, his eyes alight with mischief. "Please don't tell anyone. I have a reputation to maintain here."

"Of course," I reply, rolling my eyes playfully. "Wouldn't dream of bruising that ego of yours."

"Lucky for you, my ego is unbruisable."

"That's not a word."

He tilts his head and squints. "It's not?"

"No."

"Well, then, I just invented it."

"You can't do that."

"Sure, I can. I'm Marshal Clemmons, remember?" he gestures to the surrounding space. "Here, I can do whatever I want."

A laugh escapes me, and I shake my head, astounded by this man's audacity. And that's saying something, considering the kind of men I've known in my life.

He takes another step closer as a triumphant grin spreads across his face. "Ah," he says softly, his voice warm. "There it is. Mission accomplished."

I raise an eyebrow, intrigued. "What mission?"

He leans in, his breath tickling my ear as he whispers, "Making you laugh. It's been my goal all evening, and I have to say, your laugh is even better than I imagined."

My mouth forms a silent 'O' as I'm confused about how to

reply. It's corny, I know, but no one ever said something like that to me.

I shake my head, clearing my thoughts, as he moves back, his eyes studying my face. He's just trying to get into my pants, like all riders. "I...uh," I stammer. "I think I'll pass on the bouquet. Goodnight, Marshal." Without waiting for him to reply, I flee from the greenhouse. I toss the bag of flowers in the first compost bin I see and take the stairs two at a time, returning to my room. More than once, I imagine him chasing after me. I pause at the top of the landing, taking one last look, but there's no one.

I press my lips together and continue the rest of the way, feeling ridiculous for letting myself get carried away by such a silly notion.

Heath had made that painfully evident.

No man will ever chase after me.

Thirty-Nine

BRIGID

I have a brother.
 And if that isn't shocking enough, he's one of the most famous riders in the world, if not ever.
 I haven't built up the nerve to call my mom yet and ask her why she'd lied about my father. I want to know desperately, but a small part of me fears she knew about Sharice and had lied about that, too. The thought of her letting me believe Sharice was kidnapped or worse, when she knew all along she was part of the terrorist group, was something I was not ready to face.
 Besides, she probably wouldn't answer anyway, insisting I visit her instead, like some emotional blackmail. I had a weekend off coming up. I'd see her then and get my answers.

Marshal had a meeting after dropping the news yesterday, so he'd told me to come by his office before breakfast to talk more. I'd tossed and turned most of the night, my thoughts racing with how this could've happened. How I had never known I had another sibling out there.

I sip the cup of coffee Marshal made for me when I'd arrived. He takes it with two splashes of goat's milk and a dollop of honey, just like me. I smile to myself. What else do we have in common?

"My father stuck around just long enough to get my mom pregnant," Marshal says, "and then split. I have a few letters from him, birthday cards mostly, and when I turned ten, he sent me a printed photo, too."

"Printed? Like on paper?"

"Laminated plastic, technically, but yeah. It would have been so much easier to send through a network message, right?" Marshal hands me the square photo.

The image shows a man standing in a garden, a shovel in his hand. He looks rough around the edges, yet there's something familiar about him. His chin is round, just like mine. His eyes, though a shade grayer, mirror my own.

"I have his chin," I whisper, touching my face.

"Same," Marshal says, rubbing the scruff on his jaw. "He has blue eyes like us, too, although they're grayer."

My mind races, piecing together the fragments of my past. "My mom always said she used a sperm donor after Sharice's dad had died. She claimed she applied to Lannett after becoming a widow, and they approved her for IVF even though she wasn't married."

"Typical Circuit and their selective breeding bullshit," Marshal mutters. "From everything you've said, your mom is a top scientist with Lannett. Of course, they'd want her to reproduce."

I stare at the photo. Why would she lie to me about this? My father is alive somewhere, and I had no idea. Did he even know about me?

I look at the man in the photo again, searching for clues in the background. The sun casts a long shadow behind him, hinting at the early morning or late afternoon.

The garden around him is lush and vibrant, filled with trees and a landscape I don't recognize. His clothes are simple and practical, with no logos or labels.

My fingers tighten around the edges of the photo. This *stranger* is my father. All these years, I believed a lie. My mom's story about a sperm donor seemed plausible. But now, everything has flipped upside down.

"Why would she lie?" I ask, more to myself than to Marshal.

"Maybe she thought it was easier," he suggests. "Or maybe she had her reasons."

"Reasons," I echo. "What reasons could justify keeping my father a secret from me?"

Marshal moves to sit beside me, setting his mug on the plastic table between us. "Maybe she was protecting you. Or maybe herself."

The questions swirl in my mind, each one more troubling than the last. If my father is out there somewhere, what does that mean for me? Did he leave because he didn't want me or because he couldn't stay? Perhaps he was a criminal on the run? Or had stolen a bunch of money? I'd had a friend in college who'd had threatening calls all hours of the day when he'd racked up a bunch of gambling debt. Maybe that's what had happened? Maybe he owed the wrong person money and had fled to protect Mom and me.

I look at Marshal, seeing my confusion reflected in his eyes. "What's his name?" I blurt, remembering Rosaline's journals.

"Arlin Clemmons," Marshal says, arching a brow.

Clemmons. Well, shit. Of course.

Disappointment sours the back of my tongue, and I flip the photo over, but there's no return address. "You don't know where he is?"

Marshal shakes his head. "No clue. Mom always said he was a drifter, never staying in one place for long."

"So, he could be anywhere?"

Staring at his hands, he shrugs. "One time, he mentioned the ocean, and another a forest he hiked, but no. I searched for him on Network and found nothing either. It's like he didn't exist or changed his name."

"Why would he do that?"

"Your guess is as good as mine. But I can assume it wasn't for good reasons, hence why I didn't pursue it too much."

"There has to be a reason he wants to stay hidden."

"It seems that way."

"Did you ever think of hiring an investigator?"

Marshal scoffs. "Why waste the money? He knows where I am. If he wanted to see me, he could, so why should I make the effort?"

The bitterness in his voice is apparent, but it's hidden under a layer of resignation. He's had longer than me to process this. To come to terms with an absent father. I haven't, and the questions flutter through my mind one after another. "When was the last time he sent a letter?"

Marshal takes a small plastic container off of the shelf.

"They used to come every other month, but the last one was about a year ago." He opens the box, and I see it's full of folded papers. "Here." He takes the top letter and hands it to me.

I shake my head. "Are you sure? These are private. I wouldn't want to..."

"Nah, it's fine. He just talks about the weather and a book he's reading."

I unfold the letter, my eyes scanning the neat handwriting. It's mundane, just as Marshal said—weather reports, book summaries, the occasional mention of a new plant he's trying to grow. But between the lines, I sense a longing, a desire to connect.

"Thank you for sharing this with me," I say. "It means a lot."

Marshal meets my gaze, his expression softening. "You're my sister, Brigid. You deserve to know."

The word "sister" echoes in my mind, settling into a place that feels right. I've lost Sharice, or at least the part of her that felt like family, but I've gained a brother. And it's Marshal. We barely know each other, but he holds the esteem of every rider here. In our few interactions, I've never seen him treat anyone less than his equal, even with his high status.

"You know," I say, my voice thoughtful, "This may sound silly, but I always felt like something was missing. Like there was this piece of my life, I couldn't quite reach. Maybe this is it? Maybe finding him will help fill that void."

Marshal nods. "I get that. It's why I've kept these letters, even when I wanted to throw them away. He's a part of who we are, whether or not we like it."

I nod, absorbing this information. "We'll find him," I say again, more to convince myself than anything.

Marshal reaches out, placing a reassuring hand on my shoulder. "We will. And we'll do it together."

I glance over at him. He's different now, isn't he? I mean, I should see him differently. He's not just another rider anymore or a friend; he's my brother. Family.

Still, I'm flustered with what to do now.

"It's weird, isn't it?" he says, shaking his head and removing his hand.

"Yeah, it is," I say, laughing nervously. "What are we going to tell people?"

His eyes narrow. "I've gotten pretty damn good at smothering my bond, but they'll latch onto the shift in my emotions. So, we're screwed as far as keeping it under wraps from the other riders. I wish we could keep it hidden from the media a little longer so you can at least prepare, but I suppose since you're PR, you're more than capable of handling the barrage of interview requests."

"All right," I say with an exhale. "I'll see what I can do."

Tonight was the first time I'd seen Logan after what went down in Heath's room and him learning I'm Marshal's sister. It's not like he was big on sentimentality, but maybe if he remembered how gently he'd kissed me and how I'd looked naked, he'd make our first lesson an easy one.

Moonlight filters through the high windows, casting long shadows across the floor as I stride over to where he's clearing pads from the large mat.

"Hey," I say.

He looks up.

I slip off my shoes and pull my hair into a ponytail. "So," we say at the same time. A surprised laugh escapes me, and he shakes his head.

"You first," I say.

The muscle under his jaw flexes, and he lifts his chin. "That night... after Kaeden's memorial, I was in a shitty place, and you saved me. I don't know what you did, but I know I'd be dead if you hadn't done what you did." He pauses, eyes locking with mine. "Thank you."

My breath catches as I search his face, noting the softness in his usually guarded expression. It's the first time he's thanked me—for anything. A warm feeling blooms in my chest, spreading through me like sunlight breaking through clouds. I wish I could tell him what I'd done, but I can't. It'd been strange, like with Heath all over again at the gala. I had acted on instinct. Whatever it had been, it worked. "You're welcome. If you ever want to talk or anything—"

"Here, put these on," he says, ignoring me.

Guess our heart-to-heart is over.

He takes a pair of gloves from his bag and hands them to me. "We're going to work with batons today, and these help you with grip."

After he first told me no to helping me learn to fight on the shuttle, I'd been practicing privately in my bedroom. I'd watched every video on Network on hand-to-hand combat, martial arts, and self-defense. I'd also been working out, doing push-ups, sit-ups, and stair runs below the South wall, but he'd been on a strict workout regimen for years. A week of exercise wouldn't change the fact that I was woefully at a disadvantage.

I'd taken one martial arts class in college and attended a boxing match Vince dragged me to. I wasn't a fighter, and I wasn't even sure I had the gloves on correctly.

And as if wanting to prove that point, tonight he'd been relentless.

Ten minutes in, I'm already panting, and my sports bra and shorts cling to me while he seems barely affected.

Only our breathing and the soft thud of padded mats underfoot punctuate the gym's silence. Moonlight filters through the high windows, casting long shadows across the floor where Logan and I face each other, plastic staves in our hands.

I attack, trying with all my might to connect my baton with his body. It's not like his six-foot-five frame is a small target, but he's so damn fast. With unnatural speed, he dodges, left, right, and ducks, and I'm left feeling like a windmill swinging my arms.

"Keep your hands up," he barks, landing a blow on my left breast. I'm wearing a chest protector, so it's padded, but damn, it still hurts like a bitch. "Ow! That was my boob, asshole!"

"I told you to keep your hands up."

"At least you could be nice about it," I grumble.

"I *am* being nice. Whoever you are fighting won't be."

I widen my stance and glare at him through my gripped batons. "*This* is you being nice?"

He pivots to my right and strikes twice, and I manage to block one with my elbow. My elbow stings with the impact, but at least it's not my ribcage. "Sure is," he says. "Or you prefer the other guy?"

"No, no," I say quickly, "*this* Logan is fine."

"Widen your feet, there and again," he says, taking a step back.

I set my jaw, adjusting the grip on the batons. Four more strikes, and I'm driven off the mat, nearly tripping where the pad transitions to concrete.

I spit a curse, tasting blood from where I'd bit my cheek.

"Please," I pant, "Just tell me what I'm doing wrong."

"You're not strong," he says, twirling the baton casually like it's not some weighted weapon but a bottle of beer he's about to drink. "And you're slow. You favor your right leg 'cause you're right-handed, so you leave your left vulnerable."

I wipe the sweat from my brow, feeling it sting my eyes. I'd asked. "Okay, fine, so what can I do?"

"At Vanguard, we sparred with the same person the entire quarter to learn their habits and weaknesses. We've known each other for weeks; you've watched me spar with the other riders, and you still haven't learned mine."

Sure, I'd seen them spar at Meridian, but he was mistaken that I'd watch them to learn their strengths or habits. I was mostly there for the eye candy. I squint, wondering where he's going with this. "You have weaknesses?"

He rests his hands on his hips and gazes up at the ceiling. "Everyone does."

Fine, I'll bite. "Okay, you planning on giving me any hints?"

He lowers his eyes to mine. The intensity in his grey pupils pulls me in and I know I could get lost there. He's treating me like an equal like I'm someone worth sharing secrets with. My pulse thrums in my ears, but not from the workout. *Maybe that night had meant something to him after all.*

It's small, sure, but he's about to reveal something, something real, something that feels like it's just for me.

"When you fight me, you're chasing the flame, but the fire's already moved on."

I blink. "What fire?"

He rubs a thumb over his chin. "People are too focused on the arm that's swinging to notice my other one. No one is perfect, and sometimes, not always, but sometimes it's the second one you should be worried about."

I purse my lips and take another drink of water. "So, let me get this straight. If I want to block you, I should aim for your other arm?"

He nods. "And with a successful block, my other arm is swinging back, so there's your opening."

Oh sure, yep. That totally makes sense. A small laugh escapes me. I'm never going to get this right.

"All right, break time's over," he says, putting his mitts back on.

We go another two rounds, and while he'd probably never admit it, I think he gives me a couple when I try to do what he said and block the off-hand.

We start again, and once I'm centered back on the mat, he charges. Our bare feet thump on the pad, and I manage to block two of the dozen he unleashes. Both of which happened to be toward my head.

"Afraid you'll bruise that pretty face of yours?" he says.

I flip the end of my ponytail over my shoulder. "You think I'm pretty."

Logan grins, revealing the green rubber mouth guard and looking even more sadistic than usual. "Again," he says and steps toward me.

I assumed he'd be in a bad mood since Marshal had suspended him from drill training. But it appears I'd been wrong. He's anything but grumpy. In fact, he's almost playful, and as unnerving as it is to see him in a good mood, I don't dare question it, especially when he's got two batons in his hands.

"Tell you what," he says, letting me catch my breath. "If you hit me, I'll tell you anything you want."

Oh, I like this game. Logan is a maddeningly closed book, and this might be a chance for me to crack that hard shell. After the night of Kaeden's memorial, god knows I want to. I'd glimpsed the softness underneath, and I needed to know if it'd been an illusion or if I'd imagined it all. "Okay," I agree. We're too alike, neither one to run from a challenge. "And if you hit me?"

"You'll have to do exactly what I say." His smirk is infuriatingly gorgeous. How come I'd never noticed before? Probably cause he never smiled.

"That doesn't seem fair," I reply, adjusting my grip on the staff.

"Afraid you'll end up naked?" His taunt vibrates through the air between us.

"No." The idea makes my core turn molten, but I shove it aside.

"You should be." He laughs.

"Won't I be a distraction?"

"I have incredible self-control."

His confidence is almost tangible, filling the room. I snort, unable to contain my disbelief. "Biggest lie ever."

"All right. Question for question. Do we have a deal then, *Blondie*?"

Damn that nickname. He's trying to provoke me with it, and I stand my ground, my staff ready, and nod.

His smirk widens, and his eyes, like storm clouds, glint with a dangerous allure.

"Deal," I squeak, feeling like I'd just made a deal with the devil.

The tension between us shifts from playful to ruthless, evolving into a whirling dance of attack and defense. Sweat drips into my eyes, blurring my vision momentarily as I change my stance, readying for another exchange.

Logan doesn't hold back. Not that I want him to.

His baton taps my left shoulder, not hard enough to hurt but enough that I feel it. I wince from the sharp pain.

"Favorite food?"

"French fries."

Whack. "What's your middle name?"

"Elaine."

Whack. "Favorite color."

"Purple," I blurt, annoyance bleeding into my words. *These* are the questions he's asking. It's as if he's toying with me. I know it. The pompous ass is so confident he can beat me. He assumes he'll get endless amounts of questions so he can squander them on stupid ones.

I grit my teeth, pivoting right, then left as I swing toward his chest. He deftly blocks and counters with a blow to my elbow. "Dogs or cats?"

"Cats," I hiss, although the truth is I like both. However, cats were all that were allowed at our Uncy'lia research staff dormitories.

"When you lay in bed alone at night, do you touch yourself?"

The question catches me off guard, and in my momentary disorientation, he lands two more to my side. The air whooshes from my lungs.

"Did you get off on almost being caught in the Orchard?"

No secrets between riders. "I don't see how that's any of your —"

"Did he take you in the ass too?"

"Fuck you."

He stops. "If you don't want to participate, we can always switch to my original rules, which means." — He pauses, counting his bandage-wrapped fingers he'd used to punch through the window — "You need to ditch everything but your left sock."

I growl. "Yes, yes, and no."

Not yet.

He smirks. "Good to know Jamesy is keeping it honest with me."

"Since when are you so invested in my sex life?" I say.

He waggles a finger. "Uh huh, Blondie. You have to hit me first."

I don't know who I'm angrier with: Carter for blabbing about our intimate moments, Logan for provoking me, or myself for foolishly thinking they'd keep secrets from each other.

Either way, it doesn't matter; the irritation fuels my attack, and I charge.

The smile evaporates from his face as he's forced to defend. He raises his hands to block my upward assault, and then I snap one to his right. He deflects it.

But barely.

Arm muscles straining, I fling my right high again. However, at the last second, I pull back and swing it at his right thigh.

He's a second too slow, and I'm rewarded with a satisfying *crack* as it connects.

I hurl the question at him. "How did Galaxyla die?"

Logan stiffens, and for the first time since we've been sparring, he retreats, taking a step back. Secretly, I'm pleased that I've finally caught him off guard. Sure, it's a sensitive subject, and under normal circumstances, I'd feel guilty, but he hadn't shown any restraint in asking *me* personal questions.

"Training accident."

I keep my face passive. I'd suspected as much but still didn't understand what that meant.

He flips the baton in his hand, avoiding my gaze. "We phased together over a jump, and I miscued him when to land. We both fell on the other side of the phase, and he hit the arena wall, breaking his neck."

"Logan, I—" I say, but he interrupts me.

"Save it, Blondie. Training's over."

He tosses the staves aside.

Shit. I fucked up.

"Logan, I'm sorry, please."

He turns his back on me and strides out of the gym, the metal door slamming shut behind him.

Dammit.

As I stand there, regret seeping into my veins. The tiny progress I've made with him opening up to me disintegrates and disappears.

Forty

MARSHAL

"No more goddamn dandelion tea," Fiaro snaps at the attendant as we enter Blackhawk's largest meeting room. The tall ceilings and paintings of previous station managers are ostentatious, and yet I can't wait to sit for mine because that means I'll be dead and will never have to sit through another one of these boring ass meetings.

Manager Fiaro sits at the head of the long table. At the center of the table is a pitcher of water, a bowl of apples, and an assortment of pastries.

Carter sits next to Heath and the other two master riders, Darren and Rolan. It's odd he's here, but I suspect it has something to do with General James' recent visit.

As everyone settles, Fiaro clears his throat, bringing the low murmur of conversation to a halt. "Let's begin," he says, his voice resonating in the spacious room. "Darren, any update on the choreography?"

Darren leans forward. "It's coming along brilliantly, sir. We've made some adjustments to accommodate the added riders, and I think it's our best yet. We'll be hosting auditions for the first string in a few weeks."

Fiaro nods approvingly. "Excellent." He taps on the screen of his portable computer. "And where are we with the new treadmills?"

"They should arrive within a week," Lugsen answers. "They're a higher brand model, so I hope they last longer than the old ones."

"Good, good," Fiaro murmurs, making a note on the pad before him. His gaze sweeps the room before landing on our medical team. "Dr. Rajesh, Dr. Austin, after losing Kaeden, I know there were some concerns about riders' health?"

Dr. Rajesh speaks first. "We've had a relatively quiet week. Two dislocated fingers were easily splinted, and we've addressed a rash connected to the new detergent. We've already coordinated with the laundry staff to switch back to the previous brand."

Fiaro's eyebrows rise slightly. "And regards to brimming?"

"Encouragingly down," Dr. Austin chimes in.

"Down how?" Fiaro presses, leaning forward with interest.

"As in none for the past week," Dr. Austin clarifies.

A ripple of surprised murmurs passes through the room. I feel a surge of pride; we've been working hard to address the flaring issue, and it seems our efforts are finally paying off.

Fiaro bobs his head and grunts in approval. "Let's hope the trend continues." He turns his attention to the druadan vet, Dr. Gideon. "Any news regarding the druanera?"

Dr. Gideon's throat moves. "Still struggling to get her to eat, but progressing."

Fiaro stares at him for a moment. "I'll request Lannett send a tech at once."

"Sir, I don't believe that's necessary, I—"

He holds up a hand. "Not up for discussion. I won't have the foal starve to death under my watch."

Dr. Gideon looks like he wants to say more but doesn't.

My gaze drifts to Carter, who's been uncharacteristically quiet throughout the meeting. Something in his expression, a tension around his eyes, sets my teeth on edge. I lean into the bond but detect nothing. It's not surprising.

While we're close, the subtleties of the bond only come from riders who live together. Heath, Logan, and Carter have lived and worked together at Meridian for nearly three years, which has heightened their perception of each other compared to mine.

Even with years of practice, it's a two-way street feeling emotions in a bond.

The meeting drags for another hour, and my foot falls asleep. I wiggle it under the table, trying to make the pins and needles sensation go away. When Fiaro adjourns, I pull Carter aside as everyone shuffles from the room.

"Wait up, James," I tell him, and he stops where he is at the end of the room, turning to look at me. I'd suspected for a while now that there was something between Brigid and Carter, little looks and unspoken words that hinted at more. I'd felt similar vibes from Heath and Logan, too, but I'd brushed it off as the kind of casual lust riders often have. Now, though, I'm not so sure. I've never had to deal with this before, but things are different now. "Leroy told me about your stroll around the orchard with Brigid."

Carter laughs dryly. "That son of a bitch."

"What are your intentions?" I demand. "I've seen Heath and Logan looking at her, too."

"Wow," Carter says, crossing his arms on his chest. "I'm impressed. You've known you've had a sister for a day, and already you're playing big protective brother."

"I'm serious."

"I am, too."

I pin him with a threatening gaze. "Good. You better be. I don't want to see her hurt."

Carter laughs nervously and peers at something behind me as if anything could be more important than this. "I won't, okay?" he says, returning his gaze to mine. "I promise." He claps me on the shoulder as though we'd just had a casual chat and then darts for the exit.

I take a deep breath, letting the tension ease from my body. *Big brother.*

A smile tugs at my lips. I could get used to that.

AFTER THE MEETING, I HEAD DOWN TO THE GYM. I TRADE WEIGHTS with Darren and then clock five miles on the treadmill. I shower, change, and do a check on Nightshade. A novice has let him out in a small paddock, and he's walking the perimeter, sniffing all the other stallions that had been turned out before him.

"Anything interesting?" I ask him.

"I do not like all these new ones. Too many. Loud at night." His voice hums from across the underground space, illuminated by a series of high, narrow windows letting in the gray light of mid-morning.

"I'm sorry, buddy, but it's going to be this way for a while."

"I heard female. I do not mind her talking."

I stand a little taller, leaning my arms on the metal railing. We talk about everything: food, weather, the other stallions, and riders, hell even when I'm gone traveling for a while and come back, he's curious to know about what I've done.

This time, it feels different. This is the first time he's mentioned Oriana, and it's like he's been keeping his thoughts to himself. *"Really? Did she have anything to say?"*

Nightshade snorts and paws at the ground, looking like he's preparing to roll in the dirt.

"No. She is a hatchling. She does not know anything."

I shake my head, laughing. Really walked into that one. *"But you like her...her voice, I mean?"*

Nightshade grunts as he lays down to roll. He scratches his back, causing dust to float in the air, before standing up and shaking it off with a grunt. The reddish-brown dirt has smeared onto his dapple gray coat.

Wonder which lucky novice will get the pleasure of washing that off.

"Yes, her voice is different," he says. *"It is lighter and softer. A pleasant change from others."*

I'm thoroughly intrigued. Nightshade is far from the most aggressive of the stallions, but this is such a gentle thought, even from him. *"Wow, buddy. That's such a nice thing to say."*

He strolls, nose to the ground, to the opposite side of the fence, then lifts his head, pricking his ears in the direction Oriana is kept. *"When she is grown, I will mate her."*

I choke on my laughter as lust saturates our bond. *"I think you might be waiting awhile."* Still grinning, I pat on the bars and back away. *"I gotta go. I'll see you later."*

I head out of the underground stables and upstairs to my room, and Nightshade's effect eases the further I get from him. Heath and I had long, often hilarious, discussions about the Shade bloodline being some of the most 'lusty,' and once again, he'd caught me off guard with his comment.

Among the plethora of tests they'd run on me, they'd also

considered Nightshade had be related to my longevity as well. They took blood and hair samples and even brought a horse mare for him to mate, speculating a druadan horse hybrid might be possible.

Her name had been 2X17X since she was a Lannett lab animal. However, her nickname was Melody. With thorough supervision for three days and with her wearing a unique carbon fiber blanket to protect her, he'd been allowed to hand-breed her.

Afterward, he hadn't shut up about it for weeks.

Melody this, and Melody that. Even two years later, he'd mention her in passing, asking if she would return so he could mate her again. I didn't have the heart to tell him she'd passed away two months later when the druadan hybrid foal embryo had stopped developing.

Everyone at the lab, including myself, had been disappointed when it was concluded that whatever was allowing me to be immune to flaring wasn't connected to Nightshade's genetic makeup.

They labeled him as just another clone of the Shade line, nothing out of the ordinary.

But I disagreed.

He was bonded to me, making him more special than any other stallion.

As I push open the door to my room, I spot Finn sprawled on my bed, his massive black and brown form basking in the warmth of the wall heater. His eyes flicker open at my entrance, and he thumps his tail lazily before drifting back to sleep. He's been so much happier since Jess started walking with him.

I find my attention drawn to the hook on the wall where Finn's leash hangs neatly looped. Next to it sits a chewed piece of fabric and a note in cursive handwriting: *"Finn found this garbage on our walk and wouldn't leave it. I don't know what it is."*

My lips curl in a half-smile as I picture Jess and my dog having a tug-of-war over this dirty piece of clothing. I examine it, and it looks like part of a glove, probably from one of the security guards. I toss it into the basket of Finn's toys.

A sudden urge to see Jess strikes me. Last night, when she'd left the greenhouse, I was left confused. Torn between the desire to follow her and the need to give her space.

Tides knew I wanted to, and even later, when I was back at my place, I debated messaging her, but what could I say?

"Sorry you're going through a tough time" seemed too generic, while "I care about you" seemed too... well, that would undoubtedly scare her off.

In the end, I'd done nothing. And now, regretfully, I wish I had.

Without a second thought, I grab my keys and rush out of my apartment, my heart beating faster with each step. I have no idea what I'll say to her or if she even wants to see me, but I have to try. I make it partway down the hallway before deciding to surprise her with some butterscotch custard and fried zucchini and change direction. As I make my way to the mess hall, however, Sadie appears in the stairwell, her arms full of folded sheets.

"Excuse me, Marshal," she says, her face pinched with worry. "I was hoping to find you. It's Ms. Drakeford, she's..." She hesitates, wincing, "I was bringing her laundry, and I heard thumping behind her door. She called me a..."—she doesn't finish, letting me fill in the blank with what eloquent insult she'd said — "...well, I think she's angry. I'm afraid she's going to hurt herself. I can't get a hold of Heath."

My gut twists with worry, even as I nod to her. "Okay. I'll check into it."

Sadie murmurs a grateful thanks and scurries away. Early lunch abandoned, I hastened my step back the way I'd come, down the hallway and to her room.

I pause, listening. When I hear nothing, I knock on her door.

"I already told you, Sadie," Jess shouts from the other side. "I don't need any more *damn* towels." The door opens, and Jess appears. Her dark hair is loose around her face, and she's wearing a low-cut striped T-shirt and burgundy shorts. Her eyes widen upon seeing me.

"Oh, it's you."

I flash her a tight smile. "Sadie sent me to check everything was okay."

Jess huffs and straightens her chin. "It's fine. *I'm* fine."

She is anything but fine. Her eyes are red and puffy, and even though she's tried covering them with makeup, it's clear she's been crying.

My hands go numb, unable to process what I'm seeing. This woman that's so polished, so expertly put together, is unraveling.

I shouldn't be here. I shouldn't be seeing this. She must have a friend or... "I'm going to go get Sadie."

Her hand lands on my wrist and squeezes. "No. It's okay. Please have a drink with me?" Her touch burns, igniting the war inside me. Every instinct says walk away—I'm not the man for this, not her savior. But the quiet plea in her eyes, the desperation behind that smudged lipstick, holds me in place. I shouldn't stay, yet she clearly wants me to.

I give her a small nod, and her hand loosens its grip. "Wine?" she says, sauntering away, leaving the door open.

I step inside. At the kitchenette, she finishes the bottle she'd opened into a glass and then tosses it in the recycling. Even drunk, she carries herself with the practiced poise of someone raised in high society. She pours a glass of red wine and hands it to me.

"You know," she says, sauntering to the living room. "my team manages the majority share of Drakeford property investments." She pries another bottle from the shelf and examines the label. "We brought in four million in credits last quarter and are on track to double that." She looks at me and levels me with a gaze. "The attack at Meridian is, in part, thanks to that."

I follow her, and we sit across from each other in the pair of sofas."How?" I ask, the word escaping me before I can fully formulate my thoughts. I'm not a businessman by any means, but I understand the connection Circuit's laws can have on which industries are successful. More regulations on medicines, more money sent to Lannett for drug studies. Fewer regulations on shuttles, and so more independent shuttle manufacturers were cropping up. But I can't guess how a terrorist attack on a druadan station would have any connection to real estate.

She shrugs, appearing indifferent. "People are worried about more attacks, and the rural, isolated properties usually purchased as vacation homes are being snatched up by those wanting to make them their primary. Fear is *very* often good for business."

My body stiffens, not liking the cold, calculated way she talks about profiting off of tragedy. I want to tell her that this is wrong, that she is better than this. But I can't find the words, especially when she looks like this.

Sighing, I take a sip of wine, feeling the bitter taste on my tongue even though it's an excellent vintage. I thought I'd glimpsed a different side of her, a true side, from the way her face lit up at the greenhouse or how she'd rolled her eyes while eating the butterscotch custard.

But maybe I'd been mistaken.

I push away these dark thoughts, telling myself that she's just drunk and emotional and that she doesn't mean the things she's saying.

She flashes me a thin smile and takes my glass, topping it off with more wine even though I'd barely drank from it. "You know what I'm sick of?" she asks, but then continues without waiting for my response, "I'm so sick of these real estate agents and investors who don't know the difference between a sauna and a thermal room."

"Then why not switch things up?" I ask, "Do something else?" She's got the money and the brains. She could literally do anything.

Okay, except for anything requiring customer service. I smile into my wine glass as I take a sip, picturing Jess working retail or at a cafe.

She dismisses my suggestion with a wave of her hand. "I can't just change careers. My father would never trust anyone else to manage our properties, and besides, no one would do it as well as I do." She turns the wine glass, peering into it. "You know what I really wanted to do?"

"What?" I ask.

"Don't you dare laugh?"

"I can't promise that, but I'll do my best."

She jabs a finger at me. "That's it," she slurs. "That's what I like about you. You're so honest, you know that? I deal with these fake people every day. It's nice to be around someone that is honest with themselves and doesn't spew bullshit." She hiccups and giggles. "God, look at me, one bottle in and I'm swearing like a rider." She pauses as her eyes snap to mine. "No offense."

"It would take a lot more than that to offend me." My words linger in the air for longer than I'd expected, and I find myself clearing my throat to break the tension. "You were saying something about what you wish you could do?"

Jess' glazed eyes blink rapidly. "Oh yes, I did, didn't I? My senior year, I had a professor, Mrs. Lisbery, and she was this fantastical creature. She had long hair that reached past," — she pauses, gesturing to her lower back — "that she was always dyeing one color or another."

"I'm confused. You wanted to be a hairdresser?" I ask.

She waves the hand with the wine, causing it to spill over the top. "No. God no. Mrs. Lisbery had this greenhouse, and she let me go there to study. I'd breathe in the damp earth and flowers and wish I could stay there forever. My own secret world." A wistful smile forms on her face. "There, I dreamed of becoming a florist—making bouquets. Creating something beautiful for people, something that could bring a little light into their lives."

I study her, watching her face soften at the memory. Hell yeah, my instincts had been right, after all. It's been a while since I'd been with a woman for more than a night, and taking her to the greenhouse had been a solid move, better than I'd realized.

Still, it didn't explain why she'd run out so quickly.

She rearranges her legs on the couch, her wine sloshing in the glass and I snatch a cloth napkin from the table and pass it to her. She stares at the woven cotton rag in her hand as if unsure what to do with it, then wipes the droplets that splashed her hand. "But that would never be enough for my parents," she says, gesturing with the cloth. "No, I had to study architecture and business, all the things that would assist me in taking over the family empire."

As she speaks, my eyes linger on the elegant line of her neck and the subtle blush that colors her cheeks. There's something alluring about her vulnerability at this moment. With only the soft patter of rain against the windows to remind me of the world outside, I find all I want is to keep unraveling her, one silken layer at a time.

"That has to be shitty," I murmur, placing my glass aside to lean in closer. "Feeling trapped by those expectations."

Jess' intelligent eyes see right through me. "We're all trapped in our own ways, Marshal. You know that as well as I do."

A faint shiver runs through me at her keen observation. She's not wrong. We may have the appearance of freedom, slipping past velvet ropes at clubs, getting preferential treatment at the best tables, and doors opening for us that others can only dream of. But the truth is, riders are just as bound as anyone — shackled by a calling to live fast and burn bright.

All except me.

I'm the anomaly, the freak of nature still drawing breath while my brethren wink out of existence around me like flickering candles in the wind, their flames sputtering and dying.

"My parents couldn't have any other children," Jess continues, her speech beginning to slur further. "I'm everything to them." She laughs, but it doesn't have any warmth.

"Then you're enough," I say. "Even though I'm still here, my mom accepted long ago that as a rider, my future is here. We're supposed to live short lives. Without consequences, without regrets."

Her eyes narrow at that, two sharp emerald points piercing right through me. "Is that what you really think? That you get to skate through life without a care? Playing by different rules than the rest of us mere mortals?"

There's a slight scorn in her tone that both stings and intrigues me. The charged silence stretches out between us.

She licks her full lips, stained a deep burgundy red. I imagine kissing her, tasting the wine on her tongue.

I cross my legs to hide the growing erection. She recently was engaged to Heath. If I had any shred of honor, I'd respect that and push these feelings aside. But when it comes to her, I have no honor.

Of its own volition, my hand lifts to tuck an errant strand of hair behind her ear, letting my fingers graze her delicately flushed skin.

Her pupils dilate at the tender gesture, her plump lower lip catching between her teeth, and my dick turns to iron. There's the slightest hitch of her breath like a wild animal barely held in check, and the crackling energy in the room is undeniable.

"Marshal..." she trails off, squeezing her eyes shut. "I can't. Not yet."

I lower my hand, putting a safe distance between us once more. Raking my fingers through my hair, I struggle to collect my scrambled thoughts into some semblance of order.

It'd been fun in the greenhouse. But now she's changed. Her guard is down, and I'm taking advantage of it.

"I — I shouldn't have done that," I murmur, unable to meet her eyes I feel watching me.

For a beat, she's silent. Then, an unexpected peal of laughter bursts forth, rich and full-bodied in a way that pulls an involuntary smile from me.

"Oh, Marshal..." She looks like she's about to say something else but then stands. "Well, I appreciate you keeping me company tonight."I clearly needed to... unburden myself." She covers her mouth, concealing a hiccup.

I climb to my feet as well. Stopping before things went too far had been a smart move.

She sways and catches her balance on my arm. She gives my biceps a gentle squeeze, and her eyebrows hitch higher. "Wow," she says. "That's really all you under there?"

The light caress of her touch is all it takes to make my cock twitch in response, craving more. "Yes, it is."

Her hand lingers a little longer, her eyes fixed on where her hand touches my arm. "I'm going to draw myself a hot bath," she finally says, dropping her hand to her side. "Take advantage of those divine-smelling soaps they stock the rooms with."

With that, she rises in one effortlessly graceful movement, loose obsidian-colored hair spilling over one shoulder as she retreats to the bathroom. Pausing with her hand on the carved wooden door, she stops looking back at me, and for a fraction of a second, I think she's going to invite me to join her, but instead, she says, "Thank you again for listening, Marshal. Our little chat was just what I needed to clear my head."

And with a final small smile, she slips into the bathroom, the sound of running water soon filtering through the door. I sit there for several moments, somewhat disoriented from this whirlwind of a woman. I swallow the last of the wine and set my glass down. Ever since the greenhouse, she's had me so out of sorts that I can't think straight.

Her elegance, her wit, and the way I sense a wild current swirling beneath the calm surface of the ocean, smooth and serene.

The scar on my hand burns with a fierceness I've never felt before, almost like a confirmation.

Holy hell.

I dash out of the suite. I need a shower, too.

Forty-One

LOGAN

Judge Turner's eyebrows raise like two fuzzy caterpillars making their way across her forehead.

Heath, Marshal, and two other station managers sit on the bench to her left. As I glance around the room, spotting a few other unfamiliar figures in suits, some on their comms while others type tap on portable computers. This is just a hearing, not the trial, but that doesn't stop the tension coiling in my chest. Being the center of attention isn't something I like unless it's when I'm astride Galaxian during a show.

Hell knows if that will ever happen again.

I hate this feeling—being scrutinized and judged. This is my worst fucking nightmare. All these bureaucratic suits don't know shit about riding or druadans, and yet they feel like circling vultures. The weight of their gazes makes my skin crawl like they're already picking me apart.

"Mr. McCelroy," Judge Turner says. "This preliminary hearing is required to ensure that all parties involved are informed of the charges posed against them. Do you understand why you're being charged? Are you aware of the statutes pertaining to rogue druadan?"

"Yes," I say, then feel a kick in my shin from Marshal. "Your Honor."

She continues, her thin mouth barely moving as she speaks. "Let me be clear, Mr. McCelroy. The only reason we haven't euthanized your stallion is because I've been held up at other hearings related to terrorist attacks, including the one at Meridian. However, we must analyze all the information to determine how much of a threat your druadan is, and this assessment is well overdue."

My jaw clenches at the mention of euthanizing Galaxian, but I keep my mouth shut just as Marshal had told me to.

"We'll obtain testimony from Master Rider James," Judge Turner explains, "whose stallion was injured by the Lannett scientist, as well as from the two other scientists present. But until then, I have it under good authority that you have an admirable record of keeping the station secure. Is that correct?"

I grunt in acknowledgment. "That's right, Your Honor."

"This will certainly be taken into account," she continues. "We won't overlook your commendable service to the station during the trial," she continues. "It's important all aspects of your character and reputation are considered as we proceed."

My reputation. It's all I've got, unlike Heath and Carter, with their powerful last names to pull strings or money to smooth over mistakes.

"Since the last rogue druadan trial was twenty-seven years

ago, and the one before that fifty years prior, there is limited precedent for how to proceed," she says, her voice measured, "We will rely heavily on the rulings from those prior cases, using the established law and interpretations to guide our decisions. This situation is indeed rare, but rest assured, we will make every effort to ensure a fair trial, considering all evidence and testimonies carefully."

Fair. When Circuit pays her salary? Doubt it.

As I wait for her to continue, her assistant—a skinny man with a bulbous nose—leans over to whisper in her ear. She squints at her screen, her brow furrowing.

Marshal and Heath act like they aren't eavesdropping, but Nathan, the manager from Oak Hill on Heath's other side, shamelessly adjusts his hearing aid.

Sly bastard. I've always liked him.

The Judge's eyes dart to me, and her lips thin, making her look like the venomous snakes we had to trap on the island. "I suppose before we proceed further, there appears to be some new information presented regarding a novice rider by the name of Garret Peterson."

Fuck. Marshal had promised he'd handled that. Apparently not.

Heath and Marshal start talking at once, trying to defend me, but Judge Turner cuts them off quickly, her voice sharp. "Master Riders, we understand you want to support your fellow rider, but this is a preliminary hearing. All character testimony will need to wait until the actual trial date. Is that clear?"

Heath and Marshal nod, their eyes darkening as they turn to me. Heath's jaw tightens a hint of apology in his gaze.

Judge Turner clears her throat. "Now, Mr. McCelroy, do you have questions about how these proceedings will occur?"

I'm not educated like Heath, but I have enough common sense to know not to tug when my balls are caught in a vice. I'll play by their rules for much as it grates on me. "No questions, Your Honor," I reply. "I understand."

Forty-Two

MARSHALL

Tonight, I'm having dinner with my sister.

I haven't felt this kind of excitement in years and it's a strange, thrilling feeling, a reminder life still can surprise me.

Brigid stands in the entryway to my apartment, blue eyes reflecting the flickering candlelight. We could've eaten in the mess hall, but I'd requested a private dinner. We haven't had a chance to talk about, well, much of anything beyond that first conversation when I'd showed her our dad's photo.

A station attendant had brought in a folding table and set it with a tablecloth, real dishes, and silverware. The aroma of roasted chicken mingles with the sweetness of freshly baked apples.

"Oh, shit?" she says, glancing down at her leggings and oversized t-shirt. "I didn't think it'd be like this. I'm going to go change."

"No, it's fine. I thought since I finally have a free evening, a nice meal might be fun." I hold my hands up as if surrendering.

Brigid's sly grin tells me she isn't missing the awkward romantic setting. "This is a little over the top, isn't it?"

"I thought we wanted to keep the whole brother, sister thing a secret?" I reply, "But the staff pressed me for details about whom I was dining with, and I panicked and said, "A girl," so they did what they normally do."

Thankfully, they hadn't included the other items I asked for, like scented candles, flavored lubes, and lotions. Once there had been a pair of padded handcuffs, and at that point, I knew my attendants were fucking with me. I needed none of those extras except for the lube. Okay, and I didn't mind the candles, especially when Finny-boy was having a particularly gassy day.

She raises an eyebrow. "So, you have dinners like *this* often with women?"

I snort but then fix my face when I realize she's being genuine.

Shit.

"I'm sorry," she says. "It's just I barely know you and assumed we could get to know each other better? If it's too personal, I won't —"

I shake my head. "It's okay. I don't have," I pause, reframing my words, "There is someone, I think, but it's...*complicated*."

She takes a sip from her glass of wine. "Complicated how?"

"She's recently got out of a relationship." I pause again. God, I shouldn't have drunk half the bottle before she got here. "Well, kind of."

"Complicated," she says, stabbing at the chicken with her fork and nodding. "Believe me, I get it."

Jess's face flashes in my mind, and I wonder, not for the

first time if she'll ever see me the way I see her. It's been ages since I've navigated a real relationship. Carter often told me I'm too picky, but I'm the opposite. I'm scarred. Too many women, too many burns.

I reach for the gravy boat and pour the rich brown on my chicken, steam rising in lazy curls.

Brigid's gaze wanders, taking in the cluttered shelves and crowded walls. "You have a lot of...stuff."

I mop up some of the gravy with a bite of chicken and eat it. It's tender, seasoned with herbs that remind me of dinners back home with my mom. "I like collecting things when I travel."

"What's that one?" she asks, pointing to a tiny wooden statue of a rearing horse.

"Picked it up in a street market near Tox Zone Beta."

"From trawlers?"

"Don't knock them. Sometimes they find the coolest shit."

"And sometimes they die."

I shrug. "Risk versus reward." I gesture with my fork at a clock with birds painted on it instead of numbers. "You don't want to know how many credits that cost me."

"Really?" She tilts her head to the side, trying to appraise it. "Does it *do* anything?"

"I don't know. Probably did, at one time."

She squints and points at another one. "What about that?"

I follow her line of sight to the glass ball with liquid and a city skyline in it. In the center, lording over the other buildings, is a silver tower with a disk on the top. "Picked that up on my last trip to Canna Canna."

"Off continent? That's cool. Why were you there?"

"I, uh." Damn. "Wanted to do some hiking. The mountains there are legendary."

Satisfied with the answer, she returns her attention to her

food. We eat in silence for some time before she sets her fork down and dabs her mouth with her napkin.

"Heath probably already told you, but we've made some progress in the archives."

I lower my fork and peer over at her. "No, he hasn't mentioned anything, actually."

"Oh," she says, "then I guess you should know. We found these journals. You should see them. They're from hundreds of years ago, and they're proof women can bond with druaneras."

I chew slowly, buying time to gather my thoughts. "Bond with women? I thought you were looking into how they grow?"

Her cheeks redden. "Well, it started that way, but then when we didn't find anything useful, there were these notebooks dated during the peak of the mystyl wars. Before the bombs, and there's this rider named Rosaline Devereaux and her druanera, Solara." She starts to rise from her chair. "They're in my room. I can go get them?"

"Hold on. Just give me a minute." I dig a knuckle to my temple, trying to process this information. "Have you told anyone else about this?"

She shakes her head, returning to her seat. "Heath might have to Carter and Logan, but I haven't said anything."

"Good, keep it that way," I say, a minute amount of tension leaving my body. God dammit. I should've gone with Heath to the archives. It was supposed to be simple: learn about druanera maturation and bonding age, tell Lugsen, and then figure out which station would keep her for their novices to try to bond.

But now, a woman could bond with her? The implications are staggering. I take a deep breath, trying to organize my thoughts. This had been hidden in those journals down there all this time. How had no one found them? Probably because no one ever looked for them. Why would they? I glance over at her, feeling her contagious excitement wafting through the air.

After years as a rider, I'd assumed I knew all there was to know about druadans. Or at least all that was left to learn. But this... this was like stumbling upon a hidden grove of rare orchids in a forest I thought I'd mapped completely. I'd always thought *I* was the strangest thing connected to druadans, and, in all honesty, this is incredible.

And dangerous.

If Lugsen found out from Brigid...

I'll have to tread carefully. I'm very good at handling things on my own. However, this is not one of those times. Holy shit, I need help, and there are only three people I trust enough to figure this out and keep Brigid safe.

"All right," I say, "Bring me the journals, and let's see if Heath, Logan, and Carter are free for dessert."

Forty-Three

CARTER

"Everything we thought we knew is a lie," Marshal says to all of us, setting the book on the table. "The riders, the druadans, all of it."

We'd been finishing dinner when he'd called us to his place without telling us why.

And so, unsure how long this impromptu meeting would be, I'd brought my dessert with me. I'd been mid-chew on the brown sugar tarte when he dropped that bombshell.

I cough, sputtering on the flaky crust, and draw an irritated look from him.

Covering my mouth, I give him a thumbs-up that I'm okay. I'd done my best to avoid him after he'd given me the big bro warning. Sure, it was a chicken-shit move on my part, but now that Brigid and I were something more, Marshal treated me differently.

He'd changed. I hated it.

I'd never return to what it was, but I fucking hoped it would recover enough that things wouldn't be so damn awkward anymore. I just needed to make him see how serious I was about her. I got where he was coming from, protecting her heart, but she was a grown woman who could make her own choices.

She certainly had in Heath's room.

Unfortunately, in a way, avoiding him had worked out since I'd been preoccupied with my secret task of collecting the riders for my mom's list. I'd created a formula and scoring system that I updated her with regularly. I was actually quite proud of it, even though it sucked that no one would know for a while. Once I had the top candidates picked out, I'd have to find a way for us to meet in secret, which meant going behind Marshal's back.

I grab a glass of juice from the platter, washing down the lump in my throat as Marshal continues. "So, long story short, the agreement that only men had ever been riders is bullshit. God, historians will have a field day with this one. All the texts from the mystyl war pointed toward only men being riders."

I raise an eyebrow, processing Marshal's words. Men are riders. It's how it's always been. The idea a woman could bond with a druadan feels like it's breaking some unspoken law of nature. My eyes slide to Brigid. Her face is neutral, hands folded neatly on her lap, but her eyes flick my way for a second, and they're full of swirling emotion.

Something isn't right. Maybe the book is lying? Maybe it's all made up?

"That book is bullshit," Logan says, putting words to my thoughts. "Stallions only bond with men. It's a fact."

Marshal nods slowly. "That is true. But now we have a druanera. That doesn't apply anymore. And there's too much accuracy for it to be completely fiction. The dates, the names, the locations. It's like it matches the history texts, with the only omitted parts regarding druanera and women riders."

"Someone went to great lengths to hide this book," Heath adds.

"But why?" I ask, "What the hell would it matter if a woman could bond with a druadan?"

Marshal shakes his head. "Best guess? Circuit wanted to keep it secret for public protection."

No one replies. He's exactly right. Circuit is one hundred percent behind this.

"So, let's take a step back and look at what we do know," Marshal says.

"Druaneras existed hundreds of years ago," Brigid says, "obviously, or we wouldn't have druadans to begin with. But why did it shift to only stallions being cloned?"

"That's rider training 101," Logan says. "Hell, even I know that."

I scratch my head, trying to recall the old academy lessons. "Shit, you're making me remember what they taught us at Vanguard? I can't remember what I had for breakfast yesterday."

"Toast with apple butter," Logan says. "*My* toast."

"Oh, right," I say, without a shred of remorse. It had apple butter and the right amount of cinnamon. Fucking delicious.

Heath sighs and leans back, crossing his arms. "The reason they only cloned stallions is because the last surviving druaneras were infertile. They refused to lay eggs even after mating. In vitro was out of the question because of the risk to the female. If an ovum was planted when she wasn't precisely in season, it could kill her and the embryo. So, they started cloning them, using horses as surrogates until they eventually discovered how to gestate eggs without them and then trigger a hatch when a new druadan is needed at a station."

"And druanera always died during the cloning process," I supply. That much I *do* remember.

"At least that's what we've been told," Heath adds. The egg hatching after centuries only enforces the need to question everything we believed.

I lean forward. "What does it say about bonding with women? Is it any different? Maybe it was more dangerous or something, so that's why they didn't want the public to know. In case some woman gets it in her mind to steal an egg and try to bond to—" I trail off, suddenly aware of all eyes on Brigid.

Guilt burrows into the base of my skull. Fuck. I didn't mean to accuse her. Maybe she didn't steal the egg on purpose. Maybe it just happened. Still, I screwed up. I wish I could take it back, but it's too late now. My eyes dart between hers and Heath's and Logan's.

I'm caught in the middle—wanting to back her up but also not wanting to go against my fellow riders. I don't doubt her, but I hate that I've put her in this position like she has to defend herself.

"Please continue," she says, her gaze icy as she looks at me. "Go ahead and say what everyone is thinking. That I stole an egg to try to force it to bond with me?"

"No one is saying that," Marshal says, saving me. "This is a lot of new information for us, and we're just trying to make sense of it."

Brigid leans back, folding her arms. I can see the conflict playing out in her eyes. Her desire to push for immediate action warring with her respect for Marshal. I offer her a supportive look, and she presses her lips together before returning her gaze to Marshal.

"Back to what you were saying about what we know," Heath says. "A stallion initiates a bonding between two and five years."

"Correct," Marshal responds. "but if this journal is accurate, druaneras mature faster."

I glance at the book, feeling an urge to reach out and touch it, but I hold back. I'm not stupid, but this whole discussion feels way out of my league. I'm more the hands-on type, at times, *very* hands-on, and not exactly the sit around and discuss things type. Logan and I had leaned on Heath's notes more times than I'd like to admit, especially before tests.

I know my way around an arena and a woman's body, but old journals with cryptic notes? Yeah, nope. Honestly, I'm just trying to keep up. "Does it say how old her mare was when it bonded?" I ask.

Heath shakes his head. "I've read through it twice. Rosaline said she was twenty-two when she wrote this, so it seems average for a rider."

"So, it's useless then?" Logan says, scoffing. "Women *can* bond with druaneras, but we don't know when or how."

"You're right, we don't know," Marshal says, "but it's not entirely useless."

"For fuck's sake, Marshal. Can Blondie bond with Oriana or not?"

Marshal stretches, clearly enjoying annoying Logan, and I can't help but stifle a laugh. Logan's upper lip curls. Finally, Marshal lowers his arms. "Short answer: yes."

"And the long answer?" Brigid asks.

Marshal gives her a reassuring look and sighs. "We don't know how or when she will be old enough to bond or even if she will initiate it."

I think of all the legends, the stories of druadan riders leveling entire swarms of mystyl with their swords and guns.

The ones we replicate for exhibitions. Watching the stallions fighting during our first day here, it isn't too hard to believe. They were bred and meant to fight. Their riders were warriors. Key word being *'were'*. Now, we're just...what had my mom said? A 'cowboy gymnast?'

"Okay," Marshal says, "We need Lugsen to keep Oriana here while she grows."

"You'll never convince Lugsen with just a book," Logan says.

Marshal frowns. "Damn. You're right."

"What about the picture?" Brigid suddenly chimes in. "That woman and her druanera. He can't argue with that, right?"

"What picture?" I ask.

Brigid flicks me an annoyed glance.

Still pissed. Got it.

"There's a painting we found in one of the history books," she says, turning back to Marshal, "of a druanera rider. I saw the portrait with my own eyes. The woman's descriptions of herself and the druaneras, all match the ones in the journal. That woman is *this* book's author, Rosaline Devereaux."

Heath clears his throat. "No good. Earlier today, I tried looking for that book again and even with Yuto's help, we couldn't find it. He said he might have mis-shelved and will keep looking."

Marshal's tone is one of resignation. "I will have a word with Yuto and with the maintenance staff, as they sometimes move things to storage when cleaning."

"Talk about goddamn timing," Logan says.

"He's right," I say. "That is suspicious. Why would they suddenly move an old book that had been stored there for years when you've been looking into it?"

Logan narrows his eyes. "Exactly. Someone moved it on purpose. Hid it from us."

"Lugsen?" I ask, feeling a creeping suspicion.

"Maybe," Heath replies, although he sounds unconvinced.

"Either way," Marshal says. "It's gone for now, which means Lugsen will be a harder battle to win." Marshal refills our glasses with the pink apple wine. The color is vibrant, a personal favorite of mine in the fall. I take a sip, savoring the taste.

"So, what now?" Brigid asks.

Marshal sets down the bottle and takes his glass. "We'll have to hope the book and all of us supporting this is enough. We'll get our ducks in a row and take what we have to Lugsen. And if he's on board, we'll start basic training for you as a rider."

Brigid's eyes light up. She's fucking gorgeous when she's like this, so full of determination and resolve. It hits me just how much she's been holding onto this dream. I'm cautiously optimistic, though. There's a good chance, even with Marshal's backing, this will all go to shit, that Lugsen will shoot us down, and Oriana will be sent to another station or a lab. But looking at her now, so full of joy, I can't bring myself to say anything that'll dampen her spirits.

"Training to become a rider isn't only about bonding," Marshal says, directing her with a firm look that is nearly as good as Heath's when I'd spouted something I shouldn't. "It's an entire lifestyle change." He stares at her, measuring her resolve.

She grins. "Really? You'll help me?"

Marshal wipes the side of his mouth with a napkin. "We can start with the basics. In secret. You should start with lessons on handling and riding."

"Carter would help me with that," she says, looking at me.

Hell, it's not like I've got anything better to do.

"Count me in," I say, raising my hand.

Marshal's eyes narrow. "As long as it isn't pulling you away from his other duties." Asshole. I show up to drill practice. Most of the time.

"We have a dummy for practicing saddling and mounting in storage. I can dig out," Marshal offers. "It helps the novices get faster without the risk of burns or bites."

Brigid nods eagerly, and I crack a smile. "When can we start?"

"Next week, after Logan's hearing," Marshal replies. "But I'll have to get Fiaro's approval."

"Fat fucking chance of that," Logan mutters.

"Are you sure that's necessary?" I ask, agreeing. "I mean, there's a ton of stuff I could show her on Network. They'd never have to know."

Heath shakes his head. "Marshal's right. It's too risky to keep this from them. If Brigid gets caught, she'll be fired and blacklisted from every station. And Oriana? She could be sent to a Lannett station, never to be seen again. We have to do this by the book or not at all."

Ever since Ewensen caught him lying about the first egg being stolen, he's been playing it safe. Is this new overly cautious outlook on life aggravating? Fuck yes. But do I get it? Also, yes.

"All right," she says, tapping open her comm. "What's his favorite drink? She looks at us expectantly.

Heath cocks an eyebrow. "What does that have to do with anything?"

She tilts her head to the side, and a smug smile appears on her face. "No one said we couldn't try a little bribery. Come on, I'm in PR—I convince people to buy ten thousand credit box seats for a living. I think I can handle a station manager."

Forty-Four

BRIGID

I'm going to be a druadan rider.

Okay, not *today*. And maybe not even a hundred percent, but the odds aren't zero anymore since Marshal promised to teach me. So, if and when Oriana initiates a bond, I'll be ready.

But first comes the hard part: Convincing Fiaro.

I stand in the doorway of Fiaro's office, clutching a bottle of South Bay Scotch and wrinkling my nose at the pungent tuna wafting in my direction. Marshal had given me the unopened bottle, a birthday gift from his mom, and had generously loaned it to me on the condition: no matter how busy our schedules get, we have dinner once a week, like a family.

I'd immediately agreed.

"Come in." Fiaro gestures for me to enter, and Marshal moves in beside me. "Please, sit." Marshal points to a chair but then moves to stand behind me.

"We never had time to commend you, Ms. Corsair," Fiaro says. "Your quick thinking and decisive action saved a vital piece of Venovian history. You should be proud and know there's talk of salary advancements should you keep up the good efforts."

"Thank you," I say, then add, "Sir."

"The foal, Oriana, is what we're actually here to speak with you about," Marshal says. The sound of his periodic crunching on a cucumber slice punctuates the silence as Marshal tells him about Rosaline's journals and the capability of a woman to bond to a druanera. I'm grateful he's here, advocating on my behalf. After talking with Heath and the others, he'd been adamant we bring Fiaro into the loop, and while he'd been cautiously optimistic, he suspected Fiaro would be openly opposed to the idea. It'd be wise to 'plant the seed of possibility.'

Once Marshal is done explaining, Fiaro drops his sandwich on the plate and wads the napkin in his hands, cleaning off the sticky mayonnaise. "Let me get this straight. You believe a woman can bond with a druadan?"

Marshal nods. "Correct."

"And how did you come to this conclusion?"

"We read it." Marshal pauses. "In a book."

"A book?"

He chuckles. "You know, they're these paper things with writing inside that—"

"Don't condescend me." Fiaro cuts him off. "I know what a book is."

"Great, glad we're all on the same page."

Marshal and I both snort in unison at the terrible pun.

Yep, we're siblings.

If I thought Logan, Heath, and Carter were cocky, Marshal wore self-confidence like a jeweled crown perched on his head. I'd thought it was because he was a decade older, but I think it's just who he is. Some people are just born without fear or anxiety.

God, I wish that were the case with me.

"We understand the delicacy of the situation," Marshal says. "We have time. Oriana is still young, but we should at least entertain the idea that she could benefit the station not only as hands-on learning for the riders but as another mount instead of just breeding stock."

I nod in agreement, my heart racing. This is really happening.

Marshal is trying to keep Oriana here.

I'd ridden a druadan. Felt the rush of wind over my face, the powerful creature under me galloping across the desert, feeling as if he could do so for days. I'd witnessed the bond between riders and their stallions. Watched as Wraithwind had called to Danner—it was spiritual, as close to magic as anything I could imagine. If I had a chance to experience that, why wouldn't I take it? While I'd be content if she chose any woman to be her rider when grown, I'd be lying if I didn't want it to be me.

It'd cut my life short, but what did that matter?

Beyond this station, I had very few people who cared about me.

Truth was, my sister would just as soon kill me as talk to

me. My mother had disowned me and my father I'd never known.

The only people who mattered to me were here, at the station, and all of them were riders. Marshal included. If I belonged anywhere, it was here with them.

Just the possibility makes my palms sweat, and my breath quickens. I glance at Marshal, gratitude and uncertainty swirling in my chest. How much of this is he doing because I'm his sister now, rather than just for me? Does it matter? Isn't this how things like this get done? Having the right connections and persuading the right people?

Fiaro sets down his sandwich, his brow furrowed. "You realize what you're asking, don't you? With everything that's going on..." He trails off, shaking his head.

"Another lab was hit last night," I say, letting out a resigned sigh. It'd popped up on my Network morning news and I'd hoped he hadn't seen it. Our argument would work best if he were in a less stressed mood.

I'd hoped wrong.

His eyes snap to mine. "Exactly. And the ransacking and vandalization of Leviler courthouse. ITM is taking credit for both, demanding money be transferred to some account, or they'll release more of those dreadful creatures. Circuit is swamped, frustrated beyond belief."

I swallow hard, feeling the direction his words are going, and I glance at Marshal, seeing the muscles under his stubbled cheek working overtime.

This had been a bad idea.

Fiaro continues, his voice lowering. "President Peterson is breathing down my neck, waiting for one more slip-up before shutting us down altogether. If word got out, I was even entertaining the idea of a woman bonding to a druadan, potentially directing my attention to anything but the safety and security of the station." He makes a cutting motion across his throat. "It wouldn't be just my head rolling."

I knew it was a long shot, but hearing it laid out so bluntly is disheartening. Still, I can't give up. Not when I'm so close. "But sir," I start, surprised by the firmness in my voice, "isn't that all the more reason to consider new approaches? If things are as bad as they seem, maybe it's time to think outside the box."

Marshal shoots me a curious look, and I feel a boost of confidence. "Brigid has a point," he adds. "We're not asking for immediate action, just consideration. A willingness to explore possibilities."

Fiaro leans back in his chair, eyeing us both. I can almost see the gears turning in his head. The silence stretches, broken only by the soft whir of the air conditioning and the distant sounds of the facility beyond his office.

Finally, he sighs. "I can't promise anything," he says, and a knot burrows into my stomach. But then he continues, "However, I'll think about it. That's all I can offer right now. Think about it, and maybe…maybe we can revisit this conversation down the line."

It's not the resounding yes I'd hoped for, but it's not a hard no, either.

I'll take it. Oriana was just a baby. We had time.

"Thank you, sir," I say, trying to keep the tremor of excitement out of my voice. "We appreciate your willingness to consider it."

As we stand to leave, Fiaro holds up a hand. "This stays between us," he warns. "Not a word to anyone, understood?"

Sure, why not? What's one more secret? "Of course," I say.

Outside Fiaro's office, I exhale the breath I'd been holding as Marshal squeezes my shoulder. "That went better than expected," he says.

I nod, still processing. "Do you really think there's a chance?"

Marshal's expression softens. "There's always a chance. And for what it's worth, I'm not just doing this because you're my sister. I believe in you. Sister or not, I'd be fighting for this."

His words warm me, dispelling some of the doubts that have nagged at me since I first agreed to come with him here.

As we part ways, him going to the stables and me rushing off to my meeting with the PR team, my mind is already buzzing with possibilities. The dream of becoming a rider, of forming a bond with a druadan, feels within reach now. I know deep down that I am meant to be her rider.

And no one will stand in my way when she finally calls for me.

Logan steps closer, twirling a baton in each hand. "My turn now, Blondie."

Logan had messaged me an hour earlier he was free this afternoon. After the way our last sparring match had ended, I was surprised he was keeping his promise. I hadn't forgotten my vow to learn to protect myself, and so while I could've told him to fuck off, I swallowed my pride and went to the gym. If he was willing to move past it, then so was I.

When I arrived down here, Logan — looking one-part prize fighter and one-part Greek god — was already warming up with a punching bag, and I couldn't help but stop in the shadows and gawk. In a sleeveless shirt and shorts, his back glistening with sweat, how could I not?

But the moment he opened his mouth and called me that insufferable nickname, the Greek God turned into an arrogant jerk. I bristle. "Don't call me that."

"Make me." He smirks, then adds, "*Blondie.*"

A growl escapes my throat as I charge at him. He meets my attack with a flurry of blows, our batons clashing in a whirlwind of strikes and parries. We twist and turn, bodies coiled with exertion, sweat beading on our skin.

I narrowly dodge one of his strikes, feeling my braid bounce off my shoulders. The muscles in my arms and calves burn, but not as intensely as they once did. The consistent practice, both with him and on my own, is paying off. Still, I'm panting heavily, perspiration trickling down my back.

"Maybe it's time I came up with one for you?" I taunt between breaths, "How about... Big Bad Wolf?" I pause, pretending to consider it seriously, and he lurches toward me, hitting me on the thigh and then the shoulder. I wince in pain, stepping back. "Nah, too obvious. What about Grumpy Bear? Or wait, I've got it - Mr. Growly!"

Logan presses his size advantage, raining down a relentless series of attacks. I deflect every other one, looking for an opening to strike him back. Don't chase the flame, I tell myself, but it's so hard. It's like looking for a ship on the horizon while a wave is about to crash over you. Every instinct tells me to watch the hand coming so I don't get hit. I clamp my teeth together, trying to anticipate his offhand while not getting beamed with the other one. Three hits later, I see it.

I feint left, then whip my baton towards his exposed ribs, and they connect with a satisfying crack.

He grunts, partially deflecting the blow, but I've managed to land a glancing strike. A joyous laugh rips free from my throat at the same time; annoyance radiates across his face. I've done it. I've found a way to throw him off his game. I knew I was treading a fine line, antagonizing him like this, but wasn't this the point of these lessons? Learn how to fight using the strengths I already had. Well, words could be a weapon, and I had plenty of those.

"How about you don't call me anything?" Logan snarls, renewing his assault with even greater ferocity. Our batons are a blur of motion, the impacts reverberating through my arms.

"You put on a show," I continue, dodging and weaving. "Acting like you're all angry and scary." I duck under a wild swing, then jab at his midsection. "But really, you're just a coward."

He freezes, dropping his arms to his side. "What the fuck did you just call me?" He says, emphasizing every syllable.

I step back, chest heaving, sweat stinging my eyes. He's annoyed, but I sense I've still got room to push.

His lips curl into a snarl as we reset our stances, batons at the ready. Logan's gaze bores into me, a silent challenge.

"I said you're afraid." Our batons collide with bone-jarring impacts; however, now, I'm the one dictating the pace, driving him back with my relentless assault. With every second, my timing to hit on his recoil improves, and within minutes, I'm hitting him more than being hit. "You're afraid of letting people get too close to you," I yell between breaths. "So you lash out and close off."

I connect with his chest, and he stumbles backward, his eyes blazing with frustrated anger. I've penetrated his shell and struck a nerve. Whether that's a good thing or not, it's too soon to tell.

We separate again to catch our breaths. "Is that all you've got?" I taunt.

His jaw works furiously, but he doesn't reply. A triumphant heat warms my neck and cheeks. I've rendered him speechless. Seizing the advantage, I launch into another flurry of strikes, forcing him to give ground. My muscles are fatiguing, and the blows aren't as hard as before, but I refuse to falter. Not now. Not when I'm starting to feel like I'm not terrible at this.

Logan backpedals, deflecting my blows, but his footwork is sloppy, his guard dropping. An opening presents itself, and I don't dare hesitate. My baton lashes out, cracking against his leg with a dull thump. Logan grunts, crumpling to one knee.

I gaze triumphantly down at him.

I stand over him, casting a shadow in the overhead light. Logan gazes up, his face partly in darkness, a smug smile tugging at his lips. He's not annoyed anymore; if anything, he looks a little proud. I extend a hand, offering to help him up. He ignores it as he stands, and I step back.

Resting the baton on his shoulders behind his head, a defiant flare of challenge glints his gray eyes. "You don't know a thing about me."

"Exactly, because you won't let me," I reply.

The corded muscles in his neck and shoulders tense, but he doesn't look away.

"I know what it means to be alone," I say, my voice low. "To have no one, like you belong nowhere. To be betrayed by someone close to you. You also know what it means to care about someone who would do anything for you. You might have everyone else fooled, but I've seen you. When I kissed you the night of Kaeden's memorial, I felt you and am no longer afraid of you." It's unexpected, this newfound confidence, and no doubt piggybacking off the success at our meeting with Fiaro.

"You should be," he says, lowering the batons.

"Why?"

"Because I'm a rider with nothing to lose."

"That's not true. There's still a chance they'll let Galaxian live."

"Bullshit."

"Maybe," I say, "but it's what I believe."

He swipes the air with the baton. "That's where you're wrong. I'm not going to live very long at all, so why should I when I've got a handful of years left?"

"All the more reason you shouldn't live your life this way."

His eyes narrow, a penetrating gaze. "Fine, Blondie. What do you want to know?"

My stomach twists with nerves, feeling like it's karaoke night and I've been handed the microphone. So, all it took to get him to open up was to kick his ass. Okay, maybe not that far, but at least I hold my own against him. I can't help but smile at the thought. There's one question above all others. The one I know I'll never get to ask again.

"Tell me how Galaxyla died," I say.

Logan's eyes darken, shadowed like the storm clouds gathering outside. "I already told you it was a training accident."

"That's not what I mean," I press, willing my voice to remain steady. "Tell me what happened specifically. I want to understand."

He clenches his jaw as his body stills. He's half-turned like he's ready to leave, and if he wants to, I can't stop him, but I hope he doesn't. Things are different now. I could bond with Oriana and become a rider. Druadans were strong, fierce creatures, and yet, they weren't invincible. Injuries, even death, *could* touch them. I needed to understand how.

"We were practicing a new maneuver," he finally says. "One where we jump over a line of rails and phase onto the other side. It was routine, nothing that we hadn't done dozens of times before. But I'd been out drinking the night before and wasn't as focused as I should've been.

Galaxyla's phase distance was impressive, and he was more experienced than I. Midway through our second pass, he jumped the pole, and I gave him the wrong cue. He phased too late, and I was unable to bring him back quick enough." His voice tightens, his gaze dropping to the baton in his hand as if it holds the memory. "I realized my mistake and dragged it with me into the darkness, where I'd been powerless. For five fucking seconds, I lived with that choice, each heartbeat echoing with the regret that felt like it would never end. When we reappeared, he hit his head against the wall, snapping his neck instantly."

I'm silent for a long time. My throat tightens, and a heavy sorrow fills my chest. I can't fathom the horror of feeling so helpless. It's no wonder he didn't want to tell me before.

I see it now—why he'd been so defensive, why my questions angered him before. That guilt he carries, the weight pressing him down, makes perfect sense. He was protecting himself. But things are different now. The walls between us aren't as high, and I don't want to risk them going back up by pushing too hard.

Logan's eyes meet mine and seeing some of the storm has cleared, the ache eases in my chest. "We burned his body the next day," he says. "And two months later, Galaxian called to me."

I open my mouth to say I'm sorry and reassure him he couldn't have done anything differently, but something steals my tongue. How many times has he heard this all before? Empty words, hollow reassurances. They must mean nothing to him by now. Still, I need to say it. "I'm so sorry, Logan," I say softly, meeting his eyes. "That was a terrible thing you had to go through. You did everything you could."

His brow furrows as he processes my words. "Then why does it still hurt so damn much?"

"Because it's supposed to," I say, remembering my mom telling me something like this when I'd found the stray cat I'd been feeding dead one morning. She was old and had peacefully passed away in her sleep. Still, I'd cried for days. "Pain is proof you loved something more than yourself," I continue, "But your pain doesn't define you. Your strength does. No one will ever say you're not strong. Mistakes happen to everyone." My fingertips brush against his hand. But as soon as I do, he flinches, pulling away, and his walls slam up again.

"Fucking costly mistake," he growls, shoving his hands under his armpits. His voice is low, and his eyes harden once more, but there's a new, fresher pain behind them. "But it was a costly lesson to learn, and I'd thought I had learned it."

He's talking about killing the scientist. "Galaxian is a two-thousand-pound animal. No one could have stopped him. You did everything you could, and it wasn't your fault."

Logan scoffs. "Like hell, it wasn't. My bond wasn't strong enough. Even if I had been close enough to tell him no, it wouldn't have mattered. That scientist was dead the moment we left the station. And now my bond with Galaxian is fucked. Marshal knows it. I know it. I have lost control of my stallion."

Lost control? Is that what they meant by a druadan going rogue? I'd thought it was a way to say a druadan hurt someone, but maybe it was more complicated than that. "But what about your bond?" I ask, frowning.

Logan spins the baton as if testing the weight. "It's still there. Normally it's like a hose, water going back and forth. Now, it only flows in one direction—to Galaxian. So, I've had to shove it down, force it away, and that only makes things worse."

I tilt my head, studying him closely. There's no iridescent sheen, no aura like Heath and Carter. Maybe that's why? Because of whatever he's doing? I'm no expert, but that can't be good, right? Keeping the bond suppressed like that? "What are you going to do?"

He shrugs. "Same as I have been. Why do you care?"

I rest a hand on my hip. "Because as much as you drive me crazy, I want to be your friend."

His eyebrows cinch together. "I can't be your friend."

"Why not?" My thoughts drift to our foursome in Heath's room. He sure seemed friendly then.

"That's not why."

"Then tell me."

His throat bobs, Adam's apple shifting as he swallows hard. "I can't do this, Blondie. I can't be friends with you. Not when…" He trails off, jaw clenching, as he struggles to find the words. "Not when every moment with you makes me want things I can't have. And if the trial doesn't go my way, I'll be dismissed. I won't let myself surrender to you only to have you ripped away."

His words hit me like a punch to the gut which I can honestly say I've now experienced. This is the most he's ever admitted, and suddenly I understand. He's not pushing me away; he's trying to prevent himself from getting attached. My brain buzzes with all he said and if I should say something. Part of me wants to shout at him to let himself surrender, and we'll figure out whatever happens, but the other, practical part knows that's not how life works. If he's sent to another station or dismissed entirely, there's no way I could be with him because that'd mean leaving Carter and Heath. Something he'd never ask me to do.

"Logan, I don't know —"

But as I reply, he interrupts me. "Don't," he says, eyes sharpening. "Just don't. You got your answers. Now, we have twenty minutes before the janitors show up. How about we see how you do left-handed?"

"You're a mean teacher, you know that?" I tease, sensing the shift in energy.

A hint of a smirk plays at the corner of his mouth. "You came to *me*, remember?"

Shifting my stance, I move into an off-hand position.

"Now," he says, lifting his batons, "show me what you've got."

I bare my teeth and charge.

Forty-Five

HEATH

Today is the day of the merger.

The day Drakeford and Lockwood industries will combine.

I run the razor over my jaw, shaving away the last traces of stubble. The afternoon drills have left my muscles pleasantly sore. My light mood darkens abruptly when my comm chimes with a call from my father.

A cold dread seeps into my veins. I haven't told my parents about the broken engagement. I assumed Jess had handled it —canceled the venue, the florist, and the caterers—since nothing's shown up on the Network news. Maybe she quietly paid everyone off to keep it under wraps. Between Logan's trial and the shock of learning women can bond with druaneras, I haven't found a single moment to reach out.

This isn't the kind of news I can deliver with a short message. It's too big, too messy. If anything, I should fly to Delford and tell them in person. Look them in the eye and explain why everything they'd planned for us fell apart. Anything less would be cowardly, and I can't add that to the weight already sitting on my chest.

I click the comm on the counter, answering. "Good morning, son. I wanted to keep you apprised," my father says over the speaker. "There's been an unexpected development, and we're going to have to postpone the merger."

My hand slips, and I hiss as the razor knicks my jaw.

"What happened?" I ask, trying to keep my voice steady as I drop the razor in the sink and dab the blood with a cloth.

"God damn protesters," he says. "Half of Delford is in the streets protesting. They've blocked the entrances to the building, and when we tried to move it to another location, a bomb threat was called in. The whole city is in chaos. The police are refusing to let ours or Drakeford's representatives leave the hotel. Your mother is insisting we go to the Parnia house until things die down."

Frustration rises within me, hot and sour, as the implications sink in. If the merger falls through, Lockwood will undoubtedly have to downsize to cut costs. The filtration plant... they'll have to reduce staff. The protestors have no idea that what they're doing is hurting more people than helping.

This merger is so crucial, not just for our companies but for Venovia as a whole. "A virtual meeting? Over comms?" As I say the words, I know it's a desperate, short-term solution.

"Already working through the details, but Drakeford likes his handshakes and wet ink."

Damn him and his obsolete ways. Even if they complete

the merger, the real problem runs deeper – no one likes us. Our families. The people have lost faith in our companies and Circuit's ability to keep the country safe.

Shit.

I finish shaving and towel off my face as my comm chimes again. I sigh, expecting another grim update from my father, but am pleasantly surprised to see it's from Brigid.

> Meet me at the bridge.

Then there's a delay before she sends another:

> Bring a coat ;-)

My pulse quickens. Intriguing.

The night after Kaeden's memorial has sustained me for days.

It had been an impulsive decision spurred on by the emotional upheaval in the bond from Logan.

That was all. But god, if it hadn't been glorious and how the images of her naked body have haunted me every night since then.

Dressing quickly, I opt for navy slacks and a gray long-sleeve shirt, topping it with my wool duster to ward off the chill. It's almost childish, this excitement over our meetings, and I can't recall ever feeling this way about anyone before.

Brigid fascinates me. Her kindness and her empathy seem boundless. It's no wonder everyone who meets her is charmed. It's no wonder she excels at her job, smoothing over crises and ensuring the station's reputation is maintained.

The black stone walls of the barracks loom around me as I exit the main doors. Gravel crunches underfoot as I cross the courtyard, my steps quick and purposeful. The main gate—an imposing portcullis—remains closed, but I make for the adjacent man door, where two station security officers stand watch.

I recognize Geoff, formerly of Meridian. He'd worked under Logan. "Afternoon," I nod, aiming for casual.

"Afternoon, sir," Geoff returns. "Heading out? Storm's brewing. Wind's likely to pick up."

"Noted," I reply, grateful for the warning but eager to be on my way. "I won't be long."

As they buzz me through, I can't help but reflect on how orderly everything is here, the strict schedules and the clear chain of command. I attempted this sense of structure and control at Meridian, but with a smaller, tight-knit station and sunny climate that bolstered a more leisurely lifestyle, it had been difficult to maintain.

I miss the connection to the upper management as a manager, and yet I find I don't miss the stress or shouldering of responsibility when something goes awry. Being demoted to a Master Rider once again had its benefits.

For example, my flexible schedule allows me to meet Brigid in the archives regularly.

Through the gate, I step out into the misty afternoon. Being careful not to slip on the slick rocks, I make my way down to the old road leading to the bridge. As I approach, a lone figure in a purple coat waits for me. Her elbows rest on the bridge's stone wall, and wisps of silver hair peek out from beneath her hood, catching the fading light.

Her jacket is new and of high quality— fine wool with intricate silver embroidery along the hem. I recognize the design from a local clothing boutique in the village and feel a surge of pleasure that she's embracing the luxuries working at a station provides.

The sight of her never fails to make my heart race. I work

hard to keep my footsteps steady, not wanting to betray the effect she has on me. As our eyes meet, I'm lost. Those eyes draw me in, capturing me completely. Carter had noticed it before I did, and he'd been so right.

There's a magnetism that defies explanation, a pull that makes me regret every moment I'm not near her. "Ms. Corsair," I say, tipping my head. "No archives today?"

"No, Mr. Lockwood," she says, her tone mocking. "I needed some fresh air and thought you might, too."

"Well, then you'd be correct." I step to her, and we stroll across the cracked pavement of the partial remains of the bridge.

Finally, she stops and rests her arms on the wall, staring upstream of the rushing Northbay River. "Did you know the last stand against the mystyl took place on this very bridge?"

"Is that so?" I reply.

"It is," she says proudly.

I can't help but challenge her gently, a habit born from our shared love of historical accuracy. "There are bridges all over Venovia and three alone that cross this river. How can you be sure it was this bridge?"

Her eyes light up at the question. "They didn't have an illustration, but the journal entry was from a rider officer dated 187 AR."

"And?" I prompt, genuinely curious now.

"And he described mystyl climbing up and over the railings. He shot one off of a statue of a hawk before it landed on his stallion."

"Then you're wrong."

"What? No, I'm not."

"The statues weren't erected until years after the last battle," I reply matter of factly. "There's a plaque inside

Marshal's office with the commemorations from Circuit's first president in 378 AR."

I point at the pair of eagles perched on stone pillars behind us. "These were built then, but," I say, and slide a hand on the granite railing, scraping off the coating of moss and dead leaves. I inhale in a sigh of relief as my hand catches on to what I'd assumed was there but hadn't yet confirmed. "There were smaller ones before." I wipe away the bits of vegetation, revealing a pair of eagle-like toes carved into the stone. They're worn and cracked, but there.

She arches an ashen brow. "Impressed?"

"Very."

"Told you I'm an excellent student."

My eyes bounce between hers as I watch in awe of how curiosity lights up her face. She brings a spark to my life that I thought I had forgotten. My childhood was that of routines and schedules, each day carefully mapped out. With the ocean just outside our door, I was only allowed to walk the beach with a nanny, never to run or feel the cool water on my toes. But she—she brought back a sense of wildness, the feeling I could do anything. "I never doubted you for a second," I say, as I set my hands on the wall so they're inches from hers.

"Although, I don't know what I'm jealous of more, Ms. Corsair. That you knew a piece of Venovian history that I didn't or that Yuto got to be alone with you."

Brigid lifts her chin and sniffs. "To be fair, the man can make one hell of a cup of hot chocolate."

I chuckle. "That's true."

She gazes down at the engravings, using her thumbnail to clean out the grooves. "There was something else I found in the third volume of Rosaline's journals. She mentioned this word: Sentinels." She looks up at me. "At first, I thought it was a mistake or a code word, but then after re-reading it and making a note, I found it mentioned once more toward the end of volume four."

I sift through my memory of druadan history courses at Vanguard and everything I'd learned since sitting through station meetings and conferences. Never had Sentinels been mentioned.

I tilt my chin to better view the side of her face. "That's right before we assumed she died."

She nods. "She said the Sentinels were her guardians or like bodyguards, but then she refers to them other times as her 'heart' or 'soulkeepers.' I honestly lost track of who she was referring to half the time."

I'd only had time to skim the journals in between when Brigid and I were in the archives together, so I am grateful she had a keen eye for detail. "She got a bit rambly toward the end, didn't she?"

She laughs. "Girl was in the middle of a war. I'd be a little scatterbrained, too."

My comm dings twice, and I frown as I see another message from my father.

"Everything all right?" she asks.

"Yes, quite," I say, covering the screen. "Please carry on."

Brigid twists around and leans her elbows on the bridge. "Anyway, I did my best to connect the vague parts. In her notes, she implied she had a deeper connection with the sentinels than the other riders, almost like a bond with her druanera. She even mentions appraising her Sentinel's bonds for." She taps her chin. "How did she put it? Durability. Yeah, I think that was it."

I squint at the gondola passing overhead, pursing my lips.

I'm at a loss for how to respond, caught between understanding and confusion.

All bonded riders have a link on some level; however, I'm

aware the bond between Carter, Logan, and me is different—stronger and deeper than what is typical. Marshal had mentioned more than once that he wanted us to teach a class and show the others how to sense emotions more clearly. I was flattered, but I had to decline. The way we read each other wasn't something learned; it was instinctual and came to us naturally. How could I teach what I didn't fully understand myself? And right now is no different. What she's saying makes sense on the surface, but underneath, it feels like she's speaking a language I should know, but the meaning is just out of reach.

When I don't reply, she forges ahead. "I pieced together the information that Sentinels were three things. One, they were rare. Only some druanera riders had them and had to earn the right to them. And two Sentinels were druadan riders. They were men." She tosses her shoulders. "I know, I know, how do you 'earn' someone or even own someone in the first place? I don't have a clue, but that's what it says."

Her blue eyes are bright with excitement, but I don't feel the same. Instead, I'm overwhelmed by sadness and pity. I'd read the journals enough to know that the woman writing them was obviously mentally unstable. Even Logan had picked up on that.

Still, she's so swept up with them that I'm afraid she'll face nothing but disappointment when she discovers that most of what they say isn't true.

However, I enjoy seeing her like this, so full of hope that I don't dare burst her bubble. Besides, what harm is there in letting her continue, anyway?

"And the third?" I say as she stares at me expectantly.

Her head bobs. "Right, yeah, so the third thing is that once the druanera had enough power, whatever that means, I don't know, but like she could control the bonds of her Sentinels." She pauses, letting her words sink in.

I rub a hand over my forehead and let out a deep sigh, realizing I've let this go too far. "That's not possible."

She purses her lips. "How do you know?"

My jaw shifts as I formulate an answer. "Because although our bonds are real, saying you can change them is like saying you can control an emotion or manipulate time. The bonds exist, but they aren't physical things like this stone or that water."

She lifts her chin. "Says who?"

I blow air from my nose. "Says every scientist, physicist, or chemist that's ever studied them.

She narrows me with a look. "Sure, but their research was all done without a druanera existing. That's like aliens landing, taking a single man to study, and concluding all humans are identical to that one sample. Humans as a species differ in everything from body type, gender, and skin color, not to mention personality. How is a druadan any different?"

I pause, taken aback by the force of her argument. She has a point.

"Just cause you've never seen it done," she continues, "doesn't mean it's impossible. I mean, look at the egg, at Oriana. Both are perfect examples. We can't always trust our assumptions." She tucks a stray hair behind her ear, and her silver bracelet catches the light.

I mull over her words, feeling like I've stumbled into one of my dad's parlor room ethics debates with his fox-hunting buddies. "All right," I say slowly. "Say any of this is true. I need evidence, Ms. Corsair, and if we hope to convince anyone else of this, they will, too."

Her cheeks flush slightly, and she averts her gaze back to the river. "I can see your bonds. At least, sometimes, and don't ask me how, but I think I've already started doing it, like with Logan the other night when he..." she trails off.

When he'd tried to kill himself.

Her words sink into me. That shockwave when she'd kissed Logan—I thought I'd imagined it. I'd been drunk and terrified that Logan was about to jump. But my instincts had been right.

I'd known to call Brigid. I thought it was because of how she'd calmed me at the gala, but now it's clear it was something more. A connection like Carter had said back at Meridian. No one ever stopped Logan from doing anything he didn't want to do. But Brigid had. She'd reached him, saved him. My heartbeat quickens at the revelation. "But how is that possible?" I stammer.

She beams. "You believe me?"

"Yes."

Her smile widens, reaching her eyes so the blue irises sparkle. "Thank Tides, 'cause I really thought I was going crazy there for a minute." Her cheeks are flushed from the air whisked from the river, and I'm overwhelmed by the urge to kiss her.

"So, I guess this means more time down in the library?" she says.

"Yeah," I say. "I think it does." As if on cue, my comm buzzes with a reminder to meet the saddle smith to fit Shadowmane for a new saddle.

"It's okay," Brigid says. "You can go."

I swipe away the alert and stuff my hands in my pockets.

"Archives at seven?"

"See you then," she says.

Forty-Six

JESS

"Just *go* already," I plead through chattering teeth. "That bush. Look at that, it's perfect." I pull my hood up against the driving wind. "Would you please hurry? If I get hypothermia because you can't find a place to go, I swear I'm—." A whoosh of frigid wind swallows my threat as Finn yanks me forward.

I trudge through the damp grass, my Pinsky vintage boots sinking into the mud with each step. Callie would murder me if she saw me wearing them, but it was them or my Floriana booties.

Finn pulls on the leash, and I struggle to keep him focused on the task at hand. The chill seeps through my peacoat, and I long for the warmth of my room, the luxurious bath I could be currently taking with those exquisite soaps from Parnia.

We've been out here for what feels like an eternity, though my comm informs me it's only been forty-five minutes. Finn has marked every tree, bush, and stone pillar in sight but hasn't decided to relieve himself fully. I tap my foot, impatient, as he sniffs at yet another patch of grass.

My comm vibrates, and I see it's a call from my mother. With a sigh, I answer. Her face appears perfectly made up despite being on a shuttle.

She frowns upon seeing me. "Darling, you're going to catch a chill. Why on Earth are you outside?"

"Just taking in some fresh air, Mother," I reply, feigning a smile. "Is something the matter? I thought you were attending the merger planning meeting today."

Her tinted eyebrows furrow. "Canceled. Someone claimed they spotted one of those wretched beasts in a restroom. Don't you get the news updates there? Your father decided it was prudent to retreat to North Cliff for the weekend."

My stomach tightens. "What about Jace?" I ask concern for my younger brother, seeping through my annoyance at the merger delay. He's twelve and not yet corrupted by our parents. I'd encouraged them to send him to boarding school to keep it that way. We talked weekly, and he seemed to do well there. Mastering his classes and thriving in sports.

"We've confirmed with Judith that he's safest at Thornwick for now. The parents have pooled resources for additional security." She pauses, her lips pursing. "We'll reconvene on Monday."

I frown, puzzled. "Why not conduct the meeting virtually?"

Her sigh crackles through the comm. "You understand the delicate nature of this situation, dear. Without our families formally united, everything hangs by a thread. This is all preliminary, and nothing is set in stone until you and Heath have a child. The 'Blood and Land' act still holds sway, as much as we all detest it."

Guilt and resentment coil in my chest, tightening with

every breath. I still haven't told them about Heath's impotence or our decision to call off the wedding. I had contacted the venue myself, and after a pointed threat to blacklist them for any future events, they agreed to cancel quietly—though they kept the thirty-thousand credit deposit, of course.

At least they kept their end of the deal, as my mother remains blissfully unaware. But I know I can't delay much longer. I'll have to break the news soon so she can inform the hundreds of guests before the rumors start swirling. But clearly, today is not that day.

Tenuous indeed.

My mother continues, her voice lowering as if sharing a secret. "Circuit's reputation is in tatters. Protesters are clamoring for a new election, demanding Peterson step down as President. The audacity of it all is appalling. The power grid workers are striking, demanding increased wages, and Circuit is defaulting on their leases of the land those windmills sit on. Our land. And your father won't admit it, but unless we finalize this deal soon, we'll have to liquidate our FP portfolio."

"How unfortunate," I reply. While Circuit ran the filtration plants, they paid dividends to private equities. Investing in FPs in Venovia was both profitable and secure and provided the financial backing Circuit could draw on to build or repair the plants.

"Indeed," she replies, and static hisses through my comm. "We're losing connection, darling. Stay safe and get inside, for goodness sake."

"I will," I manage before the call cuts her off.

Finn tugs at the leash as he analyzes a corner of the outside wall. Wrapping the strap around my wrist, I open the Network news feed. Headline after headline shows images of Circuit's security forces, clad in riot gear, clashing with waves of angry protesters. Their signs flash across the screen: "God sees your lies," "Filtration failure, Circuit betrayal," "We survived the flood, not your deceit!"

My heart pounds against my ribs, panic rising like bile in my throat. This is far worse than Mother let on. I look down, ready to drag Finn back home, only to find the leash slack and the dog nowhere in sight.

You've got to be kidding me.

I call Finn's name, my voice echoing off the fortress walls. "Finn! Come here, boy!" I scan the area and spot Brigid approaching from the bridge. Her hair is in an intricate side braid, and her cheeks have a flush from the wind. She has a natural, effortless beauty, and I'm acutely aware of my appearance — sweaty, windblown, and utterly frazzled. *Why did I ever agree to this?*

"Hi there," Brigid says, climbing the path to me. "Is everything alright? I heard you calling for someone."

I straighten my posture, desperately clinging to some semblance of dignity. "Yes, everything is fine," I say, brushing past her and calling Finn's name with increased urgency.

"Finn?" Brigid repeats, falling into step beside me. "Marshal's dog?" A small laugh escapes her. "Oh no, you've lost him?"

"Don't laugh," I snap, my composure cracking.

Brigid's expression softens. "You're right, I apologize. Let's find him together, shall we?"

"I can do well enough on my own, thank you."

She doesn't relent. "It's going to be dark soon. Two sets of eyes are better than one."

I purse my lips. "Fine."

We search in silence for a few moments before coming across Finn's collar, snagged on a low-hanging branch.

"I'm going to get Marshal," Brigid says, beginning to turn away.

"No," I insist, my voice wavering. "There's no need. I'm perfectly capable of locating one dog." I stare down at the leash and collar in my hands streaked with mud. The sky opens, rain pelting us mercilessly. I feel my carefully applied makeup running in rivulets down my face, and regret grinds my teeth.

I never should've insisted on coming here or making this deal in the first place.

The walls I've built around my emotions crumble. I sink to my knees, clutching the muddy leash, uncaring the damp seeping into my pants. Tears mingle with the rain on my cheeks.

Brigid paces next to me. "It's okay. We'll find him. He can't have gone far."

"It's not the dog," I murmur as I feel my floodgates open. I pour out everything: the pressure from my family, the loneliness, the sham of my engagement. "My mother medicates herself into oblivion with her precious tea while my father drowns his worries in scotch. My entire life is unraveling, and I'm powerless to stop it."

"I...I didn't know. I'm sorry." I feel the weight of her hand on my shoulder.

"You know, if I were a man, they would have forced me to become a rider. Sometimes I think about how simple things would've been."

Brigid doesn't reply.

I sniff and look up at her. "He'll never love you, you know. Not like he loves that stallion."

"I don't know what you're—"

"Stop it. Do you really think you're that special? Darling, my cunt's brought Heath to his knees."

Her pale cheeks redden, and delight skips inside me, lifting the sadness.

Before she can process my words, a blur of fur streaks past

us. Finn — in all his muddy glory — is in hot pursuit of a terrified squirrel. The squirrel scurries up a tree and out of his reach, and we jog over to him.

"Come here," I shout, and Finn peels his gaze away to look at us. His tail wags, oblivious to the stress he induced. As I approach him, a mix of emotions wars within me. Relief at finding the dog, lingering anxiety over the state of my world, and a new, unsettling feeling I can't quite name when I look at Brigid.

I clip the collar back onto Finn's collar, my hands shaking from more than just the cold. "Thank you," I say stiffly.

"Sure," she says.

I take a shuddering breath, the cold and wet seeping into my bones. My comm chimes with another alert. A government building is in flames.

Brigid gets her notification shortly after and glances down at it. Her face turning grim.

I straighten my coat and sniff. "If Heath could give me an heir, all this nonsense would be resolved. It would solve everything for our families. The merger would proceed and avoid the layoffs."

Brigid is quiet for a moment, and I feel her eyes studying the side of my face as I walk away. "Maybe you can," she says, before I take more than a few steps. "I might know of a way."

Forty-Seven

BRIGID

Well, *shit*. The second I've spoken the words, icy tendrils of regret clamp around my throat. I never should have said anything. I should have kept my damn mouth shut. But Jess had been so vulnerable, so hopeless. Seeing her this way, so exposed, had only added to the guilt gnawing away at my insides.

Jess' eyebrows hitch up ever so slightly. "Is that so?"

I nod. "Ever since Oriana hatched, I've been looking through Blackhawk's archives for more information on her care, and I believe I've stumbled upon a way."

Jess gestures to the alcove next to us, where part of the west wing's roof overhang blocks the rain, and I make my way to it.

Out of the rain and tucked in the space, Finn sniffs around our feet before finally collapsing in a pile of dried leaves in the corner with a chuff. Jess lowers her hood and smooths her hair. "Enlighten me."

"I haven't bonded with Oriana exactly, not like normal riders, but still, I'm connected with her, and it's allowing me to sense the rider's bonds."

She wrinkles her nose. "Odd, but go on."

"Heath told you the bond causes riders to be infertile. I think I can temper it, pull it back like a curtain just enough for his body temperature to drop and—"

"And his little Lockwood legacies can do their duty," she finishes for me.

I stifle a laugh. "Yes."

"Say this is true. This is the most we've ever spoken. Why are you doing this?"

The question blindsides me, and I divert my gaze, staring at the lawn across from us that borders the tree farm. The thought of Heath being with her makes my blood boil, and I want to scream.

I want Heath. All for myself.

And I hate that I'm even suggesting this more than I've hated anything, but I could never live with myself knowing I'd walk away when I could've done something. My sister is wreaking havoc across the world. I'll be damned if I let my personal feelings get in the way of thousands of people losing their homes and jobs.

I have to do this. In some small way to make up for Sharice's actions.

Why was I given this ability to sense bonds if not to do something with it? What other purpose could it hold than this? Sure, Jess has never been overly kind to me. But there was a good chance she'd sensed something between Heath and I. Women's intuition is a powerful thing.

But I wasn't doing this to help her. I was doing this because it was the right thing to do. "My sister is the reason all of this is happening," I finally reply. "I have the power to tip the scales in our favor with at least one small part of it. I'd never live with myself if I didn't try."

"How noble of you," she says. "So, that's it then. You snap your fingers at Heath, and"— she wriggles her hand in the air — "poof, I'm pregnant?"

"Not exactly." I pause, composing my thoughts. "The text is limited, but for me to temper a bond, I must be physically touching the person."

"Hah, you can't be serious." She tilts her head back, staring at the sky. "These riders and their perversions have clearly corrupted you. No. Never. Could you imagine the scandal if this got out that I was involved in some taboo sex group?" Jess's lips twist into a snarl. "You are sick, you know that? Twisted and perverted, and—"

I clear my throat. "It's the only way. You said so yourself."

She glares at me, her mind mulling over and I can almost hear her retort, "Why don't *you* have his baby?" But she won't dare say it.

She knows why.

Drakeford and Lockwood are merging. It doesn't make sense for him to have a child with me, the daughter of a scientist and an unknown father. Jess and Heath are the heirs of the two biggest employers in the country.

There isn't a better option if Circuit wants to appease the masses and gain their support for allowing these multi-million credit companies to thrive and grow.

Finn lets out a plaintive whine as a flicker of indecision crosses her ice-blue eyes. She peers down at the dog with disdain, clearly uncomfortable with the arrangement, but she's not a hundred percent against it.

This is all performative. Her upbringing and upper-class station would never permit such indecent acts. However, I'd met my fair share of high-society even before Meridian, and none of them were free from the rumors of illicit meetings occurring behind closed doors.

This isn't all that bad, considering. If I am willing to put aside my own reservations, my own dislike of Heath and her being intimately connected via a child, then she can get over her prudish ways.

"We can do whatever makes you feel comfortable," I forge ahead. "I understand how important your reputation is, and I am familiar with discretion. We can arrange—"

"This is too much." She rubs the space between her brows. "I can't decide right now. I need time to think this over." She tugs on Finn's leash. "I need to return him to Marshal." She steps out of the shade of the alcove, then says over her shoulder. "Thank you again for helping me find him."

And then she's gone, leaving me alone. I can only imagine what she's going through. Hearing that someone can see the bonds and manipulate them had to seem like full-on magic to an outsider.

I'd hardly come to accept it, and I'd been living with it for days. She might be right about a Lockwood and Drakeford heir keeping people from losing their jobs, but she was wrong about taking time. If Venovia plunged into a civil war, no miracle babies would be enough to quench the flames of rebellion.

We were running out of time.

Forty-Eight

LOGAN

"I've got all the time in the world, Jackass," I shout at Galaxian.

Marshal finally gave me the green light to let him loose in the arena and stretch his legs, and he's spent the past hour galloping and bucking around the perimeter like he'd been shot out of a cannon. But now he won't let me catch him.

Fucking typical.

Marshal's laughter carries from the gate where he's watching from the stands. "C'mon Logan, you know how these Galaxy lines never stop testing their riders. You're demanding too much. Try meeting him a different way."

My jaw clenches, frustration bubbling up like bile. If it were anyone else, I'd tell them to piss off. But it's Marshal, and telling him off right now would be like cutting my safety harness on a rapidly descending shuttle.

Even I have more self-preservation than that. Besides, he's one of the few guys I respect.

Holding the lead in my hand, I stride forward, but Jackass tosses his head and prances just out of reach, taunting me with every step.

All right, asshole. Two can play at this game.

I turn my back on him, feigning disinterest. Reverse psychology. See how you like being ignored?

There's a confused tug on the bond blended with a flicker of anxiety.

Good. Let him stew in it.

A few heartbeats later, I feel the hair on the back of my neck lifted with warm huffs of air.

I whirl around, but the crafty bastard's already bolting. His tail flagged high like a banner of defiance.

Charging after him, I manage to cut him off in the corner, quick as a rattlesnake. Galaxian rears up, pawing at the air. Our bonding teacher at Vanguard, Professor Leon's voice, echoes in my head. The same words I repeat to the novices when they sense a bonding is near.

Don't flinch.

Don't falter.

Druadans seek strength, not fear.

The stallion's nostrils flare, steam billowing out like he's some kind of dragon. Then he charges, a ton of muscle and attitude barreling straight for me. At the last second, I sidestep, grabbing a fistful of his mane and swinging myself onto his back.

I yip with excitement as I grab hold of his mane.

Galaxian's not done, though. He lowers his head and takes off at a ground-shuddering gallop. My legs clamp down on his bare back, holding my seat, and the bond between us explodes with raw power. It's electric, intoxicating — a reminder of why I'll never give this up.

Unless you're forced to.

The thought is smothered in the mind-blowing sensations, though, as we charge around the perimeter of the arena. His body shivers, itching to phase, but I tell him no. Without a bridle, it's far too risky. My pulse accelerates as flashbacks of Galaxyla's dead body, still saddled and lying on the arena floor, bombard me.

Immediately, Galaxian senses my unease and slows to a walk. His sides heaving beneath my legs, I direct with the lead rope around his neck and guide him over to the VIP section on the north end.

Marshal's waiting, a smug grin plastered across his face.

"Not bad," Marshal says. "I was worried I'd need to get Nightshade and come rescue you."

I grunt a response and slide off Galaxian's back. He's more relaxed and lets me properly secure the halter over his ears.

Marshal hands me a water bottle. "Got some good news for you."

I unzip my gloves, tuck them in my back pocket, and savor the cold steel of the bottle under my hands.

"Yeah? What's that?" I ask, taking a swig.

"Had a chat with my mom today, and she has an attorney friend willing to help you out with your... situation."

"An attorney? What happened to this being only a hearing?"

"It still is. But figured it can't hurt to have some counsel, right?"

"I guess."

"Ken Bothwell. They're very connected and represented a rider at North Crimela station after his wife tried to take half his pension in the divorce."

Before I can respond, however, Jess appears out of nowhere, looking like a drowned rat.

She's soaked, her clothes clinging to her in ways that'd be interesting if she wasn't such a frosty bitch.

"Cunt," I say.

"Neanderthal," she replies, not looking at me. Marshal pivots to face her, and she sets a leash in his hand, giving him back his mutt, Finn.

"How did it go?" Marshal asks, ignoring our name-calling.

"How do you think?" she says, frowning. "He smelled all the squirrels and did his business, and now I'm off to take a long, hot bath."

"Sounds nice. I might join you," Marshal blurts out before clearing his throat. "I mean...take a bath in my *own* room."

Jess raises an eyebrow, a hint of skepticism in her eyes. "Sure," she says, leaving.

"Wait. I need you," he stumbles over the words, then hastily adds, "Tomorrow, I mean. I have a meeting at eight with the music director that's scheduled until noon."

She adjusts her hair under the hood of her jacket. "Yes. Eight. I'll be by to get him."

Marshal beams like a damn fool. "Eight. Yes. I'll have coffee!"

What the hell is happening right now?

She flashes him a weak smile and doesn't bother looking at me before leaving. Her footsteps recede down the hallway. There's the brief sound of rain, and then it's cut off as the outside door slams shut.

I screw the lid back on the bottle. "You've got to be fucking kidding me."

Marshal chuckles. "You know, Logan, Jess isn't all bad." He pats the dog's head. "Since she's been walking Finn, he's taken a shine to her. My boy's an excellent judge of character."

I snort, unconvinced. Heath and she had never been all that serious, and shit knows Heath never stayed faithful, so why should she?

"So, tell me about this lawyer friend," I say, wanting to change the subject from ice-queen. "What's it going to cost me?"

Marshal scratches Finn behind the ears. "No fee. This guy's semi-retired, but his nephew was a rider, so he likes to give back when he can."

"I don't need charity," I growl, turning back to Galaxian and busying myself by putting on my gloves.

"It's not charity, Logan. It's a lifeline. You'd be an idiot not to take it."

I straighten up, fixing Marshal with a hard stare. "And what makes you think I give two shits about your opinion?"

He meets my gaze, unflinching. "Because deep down, under all that piss and vinegar, you know I'm right. You're in over your head, and this is your best shot at getting out clean."

He's not wrong. I've been treading water for months, barely keeping my head above the surface. But admitting that feels like defeat, and I've never been good at losing.

I squat to examine Galaxian's legs. If I'd known he would've acted like a fool, I would have put on leg protectors. Thankfully, there aren't any scrapes or cuts.

"I'll think about it," I mutter.

Marshal sighs. "That's all I'm asking. Now, are you ready to tell me what's happening with your bond? He's as stubborn as you, but I get the feeling there's more to it."

Standing, I run a hand through my sweat-dampened hair, buying time. "Yeah, I just needed to remind him who's boss."

"Uh-huh. And how's that been working out for you?"

I glare at him. "We got it sorted, didn't we?"

Marshal chuckles, shaking his head. "Sure, if you call

nearly getting trampled, 'sorted.' You know, after a fall or accident, the connection can get scrambled. And in your case, I'd be surprised if there weren't some after-effects. If you're interested, there are easier ways to connect with him."

"Yeah? Like what? Braiding his mane and singing lullabies?"

"Smart ass. I'm talking about trust. Building it, not demanding it."

I roll my eyes, even as I know he's right. The guy's been at this longer than I have. I'll never admit it out loud, but he might be onto something. "Fine. What do you want me to do?"

As if on cue, Galaxian snorts and paws at the ground. I shoot him a look. "You got something to add?"

"*Not egg. Oriana free,*" he says in that gravelly tone.

"Tell me about it. It's all the whole station is talking about."

"*Oriana female.*" There's an odd purring noise I've never heard before, and then he adds, "*Oriana, sad and lonely.*"

"Probably, but it's for her own protection. We can't let her out yet."

Marshal laughs outright at that. "Man, I'm getting whiplash from the emotions. See? He's trying to tell you something. Maybe it's time you started listening."

The bond between Galaxian and me still humming like a live wire, I ask. "*You know we're in trouble, right? Like neck deep in shit trouble.*"

"*Kill human. Bad.*"

"Yes bad. And now the humans are going to decide what the consequences are."

There's a long silence, and I wonder if he didn't hear me until he purrs again.

"*Ember lives, I die. It is equal.*"

"NO," I blurt, and causing Marshal to look up from where

he'd been petting Finn. Since each rider speaks a different way to their mount, it sounds like garbled gibberish to him. Still, he's close enough that he can sense the tone.

"Not equal to me," I say. "You are mine." My throat clamps shut.

"Not equal." Galaxian lowers his head, scratching the side of his face on his leg.

A sigh of relief escapes me. "Yes."

"Why sad Galaxyla? I'm not equal?"

The mere mention of his name sends a jolt of anguish through me, causing my entire body to convulse with pain.

"Logan," Marshal says through the haze.

I grasp the arena wall, fingers scraping the rough surface.

Fuck. Fuck. Fuck.

I close my eyes, trying to block out the memories, but they continue to haunt me.

"Logan," Marshal repeats.

A hand seizes the back of my neck, wrenching my head upward.

Marshal's blue eyes, steeped with worry, fill my vision.

"Hey, hey," he says softly. "You with me? What was that?"

I work my tongue in my mouth, trying to quench the dryness. Galaxian's ears perk up, and he gently bumps my hip with his head. The heat wafts over the uninsulated area on my neck and wrist.

Ignoring Marshal, I rest a hand on the stallion's neck, just beneath his mane.

This is it. What Brigid had meant about me shutting off my feelings.

My ego had been the thorn in my bond since the beginning.

Well, time to pull that fucker out.

"You are not equal. You are better. You are mine."

"Mine," Galaxian replies.

The stallion snorts and cranes his neck up, his nose flaring as he tastes the air.

"Everything good?" Marshal says, visibly relaxing.

"Yeah. It's good."

"Great. Since this went relatively well, all things considered, I'll book more time for you to work with him here every day."

"Thank you," I say stiffly.

Marshal grins as he stands. "Think about what I said, yeah, about the lawyer? You've got more friends here than you know. Don't screw it up because you're too stubborn to take the help."

I grunt noncommittally.

Marshal climbs down from the bench and retreats the same way Jess had left earlier. Galaxian follows willingly now, his earlier defiance seemingly forgotten.

The barn is quiet. Most of the other druadans are taking an afternoon nap. I lead Galaxian into his stall, taking more care than usual as I brush him off and fill his feed bucket. Glowing teal eyes watch me with that curious intelligence.

"What?" I mutter, pausing in my work. "You got an opinion on all this, too?"

But as I finish up and turn to leave, Galaxian lets out a low nicker. I pause in the doorway, looking back at him. For a moment, I let myself imagine what it might be like to trust something, someone other than myself.

The thought terrifies me.

Trusting Galaxian isn't the problem. He's defiant but honest.

It's his trust in me that feels like poison spreading through my veins. I had once held Galaxyla's life in my hands and failed him. I will not make the same mistake again and let my second stallion die.

"Rest up," I tell Galaxian. "We have work to do."

Forty-Nine

CARTER

"Miss you, Jamesy," the brunette purrs at the camera, making an exaggerated kissing motion. I skip past it, feeling a slight twinge of... something. Nostalgia? Nah. As I lounge on the saggy rec room couch, my fingers lazily scroll through the backlog of messages and video clips on my comm.

"Double or nothing," Shane shouts.

"Deal," Roberts replies. We'd brought the ping-pong table from Meridian, and the two have monopolized it since we got here.

In the next video, twins with matching mahogany brown curls and thick eyeliner grin wickedly in nothing in lace bras and panties. Swipe.

Three images and a tempting offer involving stiletto heels and a ball gag later, I receive an incoming message. Hinah and Maria are Leviler Tech seniors with whom I spent a very energetic weekend in May during the peak of the exhibition season.

"Damn, Carter, you gonna hit up QR this weekend with them?" Shane's voice comes from over my shoulder as he leans in. Still holding the paddle, his eyes are glued to my projected comm screen. The Quartz Resort - the preferred base for us riders when staying in the village.

I shake my head, the stale beer smell of his breath ruffling my hair. "Nah. You want their numbers, though?"

Shane's eyes light up like it's his birthday. Shit. Maybe it is.

"Hell yeah. I'm not even itchy yet, but I ain't passing that up."

As I forward their contact info, I realize with a start that I'm not excited by these messages anymore. Fan mail never fails to lift my mood, but ever since I've been seeing Brigid, the thought of messing around with other women — or guys, for that matter — hasn't even entered my mind.

And as strange as it sounds, I'm kind of cool with it. My thoughts are interrupted, however, by Heath approaching. Discussion in the room dies down as he strides in my direction. I do my best to read his expression, but the man's a machine, and it's not until he's right in front of me do I sense the tension in the bond.

"Sorry to interrupt your free time, but you got a minute? Something's come up, and I need to talk to you about it."

I lower my boots off the beat-up coffee table with a thunk. "Everything okay?"

Heath's eyes dart around, lingering on Shane for a moment before he gives a quick nod. "Yes, of course. It's just... wedding stuff."

The pang in my chest tells me otherwise. "Oh shit, that's coming up, isn't it?" I climb to my feet.

Shane visibly relaxes out of the corner of my eye. "Catch you later," I tell him and follow Heath out of the rec room. We climb the stairs in silence to the alcove on the first floor. I scratch the scruff on my jaw. I'd been so busy with my mom's 'recruit riders agenda' I hadn't bothered shaving during our daily showers.

Maybe I'd keep it. Maybe it'd make me look older, like Marshal, more distinguished.

Once we're alone, I turn to him. "This about Logan?"

But Heath's already shaking his head before the words are all the way out. "No, no - nothing like that. Something's come up, and Brigid and I need to discuss something with you. In private."

I frown, a leaden feeling sinking into my gut. What could they possibly need to talk to me about that's so serious? Unless...

No. I force that thought away immediately. "Okay, hit me. What's going on?"

"Brigid's waiting for us in her room. It'll be easier to explain it with her." We ascend the three more flights of stairs and then down the hall to Brigid's room.

Heath knocks.

"Come in," a muffled voice says.

Heath opens the door, and the two of us enter. Brigid sits at the table with a mug in her hand. She's wearing a teal blouse that matches her eyes and white shorts that expose her long, slender legs. Instantly, there's an ache in my groin as I recall running my mouth along them, feeling the smooth skin under my lips.

My eyes drift to Jess seated across from her, also holding a mug.

What the hell is Ice-queen doing here?

She's wearing a coral jumpsuit, and her dark hair is braided down the side. Don't get me wrong, she's pretty, but you only need to have a brief conversation with her before it's clear why Heath only wants one thing in his life to have sharp, pointed teeth.

"Damn," I say, striding in. "If I knew this was going to be a party, I would've brought something."

"Close the door," Jess commands.

Heath reaches behind me, and both shut and lock it.

Brigid presses her lips together and sighs. "Thanks for coming, Carter."

My heart rate stutters in my ears. *God, is this an intervention?* I hadn't touched O-strike in months. "Anyone want to tell me what's going on?" I ask, turning to Heath.

He crosses his hands behind his back and looks at Jess.

"I assume even someone like you pays attention to the news." She twists herself in the chair to face me.

"When I'm bored enough, yeah, sure."

Her eye twitches. "Lovely. Well, to catch you up to speed, Circuit is struggling to contain the protests and strikes in response to the attacks."

Okay, so that does sound familiar. I overheard my bunkmate on the lower bunk last night. He's practically addicted to Network news. "Yeah," I say. "I heard that."

Jess's lips thin. "Excellent. Glad I won't have to spend time trying to explain it to a kindergartener."

Brigid coughs. "Maybe we move to the living room?"

"Here's fine," I say, fists clenching.

"Ms. Corsair," Heath says. "Why don't you explain?"

Brigid glances at Jess, and she gives her an approving nod. "By all means."

Brigid purses her lips and scoots back in her chair to stand.

"Look, there's this thing going on, and it could be really bad if it doesn't happen." Her eyes search mine, and I feel wafts of nervous energy wafting off Heath. "You know how I have this connection to Oriana and how Heath and I have been in the library trying to find answers?" I nod for her to go on. "Well, I might have found a way to make it possible for Heath and Jess to...have a child."

A startled laugh escapes me. "You can't be serious." I turn on Heath. "No way this is for real?"

Jess leaps to her feet. "Is it so hard to imagine that some of us do things for purposes outside our selfish interests?"

"For you? Yes."

"Please, Carter," Brigid says. "You're the final piece to this equation. We can't do this without you. If Rosaline's journals are right, I need to be in a shared mental state as Heath."

"No way." I shake my head. "You're talking about fucking with our bonds? Do you realize how dangerous this is? What if it triggers us brimming or worse?"

"I know, I know," she says, placing her hand on my chest. "I promise, if anything feels off, I'll stop."

Her blue eyes grip mine, bright with conviction. I search her face, looking for any sign of hesitation, but find only unwavering resolve. And just like that, I know I'm done for.

Who am I fucking kidding? This whole time, I've been putting on an act, pretending I could resist her. But the truth is, I'm so far gone. I'd jump off that goddamn bridge outside if she asked me to. "Okay, fine. What do you need me to do?"

"During the...act." She pauses, biting her bottom lip in that ridiculously hot way I'll never get enough of.

"This is all so new," she says. "And the one book I found mentioned that the safest way to maintain control of the bonds is by being in a shared mental state with the rider you're working with."

"So, let me get this straight. Are we talking about an orgy here? Cause, either way, count me in."

No one says anything.

Fuck me, I'm right. I hold my stomach, laughing. "Want me to get Logan? Make it a rounded five?"

"No," Jess says immediately. "We can't let anyone else know about this."

Secret orgy. Got it.

If this juicy morsel of information leaked, there'd be dozens of riders at Brigid's door, begging to do the same for them.

My mind whirs over what they're asking. Our technology isn't as advanced as it was before the ocean's rose, or so they claim, but we have flying shuttles and a connected information system. Of course, we patch together shuttles from recycled metal that run moderately well on methane, and Network is only as reliable as the nearest nearby tower if there is one. Still, there are other ways to have a baby besides doing the devil's tango.

"Not that I'm one to look a gift orgy in the mouth," I add after processing, "but there are other ways to get pregnant. Adoption. IVF."

"We considered all of those," Heath says. "None will work in our case."

"We can clone druadans, for shit's sake. I'm sure we can, you know..." I gesture to Heath's crotch and then to Jess, who immediately grimaces.

"While my science background is limited," Brigid says. "I'm certain cloning druadans and performing in vitro fertilization are two very different things. Lannett has perfected their practice for hundreds of years. Nevertheless, it involves an animal, not a human being."

"Not only that," Heath says, "Since Brigid needs to pull the bond. As complicated as this already is, imagine having to involve a Lannett scientist."

I smirk. "Depends on the scientist."

"It's too risky," Heath continues, ignoring me. "We can't involve anyone else that might leak this to Circuit or the press."

I might be flipping him shit, but he has a point. Say we found a Lannett scientist willing to do this for us. They're contracted with Circuit. And even if we agreed to pay them off and keep it secret, we don't know what contracts they've already signed. I almost certainly guarantee that any new technology or discovery belongs first and foremost to Circuit, and they are required to report it.

"If word got out that there's a way to cure rider infertility," Brigid says. "Potentially allowing the firstborn sons of wealthy families to have children, there's no amount of money that will keep their mouth shut."

"I'll do it," I say.

"This will be done only in absolute discretion and only once," Jess says. "If luck is on our side, I will announce the pregnancy once confirmed, and you will claim the baby as yours. Then we can quietly separate, citing irreconcilable differences, and you can be involved as much or as little as you want in our lives."

"Agreed," Heath says.

"Sounds like that's it then," I say, clapping my hands. "I'd offer my bunk, but with four of us, we're going to need a bigger bed. So, whose room are we using?"

"Mine," Jess says immediately. "We'll meet in mine. Tonight."

I eye her curiously. Heath always claimed she was prudish, but she was certainly an eager beaver now. I shift my gaze to Brigid's. "Works for me. And you?"

She presses her lips together and gives a curt nod. She's eager to pull off the metaphorical band-aid, so to speak, and I realize so, am I? Delaying would only cause the others to get cold feet and back out.

"Tonight," Heath replies.

"Then it's done." Jess stands. "Seven PM. My room. Make sure no one sees you." She gathers her bag and leaves.

Once the door closes, Heath and I both turn to Brigid.

"You sure about this?" Heath asks, his voice low.

"I am."

"So, I have to ask," I say, "if you're doing whatever you do to pull Heath's bond, what stops you from pulling mine?"

"Me trying my best, I guess?" She says, with a nervous laugh. "but it's okay. I'm on birth control."

It's been nearly three years since I've had to worry about this. I've been able to bed any woman I wanted without the risk of a little Carter Junior coming from it. Of course, I still took the anti-STD meds; I can't be too careful with what shit's out there. The last thing I need is to feel the burn every time I piss.

She must interpret my silence as hesitation, so she adds, "I need you to trust me." She squints at the air between us as if seeing something we can't. "All I need to do is stay focused."

"Hate to break to you," I say, scratching the back of my neck. "But if you can focus on anything besides what I'm doing to you, I'm not doing it right."

A deep rumble comes from Heath's chest as he laughs.

She places her on her hips. "I'll have you know I am *very* good at multitasking."

"Is that a challenge?"

"Maybe it is," she says, leaning closer.

Heath's forced cough breaks the tension, pulling me from my thoughts, which had already strayed to all the wicked ways

I'll draw out those sweet sounds from her lips. "Then it's agreed," he says. "We'll finish our daily tasks so as not to arouse suspicion and then reconvene back here tonight."

That's it. How can he be so nonchalant about this, like it's another meeting on his agenda?

As we exit, I can't possibly imagine focusing on anything today, knowing what awaits me tonight, but keeping busy will make the time go faster and tides how I want it to.

Fifty

BRIGID

"Shall we get this party started?" Carter says, rubbing his hands together from where he's seated across from us.

"God, yes, please," Jess says, drawing a shocked look from Carter. "I know, I agree with you. If we're going to see this through, we're going to need ample amounts of alcohol." Jess gestures to the low table between us. "It's not the best vintage, but what I could procure on short notice with Marshal's help. Heath, would you do the honors?"

Heath takes the bottle of champagne from the table and pops the cork, his eyes never leaving the ground. He hasn't looked at me once since we all gathered in his and Jess's room. I would've offered mine if it felt like more neutral territory, but theirs had a bigger bed, which, if things were going to go as we'd planned, we would need the extra room. He hands me a glass of champagne, still not making eye contact with me, and the nerves flip about like anxious moths in my stomach.

Everyone is wearing their regular clothes except Carter, who's in a fluffy white robe and slippers he'd stolen from my closet with the pink bows on the heels. Was it inappropriate attire for the occasion? I don't know.

Who am I to judge anyone's fashion choices before a foursome? Like I'm suddenly an expert just because I've done it once? Holy shit, does that sound as crazy as it feels?

My stomach flutters with nerves. I would hardly call myself an expert. Sure, by definition, it'd been a foursome. However, it'd been Logan, Heath, Carter, and I.

Not with Heath's fiancé, whom I barely knew and had spoken a handful of words to. I tried to be friendly with her, but it was obvious she didn't want to be my friend. And now we were about to do one of the most intimate things a person could do with another person, and while I knew it was for a good cause, a noble cause, it still felt like I was sixteen all over again and losing my virginity in that boathouse.

"I don't think a bottle is going to do it," Carter says and reaches into the bag that he brought. He pulls out a bottle of Delford gold. "Judging by your faces, this is going to require more liquid encouragement."

The three of us sit with our champagne glasses on the couch, keeping an awkward distance from each other. I drink mine, forcing it down quicker than I would've liked. It is very good, but I don't need it; I need it to calm my nerves, which are fraying at the edges. I can't back out; it was my idea.

I'm still not entirely convinced it can be done. But I must try. To help Heath and those thousands of people keep their jobs. Innocent families will suffer if we don't do this.

I must stay strong; I must be the one who sees this through. Without me, it will all fall apart. Once I finished my glass, I took the bottle from the table and refilled it. Jess does the same. I quickly glance at Heath, and there's a slight flush at the top of his sharp cheekbones. It's the first time I've ever seen him affected by alcohol.

Carter moves and sits on the arm of the couch next to me and rests a hand on my shoulder. I nearly jump, but I'm able to contain myself. He lets out a dry laugh. "We are all adults here. We've all decided to be here. To do this. We might as well enjoy it. Why don't we turn on some music or a movie or something to relax?"

"I don't want to relax," Jess says. "I want to get this over with and do what must be done so Venovia doesn't combust."

Carter tips back his glass. "God damn. How'd you know civil war talk always gets me into the mood?"

I clamp my lips together, stifling a laugh.

Heath sets his glass down on the table. "Perhaps Jess and I should go first. Then, after we have made ourselves comfortable...settled in the bedroom, you and Brigid can join us."

"Sounds like a plan." Carter squeezes my shoulder and looks down at me. His hazel-green irises are full of warmth and reassurance. "You sure about this?" he asks.

About what part? The group sex? Is it going to be awkward, sure? But awkward, I can handle. It's the other side that makes me the most nervous. I'd barely scratched the surface on how to sense the bonds and now I'm going to try to manipulate it. I can list about a dozen ways this could go so terribly wrong and another dozen I'm too ignorant even to fathom.

After Oriana had been born, I'd spent every free minute looking on Network for research by Lannett scientists regarding druadan bonds. I'd found a handful of thesis papers and articles dated decades ago with them attempting to infer *how* they're formed, *what* forms them, and how they're broken.

The closest they've ever come to understanding their secrets is it has some alteration with a person's DNA when a druadan bites them.

While still unclear, it's a transference of blood and saliva, but the DNA modification is so subtle they have yet to map which genomes have been changed. Still, others believe there's some aspect of pheromones at play, which makes it even more confusing. And now I've learned that certain people, women specifically, could not only feel the bonds but mold them. A tingle zips up my spine. There isn't a scientist alive today who wouldn't like to get me under a microscope.

"Yes. I'm sure." Even as my stomach twists into the tightest of knots, I wish I hadn't ever asked him to do this, to put him in this position. I'd abused the power that I held over him because I knew he wouldn't refuse me or the call he had to his duty. Even if he didn't support Circuit, he was still loyal to his duty as a rider.

And now he's wrapped up in this mess. I know this in and of itself is awkward, but it'd be so much worse if word about the four of us tied to this strange sex night involving a Lockwood and Drakeford got out. Network news channels would sell their kidneys for this information. Highly regarded and powerful family reputations would be destroyed. And more so if the other riders found out that there was a way to allow a rider to have children.

That I was capable of doing it.

All the ones that are married or want to start a family? Leave behind a legacy before their short lives ended? What if they knew I wielded this power?

As far as the limits of my ability, gift, whatever I should call it, I hadn't the faintest idea. I hadn't really put it to the test yet beyond doing whatever it was I'd done to keep Logan from jumping.

I take another drink of champagne. I'd know soon enough if I was capable of what Rosaline's journal said I was capable of.

I'm not truly bonded with Oriana, but still feel the connection, still feel that residual power. I can only imagine what would happen once she marked me...*if* she marked me and we were fully bonded.

Heath tosses back the rest of his champagne and then uses the same glass to fill it with the whiskey. Jess curls her lip at the improper use of a champagne flute. She delicately finishes drinking hers and rises to her feet. She wipes her hands on her pants and then laces her fingers together in front of her as if a teacher is about to give a lesson at the front of the classroom.

"All right. Let us go then and get this over with."

Heath stands and touches her elbow, guiding the two of them to retreat to the bedroom, leaving Carter and me alone. Carter rests a hand on my thigh and jogs the back of his fingers along the inside of my leg. Little sparks of electricity light up on my skin, and I suck in a deep breath.

"This was your idea, you know," he says.

My lips clamp down into a tight smile.

"Just imagine it's the two of us," he says softly. "Like in the orchard. I promise it won't be as bad as you think it will be. In fact, it might be a little fun."

I flash him a timid smile. "Anything involving sex is fun for you."

"With you? Always." His hand cups my chin. "As long as everyone is having a good time, I'm having a good time."

"This isn't about having a good time. This is about keeping thousands of families from starving to death and losing their jobs."

"Doing our civic duty *and* having fun? I can't see how you're not enjoying this."

I nudge him playfully with my shoulder. "Fine. I'll try my best to enjoy myself. All right?"

"That's all I need to hear."

The minutes crawl by and images wriggle their way to the front of my mind about what they're doing in there. Had they already started? Or were they still talking and not begun? I will down the flare of jealousy I knew would make a surprise appearance. The feelings I had for Heath, the ones I'd tried denying, had finally risen to the surface, and now here I was, preparing to watch him have sex with another woman in front of me.

Fuck. As if sensing my distress, Carter offers me his glass of whiskey, and I gulp down the smoky liquid. The alcohol burns the back of my throat and tongue. I'm treading a very precarious path here. I can't be so drunk that I can't control my powers to pull back the bond, but I need to be drunk enough that I don't get cold feet and run away in nothing but my bra and panties like Cinderella fleeing to her pumpkin carriage.

Carter checks his comm from where he'd put it on the coffee table. "That's long enough. Let's go." His words break the silence, and we make our way to the bedroom.

Inside, the lights are off, and candlelight dances on the walls and ceiling. Scents of lavender and lemon drift from where two candles sit inside glass jars.

My gaze flits across the room, landing on Heath and Jess. Their faces are serene, almost unnaturally passive beneath the flickering candlelight.

I don't dare meet her gaze, instead shifting to meet Heath's. My breath whooshes from my lungs. He's shirtless, a few black curls dotting his sculpted chest, and taut skin stretched over the rock-hard muscle of his arms and shoulders.

But it's the deep brown of eyes, so full of hunger, so full of unfiltered lust that it makes the space between my legs bloom with heat.

Jess adjusts the covers, giving me a glimpse of her naked body under the blankets. The peaks of her sun-kissed cleavage are visible over the edge of the blanket. Where my half-hearted tan was already fading from my short stay at Meridian, hers was glowing. Freckles dotting her shoulders and chest, no doubt from her frequent travels to the sunny Parnian coast.

Darling, this cunt has brought Heath to his knees.

I avert my eyes, determined not to let the memory of her insult sway me.

Holding back his bond is a skill that requires precision and focus. Any slip-up on my part could permanently damage his or Carter's bond with their stallions. I cannot allow myself to be distracted.

"Here we are," Carter says, handing me a silk scarf before giving one to Jess as well. "Put those on, and Heath and I will do the rest."

From the edge of my vision, Jess fastens it over her eyes, ties it quickly behind her head, and then leans against the headboard. Her expression is passive and unbothered as if she is awaiting a pedicure.

I take the black fabric from him, hesitating. "Figured it'd make everyone more comfortable," Carter says. "If you don't want to, you don't have to —"

I shake my head, "No, it's...fine." I should have thought of this myself, to be honest. The anonymity will make things so much easier.

Carter tugs his shirt over his head, revealing the toned physique I'm sure I'll never get enough of, then bends to kick off his boots. As he does so, I get a full drool-worthy display of the flexing of the defined muscles of his torso and back, which sends another jolt of electricity between my legs. Then, without hesitation, he sheds his pants, revealing his toned ass and thighs.

He catches me staring, shocked by the lack of underwear beneath.

"We both knew where this was going, so why bother?"

I laugh, and hysteria fringes its edges as I realize it's my turn.

With Carter standing completely naked beside me and Heath watching me, waiting, I slide the straps of my tank top off quickly, letting it fall to the floor, before slipping my shorts down.

I feel Carter's heated gaze on my cheek, and my eyes lock with Heath's again. The effects of the whiskey overpower my self-consciousness to stare at the wall or something instead of Heath. But it's not like it matters where I look. He'll still see me, and I see *him*. I unfasten my bra, feeling the weight of my freed breasts on my chest. My eyes never leave him; I lower my panties and step out of them.

Both men inhale sharply.

As the last piece of clothing slips from my body, I clutch the blindfold to my chest. The lavender scent swirls around my naked body, grounding me in this moment and reminding me of the power I wield.

My breath comes in slow, steady rhythms, each inhale and exhale a tether to the calm that lies at my core. I am the eye of the storm, the master of forces that could so easily spiral out of control. Heath and Jess lie beneath the covers, and I move to the bed. Carter wastes no time following me.

I take a deep breath, pushing aside any lingering doubts or hesitations. This is the decision we have all chosen, and as long as they are all willing, I will see it through to the end.

Carter sits on the edge of the bed and takes the scarf from

my hands. "Here, let me." I feel the cool fabric press against my face as I close my eyes. The dim light of the room disappears, replaced with a soothing blackness.

Carter's warm fingers caress my chin. "You can trust me," He murmurs. "Just lay back."

I do as he says, feeling exposed as I lay my head on the pillow. The bed shifts, as I assume Heath is making room for Carter on the bed. My elbow accidentally brushes against Jess's, and she quickly scoots away.

The bed shifts again, and my mind blurs with what could be happening.

There's a cool breeze as the covers are lifted off me, followed by the heat of a body above me.

"It's just me," Carter whispers. I feel his arousal pressing against my thigh. The alcohol in my system makes my head spin.

This is really happening.

My heart sinks as I imagine Jess and Heath doing the same. His lips on hers. Hands in her hair.

Carter's hand on my chin brings me back to the present. "You can do this," he says softly. "I'm right here."

His face drifts close to mine, and he kisses my neck. His lips are warm and inviting, and I feel myself relax into the sensation.

Soon, I feel the tip of Carter's erection pressing against my center. His hips move slightly, positioning himself, then sliding easily in, confirming the wetness I knew was there. Sure, this is the most unusual sexual encounter I've ever experienced, but damn if it didn't turn me on.

I stretch deliciously as Carter seats himself inside me, letting out a soft groan in my ear. "Fuck me, Brigid. You don't know how much I want you."

A moan escapes my lips as my head moves up and down on

the pillow, each thrust from Carter pushing me and pulling me, tethering me to the present moment. In the darkness, my body is on fire, aching for release, and the feeling of Carter's skin against mine consumes my mind. His hands are everywhere: my breasts, my hair, my face, driving me to the edge of ecstasy. Above me, I hear him place a hand against the headboard, his fingers digging into the wood.

But it's not just Carter's energy that has me in a frenzy. I feel Heath's heat next to me. Even with the blindfold, I can make out the auras of their bonds. It shimmers and glows, coalescing brightly until everywhere above me is a flickering iridescence. My hands grip Carter's back, feeling the muscles flex as he fucks me.

The intensity of his movements steals my breath, and I moan. The bed moves suddenly. My hands are caressing another set of shoulder muscles. Incessant fingers slide into my slick core, caressing, moving, thrusting.

I drop my right hand to the bed and arch my back. Someone's hand touches mine. Slowly, I let my fingers drift over it, feeling the crescent-shaped scar.

As if sensing what I'm doing, the hand retreats, and a second later, it laces its fingers with mine.

Carter.

Heath.

It doesn't matter.

They're separate, yet the same.

Riders.

Mine.

Like a breach in a dam, I'm unable to stop the tidal wave of his own desire flooding through the connection I've created between us.

I crave more. Touching, licking, kissing.

Strong, purposeful fingers continue to move inside me,

pushing me close, higher. I grit my teeth, focusing on the illuminated pulsing aura. Drawing in a breath, I mentally tug the bond toward me. The light wavers, fading from the brilliant golden yellow to a deep orange.

It's not enough.

A thumb circles my clit, and a person gasps from somewhere in the darkness.

Or was that me?

Teeth nip at my neck, and heat radiates from his presence.

"Ready?" a husky voice says.

Heath.

"Yes," I breathe.

The fingers retreat from inside me, and I'm left feeling empty and craving more. Again, the mattress moves, and I imagine Carter and him switching places.

The aura continues to glow a steady orange, and as Carter lazily rubs his cock on my entrance, I focus again through the blindfold. The aura flickers, and then, like a light switch, it disappears.

"Now," I gasp, and Carter plunges into me again.

Fifty-One

Heath

I've ascended.

Nothing exists outside these bedroom walls. Nothing that compares to this...awareness.

The coolness of the sheets. The warmth from our bodies. The scent of jasmine and roses; Jess and Brigid.

Brigid's urgent *"Now"* fuels me, pushing me towards my climax as Carter's movements become more urgent. Brigid had warned us the mindset must remain locked with hers, and I'd been worried the passion wouldn't match if I were with Jess.

How I'd been wrong.

Already, the pressure builds within me, my body becoming taut and slick with sweat. Jess's lips are hot against mine, her hands firm on my hips.

But it's not just Jess that I feel.

Brigid's hand rests in the space between us. Her fingers glide seductively over my palm, awakening every nerve ending, and I gasp as her pleasure coalesces with mine.

And then there's Carter.

Desire, lust, and heat all surge through the bond. Like a warm glow, it envelops us all. I feel connected to all of them, even Jess.

"I'm close," I groan and grip Brigid's hand.

Jess arches her hips, inviting me to go deeper, and instinct takes over. The walls I'd built to keep Shadowmane's urges from crowding my mind collapse. The wanton need from my stallion roars into me. Our connection illuminates, and the cord bonding us solidifies. I gasp at the intensity of the sensation.

"Fuck," I murmur, but the second the word leaves my mouth, something clamps down on the bond. Frigid cold seeps into it, radiating both directions on the teether. Even though I can't see it, I feel the numbing sensation as it penetrates my chest just above my heart.

My eyes dart to Brigid. Face flushed, eyes hidden behind the black silk, her body rhythmically moves with each of Carter's thrusts. Silver hair splays out around her head on the pillow. As if feeling my gaze on her face, her hand caresses mine, and the numbing feeling grows.

It's gone.

The subtle tug of the bond that's always there, always present, no matter how far I am from Shadowmane, disappears.

A slight crease forms between her brows.

"Now," she repeats. The heat in her voice is like a trigger. I'm too close to stop even if I wanted. With one last thrust, I shatter, my body trembling as waves of pleasure wash over me.

Carter follows closely behind, his moans mingling with Brigid's as he finds his release.

As we both catch our breath, I roll to the side while Brigid lets out a small gasp. The bond between us reignites, and Shadowmane's presence returns like a rubber band snapping back into place. Jess takes off her blindfold and breaks the silence. "Well, that was...something," she says breathlessly. We lay in silence for a few minutes, recovering from the intense experience. Then Brigid carefully removes her blindfold, and we all stare at each other, a million unspoken words passing between us. Nothing could compare to what had just happened.

After a minute, Jess gets up and puts on her robe. She pauses at the door, looking back at me, her face a veiled mask. Her mouth twitches like she's going to say something, but then she opens the door and is gone.

Carter, Brigid, and I remain on the bed, spent and breathless.

Carter's voice breaks the silence. "Come here," he says, voice a murmur. "Let me hold you both."

Fifty-Two

BRIGID

Two nights in a row.

I'll be damned. Look at me making up for my dry spell.

Carter, Heath, and I fell asleep shortly after Jess left. When the first morning light streams through the ruffled curtains, I awake to find both gone.

There's a message on my comm from Carter saying he had a meeting but would meet me for lunch. I, too, have an early meeting, so I begrudgingly get up and dress even as the euphoria and dazed state haunt me.

I'd done it. I'd pulled back a bond and *not* broken it. Already, my mind churns with the different ways this can benefit riders. However, since I'm not eagerly volunteering to have group sex with couples, there must be other ways beyond fertility enhancement.

Say, during painful medical treatments where the rider's pain could upset their stallion and keep the druadan from doing something regrettable, as Galaxian had.

It'd been a fraction of a second, and among people I trusted. I am in no way prepared for longer sessions with strangers.

So, until I can figure out how to practice it safely, I'd hold off doing it again.

I set off to the gym when Logan had messaged me that the gym was free that afternoon.

Most riders had the day off because Lugsen and Marshal were preoccupied with the trial. After changing into leggings, a sports bra, and tennis shoes, I opened the door to the underground gym.

"You're late," Logan shouts as I approach and set down my water bottle by a bench.

"Sorry, had a memo I needed to write up for the security team." A slight crease forms between his brows. Apparently, it's still a sensitive subject that he's lost his old position. "It was nothing," I hastily add. "Just options to work overtime."

"Makes sense," he says, peeling off his punching gloves.

I try to shake off the strange feeling of unease that's settled over me. Maybe it's the stress of everything, Kaeden's death, Oriana, his trial, but it's undeniable. This hint of irritability simmering beneath my skin. I'm unable to ease it no matter how many long baths I take or how many glazed donuts I swipe from the mess hall.

I slip off my shoes and wander to the weapons rack. "No batons," he says, tossing me a pair of gloves. "It's time for you to learn to throw a punch."

He has me start with the punching bag, teaching me where to place my feet, elbows, shoulders, and hips. Three rounds later, I'm clutching my stomach, trying to keep from throwing up from the exertion, and I am rethinking all of my life's decisions.

Once he's thoroughly satisfied my heart rate has reached that of a hummingbird's, he puts on a pair of padded mitts for me to aim at, and we start the lesson all over again.

Logan starts with them centered, then moves them up and down and side to side, trying to increase my speed.

He swipes the top of my head with the punching mitt. "Focus, Blondie."

"I'm trying," I say through gritted teeth.

"Not hard enough!" he yells, his voice echoing off the walls.

We continue until my arms feel like jelly and I can barely lift them.

"Five minutes," he says, gesturing to the bench and my water bottle. I sigh and tromp over, collapsing onto it as I tug off my gloves. I flip open the cap and gulp.

Logan moves closer, standing sideways and gazing over the dark gym. "Believe it or not, I think you're improving."

"Really?" I say, wiping the excess water from my chin.

"Maybe against a pack of middle schoolers," he says. "you might hold your own until a teacher arrives."

"Gee, thanks," I say, rolling my eyes at the short-lived compliment.

I slip on my gloves, tighten the straps with a sharp tug, and step back onto the mat. Logan switches out the punching mitts for a square-padded target. I jab left, quick and precise, then follow with a swift right hook, feeling the satisfying thud as my glove connects. Logan grunts, nodding, urging me to focus and stay light on my feet.

"For fuck's sake, keep your wrist straight!" he grumbles as I throw another punch. "You're going to break your hand, and then how will you entertain yourself at night if Jamesy can't come to you?"

I curl my lip into a smile. "I could always call you."

Logan's expression hardens, the playful glint in his eyes vanishing as if it had never been there. His jaw tightens, and a shadow crosses his face, his features growing cold.

Shit. He'd been the one playing around, and yet, somehow, I'd overstepped.

I couldn't help it. As much as I'm trying to focus, my thoughts keep drifting to last night. The erotic as-hell moments with the blindfolds, the feel of Heath and Carter's breath on my skin, even Jess's moans.

"I wouldn't answer," he finally says.

His words hit like a slap, cold and cutting. What does that mean? It's harsh, even from him. Something in me snaps and I lower my fists, taking a step towards him. "I'm sorry. What the hell is going on with you?"

He glowers at me and raises his mitts. "Get your hands up."

"No," I say, as sweat stings my eyes. "Tell me. I know the trial is coming up, so if you need someone to talk to."

He lowers his mitts, his gaze like daggers. "If you think you're going to get me to talk because you've seen my dick, you're wrong. There's no us, Blondie. There never will be. I'm a rider, remember? There's me and Galaxian, and then the rest of the world. So the sooner you get that in your pretty little head, the better."

I feel anger rising in me, matching his intensity. "I don't care that you're a rider. Isn't that obvious? I want you like I want Heath and Carter."

Logan's eyes flash. "There's an oath we say when we leave Vanguard, a promise we make to ourselves. Do you know what that is?" He pats his chest. "We put our druadans first, always above everything and everyone else. That's what being a rider means. It means there's no room for," — He gestures between us — "This."

"That's bullshit," I spit out. "Carter and I make it work, and Heath will—"

"Will never see you as more than a fun distraction. A way to pass the time and entertain until they flare out. It's how all riders are."

I bite back at the sting of his words. He's wrong. Carter and Heath had both told me they cared about me. Loved me. "You're wrong," I forge on. "You might be a rider, but that doesn't mean you can't care about other people. You can't use your bond as an excuse to shut everyone out. That's not living, Logan, that's existing."

"Maybe. But it's the way it has to be," he says, his voice cold.

It's like we're back on the window ledge all over again. My heart sinks, the familiar ache creeping in and squeezing my throat like a vice.

I thought after that night, after everything, I'd made a difference—made him see things differently. And yet here he was, shutting out the world, ready to give up.

I was wrong. I hadn't made a difference at all.

Pulse clamoring in my eardrums, I suck in a shaky breath.

I can't stand here and watch him self-implode while I'm powerless to stop it. "I've had enough of this," I shout, feeling like we're running in circles. "I've tried. God knows how I've tried to reach out to you as a friend. Well, I'm done. If you want to be alone, then so be it."

I toss the baton on the ground with a thud and spin on my heel to leave.

"We were better off before you," he says to my back, so soft I almost miss it.

My footsteps falter, but I continue stomping to the exit. Without a backward glance, I storm out of the gym, slamming the door behind me as my heart feels like it's been torn clean from my chest.

How could it hurt this much to lose something I never really had in the first place?

∼

ONCE I RETURN TO MY BEDROOM, I STRIP OFF MY SWEATY CLOTHES and retreat to the bathroom.

I sit in the shower until the hot water runs out, and I emerge teeth chattering.

The fight with Logan had left me shaken and my head throbbing. I was used to Logan's asshole ways, so why was I letting him get to me *this* time?

Because this time, it hadn't just been him and me in the tug of war. He'd aimed below the belt. He'd meant to hurt me.

This time, he'd gone too far.

And to make matters worse, I think I'm going to start my period. I retreat to my bathroom to look for feminine hygiene products when there's a knock at the door.

Irritation gnaws at the back of my throat. Maybe it's Logan coming to apologize?

I don't know if I had it in me to forgive him, though. I steel myself to tell him to go to hell, but when I open the door, Heath is waiting for me.

"Hey," I say, swiftly shoving away my sour mood. "What's up?"

"There's something I need to tell you, and it can't wait any longer."

I step backward, letting him in. A smugness settles over

me, and I wish I could take a picture of this to wave in front of Logan's face like a *'I told you so.'*

The smokey sweet of whiskey drifts in with him as he enters and his eyes are storm clouds of emotion when he turns to look at me.

"About last night," he says, his throat bobbing. "I never should've asked you to do that. It was wrong. I know that now."

Okay, maybe I'd jumped the gun a little on the whole 'I told you so.' Dammit, could this night get any worse?

"You didn't ask me. I suggested it," I refute. "Remember? It was my idea, so don't you dare try to take credit." I giggle, trying to lighten his mood, but his face remains somber.

"Be that as it may, it did provide clarity to the dilemma I've been struggling with."

A vice compresses around my heart as I brace myself. This is it. He's decided to go back to Jess. Logan was right. I am — scratch that — *was* just an infatuation.

Heath clears his throat and steps closer, resting his hands on my shoulders.

"Brigid Corsair, it has come to my attention that I'm yours and will only ever be. Jess means nothing to me. You are the air that fills my lungs, the force that slows the passage of time so much that I feel I've discovered a newness to my life."

My heart is beating so frantically I'm afraid it's going to burst from my chest.

"*You* are all that matters to me now. The engagement with Jess and I is over. If she is pregnant, then we know we've done our part, and I will support and raise the child, but that will be the extent of it." At the mention of becoming a father, a deep crease appears between his brows, and he hesitates, composing his thoughts before continuing. "I won't walk away from being a father, but I also refuse to walk away from where my heart leads me."

"Heath, I..." I say, my voice barely above a whisper.

"It's with you, Brigid. My heart lies with you." And then he's kissing me. Unbridled, uninhibited, passionately, so much so I can barely catch my breath, it's like he's waited centuries to do this. His tongue rubs my lower lip, and I part, letting him in. He tastes of whiskey, and goosebumps prickle my arms as his hand strokes my back before pressing me closer to him.

Finally, we break apart, both of us flushed and panting. I peer at him and run a thumb over the permanent crease on his brow, trying to smooth it.

"You will make a wonderful father," I murmur. "And I hope she is pregnant, truly for Venovia's sake and yours."

A flicker of emotion crosses his face. "Even if she is not, I will never ask you to do that again."

I take a deep breath, realizing he misunderstood me. "That's good." A nervous laugh escapes me. "Cause I don't think I can physically pull the bond back again."

Heath's eyebrows shoot up. "Did something happen?"

I twist my mouth. "I don't know, but my connection... it's as if it's not as clear. I can't see your bonds anymore," I explain, feeling a lump form in my throat. I've denied it long enough. The auras I'd seen had faded, and even if I squinted, there was nothing there.

Whatever gift or ability I'd had was gone.

Heath leans in closer, his voice soft. "Have you spoken to anyone about this?"

I shake my head.

He takes my wrist in his hand and I don't pull away, instead looking up at him. "I'm sorry I didn't tell you before, but I wasn't sure."

His throat moves as he swallows.

"What is it?" I ask, even though the tone of his voice tells me I'll not like the answer.

"I saw Oriana this morning. She's sick." He pauses. "Dr. Gideon thinks she's dying."

I blink, not fully registering what he said. "Sick? No, that can't be right. Gideon's last report said she was eating and growing like normal. They could barely keep her in the stall because she was phasing so often." The disbelief twists in my voice, and my mind grasps for any other explanation.

"Not anymore," Heath says slowly. "She's refusing to eat, and they've started tube feeding her."

The floor tilts beneath me. Heat rises in my chest as my breath quickens, the air suddenly too thin. "I need to see her. Now." I'm not allowed in the barns, but I can't trust this secondhand. Not with Oriana. Not with her life.

"You know the rules."

"Screw the rules," I snap. "Either you take me down there, or I'll go myself."

Indecision flickers in his eyes, but he knows I'm not bluffing. "Fine," he says, and we hurry to the barn. It's late enough; we're able to slip in undetected, and as we approach Oriana's stall, Dr. Gideon is waiting for us.

She's hardly a week old, and already we've fucked it up.

His face is sallow, and his coat is askew where he missed a button.

"She was eating before, but now she's refusing to eat altogether. Her temperature has dropped, and she's lethargic."

I peer into the stall, my heart breaking at the sight. Oriana lays in the corner, her long legs wrapped around her and her head on the ground. Her once shiny gold coat is now dull and her eyes appear partly closed. The bowl of raw venison and water are untouched.

"How long?" Heath asks, his voice tight.

"I'm not sure," Dr. Gideon says.

My fists clench the bars, turning my knuckles white. "That's not good enough. Tell me, how long does she have? How long can she go on like this, not eating, not drinking?"

Dr. Gideon sighs. "I'm not sure. There's so little we know about the female foals, but if she were a druadan in this state, I'd give her a week or two, maybe."

Oriana shifts slightly, her eyes barely opening.

"We'll do our best," Gideon says. "Other vets have suggested we treat her for a viral infection, and we're running fecal samples regarding parasites."

"Meridian had a parasite infection ten years ago," Heath says. "Pilchuck quarantined everyone and sanitized the protein pellets with UV light. Perhaps this is similar?"

"Perhaps, but it's presented differently. The druadans never went off their feed," Dr. Gideon replies grimly. "I will ask for additional testing for parasites just to be safe. And as far as viral, I did contact the other stations to ask. I'm not seeing any markers. No elevated white blood cell count or anything else that leads me to believe that it's a contagion, so the stallions should be safe."

"So, what is it?" I ask.

"I'm not sure," Dr. Gideon admits. "I've seen nothing like this before. It's as if she's failing to thrive like an infant."

"So, we're gonna just watch her die?" My voice rises an octave higher.

"No, absolutely not," Dr. Gideon responds firmly. "I will do everything in my power to help her."

Heath turns to me, chestnut eyes clouded with resolve. "Starting tomorrow, we can pour through the annals in the archives. There must be something that talks about this."

I nod, plastering a reassuring smile on my face.

It's an empty promise.

He knows as well as I do we were fortunate to find scraps of anything pertaining to druaneras in those journals.

We'd run the well dry.

There are no answers here. If I want to save Oriana, I need to find them elsewhere.

Fifty-Three

MARSHAL

"If *you* can't find them," Jess says over her comm while standing on the gondola platform, "then pass me to someone who can."

Some poor store worker desperately apologizes. "I don't want to hear it. I expect my package expedited and delivered to me tomorrow." She doesn't wait for them to finish and ends the call.

"Pleasant surprise seeing you here," I say, holding my hands behind my back.

"I suppose so." She tucks a loose strand behind her ear and straightens her shoulders.

I eye the shopping bags hanging from her arms. "Successful day?"

She looks down the line of cable, searching for the gondola. "Yes, as a matter of fact, it was." She sighs. "Except for the woefully pathetic selection of sandals here."

I motion to the gray sky, threatening to break. "Not a lot of demand, I guess."

Finally, she shoots me a sideways look. "I'm surprised to see you here. I thought you'd be busy with the rogue stallion hearing."

"I made my statements, but I will be there when they decide later today."

She eyes the small plastic sack in my hands. "Bones for Finn. The local venison butcher saves them for me."

She sniffs. "He prefers those over the pig ears."

I blink, surprised. Her attention to Finn pleases me more than I thought it would. "He does," I say.

The machinery's thumping grows louder, and the gondola cabin appears. Jess strides forward, then struggles to force her way in with the bags.

"Let me help you," I say and take some from her arm.

Once we're inside, Jess heaves her bags on the empty bench, but neither of us sits even though we're the only passengers. I grab the strap hanging from the ceiling, and the doors hiss close. The gondola lurches forward, shuffling along the cable and staying low until clear of the platform before ascending a good twenty feet up, soaring over the roofs of the village.

Rain splatters the windows, and flashes of lightning highlight the horizon to the North, where a storm has formed over the sea. Seconds after, the rumbling of thunder reaches us.

Soon, the buildings disperse, and we glide above the old road that used to cross the bridge. Jess hugs her coat a little tighter around her and sniffs, staring out the dark window and watching the storm. I can't tear my eyes away from her flawless olive skin and long black hair—the contrast is breathtaking.

Heath is my friend, but he's a fool not to see her for what she is.

I try not to stare too openly, but it's impossible. Her intelligent gaze has always felt like it could slice right through me if she wanted it to.

And hell, part of me wishes she would.

Maybe then I would finally have closure instead of this endless cycle of uncertainty.

I want to be the one to tear down those walls she's so carefully constructed. I want to see what's underneath.

As we approach the mid-way point, the lights flicker and then go out completely as the gondola shudders to a jarring halt. In the seconds of total blackness, my heart hammers in my chest—not just from the sudden stoppage but from being trapped here alone with Jess.

Jess lets out a slightly manic laugh, her face made more unsettling by the eerie red glow cast by the emergency lights. "Well, why not? Isn't this my goddamn luck?"

"Maybe it's the universe telling you something," I say, aiming for a nonchalant tone despite the storm of emotions inside me rivaling that of the storm outside.

One of her finely arched eyebrows arcs upward. "Oh? And what might that be? That I'm doomed to be trapped forever?"

Taking a risk, I close the distance between us until I'm near enough to make out the glacial blue swirls in her irises. "That you shouldn't leave," I murmur.

The overhead lights continue flickering, casting dramatic shadows that accentuate the sculpted lines of her face. I imagine pulling her against me, pressing her back to one of the floor-to-ceiling windows that make up the entire cable car. Getting so close that I'd feel the warmth of her breath, smell the faint sweetness of her shampoo. Finally, allowing the dam holding back my feelings to break.

A boom of thunder shakes the car, and I glance around, abruptly aware of our surroundings again.

The night sky visible through the curved wall of windows is a churning storm of black clouds lit from within by the explosive flashes of lightning.

Far below, I can make out the arched silhouette of the stone bridge spanning the North Bay River that we're currently suspended above.

Another rumble of thunder, this one much closer, and Jess jumps ever so slightly. I don't miss the flicker of trepidation that crosses her features before the impassive mask slams back into place.

I sit on the bench. "Might as well get comfortable. Could be a while before they get this thing working again."

Jess gives me a guarded look and then claims the bench next to me, gazing out at the storm.

Women throw themselves at me. It's never been a challenge, but she's different. Maybe I'm a masochist, but there's something about the way she resists that makes me want to break through. The challenge she poses—no, the *allure* she holds—it's intoxicating as hell.

She flinches at the crack of thunder, instinctively pressing against me before realizing what she's done. Her eyes widen in surprise, and she pulls away, but only for a second. After a brief pause, she leans back in, resting her head on my shoulder. It feels surprisingly good, natural even.

A gust of wind shakes the cable car, and without thinking, I reach for her hand. It's cold. She stiffens at the touch but doesn't pull away.

"The cable and car was built to handle this. Storms come through here all the time," I say as her hand trembles in mine. "You know, once I was so hungover, I completely missed my call time for a performance."

Her grip on my hand eases. I keep going. "Lugsen looked like he was ready to blow a fuse when he saw me galloping past him, but Nightshade and I wove in with the group on the third lap. No one in the audience had a clue." Thunder rattles the windows, and her grip tightens. "But there was no point in stressing. I figured it was too late to fix anything anyway, so I didn't. I showed up, shrugged it off, and somehow, it all worked out. Ended up being one of my best performances."

Her lips twitch slightly, almost like a smile. I lower my voice like it's a secret. "The best part? My boots were on backward the entire show. Didn't even realize until after. But hey, no one ever noticed."

"You've got it all figured out, don't you?" she says, her hand still in mine. "Must be nice to be so sure all the time."

"Can't complain," I say. "Living every day like your last has its benefits." It's true, although surviving past my expiration date has made some of the shine wear off.

"You know, it's funny," she begins, her voice taking on a harder edge. "Ever since I was a little girl, I've been told what I want, what my purpose in life should be." She gestures vaguely with one hand. "I'm the first-born in my family. If I wasn't a woman, I should have been a rider—at least, then I would know what my future holds. Not this *uncertainty*." She scoffs. "I'm a Drakeford. The property management is just a placeholder until I marry and produce an heir, which will be when —" She snaps her mouth shut.

My mind leaps ahead with where she'd been going. "When what?"

"Forget it. I shouldn't have said anything." She picks her head up and stands, letting my hand slip from hers.

I follow, stepping in front of her. "No, Jess. You don't get to do that. You don't get to shut me out. Tell me."

She braces her shoulders, but her eyes stay locked on mine,

searching to see if I'm really backing my claim to keep her from shutting me out. "Heath and I, we discovered a way to have a child."

In the realm of all the things I imagined her telling me—she's moving off-continent, she's with another man, or worse, that she's terminally ill—this beats them all. A sharp ache I can't ignore pierces my chest. It's not possible. "But I thought Lockwood and you were finished?"

"We are," she says sharply. "This was just about having a baby. Strictly transactional."

Transactional. The word grates in my mind. They were supposed to be done—she'd told me Heath was over when I found her stress-eating in the cafeteria. And now what? They hook up one more time to make a baby? The emotional whiplash is giving me a headache. Still, I can't deny the idea that a rider can become fertile is intriguing as hell.

"How is this possible?" I ask finally.

"I'm sorry." She shakes her head. "I can't tell you."

I want to press her for details about this revelation of the century. And that bar was already set pretty fucking high, considering I recently learned women could bond with druadans. But the pain in her eyes stills my tongue. I'll get my answers from Heath.

"Can I ask why you needed to do this?" Even as the question leaves me, I regret asking it. It feels too personal. I've barely known her for a week. It's unfair of me to ask, but it's too late now.

She sniffs her voice tight. "Something with our family's merger has come up, and if we have a child, we can keep Venovia from tearing itself apart and a lot of people from losing their jobs."

Her words hang in the air, cold as the cable car's interior. "I still don't understand how a baby will help with that?"

"The Bloodland Act," she says flatly. "Any amount of land over a certain amount requires a blood relative to own it, and since both our families have acquired hundreds of thousands of acres, the merger and combining of the land won't be seen as official by the shareholders unless we have an heir."

Fucking Bloodland Act.

Some of Circuit's most archaic bullshit. I bite back the rush of words I want to say. "That's all noble and shit," I mutter, forcing a calm I don't feel. "But it doesn't change the fact you're going to be tied to someone you don't want to be. For the rest of your life."

"I know," she says, defeat creeping into her words.

The flare of jealousy burns hot, even as I try to smother it, but it's no use. The thought of her carrying his child gnaws at me, unraveling everything. A door slams shut in my mind—us, whatever chance we had, closing firmly, leaving me on the wrong side of it.

"Do you." I start, then pause, swallowing hard before finishing my question. "Do you want to be a mother?"

"I don't know," she murmurs. "But the deed is done. We'll know in a few days."

The thought of their baby—*his* baby—saving the future of Venovia, securing alliances, jobs, and stability. It's all too damn much to process.

I study her in the dim light, the gravity of the situation bearing down on us. It's hard to see beyond the immediate shock, the confusion twisting between us, but I have to, for her.

Searching for the right words, I draw in a slow breath. "So, say you *are* pregnant," I begin carefully. "That doesn't mean your life is over. It doesn't mean you're trapped forever."

Her gaze snaps up to meet mine — a flicker of defensiveness mixed with uncertainty—crossing her face.

"Look, I get this is huge. But it's not everything. Not the end of you. After this—after the merger, after the baby, if that's what happens—you still get to decide what comes next. What you do. Who you become. You don't have to let them dictate your entire life."

She considers my words, pressing her lips into a thin line.

"So, tell me," I ask, my voice low, almost breaking. "What do you want?"

She stares at the fists in her lap. "Freedom," she finally breathes. "I want the freedom to live my life however I want. Try new things. Travel whenever and wherever I want. " She pauses, her icy-blue eyes finding mine. "Be with whomever I want."

"Then why do this?" I ask as the intensity of her gaze spikes my pulse. "Why do something if you don't want to?"

"Because." She bites her lip, and a single glistening tear descends her cheek. "Because if I don't, I know every day I will live to regret it. Because if I don't see this through, I'll never have the courage to do it again. Heath and I—" her voice cracks. "I've given him years of my life. My love and loyalty, and it was all for nothing. Time I'll never get back, so at least this means it'll have been worth it. It won't have been for nothing."

Her words hit harder than I expected. *Shit, I get it.* Everything she's done, everything she's given, feels like it's amounted to nothing. It's the same way I've felt about riding—years of pushing myself, giving everything, only to feel stuck. Coasting without direction, wondering if any of it even matters. The same empty ache, the same fear of wasted time, wasted purpose.

Was I taking full advantage of the extra life I'd been given, or was I squandering it? I've lived longer than I was supposed to, longer than anyone expected. That question's been in the back of my mind for years. Was I making it count, or just drifting, letting the days blur together? Late at night, when everything goes quiet, it keeps me awake. I stare at the ceiling, asking myself *why*. Why had I been given this extra time? Was there a reason, a purpose I still hadn't found? Or had I already missed it?

I offer a soft smile. "Well, if seeing you with Finn is any indication, you'll be an incredible mother."

She stares up at me, and I'm acutely aware of how stunning she really is. "Do you really think so?"

"I know so." I pause, looking straight at her. "You've never backed down from a challenge, Jess. I've seen it. Hell, I've been on the other side of it. You don't let anyone, or anything, decide your fate for you. This isn't any different."

A faint blush tinges her cheeks at my words, and she ducks her head almost shyly. "You have far too much faith in me, Marshal."

"Not at all." I rub a thumb over her cheek, wiping away the tears. "I'm simply seeing you for who you truly are."

She places her hand on mine, and I let her fingers intertwine.

My mouth hovers inches from hers as I press her back into the window. Even through my jacket, I can feel her chest rising and falling. She tilts her chin. An offering. And I lean even closer.

Our lips barely brush each other's before the lights flicker on and the gondola begins moving forward.

She pulls away, letting my hands fall. "I...I can't. I'm sorry." She turns away from me.

The moment is gone.

The remaining ten minutes pass with us in silence, and I'm desperate to know what she's thinking. Why had she pulled away? What harm was a kiss? Was she mad I waited so long, or was it a hesitation to be this way with another rider?

When the doors open at the landing in Blackhawk, she grabs her bags in one swift motion and walks away, not looking back.

Unsure if she can even hear me, I say softly, "When you're ready, I'll be here."

Fifty-Four

BRIGID

My comm buzzes with a message from Heath.

> Dr. Gideon is doing two-hour checks on Oriana. She's resting but comfortable. I'll notify you if anything changes.

I scowl at the screen on my wrist. Resting is all she's been doing for days. She shouldn't be sleeping; she should be a ball of energy like before, bouncing off the walls and doing her little baby phases for Dr. Gideon when he tries to examine her.

They'd done everything they could for her, and now we're just going to watch her die.

I refuse to let that happen, not when another option exists.

I tap on my comm, entering the number I'd been given during my interrogation.

"Agent Zane," a man's voice sounds from my comm.

"It's me. Brigid Corsair. I'm ready to talk now."

Agent Zane chuckles. "You're about the last person I expected to call. What changed your mind?"

"It doesn't matter," I say dismissively. "I'll tell you anything you want to know about my sister in exchange for a favor."

There's a weighted pause, and I brace myself for him arguing, but instead, he says, "Fine. What is it?"

I lick my lips, blood rushing in my ears. "I know you caught one of the rebels and are holding them at Delford police station. I want to talk to them."

Another pause. I'd chosen this to be a voice-only call, preemptively fearing I'd get cold feet if I saw the snide grin on his face, but now I'm regretting the decision. I'm gambling everything on this, and if he could see my face, maybe he would recognize and take pity on me.

"A police shuttle will be there in two hours. Be on it."

As the police shuttle hums through the city skyline, I gaze out the window, fixated on the towering brick buildings that pierce the low-hanging clouds. My mind, however, is a swirling vortex of thoughts and emotions. I knew what I was doing was risky. Leaving the station right now alone was risky, and I'm sure I would get an earful from Logan and the others when I got back. We'd tried their methods and had failed. Now, it was time to try mine.

But the risk was worth the payoff. The answers to helping Oriana awaited me in the interrogation room.

Oriana's deteriorating condition had become a constant weight on my chest, a helplessness that was threatening to consume me.

The shuttle descends into the walled-in landing pad outside the police station. As I emerge from the shuttle, I spot Agent Zane standing at the edge of the pad, jacket billowing in the blisteringly chilly wind. I wrap my sweater tighter around me as Agent Zane leads me through the winding corridors of the Delford Circuit jail.

"You're lucky you called me when you did," Zane announces, his voice echoing against the concrete walls. "The rebel we caught is currently being detained, but since they confessed, the judge rushed their trial, and he's already been going to Tox Zone Alpha."

Shit. A death sentence. Images of the attack at Meridian flutter before me, and I swallow the pity for this man. I'd seen the faces of everyone in Sharice's group. None showed an ounce of remorse, so why should I?

"You've got ten minutes," Zane says, sneering.

My skin crawls, and I involuntarily shudder.

God, I hope this is worth it.

As I enter the interrogation room, my eyes lock on the man's cuffed to the bracket on the table.

Recognition sends a jolt through my body and my pulse quickens. Marcus. He's shaved his head and grown out a beard, and there's a zig-zagging pink scar on his left cheek, but it's him. I know him, or at least I think I do. If anyone can lead me to Sharice and the answers I so desperately seek, it's him.

He must recognize me, too, because the defiant gaze melts away as he looks up at me. His bottom lip is busted, and blood coats his lips.

The brief, unsettling look in his eyes disappears, and a

smirk plays on his lips as if he knows something I don't. "Lil sis, Bridgie. What good fortune this is meeting you here."

"Where is Sharice?" I demand, my voice steady despite seeing someone I knew and trusted in handcuffs. I'd been so preoccupied with getting the answers to my questions that I hadn't stopped once to consider I might have to ask someone I know. The conviction I've been clinging to seeps out of me. It'd been so much easier to prepare myself for this when I'd assumed it would be a stranger I'd be facing.

"So, what, you wanted to come tell an old friend goodbye?"

"You were never my friend," I say.

He bows his head. "True. However, I still know you. And you wouldn't come here unless you needed something," Marcus tilts his head. "Oh shit. Something *is* wrong."

His lasering in on the truth cuts deep, striking at the very core of my vulnerability. He's right. I wouldn't be here if I had any other options. "Tell me where she is," I press, placing my hands flat on the table. "I need to find her."

"Oh my. Look at you. So.... *desperate.*"

I don't respond.

"Answer me. Why are you doing this?" I snap. "Why are you releasing those horrible creatures into the world? What possible benefit do you guys get if the world is in shambles and we're fighting them again?"

"Boring."

I narrow my eyes and place a hand on my hip, refusing to engage.

"Come on, Bridgie," he says, using the pet name mom used to call me, and Sharice obviously told him. "Tell me really why you're here?"

"I already told you I need to find Sharice," I say through clenched teeth.

He pouts. "Ah, playing hard to get, huh?" He glares at me.

"Fine. You know, everyone thought I cheated because I won the charades at parties, but there's no cheating. I have a knack for reading between the lines." He pauses again. "You should have played with us more often. We learned our lesson when you were on your sister's team. That was the one time I lost." He leans back as far as the cuffs will let him. "If I were to guess, I'd say something has happened." His eyes appraise me, and I bristle, using all my strength to keep my face a mask. When I don't respond, he laughs dryly, then winces and coughs. Blood splatters his grass-stained shirt. "You're just like her, you know. Sharp, calculating, and stubborn as hell. If Sharice knew we were having this conversation right now." He whistles. "Man, she would be —"

"Where. Is. She?" I enunciate each word, irritated at his deflection.

He clicks his tongue. "Come on. Don't make me take back what I just said. You're smarter than this. Ask me the *right* question."

My stomach tenses feeling as though I've been called out in class to answer a teacher's question. But he was wrong. I wanted to know the answers to those questions. Desperately. The ITM was so hellbent on the destruction of the world; there had to be a reason. Something that I and the collective of Circuit weren't seeing. Or perhaps it's not that complicated.

Perhaps they were all just plain crazy.

So, if that were the case, how could we even fathom to reason with them?

We couldn't.

Which meant the only chance we had to stop their assaults before they morphed into something more catastrophic was to go straight to the source. The leader.

I draw in a shaky breath. "Is Sharice your leader?"

He makes a buzzing noise like when you get a wrong

answer in that Network trivia game that's programmed in all our comms. "Try again."

My fists curl so tightly my nails dig into my palms as I grow increasingly annoyed every second I am here.

"Why is ITM doing this?"

"*Wrong*," he belts. "Try again."

Frustration surges through me. "This is a waste of time." I spin on my heel to leave.

"Come on now, don't tell me you're giving up that easily. This is just starting to get fun."

Ignoring him, I move to the door.

"Sharice would've guessed it by now."

My hand pauses on the handle, my distorted reflection staring back at me from the polished steel door.

I won't do it. I will not let him get under my skin. What did his words mean to me? That's all they were. Just words. I get to walk out of here while he's a dead man walking. In three days, he'll be dumped in the tox zone, and within days, he'll be dead.

Fuck, I curse under my breath as the realization settles over me. And as much as the image of him choking to death on his own blood satisfies me, the answers to how to save Oriana will die with him.

Slowly, I pivot to face him.

A sadistic smile spreads on his face. "Oh, goodie. You've come to your senses. I was hoping you would. It's not like I'm going anywhere." He rattles the chains connected to his cuffs. "And was rather enjoying our little talk."

"Screw you," I spit. "No more of your sick games. Tell me what I need to know."

The smile falls from Marcus' face. "Very well, no more games. You ask, and I'll answer."

My thoughts buzz with anticipation. Finally, we're getting somewhere.

"The other egg? Why does Sharice want it?"

He shakes his head. "Above my paygrade, sorry. Your sister likes to keep her plans to herself, you know that."

I take a step closer, feeling like I'm on the verge of asking what he'd wanted me to ask all along. I retrace our conversation back to when he'd concluded that our egg had hatched. That had been it, the key I'd been missing. He'd inferred that the egg had hatched, which could only mean...

"The other egg, the one Sharice took. Did it hatch?"

"Ding ding," Marcus says triumphantly. "That's the one." The chain jangles around his wrists as he attempts to raise his hands in celebration but can only manage to lift them a few inches off the table. "You aren't as dumb as I thought. Well done."

"Tell me," I growl.

He stares down at his hands, picking at the dried blood under his fingernails.

He's testing my patience, but I refuse to back down. Not when I'm this close. I chew the inside of my cheek and fold my arms, waiting.

When a minute passes, he peers up at me. "As a matter of fact, it did."

I like my lips, eager, and slingshot him the next question. "And is it still alive?"

"Last I heard before these assholes snatched me was, yes, it was alive."

My heart races, a frantic rhythm in my chest. "Is it a male or female? How has it survived this long? What is she doing with it?"

"Sorry," he says. "No one gets to see it, even me. So much for best friend perks."

I slam my lips together, feeling the icy trickle of frustration creeping back up my neck. There aren't many more questions I can ask without revealing more than I already have. But what does it matter? He's being kept in a private holding cell and soon will be transported to a tox zone. If I'm being completely truthful, I'm desperate for this ordeal to be over. Every moment spent here is a moment wasted when I could be back at Blackhawk with Heath, poring over the archives. I take a deep breath to steady my racing nerves.

"Ours is a female," I say, using every ounce of willpower to keep my voice from shaking. "And it's sick. Nothing we've done is helping her. I need you to tell me why?"

His face remains neutral, but he ceases the picking at his nails. "Interesting. A female." He sighs and resumes prying the dried blood out from under his ring finger. "Afraid I can't tell you," he says flatly. "So sorry. Seems a shame. If only you could ask someone who also has a newly hatched druadan..." He trails off, letting me fill in the blank.

Sharice.

I brace my shoulders. "Where is she?"

"She's your sister. You know better than anyone how to find her."

He's right. I do.

Fifty-Five

CARTER

"Brigid is going to lose her mind over this," I say, grabbing the extra chair Sadie had brought to the room. I rotate it around so it fits evenly with the other three by the table. I'm far from Brigid's or Carla's event-planning skills, but I'd seen enough fancy dinners and fundraisers to know how to balance a room.

Heath nods absently while staring at his wrist comm. "The kitchen said they were able to find some scallops on short notice."

"Fuck yeah, and how about the oysters? We're going to need them."

Heath swipes his screen closed. "This is just a celebratory dinner for Logan."

"I know," I say, ignoring the exasperated look on his face. "But why can't it end up being more?" Ever since the day in the orchard, my fucking hormones were in overdrive. My dreams were so lifelike that I'd awaken with a dick hard enough to punch a hole in a wall.

He slides me a sideways look, and a hint of a smile tugs at the corners of his mouth. "We'll see."

I clap my hands together. "That's what I'm talking about!"

"Once Logan is acquitted and we have properly celebrated."

I perform a mock bow. "Of course."

Heath sighs and turns away from me. He sets out the napkins and flatware next to the plates on the table. Since Jess had found a place in the Village and Heath was continuing to sleep in the barracks, it'd left this one temporarily vacant. It'd been partly my idea to surprise Logan, but it'd been Heath who insisted we include Brigid.

My man has had but a taste of that glorious nectar and wanted more.

I totally get it.

And with Jess out of his life, at least in that way, he is finally free to take a bite.

The case of wine and champagne sits on the entryway table, and Heath saunters to it. He pulls out a bottle of champagne and reads the label. He tsks under his breath, then swipes his comm.

He catches me staring. "It's too dry. Brigid prefers sweeter ones."

I nod. "You know she never had champagne until Meridian?"

"Not surprising. It's as rare as it is expensive. The grapes in the west struggle in the humidity." He places the bottle back. "I'll have Sadie exchange this out for a Newberrit or Hùza."

This is what it's all about. The good life. The early mornings, the long hours in the gym, and longer in the arena drilling, practicing, and honing our choreography, all of it is worth it in exchange for the sizeable weekly credit deposits, unlimited food and beverage requests, and all my fans.

All the shit we'd been through in the past few weeks, Brigid's missing sister, the station attack, and Logan's trial, it was so fucking close to being over.

Soon, the four of us would be free to savor it finally.

"I saw Brigadier General James on the shuttle intake list. She'll be arriving tomorrow afternoon."

I scratch the side of my face and slump onto the couch. "She's wanting to finalize my picks."

"And?"

"And *I* haven't finalized them yet."

"Carter, you're running out of time." He pauses, pursing his lips. "Who do you have so far?"

I rattle off the names in my head. "Logan, me, you, Shane, Liam and Luke, Ve'loth, Marshal—"

He shakes his head, silencing me. "Marshal can't. He's too valuable."

"What does that matter?" I say. "They've done every test imaginable and still don't know why he's still breathing. So, what does it matter if he's on the team? If anything, he's got more experience than us and would make us better."

His lips turn down in their usual scowl. "We'll clear it with Fiaro. Who else?"

"That's it. I'm stuck between Taylor and Roberts."

"Neither, choose Garret."

I choke on a laugh. "Fuck that. No way am I going to pick him."

"He's the president's son. Having him will be an ace in your hole later."

"I'll add him to the maybe pile," I grumble, knowing that Heath is, once again, right.

"What happens once you submit your list?" Heath asks.

"She'll sign it, and we'll keep training here for the time being," I say, setting down a fork. "But she wants to send us to the Circuit training facility outside Delford for," — I pause, making air quotes — 'supplemental specialization.'"

Heath's eyebrows raise. "Clearwater Base? That's serious, Carter. What kind of specialization are we looking at?"

I take a deep breath, recalling my mother's words. "Fuck. I don't know. Riot control, guarding, patrolling... none of it seemed off the table. She wants us prepared for anything."

Fifty-Six

LOGAN

This room feels like a goddamn cage. The walls seem to close in as I scan the room, my eyes locking onto the sniveling fools seated in the other chairs—Dr. Langley and Dr. Chelsea, the so-called witnesses to the incident. My gaze drifts to the woman crying behind them, and I assume she's the widow of the idiot scientist who got himself killed.

Four station managers sit next to Marshal, their faces expressionless. It's a closed affair. The public shut out from watching me get railroaded. Carter and Heath sit behind them among a handful of other riders who've come to support me. Like me, they're wearing their formal riding jackets. Heath catches my eye and gives me a subtle nod.

Like that means a damn thing.

Anger burns through me at the thought of losing Galaxian, and it makes me want to punch a hole in this table.

"All rise," a man with a gray mustache and a brown suit says. "For the honorable Judge Cynthia Apatow."

Everyone stands in the meeting room. Tables were arranged around the perimeter, and a podium sat on the far wall.

"I have reviewed the testimony and the evidence provided by the Lannett scientist witnesses," she drones, her voice echoing through the room.

"The charges are as follows. A druadan stallion, Galaxian-028, and his bonded rider, Master Rider Logan McCelroy, are charged with the murder of Frederick Ellingston, a biology graduate student currently performing his internship at Lannett."

"Mr. Ellingston's family has pressed charges against Meridian and the station oversight committee. Previous incidences of a druadan harming or killing a human are rare, and the most recent records involve unbonded stallions or stallions who have recently lost a rider and are hyperreactive."

She laces her fingers together on the table. "Of all these documented cases, the druadan is euthanized. However, as this is an unusual case where a druadan was trying to protect another rider and druadan, this will require special consideration."

She swings her gaze to me and lowers her glasses on her nose. "Master Rider McCelroy, I have heard testimony from the other scientists present and other riders, including Master Rider Carter James."

I resist the urge to look at Carter seated off to my right. "And using only this as evidence, the verdict is clear. However, in light of recent events involving you and a novice rider, Garret Peterson, I cannot ignore the suggestion made by experiential witnesses that this is beyond a textbook rogue druadan case."

Fucking Peterson. I knew that'd come back to bite me in the ass.

"Therefore, I would request you supply me with the answer to one very simple question." She rests her hands on the podium, leaning forward slightly. "Do you believe that your stallion acted of their own accord, or do you claim responsibility for his actions?"

Not one of the twenty people coughs, shifts, or moves in their seats, and even the automatic fan from the wall heater switches off as if awaiting my answer.

I knew it would come to this. Whether it's my fault or Galaxian's, we're in trouble. If I take the blame, I'll be punished, but at least they'll drop the rogue allegations against Galaxian. But if I say Galaxian did it on his own, he'll be killed.

It's not even a choice.

Judge Apatow clears her throat. "Master McCelroy. Please answer. Did you command Galaxian to harm that scientist? Yes, or no?"

"Yes. It was me," I lie. "I commanded Galaxian to attack the Lannett scientist."

"This is a very serious statement, Master Rider. You are certain this is the truth?"

"It is."

She frowns, the wrinkles on her forehead deepening. "Then it is without further evidence decided that rider McCelroy be stripped of his rider status. His stallion will remain in protective custody, unavailable for him to access, until McCelroy's term expires and another suitable rider is found to take his place."

A deafening silence falls over the room. Those words hit me like a sledgehammer to the gut. That's it.

But as shitty as that is, it's the best outcome because

Galaxian will live.

"This hearing is adjourned. Everyone is dismissed. Manager Fiaro, I would like to speak with you please privately."

Chairs squeak as everyone shuffles out of the room.

Heath and Carter rush over, flanking me before I can leave.

"What the actual fuck, Logan," Carter says. "Why did you say that?"

I brush him off. "You know why."

"I won't let this slide." Heath moves closer. "I'll speak to Fiaro. I'll fix this."

"It's fine," I snap. "I made my choice." I search the faces of people making their way to the door. "Where's Blondie?" I ask. "She said she was going to be here."

"Haven't seen her," Carter says, searching the crowd too. "Maybe she's with Marshal?"

All three of us look in Marshal's direction and see him standing. Two station managers crowd near him and talk in hushed tones with him.

After a minute, they excuse themselves and break apart. Marshal takes off his jacket and, upon seeing us, approaches. "That could've gone better. You all right?"

I ignore him. "Is Brigid with you?"

"Yeah, she was here earlier," he says. "But told me she had to step out to answer a call from a Delford News channel."

I storm out of the trial room, and I search the hallway for any sign of her.

"Logan, wait up!" Carter calls out.

I whirl around. "Where the hell is she?"

Carter holds up his hands placatingly. "Hey, man, take it easy. Brigid's here, somewhere. You're overreacting."

"Am I?" I growl, raking a hand over my buzzed-cut hair. "She said she'd be at the trial."

Heath frowns. "Let's check her room first before we jump to conclusions."

With a grunt of begrudging agreement, I stalk off towards the residential wing, my friends following close behind. Carter tries to lighten the mood with a joke, but I'm in no state to find any humor in his words.

We reach Brigid's door, and I glare at the lock.

Carter gives me a knowing look and keys in the number. Without waiting for either of them, I burst open the door. My eyes frantically scan the empty space, taking in the rumpled bedsheets and a few scattered personal items.

"See? Everything looks normal," Carter points out, but then his brow furrows. "That's odd."

"What?" I bark.

"I don't see her comm charger, and her shoulder bag that always hangs on this chair is gone, too."

Heath steps forward, picking up a small note left on her nightstand. He curses under his breath. "Look at this."

I snatch the note from his hand and read the hastily scrawled words.

I'm sorry. There's something I need to do. Please don't follow me.

The note slips from my grasp, fluttering to the floor as the weight of her absence hits me. She's gone.

"This doesn't make any sense," I growl through gritted teeth. "Where the hell would she go?"

"I'll check the flight logs." Heath taps his comm. There's a chime as the computer confirms his passcode. A second later, he sends a copy of it to mine and Carter's.

A police shuttle left with her name as the only passenger.

It'd departed for Delford and never returned. Guilt coats my tongue like sour milk. I'd done this. I'd pushed her too far.

Fuck.

"Logan?" Heath's voice cuts through my spiraling thoughts.

"What?" I snap.

Heath narrows his eyes. "It's too late to check tonight, but I'll make calls in the morning."

Carter sinks into one of the chairs at the table, defeat etched into the lines of his forehead. "Why would she just leave without telling us?"

I straighten my shoulders, forcing my features into an impassive mask. "Who the hell knows, but she's wrong to think we won't look for her."

Fifty-Seven

BRIGID

Bag slung over my shoulder, I stand in front of my childhood home.

The salty sea breeze carries the scent of home, stirring up a bittersweet ache in my chest.

Two shipping containers, their hinges and rivets rusted, are stacked atop each other. My eyes trace the familiar lines of the metal buildings. Ours was just one of the dozens that are down here. They're all interconnected, forming a sprawling complex of labs, apartments, and schools.

The containers, once plain and industrial, have been transformed into a community. Some are stacked two or three high, creating multi-level structures that gleam dully in the sunlight. Narrow walkways and stairs connect the upper levels, while small porches jut out from the ground floor units, each one a tiny oasis in the sea of metal.

My gaze falls on my mom's house, and my breath catches. It looks the same as when I left. The single plexiglass window reflects the afternoon light, and I can almost imagine her silhouette moving behind the curtains. The familiarity of it all hits me like a physical force.

I climb the white railing stairs, my fingers automatically reaching out to touch the spot where Sharice and I had pressed our thumbprints into the fresh paint years ago. The memory floods back: Our laughter, the sticky feel of paint on our skin, Mom's mock scolding that quickly dissolved into a warm smile.

As I reach the small porch, the wind chimes flutter and sing, their gentle melody a welcome I didn't realize I'd been longing for. I pause at the door, overcome by a wave of homesickness so intense it nearly brings me to my tears.

Taking a deep breath, I step inside. The interior is surprisingly cozy, defying the stark metal exterior. Crocheted blankets drape over well-worn furniture, adding splashes of color to the space. Potted plants and flowers line the shelves, bringing life and a touch of nature to the metal box we call home.

My eyes fall on the old music player sitting on a side table. I remember winding it up every day, filling our little home with tinny melodies that somehow made the space feel warmer and more alive. The urge to cross the room and wind it now is almost overwhelming.

Through the window, I can see rows of similar containers stretching out, their small porches dotting the landscape like islands in a sea of beach grass and sand. Each one holds its own stories, its own version of home.

Standing here, surrounded by the sights and smells of my childhood, I'm struck by how much I've missed this place. The familiar scent of home washes over me. My mom stands by the kitchen counter, her hands fidgeting with a dish towel.

"Bridgie," she says, her voice lifting, but it's hard to tell if she's actually happy to see me or just surprised. "I wasn't sure you'd come."

"I told you I would," I reply dryly.

"Ah, yes, well, you look well. I'm happy to see you let your hair grow out again. I didn't like it last time."

Ever since I could remember, she'd hated it when I did anything to my hair, cut it, dye it. One time, my friend had braided it in pigtails, and she'd sent her home immediately. So, as any rebellious tween would, I found the scissors and gave myself bangs.

I'd been grounded for a week.

"Go take a seat in the living room," she says. "I'll make us some lemonade."

I move to the adjacent rectangular room. A pair of padded sofas and an armchair sit on the walls, encircling a gray plastic coffee table. Two portable computers, with their charging cords, and three mugs with coffee rings inside them clutter the surface.

My eyes take in the room. It's as it had been when I left six years ago.

The same framed art on the wall, the same broken cuckoo clock, the same bookshelf with the handful of books and scientific journals.

It even smells the same: Musty furniture and stale coffee.

Soon after I settle into the sofa, she enters with a tray of lemonade in a pitcher and two mismatched glasses. There's a small plate with sugar cookies, and despite my best efforts, my mouth instantly waters. She might have many faults, but she is a phenomenal baker.

"Here," she says, pouring me a glass and handing it to me.

"The citrus tree your sister planted before you left is quite popular."

I take a sip, savoring the fresh lemon and hint of sweetness from the sugar and something else, floral. "Honey?" I ask, arching a brow.

Her pale lips form a smile. "Excellent palate. Indeed, we have a small hive, fully enclosed, of course, that proved to be resilient to the fungus that we've been working to isolate the genome of and allow it to splice into—"

She stops mid-sentence and frowns. "Sorry, Sweetheart, I got carried away."

"It's fine," I reply as I had so often before when she'd tried to talk to me like I was Sharice.

I take a cookie, eat it, and then take another as a long silence stretches between us, filled with a thousand unspoken words. Finally, Mom clears her throat. "Did you see the damage from the storm? It really did a number on the east side of the compound."

I nod, not quite meeting her eyes. "Yeah, I noticed."

"I had to take out that old berry bush out back," she continues, her words coming faster now. "It was barely hanging on after the wind—"

"I'm not here to talk about the garden, Mom," I interrupt, my patience wearing thin. "You know why I'm here. Where's Sharice?"

She sighs, her shoulders slumping. "Oh, sweetheart. You just never come to see me. Is it wrong for a mother to want to have a polite conversation with their daughter?"

My throat tightens as I'm put on the defensive. I used to be surprised when she'd manipulate me into apologizing for nothing, but not anymore. I'm not that naïve little child. I see right through her act. "No," I say, my voice sharper. I need her help, and starting a fight now would be a bad idea. "I'm sorry I haven't visited. I've been busy with work."

"At the druadan station?" she says softly.

"Yes. Actually, that's why I am here." I hesitate, drawing in a breath to settle my nerves. "I know Sharice was part of the attack, and I know you know where she is."

Mom's face crumples, and there's age etched in the lines around her eyes. "Oh, Brigid," she whispers, reaching out to me.

"No." I shake my head. "I need to talk to her. It's important, please."

Mom frowns. "Oh, Bridgie. There's so much you don't understand."

"Then help me understand," I plead, my earlier anger giving way to desperation. "Please, just tell me, and I'll leave. I promise."

She takes a deep breath as if bracing herself. "I wish I could explain, but it's not that easy."

I blink, trying to listen, but her words sound muffled, like I'm underwater.

"What did you—" I think I say, then am slumping forward. The glass slips from my hand, and still, my mother's voice echoes somewhere in the distance.

"You should have stayed at the station, sweetheart."

My eyes droop. Holy shit, I've been—

But before I can finish the thought, the threatening black rings close in, plunging my vision into blackness.

My head feels like it's going to explode.

Every nerve fiber in my skull is on fire, and I'm paralyzed, unable to move to get comfortable. I must be dead.

But if you're dead, you can't *feel*, right? And I feel everything. The ache in my head, the soreness in my shoulders, the humid air clinging to my face and body.

My eyes snap open, and I stare at an unfamiliar ceiling of chipped plaster and peeling wallpaper angled from the corner like shredded pieces of fabric. I wiggle my fingers and toes, trying to bring myself into reality. Whatever reality *this* is. It hurts to think, but thinking is survival, and I want to survive. But why? For what reason? Panic pours ice into my veins as I fail to find a reason. No memories exist. Only this.

Desperately, I claw my way to the surface, yanking back the fog surrounding my mind. The second I focus on my heartbeat, my mind clears. Visions of my mother's face swirl and blur with a blue liquid.

I'd been sitting with my mother. But that can't be right. I hadn't seen my mother in years.

I bolt upright and instantly regret the decision. A jolt of pain ricochets up my spine into the base of my skull. I collapse forward between my knees, wincing in agony.

"The headache will pass," I hear a woman say. "Once you're more alert, I can give you something for the pain, a tea elixir, but we want to make sure you're swallowing correctly before doing that."

I don't recognize the woman's face. She has kind eyes, almost grandmotherly, but then my gaze falls to the laser pistol on her hip and the jagged scar along her collarbone that reaches all the way up past her ear, disappearing into her hairline.

This is one of the rebels. I'm certain of it. Suddenly, wave after wave of memories flood back into me: me flying to Uncy'lia, meeting with my mother, and the lemonade that she'd drugged. My hand flies to my wrist. My comm is gone. Shit.

My eyes dart around the small room, seeing no sign of it or my bag. Anger rises in me, overriding the momentary disorientation.

"Why am I here?" I snap. "Who are you? Where is my mom?"

"I'm Regina." She purses her lips and gives me a sideways look at the closed door I hadn't noticed. "And I'm sorry, but I can't answer any other questions." She offers me a small smile. "All you need to know is that you're safe, and I am here to make sure you recover from the medication we gave you."

"Please tell me why am I here?" My mouth feels like it's full of cotton, and I stumble over the words, even as I try desperately to make them clear.

The woman wines, and I choke down the ounce of remorse it induces. These are terrorists. People who want to destroy everything in their path. I won't feel sorry for them.

"I don't know anything. They just told me to look after you. I was a nurse before." Her hands fidget with the drawstring on her pants, which I realize now are loose cotton scrubs. "I've been assigned to your care. I need to check that you're alert and see if you need anything."

"I need to leave."

She bows her head. "I'm sorry, but that's not an option."

The fury-fueled beast, now fully awakened, spurs me on. "So, what, I'm a prisoner here? Did my sister put you up to this?"

Regina recoils, and a single tear drips down her cheek. She spins, making a beeline for the door. Damnit. I'm scaring the one person I might get answers from.

I need to change tactics. Clearly, this woman is sensitive; maybe she's a new recruit or doesn't get to see any of the actual combat. Whatever it is, my intimidation plan isn't working. "Look," I say, softening my tone. "I don't know why you're here or what they have on you, but you clearly are a good person; otherwise, you wouldn't have gone into the field you've gone into. Nurses are supposed to help people. So, help me? "

"She opens her mouth as if ready to say something, but before she can, the door opens, and Sharice appears.

"Hello, sister," Sharice says. "You have no idea how happy I was when Mom told me you came here. Finally, you came to your senses and decided to join me. Join our cause."

She stands there in her dark brown jumpsuit, a laser pistol strapped to her hip, goggles resting atop her head. The wind has burned her face and left her lips chapped and cracked. Her dark brown hair is pulled back into a tight braid, held together by a worn plastic cord.

My eyes land on hers, still cold but with a fire behind them, a burning energy I hadn't noticed that night at Meridian. She's a handful of years older, yet this past year has aged her more than I expected. Her cheekbones are sharper, her body thinner, as if she's been carved down by exhaustion. Dark bags sit under her eyes—she isn't sleeping well, or she's sick.

My heart clenches. She looks like hell. Still, I prepared for this. Okay, not to be drugged and locked in this room, which I am still super pissed about, but I was prepared to face Sharice *again* more than I had at Meridian. I brace myself. "I'm not here to join your cause."

She pulls a chair from the corner and straddles it. "Then why did you come here?" she asks. "Why did you look for me? Mom said you barely talk to her, and you've never once shown any interest in science or politics, for that matter. So, why now?"

"It's about the first egg you stole," I say. "I talked to Marcus. He said it hatched. I need to know how you've kept it alive."

She leans her arms over the back of the chair and picks at some dirt crusted under her comm band. "I saw you in the Blackhawk ad," she says, not answering my question. "On Network. It was such a line of bullshit. Circuit's unity. Circuit's strength. It was all one big ego stroking, cool aid drinking, circus." She laughs. "And there you were, right in the middle of it. How can you be so stupid? They're hiding the truth from us. Blurring the facts to make them look better. Let me show you exactly what Circuit is doing in the name of protecting Venovia."

She pulls up a shaky video on her comm and taps it to project in the air between us. It shows workers at one of Circuit's filtration plants, sweat staining their coveralls as they rush between towering machines pumping out fumes. Their faces are drawn, exhausted as they struggle to keep up with the malfunctioning equipment.

"Look at them," Sharice demands. "Working themselves to death while the wealthy asshole owners cash in."

In high school, we were shown filtration plant recruitment videos, in which plant managers showed pictures of the giant filters, piping, and a bottle of tox zone air. The last one fascinated me the most. The brownish-orange-tinged air inside it turned clear after processing.

She swipes to another clip, this one showing a dimly lit room where two scientists in lab coats sit handcuffed to a table. A harsh light shines on their faces as they stammer their confessions.

"My name is Dr. Taliya Fazil," an older woman says. Her voice is hoarse, and her hair is a tangled mess. How long had she been kept in that tiny room? Had she been tortured? Starved? Clearly, she had been coerced into what she was saying, so there was no way it would hold up in a Circuit hearing. However, it didn't seem to occur to Sharice that this was the case. Her gaze never wavers from the screen. "Lannett ordered me to falsify the air quality data reports."

The other mumbles a similar admission about tweaking the numbers.

Sharice's eyes blaze as she looks back at me. "And this is what our joke for a government is doing behind closed doors. Poisoning Venovia while arresting anyone who tries to expose the truth." She jabs an accusing finger at me. "Venovia has one year before the air is completely unbreathable. One year until all of us are dead, including your beloved riders."

My riders. Wait, how does she know about them?

The world tilts on its axis, and I grip the seat of my chair for fear of falling out of it. *Unless Zane had been right about Sharice having connections with Blackhawk.* A mole had been spying on me the whole time. My pulse pounds with terror at the horrifying realization the others are still there being watched.

Sharice stalks to the door, pausing with her hand on the frame. She glances back at me, her lips twitching into a hard smile. "I meant it when I said I'm overjoyed you're here. I was starting to worry you'd never come. You have no idea how much I've waited for this." Her eyes narrow, and she sighs. "I know you have questions, and I'll get to them in due time. But now that you're here, there's so much to do. So much to prepare for."

She hesitates, then adds, voice lowering, "You're the key, Brigid. You just don't know it yet. But I'll show you. It's what big sisters are for, right?" Before I can answer, the door slams behind her. I hear the jingle of a locking mechanism, snuffing out any chance of escaping.

I pull my knees up, hugging them tightly. The sapphire stone on my bracelet presses into the sensitive skin of my wrist, its sharp edges digging painfully. Gritting my teeth, I slip my fingers beneath the delicate chain. With an angry shout, I tear it free, the stone biting deeper as it snaps. A sharp pain flares up my arm as I hurl the broken bracelet at the wall, where it strikes with a harsh crack.

Anguish clogs my throat as I sit alone in this tiny, windowless room.

No one knows where I am. *I* don't know where I am. I am doomed to this godforsaken place for what? For forever? A cold wave of despair washes over me. I've failed; Oriana is going to die because of me.

I close my eyes, feeling the gravity of my situation seep into me. My riders, the men who've become my world, will forever believe I abandoned them.

I am going to die here, and they will never know the truth.

THE END

AFTERWORD

Stay tuned for DRUADAN LEGACY Book 3

Keep up to date with the latest announcements from me by subscribing to my newsletter
Join my Amelia Cole reader Facebook group! https://www.facebook.com/share/g/gVyHbvQXM1cKB1Ei/
Visit my website at:
https://www.ameliacolebooks.com/
Questions/comments?
Email me: contact@ameliacolebooks.com

Acknowledgments

Thank you so much for reading SOULBOUND!

Soulbound and this world was a challenge, and I can't believe how much this story has bloomed and grown. These characters all share parts of my soul, and I hope I did them justice.

Starting with the first page, I poured myself into it, pushing it to be the perfect version you see today.

This book never would have seen the light of day if I hadn't been surrounded by many supportive people in my life.

To my agent, Morgan Hughes, for being patient, kind, and supportive.

To my mom for tagging along as my assistant at book signings.

Love you, Llamaquad pals! You're my go-to friend when I feel like the words aren't wording and I need a boost of encouragement.

To my rockstar team of Beta and ARC readers. Morgan, Sarabelle, and many others. Your first reads helped me shape this story and cheered me and the characters on, pushing me to finish this book.

To my amazing PA, Alyssa. Thank you for doing the behind-the-scenes lifting to make sure my newsletters go out and crafting all the pretty pictures of my books.

To Michael, Kian, and Megan, you are my whole world.

Thank you for bringing me snacks while working and listening to me talk about characters on long car rides.

About the Author

Amelia Cole is a fantasy and sci-fi romance author. She enjoys guessing twist endings of movies, rolling D20s with her friends, and pretending to be an elf archer at ren faires. She's a short story contest winner and has been published in magazines and anthologies.

She lives with her family in Washington state.

www.ingramcontent.com/pod-product-compliance
Lightning Source LLC
LaVergne TN
LVHW010305070526
838199LV00065B/5450